KYZYL KISHLAK

REFUGEE VILLAGE

Books by Herman Taube:

Novels
The Unforgettable (with Susan Taube)
Remember (with Susan Taube)
Empty Pews
The Last Train
Kyzyl Kishlak, Refugee Village

Poetry
A Chain of Images
Echoes
Questions
Jerusalem — We Are Here
Between the Shadows: New and Selected Poems
Land of the Blue Skies
Autumn Travels, Devious Paths: Poetry and Prose
A Herman Taube Reader
The Blizzard (a play)

KYZYL KISHLAK

REFUGEE VILLAGE

a novel

by Herman Taube

OLAMI PRESS
Washington, D.C.

Acknowledgements
I am indebted to Joy Gold for typesetting, and to Michlean Amir, Tahma Metz, and Irene Auvil for reading the first draft of this novel.

Olami Press extends its appreciation to Shelby Shapiro who helped support the production of this book.

Library of Congress Catalog Number: LC 93-084228

ISBN 0-931848-88-1

Olami Press
Distributed by Dryad Press
15 Sherman Avenue
Takoma Park, Maryland 20912

Contents

Dedicated with affection to
my friend Merrill Leffler

KYZYL KISHLAK
REFUGEE VILLAGE

Prologue

*"Man is led along the road
which he wants to follow."*
Makkoth 10B

Prologue

Volodia Tarko, a medic in the Tyumen, Siberian Regional Clinic, was called to the Regional Military Commandantura for a temporary reassignment to the *Teritorial Bolnitza* -- a hospital in the town of Irtish in Siberia.

He was led into a small room with pictures of Lenin and Stalin and an oversized map of Siberia on the wall. A tall man in a military jacket without insignia greeted him politely, saying, "Comrade Tarko, we called you here on short notice on a very urgent matter. You will escort a transport of volunteers. going to work in the shafts in the Irtysh Basin. Your superiors were already notified about your transfer. The transport is leaving tomorrow at midnight; our own nurses and medical personnel are needed on the Finnish front. We give you, Comrade Tarko, a *biwshy Polski grazdanin* -- a former Polish citizen we liberated from oppression -- the opportunity to help the motherland. You will accompany this transport of patriotic volunteers to their new place of work. As soon as they are settled in their new place, you will be able to return to Tyumen."

"How long do you think this assignment will take?"

"Three to four weeks. Here are your *commandirowkas* -- travel orders, food cards. You will be cared for by our escort leader, Major Yuri Vasilov, who will provide you with a warm overcoat, valenki boots and warm underwear -- a gift from our great leader, Comrade Stalin."

"Spasibo bolshoye -- great thanks."

"You are welcome, Comrade Tarko. The territory you are going to is rich in rare metals and much needed for our economy, but the climate there is severe, cold. So keep yourself warm. Good luck."

Volodia's vigor served him well in the six days of travel with the transport of volunteers who were a mix of tall, broadshouldered, athletic, Nordic Russians and slender Mongoloid Yakuts. The temperature was 20 degrees below zero, but the people were warm and friendly. The transport made many stops, letting scheduled trains go by, taking on coal and water, adding wagons with prisoners for the taigas and gulags. But the volunteers never complained. Some even sang songs.

The four-week assignment turned into fourteen long months of total isolation in a Siberian village with below zero temperature even on summer nights. Volodia worked twelve to fourteen hours daily in the small medical station that served the entire region.

The patients -- even the sickest of them -- waited long hours to be seen by a doctor, nurse, or a medic. But they never complained. The patients, like the volunteers, came from all parts of Eastern Europe. They were deportees from Latvia and Eastern Poland, Chechen and Ingush people, Balkaris deported from their autonomous republics; Jews from Central Poland, arrested for applying for travel permits to occupied Poland to save their families from the Nazis.

Until the Hitler invasion of Russia in June 1941, there was no hope for the Polish prisoners to be freed from banishment. The *Natchalniks* -- camp commanders -- in charge of the Polish barracks kept saying, "You Poles will never again see your homeland. You are here *na wsegda* -- forever."

Many of the Poles, Polish Jews and Latvian, died from hunger, cold, sickness, many froze to death at work in the forest, many committed suicide listening to the radio loudspeakers to the news broadcasts, to what was happening to their families in Poland, Ukraine, and the Baltic areas. Many of the deportees suffered from severe depression and fear, doubting that they would ever live to see an end to their misery.

But, in the fall of 1941, after the Soviet Union established relations with General Sikorski's Polish government in London, orders arrived that all former citizens of Poland should be freed from the detention camps and allowed to settle anywhere they chose except for strategic areas and capital cities of the Soviet Republics.

Volodia transferred his responsibilities to newly arrived demobilized nurses and medics, wounded in the war. Their former homes devastated by the Germans, they came to live and work in Siberia.

He was given *characteristicas* praising his work at the Tyumen Medical Center, travel permits, food cards, and a railroad pass 'good for thirty days.'

During his stay in Irtish, Volodia lived in a room in the small old home of Sergei and Ludmila Berdayew. Sergei was a retired railroad worker and Ludmila, a former elementary school teacher. Poor as they were, they always insisted that Volodia share some warm soup or borscht with them, and Volodia reciprocated by sharing his food allotment with them.

He helped around the house on frigid winter days, shoveling snow, chopping wood, picking up their coal allotment. Ludmila, a childless woman, was kind and intelligent. She shared her library of old books by Dostoyevski, Tolstoy, Turgeniev and their namesake, Berdayew, with Volodia. On cold nights, Sergei played the *Harmoshka,* and Ludmila sang sad, romantic songs about Mother Russia. Sergei always boasted how he helped build the Trans-Siberian railroad, his contribution to his beloved motherland. Sergei and Ludmila loved their village and the surrounding nature, the forests, the taiga, the frost. So long as they had wood, coal, food, and their radio loudspeaker, they were content.

They could not understand why Volodia wanted to leave such a serene village. "Why, Volodinka, are you leaving us? Look at the beautiful trees. Look at the pure, white snow, the quietness and tranquility here ... "

"Dear Sergei and Ludmila, everything is beautiful here. You treated me like a son, but I need more people and less snow."

"You have a good profession which is much needed here. Your occupation will secure you a good livelihood here for a lifetime, a steady base under your feet. We're old. We will leave you our humble home. Please stay."

"But, dear Sergei, what I need is my own roof among my own people."

Volodia convinced them that this was a time of war and that he was determined to join the army to fight the bloodthirsty tyrant who had invaded the Russian motherland.

On the day of his departure, Ludmila gave Volodia some home-made sugar cookies. Where she had gotten the flour to bake them Volodia could not imagine.

"Volodinka, may God watch over you. Please write to us," Ludmila said, hugged him the way a mother hugs her son when he goes off to war.

For seventeen days he traveled, on transport trains in freight cars with refugees from all over the Soviet Union, in horse wagons, lacking the most elementary of comforts, waiting in overcrowded railway stations for connecting trains, living on hot water and dried fruits. Finally, he reached Andizhan, a town in the Fergana Valley of Uzbekistan.

He reported to the health department, where he received bread cards, a place to sleep, and a promise of a job. After four days of waiting, he was sent to the malaria station in the village of Kyzyl Kishlak.

* * * * *

CHAPTER ONE
Refugee Village

Refugee Village

A two-wheeled cart harnessed with a camel moved, drifting slowly on the sandy road, raising a thick cloud of dust. The wheels squeaked loudly, stirring the dogs in the courtyards beside the roads and fields where cotton shrubs lay drying and poppy flowers with their musty sweet smell tickled the nose like the taste of thyme and made you sleepy. The driver, a man with a cap on his shaven head, slept while the cart carried its passenger, Vladimir (Volodia) Arionovitz Tarko, to Kyzyl Kishlak, a remote village at the crossroads of three worlds: the Soviet Union, China, and Afghanistan.

The camel must have known this road. While the driver was dozing, he inched his way past plum groves and cotton fields into the main street, turned into an alley and then into the courtyard of a large, white building, decorated with a red banner and a sign reading: "SEL SOVIET -- VILLAGE COUNCIL."

It was a long, all-night journey from Andizhan to Kyzyl Kishlak. They had left in the darkness of the evening, clattering through sandy dunes, plains, cotton and rice fields, across the Syr Darya River, and past the towns of Chakulabaad and Chinabaad, where fields were irrigated with artificial basins, and past areas green with orchards and wild plants.

The clouds disappeared and a clear, bright sky unveiled a horizon of mysterious snow-bedecked mountains.

"Comrade." Volodia touched the shoulder of the napping camel driver, "See!" Volodia's touch awakened him. "Thank Allah!" said the driver. "We are home ... the sun will rise soon from the mountain."

The driver handed Volodia his belongings. "You can clean up in the *arik* -- the little stream behind the building. May

2

Allah bless you with a good life here. I will go home and rest now from the long ride."

"Thank you for the ride and fruits, *Salaam!*"

"*Aleikum Salaam.* Good Luck, *Chozain* -- God is Great!"

Volodia opened his travel bag at the stream. He washed his dirty, sunburned face, brushed his teeth with his fingers, and changed to the only clean shirt he possessed. He felt a desire to look his best when confronting his new employer. It was full daylight by the time he looked at his reflection in the water -- a face of complete weariness, burning red eyes, and skinny sunburned face.

The village *muezzin,* holding a long instrument resembling a horn, sounded a melodious tune from the top of a mosque. His call to the faithful for prayer echoed back from the Tien-Shan Mountains to the village.

A security guard came to the stream, washed his face and hands, kneeled on the ground and said his morning prayers. After getting up he turned to Volodia, who was sitting on the sand with his feet out straight and eating old, dry bread.

"Peace be upon you stranger, *Salaam Aleikum. Yakshi misis?* What brings you to our village so early in the morning?"

"*Aleikum Salaam,*" Volodia said, swallowed his last bite of bread. "I came here to see Dr. Chaidarov. I was sent here from Andizhan."

"I saw you coming on the cart. I have been watching you since. If you want to see Dr. Chaidarov, come, I will take you there. It is on my way."

The alleys leading to the bazaar were coming to life. From the narrow, crooked lanes and side streets came the children, strolling on their way to school. Uzbeks were leading donkeys loaded with heavy bags, fruit baskets, loads of wood, vegetation and a variety of tulips, violets, and lilies. Women wearing *parangas* -- black face masks and special native dress -- carried baskets and milk jugs on their heads. Ragged refugees from many parts of Russia, some barefoot and dirty, walked slowly to the bazaar. The aromas of fresh peaches, apricots, apples,

dates, and melons mixed with that of the garbage around the
ditches by the road. Around a large building decorated with a
portrait of Lenin and a red flag, people gathered to listen to a
loudspeaker blaring the morning news:

"The Army of General Sokolovsky is gradually grinding
down the Wehrmacht Divisions. Our heroic defenders of
Moscow stopped all desperate attempts by the enemy to come
near the city. The 41st German Tank Corps was driven back
with heavy losses to the enemy."

Volodia walked in silence along the sandy road, anxious to
hear more of the morning news. The loudspeaker was drowned
out by the clatter and noise all around -- donkeys shrieking,
dogs barking, cart wheels squeaking, and wagons loaded with
cotton rattling by. The guard led Volodia into a tiny alley
with mud houses perched along a crooked street. The tiny huts
were huddled together, touching each other, separated only by
mud walls. Sunrays were flickering through the fruit trees
between the walls.

The sky was clear; the air and heat were as stifling as a
blast furnace. Volodia was hoping it would be a short walk.
Finally the guard announced: "This is your clinic, Comrade."

"Thank you for your kindness, Comrade Guard. *"Salaam!"*

"Salaam. Allah Akbar -- God is Great." The guard bowed
and vanished.

The line of people waiting in front of the medical center
stretched from the gate, down the alley, and around the huge
building. Volodia, with his bundle of belongings on his
shoulder, passed through the gate. Someone shouted, "Hey,
Citizen. Where are you going?"

"To see Dr. Chaidarov."

"What do you think? I am an idiot? We know those
tricks. Stay in line like the rest of us. If not, we will fix you
so that you will be dragged away."

"I am not a patient. I will work here."

The man noticed the Red Cross badge on Volodia's arm.

"Oh, excuse me," the man murmured.

An old *Uzbek* came to the gate.

"Salaam Aleikum. Yakshi Misis? Tuzuk? I am Aziz Ali."

The man offered Volodia the tips of his fingers. Dr. Chaidarov
is aware of your arrival; follow me." Aziz Ali admitted
Volodia to a small office. "Please wait here. Dr. Chaidarov
will soon come. Are those your belongings? Let me take
them. I have arranged a special room for you."
 Time passed and Volodia felt quite forgotten. He sat down
on a bench. Before he had time to look out of the small
window, he was deep in sleep. Moments later he heard a
voice call his name: "Welcome to Kyzyl Kishlak. I am
Muhamoud Achmedovitz," Chaidarov's voice spoke in correct
Russian. The short man with close-cut graying hair and
feverish black eyes greeted Volodia with a gracious smile and
strong handshake. Dr. Chaidarov's voice was soft, warm, with
a sound of familiarity that made him feel welcome.
 Volodia presented his documents and the appointment paper
from the Andizhan Health Commissariat.
 "We know all there is to know about you, Vladimir
Arionovitz. We're glad they sent you."
 "Thank you, Dr. Chaidarov. I consider the position you
offered me here a most important responsibility. I look
forward to working with you."
 "You have an enormous job to do. This area is one of the
worst malaria-infested regions in our republic. Also, there are
many things you will have to learn about our people."
 "Dr. Chaidarov, I hope that I can be of help to you. I
know I have much to learn. I will try to follow your advice
and orders."
 Aziz Ali served tea. Dr. Chaidarov sat at his desk and
sized up the tall, slim young man on the bench. He looked at
Volodia's documents: age, twenty-three; experience, clinics,
front-line duty in *lazarets;* mature, keen mind, fast-thinking in
difficult situations.
 While reading, Dr. Chaidarov kept glancing up at Volodia.
He watched his open face and dark brown eyes. When he
spoke, he looked at him directly. Volodia's voice was clear,
deep, with an emotional warmth that develops an immediate
feeling of trust. Dr. Chaidarov, the skilled general practitioner,
was an Asian, an *Uzbek,* a party member who had an inborn

mistrust of strangers and foreigners. He was a sensitive man who depended much on his intuition and personal insight in evaluating people around him. He offered his hand to Volodia.

"Glad to have you on our staff."

Volodia felt a pleasant flutter of gladness in this handshake.

"I hope my work will justify your trust."

"Your job will be supervising the malaria center and overseeing the sanitary conditions of all public establishments in our area. You'll have problems. Food allotments always reach our health complex late. We lack essential drugs, food, salt. Malaria, as you know, makes people anemic and weak, leaving them with no resistance to other diseases. Production in the cooperatives is down, while the government demands prompt deliveries of cotton, rice, and *Dzuqara* barley for the Red Army. It is a vicious cycle."

A tall, light-haired nurse entered and announced that a patient was having convulsions.

"Vladimir Arionovitz, look around the village, visit the health complex, register in the militia and draft board, meet our staff. You will report for work on Monday. After you are settled, please accept my invitation to dinner. Good luck."

"Thank you, Dr. Chaidarov."

"Aziz Ali will get you all your personal necessities."

"Thank you."

Volodia was exhausted from the long days of travel from North Asia to the remote little village in Central Asia, but his spirits were up. He felt that he had made a good impression on Dr. Chaidarov. His morning meeting with the friendly guard, and with Aziz Ali, made him feel welcome in this little oasis at the foothills of the snow-bedecked Tien-Shan Mountains. Aziz Ali was waiting for him.

"Chozain -- is tired? Your room is ready."

A loudspeaker blared the special news: "Japan has attacked Pearl Harbor." "The Red Army has repelled attacks by the Germans near Moscow." "The German Air Force is bombing Leningrad." "England has declared war on Hungary, Rumania, and Finland."

The room had a small window with no glass; the door had

no lock. The bed was covered with a straw sack as a mattress. The white-painted walls had some rusty nails sticking out to be used for hanging clothes. A big, wooden box served as a table. There were clean bed sheets, a pillow and a pair of towels on the only chair in the room. They smelled of carbolic acid and were stamped: "Property of Kyzyl Kishlak Health Complex."

Volodia unpacked his bag. Everything was dusty and sweaty. He looked sadly at his belongings and smiled -- what possessions! Two shirts, one undershirt, one pair of pants, books on malaria, sanitation and public health, a small cotton document-holder, and a folder with notes and poems. Everything needed mending and washing. He had a toothbrush, but no toothpowder. He had some green soap in a jar which he needed to wash his face and body. He had a piece of a mirror, a metal comb, and a razor with rusty old blades. He was tired from his long journey. All he wanted now was to take a shower and rest.

The shower room and toilet were down the hall from his room in the malaria center building. It was not ideal, but much better than walking to the bathroom in the hospital building or using the public lavatory in the backyard.

Volodia showered, shaved, picked out a pair of white pants and a white jacket from the warehouse, signed a receipt for it, attached a little red name badge to his lapel, and went back to his room. In minutes he was asleep.

Volodia dreamed ... It is Friday afternoon in 1937. He was rushing past the tall buildings on Legionow Street in his home town of Lodz, Poland. He had just returned home for the weekend from the clinic in the nearby town of Konstantin where he worked as an orderly. He dashed up four floors to his grandparents' apartment, handed his grandmother his pay envelope, washed, and sat down to read the local newspaper. His grandfather returned home from synagogue wearing his long, black Saturday-coat and round, black hat. He said *Gut Shabbos* and *Shalom Aleichem* and recited *Kiddush* -- the blessing over the wine. During the meal, he sang Sabbath songs with a tired voice:

"Though we on earth a thousand years should dwell,
Too brief the space, thy marvels forth to tell!"

After the meal was over, Volodia was ready to leave.

"Wait, Velvel. I want to talk to you."

His grandfather was looking at him across the table waiting for grandmother to remove the dishes. He kept stroking his long, gray beard and did not know how to start.

"What is it, Grandfather?"

"Are you in a hurry to go somewhere?"

"No, but I work hard all week long and Friday evening is the only time I see my friends."

"Friday night we should stay home and study the *Sedra* -- the portion of the Bible.

"Is this what you wanted to talk about?"

"No," he sighs. "It is about your job."

"I like what I am learning."

"Why did you not tell me you work in a hospital?"

"I didn't want to upset you. I was afraid it would make you sad. I care about you."

"I know. But why does it have to be a Christian hospital?"

"In a hospital there is no difference between Christian and Jew. We learn to like and help all people."

"Someone of my congregation sees you regularly on the streetcar talking to nurses, nuns, and a priest."

"Is that a sin?"

"No. He said he saw you reading a book with a cross on it. He saw the priest put his hand on your shoulder. Is this the truth?"

"Yes. The book is about the Red Cross, and the priest is my friend. We work in the same hospital."

"Does he teach you about their religion?"

"Not at all, Grandfather. We only talk about our work, our patients, how to help people."

"Velvel, I want you to promise me something. Regardless of what you do, wherever you are going to work, remember who you are. Remain a Jew."

"I will."

"God forgive us. We promised your parents -- may they rest in peace -- to raise you to be a good man and an observing Jew. You can go now. Don't come home late. I want you to come to synagogue with me tomorrow morning. I want to show them that my Velvel is still a good Jew."

Next morning, in the small, crowded synagogue, Grandfather was sitting in his long prayer shawl. He swayed back and forth chanting:

> "The Lord slumbers not, nor sleeps;
> He arouses the sleepers and awakens the slumberers;
> He makes the dumb to speak, sets free the prisoners,
> Supports the falling, and raises up those who are bowed down."

Grandfather kept swaying, holding his hand over the hand of his grandson. He had a smile on his face.

Next morning, rested, shaven, Volodia made his first visit to the center. He walked around the long ward looking at the charts written in Russian and Uzbekian. The Uzbekian alphabet had been changed from Arabic to the Cyrillic, Russian. It was not difficult for Volodia to read the charts in Russian, but the Uzbekian was totally strange to him. He observed the patients, most of whom were Uzbek, brown-skinned, round faces, mongol eyes, and shaven heads. There were also many Tatars from Crimea, Poles, by-Volga -- Germans and Jews.

He looked at the faces of the patients in beds, on crutches, in wheelchairs. He wanted to talk to them. He heard a variety of languages, moaning, gurgling, breathing. There was only one nurse in the ward, and the old man, Aziz Ali, serving the forty-bed center.

Aziz Ali was a short man with almond-shaped eyes, high cheek bones, and an enormous mustache. His head was shaven and covered with a *tubiteika* -- the traditional Uzbekian cap. He greeted Volodia in a drawling voice.

"Salaam. Yakshi Misis? How is your health? Did you rest well? This is our Center, *Chozain* Tarko. I am the

caretaker here. The nurse is my daughter, Fatima. She will be a good assistant to you, but anything you need, *Chozain* Tarko, you call me."

Aziz Ali proudly presented his daughter.

"*Chozain* Tarko, my Fatima."

"I am please to meet you, Fatima. Dr. Chaidarov said that you are very dependable."

Her father's introduction and Volodia's compliment pleased her. She responded humbly.

"Dr. Chaidarov said you are coming to work on Monday." Her voice was warm. Her smile displayed a full mouth of strong, white teeth. "I will be very pleased to work with you."

"You have a very nice daughter, Aziz Ali, and everything here is very clean. I am very much impressed."

Fatima grinned with pleasure, her oval face blushing with an innocence quite at odds with her voluptuous figure.

"I will get a new rug for your room, a new wash basin, and a lamp. My father will get a new lock for your door."

"Thank you, Fatima. By the way, how do you register for bread and food stamps?"

"You give me a note with all the things you need from the local cooperative. My father will register all your cards for you. You will receive bread here at work."

A patient was calling and Fatima left quickly. Aziz Ali took the list and the cards from Volodia,

"I can't read or write, but I can speak Russian," Aziz Ali continued. "All my children are well learned. My youngest son -- Allah bless him -- is now an officer in the Army School in Frunze. Fatima is a good nurse, and someday she will marry a good man here, *Inshallah* -- God willing."

"May God bless you for raising such fine children, Aziz Ali."

"May your coming to our village be a blessing from Allah to all of us."

Aziz Ali touched his chin, said a prayer in his native Uzbekistani; his face was glowing with fatherly pride.

Salaam, Aziz Ali. thank you for cleaning up my room. See you Monday."

"Inshallah!"

Volodia strolled down Lenina Street, the main roadway of
the village. The street w:.з a mixture of diverse mud and brick
houses, vineyards, cooperative shops, a bazaar, tea houses, a
parikmacherskaya -- barber shop, a *stolova* -- restaurant -- and
an old mosque which had been converted into a public bath.
Most buildings were being used by the local militia, military
draft board, and the village council. Some of them were old
remains dating back to the late '90s, when this was a border
village and Tzarist Cossacks fortified the border area.
Volodia walked into the only new two-story dwelling. On
the door was a metal plaque saying:
ON THE TENTH ANNIVERSARY OF UZBEKISTAN,
THIS VILLAGE DEDICATED FOUR BUILDINGS
TO THE SERVICE AND PROTECTION OF THE
VICTORIOUS WORKERS AND BUILDERS OF
REVOLUTIONARY UZBEKISTAN.   MAY 1, 1934.
Volodia walked into the office of the draft board and
presented his papers. The woman at the desk hardly looked at
him. She stamped his documents and entered his name in a
huge register.
After registering with the draft board and militia, he
stopped by the school building and read a big poster: "School
Drama Club presents a play ... " He thought: Here, in a
remote village more than thirty kilometers away from a railroad
station, in a desert land at the end of the world, in a period of
war, in a time of a malaria epidemic, children in a school
present "Episodes from Sholochov's Quiet Flows the Don."
He walked back to the health complex. Aziz Ali was
waiting for him.
"Chozain Tarko is still tired? I got your food stamps. I
fixed the lock on your door."
"Thank you, Aziz Ali."
Volodia looked out of the small window of his tiny room.
The view was startling. The serene mountains covered with
patches of snow struck him with their beauty. He was
enchanted by this small, picturesque hamlet with its exotic

bazaar, friendly people, tiny houses, unpaved streets, flocks of goats, sheep and donkeys grazing on thin patches of grass. This place would have been a paradise if it were not plagued by malaria.

With the building of the Fergana Canal, which dramatically changed the land of Uzbekistan, came a one-celled parasite that multiplied by the billions, spreading malaria in epidemic proportions. Around the streams and swampy grounds of the Darya River, people suffered and died by the thousands every year.

Volodia was to educate the people in the area about the importance of destroying the mosquitoes' breeding places. He was told that his job would be difficult, almost impossible. He would get no cooperation from the local people. They would not let him inspect their homes or backyard streams until they had chills and fever.

The women suffered more than the men. For religious reasons, most married women would not go to public clinics or to the malaria center, where male doctors treated them.

Volodia could also see the dangers of a typhoid epidemic in the overcrowded teahouses and the public places where homeless, starving refugees lived in filth.

"The first thing I will do is get some cans of road oil and spray all breeding nests where the mosquitoes lay their eggs," Volodia wrote in his notebook. "Then I will advise them to drain all barrow pits and shallow ponds. I will dispose of all the artificial water containers around the public buildings and houses."

He slapped the notebook shut and strode the few blocks to the village council office. The village council secretary, Comrade Kozlov, a heavy set Russian with horn-rimmed glasses and an enormous red nose, greeted Volodia with a look of contempt.

"What are you looking for, Comrade?"

"Tarko. Vladimir Arionovitz Tarko."

"I know. We approved your position here at last night's council meeting."

"Thank you. I would like to see the records on health and

diseases, reports on sanitary controls, enforced quarantines, and immunization statistics."

"Tarko, there is nothing here but dusty, empty shelves. You better ask Comrade Chaidarov. Maybe he has some information. Here someone used all the material for cigarette paper."

"Thank you, Comrade Secretary."

The massive figure of Kozlov sat there looking at some papers and did not say a word. Feeling intimidated, Volodia left.

Monday morning Volodia started to work. In his first visit to the hospital he was confronted by the shortage of food and drugs. He introduced himself to Dr. Tatyana Ivanovna, the only doctor at the hospital. He met her making her morning rounds, talking to Vera Alexeyvna, the tall nurse he had seen at Dr. Chaidarov's office. She hardly raised her face from the patient's chart given her by Vera.

"We have too many patients."

"So does the center, Dr. Ivanovna."

She finally greeted him with a hearty handshake.

"Dr. Chaidarov told me about you. Glad you're here. We need so many things: instruments, fixtures, drug supplies. We ordered them, but they were never delivered. I need some simple things like thermometers and a new stethoscope. I hope you will get it for us."

"I will try, Dr. Ivanovna. I will see you later."

"Better make it tonight at my home. We will have some tea."

"Thank you, Dr. Ivanovna."

He walked from the hospital building to the malaria center where the ward was thick with pitiful people shivering and burning with fever.

Fatima, unaware that Volodia was right behind her, was arguing with a patient who wanted the loudspeaker turned on.

"You better go back to bed or I will call the doctor and we will kick you out."

"I must listen to the news. My son is on the frontline, my

husband ... they are together. I must follow the news."

Volodia walked to the bazaar. He looked at the refugees around the teahouse. Russians, Ukrainians, Jews, Tatars, were crowded together on dirty blankets, sick, exhausted. He came upon trucks and wagons standing in the open field around the bazaar. A seething mob of women and children were carrying piles of luggage, dirty, dusty bundles of their belongings -- looking for a place under a few shady trees in the field. Women screamed at the drivers, begging not to be discarded there. Children were crying for water, but there was none except at the muddy stream. The white dust, from the sand on the unpaved street and from the road dust, was on the people's hair and eyebrows making them look like ghosts.

Volodia found the stench from perspiration and unwashed bodies almost unbearable. Most of the mixed crowd were Tatars from Crimea. Wherever they stopped, they were unwanted. The Russians looked upon them as enemies and collaborators. A militiaman would force them back on the trucks and wagons, and they would take off for another destination.

Volodia walked around the alleys, the low *kibitkas*. He rapped on doors and asked questions.

"Are there any sick people in the house? Does anyone have malaria?"

People looked at his white uniform and Red Cross badge with fear and respect. Women covered their faces and hid behind doors.

"No sick here, thank Allah!"

Tall and thin, Volodia suspected that his pale, lean face, dark hair, and foreign accent frightened some of the people.

Everything about him contrasted with the local inspectors who used to roam the area from time to time. For hours he walked in the sandy alleys. Sometimes an Uzbek would invite him to his vineyard and offer him a glass of milk or a bowl of tea, exchange a friendly greeting and good wishes. When Volodia was just about to call it quits for the day, he came upon a small house hidden by trees, plants, feather grass, and poppies. A young Uzbekian girl with thin, black strings of hair braids, dressed in a long, multicolored, silk dress greeted him with a smile.

"Comrade Tarko, come to see us? I am Fatima. You don't recognize me? Dr. Ivanovna lives here."

"Here?"

"Yes. This house belongs to our medical complex and is used for personnel."

Dr. Ivanovna came to the door.

"Oh, welcome. You're early. Come in, please. Welcome to the team, Comrade Tarko. Would you like some tea?"

"No thank you. My sandals are full of sand. We can talk here, a nice veranda, beautiful view."

"Take off your shoes and leave them outside. We have a shower room attached to our yard-stream. Would you like to wash yourself?"

Dr. Ivanovna said this with familiarity as if she had known Volodia for years. Volodia carefully pushed off his sandals and left them standing at the door.

"It is almost a dream."

"What is? Your job? Your coming here?"

"No. Your offer of a shower in this hot place."

* * * * *

CHAPTER TWO
Tanya

Tanya

Volodia followed Dr. Ivanovna into a cozy room lined with bookshelves. A very old, but clean, carpet covered the floor, and an 'ancient' sofa with two matching chairs surrounded a small, round table.

"Forgive me, Comrade Tarko, for the way everything looks. We seldom entertain guests in our home."

"Please, call me Vladimir or Volodia."

"If you will call me Tanya."

Fatima served tea and *urug* -- dry plums.

"Fatima, I am very impressed with your father. He is very efficient and helpful. He fixed everything in my room exactly as he promised."

"Thank you, Comrade Tarko. I am blessed with a good father."

"You know, Volodia," Tanya made herself comfortable on the sofa, "Aziz Ali had a big home in a *kolkhoz*. He lived there with his two wives and family. When Fatima decided to become a nurse, he lamented over her departure to Samarkand. When Fatima returned from school and was offered a job at the malaria center, Aziz Ali gave Dr. Chaidarov an ultimatum: Aziz Ali would allow his daughter to work only under one condition, that he must stay with her."

"I don't blame Aziz Ali for wanting to protect his daughter. Fatima is a very pretty girl."

"My father loves me like his sons," Fatima said proudly, and sipped her tea.

Fatima left the room to prepare the shower for Volodia. Tanya sipped her tea, holding the bowl in both hands, and gazed affectionately at her guest who in her eyes was irresistibly handsome. Volodia sat quietly, thinking how different

18

women can look, how they can change with the hours in manners and in varied uniforms or clothes. He looked at her brightly colored pink housedress, so totally different from the white uniform she wore at the hospital. Her beauty was overwhelming, with her light skin and golden blond hair, her lively eyes and full mouth. Her voice had a sound of sweetness that demanded attention. He felt genuine joy just sitting there in that room with the old fashioned sofa and books.

"You have a lot of books here."

Tanya moved closer to him. He could feel her breath. It made shivers run over him. She whispered, " It gets lonely in this village. I like to read. There is not too much to do in this village after a day's work ... How about you? Do you like to read?"

"Very much so. I like to read and write."

"What do you write about?"

"I like to scribble all sorts of things, poetry about people, nature."

"So, be my guest. Come here anytime ... read, study, write, talk. I like to talk."

Volodia sipped his tea and interrupted the silence: "Sitting here is very heartwarming."

"Thank you, Volodia. It is pleasant to have a man for company."

Fatima came back. The shower was ready.

When Volodia came back from the shower, the two women were sitting on the sofa still holding the bowls of green tea.

"Thank you very much for this treat. I enjoyed it immensely."

"You're so welcome, Volodia. Here is some bread and *katik* -- yogurt. After you eat, we will talk about our work."

Fatima placed a plate full of fruit on the small table.

Tanya's blue eyes shone as she invited him to sit near her. "Sit down here, Volodia. Let me teach you how to eat yogurt without a spoon." She dipped a piece of flat bread in the bowl and artfully offered it to Volodia. "Come on, hurry ... Open your mouth, wide." The closeness of Tanya awakened a craving in him to move closer and touch her hand.

Something suddenly occurred to Volodia. He was aware that she might feel him too inquisitive, but he had to ask her. "Tanya, why did you come to this village?"

"Everyone asks me the same question. Eat, Volodia."

While eating, Volodia kept looking at Tanya. The two braids on her head sat like a crown. Her big, blue eyes sparkled.

"Yogurt will give you energy. Eat."

"I have all the energy I need."

Tanya smiled. "I meant to say, 'masculinity'." She smiled and blushed, showing two lines of pearl-white teeth and full, lusty lips.

"You see, you hold the bread with the tips of your fingers ... like this."

Her manner was natural, honest, open. When she smiled, it was with her whole face, even the corners of her mouth.

Tanya continued feeding Volodia pieces of melon. Her housedress did not conceal the snow white color of her full bosom. Tanya was pleased knowing that Volodia admired her.

"I'll give you a *kopeck* for your thoughts."

Volodia, hesitating to say anything, blushed.

"I know what you want to ask me."

"You did not answer my question. Why did you come here?"

"The people here need me ... need us. They still live in the past. The revolution has not reached this area yet."

Fatima came back with a small tea tray. She must have heard what Tanya said, and remarked, "We are making great progress here. Eighty percent of our young attend school. Some of us speak Russian fluently. In a few years, with the new irrigation in this area, we will indeed prosper."

Tanya interjected, "Fatima is obsessed by the importance of her profession. In the meantime, we must give them all the help we can. What did you accomplish today, Volodia?"

"I made many calls. Only four homes admitted that they needed help, and the rest hardly talked to me. One Uzbek was very friendly. He was standing in the gateway of his *kibitka* and called for me to come in. When I explained what I am here for, he said, 'My whole family suffers from malaria. We don't care. All we worry about is our oldest son who is far away in Russia, fighting in the war.' His parting words were, 'Come to see us again.' I invited him and his family to visit us at the clinic."

"You're lucky. When they first saw me, they slammed the door in my face. It takes time. Now, all the village people are my friends. I can assure you they will be your friends also."

"Our people are good people," Fatima said earnestly. "An Uzbek is friendly, honest, but mistrusts strangers."

The phone rang. Fatima answered in Uzbekian and turned to Tanya. "Vera says that the Russki woman is having difficulty breathing."

Tanya took the phone. "Verotchka, I will see you in minutes." Volodia offered to accompany her.

Outside it was very dark. No street lights, no sight of the mountains, the city. The air was cool, dogs were barking, and a shred of light came from inside buildings they passed. The magazines -- store buildings -- were in disrepair, the fences tilting. As they walked hastily toward the Center, Volodia noticed that Tanya limped. Tanya unceremoniously took his arm with her soft hand.

"Forgive me, Volodia. I can't walk as fast as I'd like to. I have a 'souvenir' from my military service in the Finnish War," Tanya explained matter-of-factly. "Sometimes I am desperate, when there is an emergency and I have to hurry, but generally I have learned to live with it. Sometimes it hurts, but I have learned to bear that also."

Volodia was moved by Tanya's familiarity and openness. He could not find the right words to answer her. He just took her arm and they walked hurriedly to the center.

"Volodia, when I saw your documents on Dr. Chaidarov's desk, I felt sorry for you in a way. There are so many difficulties and problems here. We have a shortage of beds and a short supply of almost everything. That is why no one

wants to come here. I like it here. Dr. Chaidarov is a good
man to work with. We both are determined to succeed.
Because of the war, many departments in our health
commissariat are mismanaged. Medical assistance is free here
and the population knows it, however, they never come to us
until it is too late. When they do come, we are short of the
most essential medications. Sometimes it is almost impossible
to get even an aspirin or headache powder. But despite all the
hindrances we stay on. For us this is 'Mother Russia.' We
have learned to live with the shortages we have, slackness,
mismanagement and often corruption of some bureaucrats in
our system. But you? What can keep you here? Now, after
meeting you tonight, I feel that you can be a great help to us,
to the poor refugees here. They need you, they need us. The
woman I am going to see now is Jewish. She is a widow with
two children here; her son is in the army and they seldom get
letters. Come in with me. Talk to her in your own language.
It can help her, I hope."

Vera greeted Volodia and helped Tanya change into a white
coat. They rushed into the ward toward the woman's bed.
The room reaked of Carboline.

"What was she complaining about?" Tanya asked.

"Chest pains and breathing difficulties. I gave her nitrostat
and some oxygen, but all the tanks are almost empty."

Tanya turned to Volodia. "You see what I mean by
problems?" Volodia asked the woman in Yiddish *"Vos Macht
ihr?"* She opened her eyes and said quietly, "I am not feeling
too well tonight. I feel pain in my chest and shoulders." She
closed her eyes again.

Volodia was invited to speak at the meeting of the village
council. It was Dr. Chaidarov's idea to introduce him to the
area chairmen and secretaries. He arrived at the meeting
promptly and stood in the back of the room, observing the
noisy, mostly-male crowd of Uzbeks and a few Russians. Two
servants waited on the guests, serving bowls of tea. Volodia
was nervous; it was his first exposure before an Uzbek
audience. He looked at the faces of people he had never met.

They were so different from the Poles and Russians he had worked with before.

For a moment he saw himself four years ago, when for the first time he entered a hospital ward in Poland -- one Jew-medic within a staff of nurses, nuns, priests, servants, orderlies, all of them Christians. The hospital walls were filled with pictures of the Pope, wooden crosses, paintings of Mary and Child. He felt strange there, until he finished his first week of duty. Meeting the patients and the staff changed his attitudes and made him realize it was the way he performed his duties that formed the impression these people had of him. This thought helped him now as he looked at the faces of the Uzbeks. All of them were Moslems. These people looked like Mongolians -- with almond-shaped eyes, straight black hair. They sat on small carpets crosslegged, forming a ring around the center.

When the chairman opened the meeting, they applauded enthusiastically. He said something in Uzbekian about health problems, epidemics, malaria. Volodia could not understand his fast speech. Then the chairman introduced Dr. Chaidarov, who received a tremendous ovation.

Dr. Chaidarov was reading from a paper in Uzbekian, but Volodia realized that he was talking about him. Then, turning to Volodia, he said in Russian, "Comrades, this is Vladimir Arionovitz Tarko, my new assistant at our malaria center."

Volodia briefly discussed the need for prevention of epidemics and urged everyone to mobilize and fight against malaria, typhus, and yellow fever.

"Very good," said Dr. Chaidarov, "but by the end of your speech you should always utter some praise for Comrade Iosef Vissarionovich Stalin."

Volodia started his work by making changes. Instead of the *kolkhoz* sending their malaria sufferers to the center, he arranged for Vera, Fatima, and two aides to travel to the *kolkhoz,* field-brigades and the villages.

Often, Volodia, Fatima, and Vera were offered gifts or free foods but they politely refused, explaining, "Our patients need

the food more than we do. You want to help us? Send us
fresh straw, blankets, eggs."

One morning, Fatima surprised him with a smile and warm
greeting. "Comrade Tarko, your name is in our local paper.
They printed Dr. Chaidarov's 'Rules and Regulations' and they
are quoting your speech at the village council meeting."

"Would you like to translate it for me, Fatimà?"

"I'll try." Fatima slowly began to read the story which
talked about the proud Uzbek nation, its grand Fergana Canal,
built by the people. "This canal will become a blessing for
this area. You will have more prosperity for yourself, your
children, and your country. But you must kill the mosquitoes.
You must not drink the water from the stream without boiling
it. When someone around you is sick and in need of help,
help them. Your sons will return home unhurt and proud of
their village, of Uzbekistan their great country, and the leader
of our Great Fatherland, Iosef Vissarionovich Stalin, will be
proud of us."

"Hmm," Volodia wondered, "When did I say all this?"

"You must have said it, Comrade Tarko. This is our Party
paper."

When Volodia got back to his room and glanced again at
the local newspaper, he was ashamed of all the big words in
the article credited to him.

He was upset at the way the article was written. He felt
like writing a letter to the editor complaining about the real
indifference of the local people to the unfortunate refugees
living in misery, of fellow human beings walking by and not
even stopping to look in their direction. But why accuse
them? Where is he, Vladimir Tarko, the homeless refugee
himself, with all those bynames, with all his ideas of mercy
and compassion for the ill-treated? Whose gratitude does he
try to find? Dr. Chaidarov's? Tanya's? Or is it all for his
own personal comfort? Whom does he want to impress with
his speeches? How will this help the mass of refugees?

Why not get up and take some food to the refugees, go
and talk to them, help obtain for them residence permits so
they can receive breadcards?

A voice in him kept calling, "Volodia, Wolf, you dreamed of becoming a medic to help your people. They are here now ... waiting for you. They lie there on the bazaar, hungry and in pain. Your ideas, your words will have meaning only if you prove with deeds what you say and believe in."

He got up, got dressed, took his bread portion and went to the bazaar. Merchants in black coats were sitting in the shade beneath verandas sipping tea, chewing tobacco, or passing a pipe. The refugees looked for tobacco and crumbs of bread or some half-eaten melons in the wastebox in the courtyard. Merchants walked around selling spices with an indescribable scent that made the refugees even hungrier. Around the shops and stalls, vendors were mopping their "space," the pavement around their stalls. The dust rose from the unpaved ground and covered the refugees lying on their bundles under the bazaar's mud walls.

A merchant was chasing a barefoot little girl. "Move on, little thief, or I'll spank you!"

"I'm hungry. Let me pick up some of the raisins from the ground."

The merchant picked up a handful of dust and aimed it at the child. "You stupid kid. I'll blind you if ..."

The little girl walked away. Volodia followed her.

"What is your name, little girl?"

"Halina. I'm so hungry."

"Halina, here is some bread for you."

"Can I give some to my little sister?"

"Yes, Halina. How old are you?"

"Six. My sister is two."

Under the veranda of a teahouse, refugees huddled together on bundles of their belongings. Halina ran to her mother and grandmother.

"Mama, Mama," she yelled in Polish. "This man gave me some bread ... real bread."

"Where are you from?" Volodia asked the young woman.

"From Podole. We are Poles. They brought us here from the Far East. They promised to take us to a collective farm."

"Are you sick?"

"No, God forbid. Just exhausted and hungry."

Volodia gave her all the rubles he had. "Go, get some food."

"Thank you. God will reward you!"

Volodia left the teahouse. He was depressed, and grumbled to himself. "All their talk of freedom, of brotherhood for all nations. Perhaps there is freedom here for the local people, but the refugees? They are free to suffer, to die. Why did they send Halina and her mother here? Why did they dump all those people here, thousands of miles from Europe?"

A sadness overtook him. He returned to the center and made out a list of next morning's needs. Fatima had a message for him.

"Dr. Ivanovna asked me to give you this note."

"Thank you, Fatima."

Volodia unfolded the note written in pencil.

"Vladimir Arionovitz. Saw the article about you. Good start. Would like to see you. Perhaps tonight? T. I."

* * *

Volodia wrote in his notebook:

> *"I've just come back from Tanya. We are facing here formidable obstacles in our work even before I start anything.*
>
> *I am waiting impatiently for my first directives from Dr. Chaidarov. Tanya is a conscientious doctor, an enthusiastic patriot torn between the war affairs of her country and the interests of her clinic and health center. We spent until past midnight talking about her plans for the isolator attached to the ward. I am fascinated by her optimistic spirit, by her matter-of-factness. When I was ready to leave, she said quietly, 'Would you like to stay overnight? I am very lonely. Fatima is on duty.' I never expected anything of this sort. There was no shyness in her request*

and for a moment I was silent from the shock of surprise. She turned off the light and we undressed.

Her warm, full body aroused my desire for her. My hands trembling with excitement started to caress her shoulders and pull her closer to me. She put her fingers on my lips. "Not now, Volodia. I feel very, very tired. Just hold me like this ... I am very lonely ... You can wake me later."

I moved away from her swiftly. At dawn in the profound stillness, she came to me, into my arms, cuddled, affectionately caressed my face, my chest.

Tanya displays an unwavering hunger for love. She is a warm creature and likes to play like a little girl. This morning, she forgot her age, position, all worldly wisdom, and was all woman.

"You are the first man I've slept with since my Mischa left. He was a refugee like you. We met on the refugee train from Kuibyshev to Andizhan. He is at the front now fighting our common enemy."

"And here we are stealing his love."

"No, we are sharing hunger, loneliness. We satisfy a longing."

Tanya got upset by our conversation. We washed and dressed. Her silence began to worry me. I took her in my arms and she quieted down.

"I am a durak *-- a fool -- for saying all those unpleasant words."*

"They depressed me very much. They made me feel guilty," she said in a meek voice. "I am a woman and very lonely."

"I understand. Are we still friends?"

"Yes. When you are lonely, come over. I am always ready to receive you."

Volodia started to implement Dr. Chaidarov's directives.
Every morning, after he checked the inventory with Fatima and
gave Aziz Ali his daily assignments, he visited kitchens,
restaurants, and teahouses and ordered improvements.
He was inspecting the local bakery yard and was about to
write a report about its unsanitary conditions. The bakery
manager pleaded with him to give him three days to clean up
the yard.
"I will do anything for you, Comrade Inspector. Maybe
you need some flour? Salt? Some extra bread? Just don't
write this report."
"I don't need anything for myself, but you can do us a
favor. We get our bread ration delivered at noontime. Can
you arrange to deliver bread to the hospital and center early
every morning?"
"I promise."
The manager wrapped two loaves of bread in a newspaper.
"This is for you, Comrade Inspector."
"Are you trying to bribe me?"
"Oh, no! This is just a favor for a favor."
"I can't take this bread with me. You can deliver it to our
center and give the bread to Aziz Ali."
"I will deliver it myself. I promise to clean up the bakery
in three days ... I swear."
Volodia, with the help of Dr. Chaidarov, forced the village
council to open the public bath three times weekly and invite
all refugees to come for free baths and clothes-disinfection.
His evenings were divided between the refugees from
Poland and the Ukraine, visits to the center ward, preparing
requests for the Andizhan Board of Health, drinking tea with
Dr. Tanya Ivanovna, or writing poems and his memoirs.
Tanya was lonely. She liked books and magazines, but
she was a young woman longing for company. Volodia was
a few years younger than Tanya, and was just as lonesome.
Volodia reminded her of her friend, Mischa Wengrov, a Jew
from Germany. She had met him on the last train of evacuees
from Russia. He was away at the front. Tanya was reading

Mischa's letters to Volodia, short accounts of frontier life.

"We had only a few weeks together, but they were happy moments in my life. I love him ... even though I know I will never marry him."

"Are you going to live alone the rest of your life?"

"Yes. I'm married to my work."

After conversations like these, they sat quietly listening to the radio, reading outdated papers, or Volodia would write his diary. Sometimes Tanya would simply ask Volodia to please stay for the night.

Her startling directness always made him sentimental. Here she was, a beautiful woman, a mature person, a strong-willed, energetic doctor, and so terribly in need of someone to talk to.

There was another lonely woman at the hospital complex, the nurse, Vera Alexeyvna Kenegina. Volodia asked her one evening, "Vera Alexeyvna, you never go anywhere?"

Vera was a young White Russian woman. She graduated from the Nursing School of the Minsk Medical Institute and had come to Kyzyl Kishlak before the war. Vera had a light complexion, white-blond hair, green eyes, a flat chest, and masculine arms. She was tall, strong and efficient, but had no friends. The local young men who tried to make advances were disappointed. They called her "the girl with the warm heart and cold body."

Vera lived alone in a small room at the hospital building. Tanya had invited her to move in with her but she politely declined. She spent her evenings reading medical books. She was friendly but reserved, especially with men, and habitually showered with strong disinfectant, a repulsive odor that drove men away.

Volodia made friends with her from his first day of work.

"Hmm. Vera ... I like the scent of Carbol. You remind me of the hospital where I worked." Volodia closed his eyes, inhaling the Carbol-filled air drifting from Vera's uniform.

"Thank you, Vladimir Arionovitz."

"For what?"

"People hate to stay near me, but this is my best protector against men."

"You hate men?"

"I don't hate them. I just don't like them ... or need them."

"We must talk about it sometime."

"Why? What for? Why relive fear?"

Volodia mentioned Vera to Dr. Chaidarov.

"We are fortunate to have such an efficient nurse on our staff. But she is separated from us all, withdrawn."

"Vera has her reasons. Solitude is sometimes better than bad company."

"I could never live in such isolation. People need people."

"So why don't you come to us one evening? Babachan, my wife, would love to have you and Dr. Ivanovna for dinner."

"You let us know when, Dr. Chaidarov. It will be our pleasure to spend an evening as guests in your home."

"I will invite Dr. Ivanovna myself." Dr. Chaidarov's eyes rested for a moment on Volodia. "You know, I'm so glad you came here. You care about people."

Volodia was overtaken by Dr. Chaidarov's words, deeply moved by the invitation. But his feelings of fondness were mingled with genuine fear of the menacing dangers that confronted the village now that thousands of homeless refugees, rag-clad, half naked, hungry and sick older men, women, and children had arrived. He could see that the village, overtaken by the homeless, was sliding toward sudden, widespread typhus, diarrhea, and scabies epidemics.

He felt like a mountain climber on the edge of a slope who was in danger of rolling down, sinking downhill to the bottom of a menacing reality: the incomprehensible Soviet system.

* * * * *

CHAPTER THREE
Uzbekian Hospitality

Uzbekian Hospitality

Tanya was upset at not having a proper dress to wear, her only blouse was too tight, her only dress worn out. She kept changing her hair style and constantly asked Volodia how she looked. "You look great, delightful, time to go. We are late ... " Finally she decided to wear her army uniform.

They walked through the quiet alley to a little house with a vineyard and a veranda covered with violets and tulips. Dr. Chaidarov greeted them and introduced them to Babachan, his wife, a small woman with a girlish face, big black eyes, long eyebrows, and a tiny mouth. She looked like a princess out of a storybook, clad in the garb of Uzbekian women -- a multi-colored long silk dress, silk trousers, and sandals. In a gentle voice, Dr. Chaidarov complimented Tanya on her good looks. "Tanya, you look truly beautiful. We are honored and glad you came."

Babachan invited her guests into a large room. The walls were covered with tapestries. A huge carpet rested on the floor with many pillows, cushions, and soft mats. The dim light from the small window made the room look intimate. Babachan and Ninotchka, a refugee girl who lived with them, spread an embroidered cloth upon a round, low table. Ninotchka placed hot, thick *lepioshkas* -- round shaped bread, bowls with *katik* -- curdled sour milk, and dishes with pink and blue berries on the table. They all sat on cotton-stuffed cushions of different sizes and shapes, embroidered with scenes of Samarkand palaces, Uzbekian inscriptions, and colorful designs.

Dr. Chaidarov showed special interest in finding out what all the ribbons on Tanya's uniform were for.

"You must have been some brave officer, Tatyana

Ivanovna."

"Dr. Chaidarov, we all did our duty. You have a nice record of service yourself."

"We got Viborg, the Karelian Peninsulas, and some holes in my lungs," Dr. Chaidarov said modestly. Tanya appeared to be uncomfortable sitting on the cushions. Complaining would make her look clumsy, so, like a good soldier, she pretended to be comfortable. She did not say a word, and instead turned to Dr. Chaidarov. "Dr. Chaidarov, you have a very nice home and a very beautiful wife," Tanya remarked in order to change the subject.

Dr. Chaidarov beamed.

"We have a great love for this house. It was my father's and grandfather's home for generations. In fact, my great grandfather lived here before the Russian Czars came. My folks were herdsman, living in tents and travelling from place to place in the hills and in the desert around here. They settled here because they found enough water for grass and rice. My grandparents built this little house with their own hands and I rebuilt it." They all sat silently while Dr. Chaidarov continued.

"Here, in the shadow of the Tien-Shan Mountains, I was born and grew up. When I left for the medical institute to study, I always came back here for my vacation to work in the *Kolkhoz* Village Council. My entire life has been centered around Kyzyl Kishlak. I love the sight of the mountains, the mild climate. I call it, 'our paradise' ... "

Babachan and Ninotchka served a steaming *pilaff* -- rice with bits of lamb. The aroma of the diced mutton cooked with carrots, onions, and spices teased the appetite. Ninotchka returned with a pitcher of water, a small basin, and long towel. They all followed Dr. Chaidarov, washed their finger tips and waited. There were no forks or spoons, and again they imitated Dr. Chaidarov and Babachan and ate with their fingers.

Volodia watched Babachan pick up some rice, roll it into a ball, and snap it neatly into her little mouth. Tanya also looked at them in wonderment. The Chaidarovs ate without losing a grain of rice, without soiling more than the tips of their fingers. Volodia was reluctant to display his clumsiness. Dr. Chaidarov must have noticed this because he kept rolling rice balls and pushing them in his direction.

Volodia complimented Babachan on the meal.

"The *pilaff* was delicious ... Everything tasted so good."

"Thank you, but the credit goes to my husband. Muhamoud cooked the *pilaff*," Babachan said humbly. "He is a better cook than I am." Her eyes turned proudly to her husband.

"In that case we will make him chief inspector in our hospital's kitchen."

"That's all I need!" Dr. Chaidarov laughed heartily.

While Volodia and Tanya drank their strong green tea, Dr. Chaidarov, in an intimate voice, continued.

"Originally this area was desert with only small farms from here to Chinabaad. On land where a little water was found, our government built water canals. The new irrigation system supplied us with plenty of water; our *kolkhoz* -- cooperatives -- produce barley, vegetables, fruit, rice. Our area is now a leading producer of cotton."

"But we are so far away from any road ... almost at the end of the world," Tanya commented.

"Yes, our main problem is transportation. We are hampered by bad roads, and we're far away from a railroad. Still, in the last eighteen years we've come a long way. We've built a new school, hospital, pioneer club house, the malaria center, and a new road to Chinabaad. Most of our homes in the village have electricity. When the war ends, when our boys return, we will build new, better roads. Our government had to combat many problems here. All important buildings must be reinforced with concrete and only built to a limited height."

"Why?"

"The crust of our area is shaky. We often have earthquakes and some of our houses are built only from mud. Across the border in China, Afghanistan and Iran people die by the thousands yearly. Whole villages disappear in the earthquakes. Our government builds reinforcements, artificial mountains and bridges to protect us from such natural calamities."

"You have a nice place here. The whole panorama of the valley and the mountains is majestic and pleasant," Volodia remarked earnestly. "It's a pity that the people here must suffer so much from malaria."

"Yes, it's more than pitiful. It is pathetic," Babachan said in a quiet voice. "There is sometimes a fifty percent absentee rate among students and teachers in my school. Our problems as a new village cannot be blamed on the war alone. Our growth has not been orderly or properly planned." Babachan spoke in very articulate Russian, almost without accent. "In the past we had no qualified leaders. They were good workers, farmers, devoted Party followers but with little or no experience in the field of village development."

Babachan's little face got very serious. Her voice became harsh, scornful, "We still have a long way to go to educate our people. We must have patience until the war ends, and the arrival of so many refugees does not help us either ... "

Tanya got up. "Forgive me, my legs stiffened ... Babachan, dear," Tanya's voice trembled slightly, "we can't drive the refugees from our midst. They are Soviet citizens. I am also a refugee but not a stranger here. You, as a school principal, can call for patience in developing your cultural programs. But we, in the medical field, cannot wait until the war ends. We deal with health problems, with undernourished children, with a shortage of medicines. I checked the tractor brigades in the *kolkhoz* here. The majority of them suffer from deficiencies and sicknesses. We have a war right in our midst. Malaria is the enemy. It spreads like wildfire."

Volodia interjected, "We are also worried about a typhoid epidemic among the refugees. There is no soap, no disinfectant available for the refugees, and they keep sending more and more refugees every week. Visit the village bazaar and you will see and hear the lament, the wails of misfortunes."

"The most important factor contributing to this situation," Tanya continued, "is the lack of salt, fat, and much needed drugs. I'm glad you raised this question, Vladimir Arionovitz. Dr. Chaidarov is undoubtedly aware of the unfortunate circumstances in which the refugees live. We are grateful to the local Uzbek population and leaders for their help, but the misery of the refugees cries out for more help. There is no healing we can offer without food and medications. Many of our people will perish here.

"Yes, I know," Dr. Chaidarov put aside his bowl of tea. "Our people were always friendly to strangers. It's part of our way of life. But some functionaries in Tashkent, in Andizhan, are overdoing it. They don't ask for our opinions. They just dump a mass of people here with many problems. We've already had complaints that the refugees are buying up all the food from the cooperatives and markets. Prices are rising on everything in the bazaar, and they keep sending those unfortunate homeless people."

Tanya again interceded. "Forgive me, Dr. Chaidarov. This steady increase of refugees in our center and clinic requires more personnel. Our equipment is outdated. We have patients, war veterans, who need help. We don't have enough sterile instruments for one day's work. Sometimes, we are so exhausted that we can't go on. I'm not easily discouraged, but I get depressed when I see patients lying on the bare floors for lack of mattresses, beds. We have cases of scorpion and spider bites. It's hard to work under those conditions."

There was a long silence. Nonitchka removed the tea bowls and dishes. Tanya and Volodia followed the Chaidarovs to the veranda and sat down quietly, listening to the daily communique.

"Our troops continue to counter-attack on all sectors of the front. Thirty-one enemy planes were shot down. We lost seven planes. Our forces in the area of Mozaisk made a break in the enemy's main defense and our forces silenced the German artillery.

"Our units under the command of Comrade Panfedoff in one battle stubbornly overcame enemy resistance, capturing many guns and other ammunition, fifty horses and other booty. The enemy lost two hundred fifty soldiers and officers."

Ninotchka and Babachan served honeydew and grapes. No one ate. Dr. Chaidarov broke the silence. "I asked the village council to give us the old school building."

Babachan's face got sad again. "This is no solution to the refugee problem. It will hamper the activities of our young students ... They will leave the area if the school building is taken from them. They take advantage of the school grounds, play ball, and have cultural activities there. When the subject comes up for a vote at the council, I will vote against it."

Tanya, surprised, looked at Babachan. "You're going to vote against your husband?"

"At home he is my husband, the authority, the master of the house. But this question cuts deeply into my convictions. I'm a school principal and I consider the education of our children the most important thing in our village. We women were treated as slaves. Now we are equal to men by law, but men still don't recognize that we are on par with them. The only way we will get recognition and equality is through education. When I feel that the interests of my students are at stake, I fight for them. I'm sorry my husband thinks otherwise. Instead of seeing our children leaving their *kishlak,* I'd rather see a stop to the flood of more and more refugees."

Volodia's face turned red from shock. He suddenly realized that this woman was part of the village facade who, under the banner of 'Party, Government, Constitution,' pursued her own parochial interests. All that she and the others cared for were their own children and their own people. All strangers, refugees, were the intruders who trespassed on their way of life, invaders forced upon them, a burden, a curse, a plague on her village.

"Forgive us, Dr. Chaidarov, for bringing up all these problems at your dinner table," Tanya said in a friendly manner. "I should not have spoken here about this situation, but their pain is ours, and if a typhoid epidemic will spread, it will destroy us all."

Dr. Chaidarov, a little embarrassed by Babachan's scornful remarks, stood up. "Tatyana Ivanovna, you're the best doctor

we ever had in this area. I hope we will be able to say the
same thing about you, Vladimir Arionovitz. May I say,
frankly, I'm glad to see that you two are friends fighting for
each other's needs. Your needs, your problems, your anger, are
mine also. We all have a hard job ahead of us. Together, we
can overcome it."

I'm sure we will," Volodia said humbly. Tanya and
Babachan hugged each other.

"Thank you for a most delicious meal and a most pleasant
evening."

"Sorry I got carried away," Babachan said smilingly. "I
am honored that you came to my home for dinner. I'm
pleased to see how much you two care about the Uzbek
people."

"They are also my people," Tanya answered.

Dr. Chaidarov walked his guests through the narrow alley
to the street. "Come again ... We were pleased to have you.
We must meet like this more often. We can't solve all our
problems, but surely discussing them can't hurt."

"We will be glad to come again. Thank you."

"Dosvidanya."

"Salaam!"

From nearby houses, women and children peeked through
holes in the gatedoors and through leaves of trees at Volodia
and Tanya -- the strange Europeans walking their street.
Volodia greeted them with a friendly *"Salaam,"* but they ran
away for fear that he might see their faces, quite an improper
thing in an Uzbek village.

Tanya and Volodia walked leisurely to the clinic. It was
late evening. Groups of people were still sitting outside their
houses talking. The night was cool. Tanya was tired, but still
felt like talking.

"I really would have nothing against having a meeting like
this once a week."

"I had the first decent meal in weeks and a good discussion
with dedicated people, and besides, I was in the company of
two charming women."

"Volodia, stop your flattery. I don't need adulation or

buttering-up. You still have your capitalistic mentality of coaxing the madame. Our discussion was deadly serious."

"So was I."

"Stop being cynical and don't make fun of Babachan and me."

"I really think you are two pretty, charming, outspoken women. Is something wrong with that? You spoke the truth without restraint, and Babachan, I believe, is more Uzbek than a Party Communist."

They walked in silence for a while, looking at the houses, the flat roofs and mud walls. Women were sitting in front of their porches turning round, flat stones with a hole in the middle pouring handsful of barley between them, grinding the barley into flour.

"They work like this almost all night to grind enough flour for their daily needs. Oh, how primitive we still are," Tanya said quietly. "But they are happy this way ... They can take the barley to the *kolkhoz* and have it ground. Still, they like to do it themselves. Have you seen the ovens in which they bake bread?"

"No. What about them?"

"See the smoke coming from the yards? They all have ovens made from clay and mud shaped like beehives. They make a fire with cotton wicks or dried dung mixed with straw. When the oven becomes very hot, they take the dough and slap it against the oven walls. There it sticks until the *lepioshka* is baked and falls down when it is ready."

"They've done this for thousands of years."

"How do you know?"

"My ancestors in Egypt baked bread the same way."

It was a long walk to the clinic. The smell of the streams combined with the smoke of the burning ovens left a disagreeable odor. It got very dark and the streets were emptying. Dogs barked. Tanya held onto Volodia.

"Why do they have so many dogs?"

"Dear Tanya, the dogs work for us ... for my malaria center."

"How?"

"These dogs are never fed. They simply live on the refuse and waste which people throw into the streets. If it were not for the dogs, the people here would suffer from many more diseases than they do now. The dogs eat up all the trash which would otherwise decay."

"Where did you learn all this?"

"By reading, observing."

"You're some man. I wish I were a man."

"What's wrong with being a woman?"

"Sometimes I hate myself. I'm getting older. I have gray hair. I'm scared of getting old and sick and not being able to work, to serve my patients. As a man I would have been physically stronger."

"Tanya Ivanovna, you are talking like a child. You're the equal of any man I've ever known. You are dedicated to your profession. Everybody respects you. Nature has rewarded you in so many ways. You're a delightful, beautiful human being. How can you talk like an immature little girl?"

"You know, Volodia, sometimes I wish I were an immature girl working on a farm, in love with a tractor driver, with two or three children, washing and mending my husband's socks, loving, living with him, sharing, giving. Being happy."

Again they walked in silence.

Volodia remarked, "What a crazy world."

"You say I'm crazy?"

"God forbid! I said, what a crazy world."

"Why?"

"Here we live in a time of war, millions of young people dying in battle. Here people are collapsing and dying from diseases, epidemics, hunger. We just had dinner where a doctor claimed that he was satisfied by the great service you are performing here. We almost spoiled a good dinner by talking of our own insufficiencies and shortcomings and offering our ideas on how to overcome them. And here you are walking beside me, an honored officer, telling me that you dream of a tractor driver in a *kolkhoz,* a half dozen children, and hate being a woman."

"This damned, inferior clinic and our lousy center with no

beds depresses me. I don't think I can take it anymore."
Tanya started to cry. For a while, Volodia let her weep,
then he gave her his handkerchief and she wiped her nose.
They came to the clinic. Tanya took off her uniform and
changed into a white coat.
"Volodia, wait for me here. Don't leave me alone tonight.
I'm going to see a few patients and will come back soon.
How do I look?"
"Beautiful, as always."
"No, will they notice that I cried?"
"So what? Sobbing is human."
"I don't have to add worry to their misery."
Volodia fixed the hair-crown of her thick braids on her
head. "You look good now, honestly."
"Thank you. I will be back soon. Will you wait?"
"I said I would."
Again she came over, put her arms around him, and kissed
him. "Sorry I was carried away ... You know I did not mean
it."
"I know."
"Please wait."
"I will, I will," he whispered.

It was a sad morning at the hospital. Four patients had
died during the night. All of the deceased were women,
refugees from the Ukraine. Volodia's face was chalk white.
Dr. Chaidarov looked ill and nervous. Tanya was upset. Vera
was biting her upper lip and her eyes were dark with sadness.
According to one youngster whose mother was among the
patients who had died so suddenly, all the women and their
families lived together in a nearby *kolkhoz*.
The women became ill, stricken with severe stomach pains
two days before. Alarmed by their cries and pains, the
kolkhoz secretary sent them to the clinic. Vera had given them
some medication and told them to go back home. There was
no room in the hospital. On their way back home all the
women felt severe pains in their legs. They had turned around
and dragged themselves back to the clinic, sitting there, waiting

all night for a doctor. Tanya was busy at the center. Dr.
Chaidarov was away in the village. In the morning, when he
returned, he pronounced them dead.
    Tanya was defeated. "Those four women will weigh on
my conscience."
    "No use blaming yourself, Tatyana Ivanovna," Dr.Chaidarov
said sadly. "We have an epidemic on our hands. We are
short of most essential supplies. Vladimir Arionovitz, please,
get some anti-typhus serum and camphor immediately."
    "There is no place around here that I can get it."
    "I will get you a horse and you can go down to
Chinabaad."
    Dr. Chaidarov called the local bank director Naimov. By
directive of the village council, the hospital complex had the
right to use the horses in case of emergency.
    "I can't give you horses this morning but we can take a
passenger to Chinabaad. Our bank accountant is leaving for
Chakulabaad and Chinabaad."
    "How will Comrade Tarko get back?"
    "Our accountant will pick him up."
    Dr. Chaidarov hung up the phone and turned to Volodia.
"Tell them we are furious at the way our quota of medicines
and supplies is being stolen en route to our village."
    "How will I get there?"
    "The bank's accountant will pick you up here any minute."
    Vera wrote down a list of needs for the hospital emergency
room. Dr. Chaidarov signed and stamped the request. Outside
the buggy was waiting.

    "So you are the bank accountant? Good morning. I am
Tarko. Haven't I seen you before?"
    "Yes ... I am Eva. My mother is Celia Markes, a patient
at the center. You are the Pole my mother told me about."
    "My name is Wolf Tarko. Here they call me Vladimir or
Volodia."
    "Some name for a Jew from Poland."
    "I have had many names: Velvel, Vladislaw, Volodia. You
have one name?"

"Yes ... Eva."

"A beautiful name for an attractive girl."

"Some bargain. It doesn't help at the goods storehouse and you don't get an extra bone in your borscht in the restaurant."

"How long have you been an accountant?"

"Since 1939. I graduated Teachers Technikum in Zhitomir, but my father was killed and I had to return home to help mother. I got a job in the Malichov Bank. Where is your home?"

"In Lodz, a big industrial center with large factories. It is the second largest city in Poland."

"Anyone left from your family?"

"My parents died when I was a child. I was raised by my grandparents."

"Any relatives left?"

"I hope and pray. I don't know."

"You believe in prayer?"

"Yes, I believe. Sometimes I have doubts. I guess sometimes I use the expression because I was raised to believe."

"I am Jewish and proud of it. I don't know anything about religion, but I pray every moment for our soldiers to return home."

"Such prayers are noble, but with prayers we must have action. When an enemy attacks, regardless whether Nazi or typhus bacteria, we can't just pray. We must fight back with all the power we have."

Eva's look changed from a reserved appraising one to a warm, animated expression of kinship. "My brother is doing the fighting and I do the praying. My brother is only nineteen."

"Tell me more about yourself, Eva."

"What is there to tell?"

"Recite something to me in Yiddish."

"What would you like to hear?"

"Anything to remind me of home ... school ... "

The buggy moved slowly on the dry, sandy road; around them was dust and the hot sun. They passed fields of cotton,

Volodia was holding onto the whip and reins. From time to time he glanced at Eva, who was singing a popular Hofshtein poem in a subdued voice,

> *On Russian fields, in the winter twilights,*
> *Where can we be lonelier?*
> *Where can one be more lonesome?*
> *Our world is so confined, my circle so little --*
> *On the bright Russian fields I am starved for space.*

"You sing beautifully, Eva. Please continue."

"I don't remember the rest of the poem. I just remember the melody."

"Please tell me more about your family."

"My father was a master mechanic at the local brewery in Malichov, a small town near Zhitomir. He died in an accident in the brewery boiling room. My mother lived on a small pension and worked part-time in the local brewery-canteen as a cashier. I worked in the bank; my brother, Boris, studied at the FZO Technical School. He was a bright student, and hoped to become a qualified mechanic. The brewery promised to give him my father's job when he graduated, but the war started on June 22nd, and the next day my brother was mobilized. We did not hear from him for months. My mother, my younger sister, Anna, and I were evacuated to Kamishin, then, by barge on the Volga River, to Kuibyshev.

"We liked living in the Kuibyshev area, but the cold weather was too much for my mother. After we got the first letters from Boris we decided to ask for permission to travel to Uzbekistan. We hoped they would let us stay in Chimkent, Tashkent or Samarkand, but the train did not even stop at those stations. They sent us to Andizhan. The State Bank offered me this job in the Kyzyl Kishlak branch. They said that this was 'the most beautiful oasis in the Fergana Valley.' We were tired of wandering. Mother was sick, so I accepted the job and here I am. Our hut is small but safe. Anna has a job in the local restaurant after school hours. We get some letters from Boris and this keeps us alive. My big worry is mother, she has asthma and malaria. She keeps telling me that you keep her alive with hope."

"Sometimes people feel a need for encouragement. Here in our center there are people with no friends, no families, no loving daughters. So, they have me, just a symbol, a landsman they can freely talk to me about their pains, failures, despair, longings. I stay by their beds and listen to them, pray with them to our 'God of Mercy' who has no mercy for them. I let them hear the words they desire. Sometimes I get the impression that God really hears them. They smile, they fall asleep peacefully."

"Don't apologize for praying with the sick ... as long as it helps them in some way."

"I just wanted to explain, Eva. Tell me, where did you learn to handle a horse?"

"No big deal. I can even handle a donkey."

"You often travel this road by yourself?"

"Yes. The first time I was scared; there was staring from every hut and every corner. Men, women, and children all gathered around me, shaking my hands, even pinching, but after awhile they knew I was with the bank and they became used to me."

They reached Chinabaad. Eva stopped her buggy in front of the hospital. A long line of people in rags, shivering from malaria, surrounded the region hospital, begging for food and money. Women in dresses that covered their faces and men in black cotton overcoats with small skullcaps on their shaven heads were busy selling and buying sour milk, dry fruit, raisins -- chewing tobacco, arguing, bargaining and shivering, always shivering, while waiting in line to get into the outpatient clinic.

Volodia stepped down from the buggy. "Thank you, Eva." He said in Yiddish, "I will wait for you here. When do you think you will be going back?"

"It will not take me too long ... about two hours."

* * * * *

CHAPTER FOUR
Eva

Eva

Eva was late. Volodia waited in front of the clinic, listening to the daily broadcast. "On the sector of the Kalinin front our rifle battalions were attacked by numerically superior forces. After crippling several enemy tanks, the Red Army, with well organized fire, confused the enemy and then made a bayonet attack. The Germans retreated. Our orderlies counted 450 dead German officers and soldiers on the battlefield."

The news upset Volodia, as always. There was a war going on against the savagery of the Nazis with hundreds and thousands of soldiers wounded, and he, a medic, willing to help on the battlefield of Europe, was looked upon as an untrustworthy refugee, left at this remote village fighting mosquitoes and ticks.

He was in an exceedingly bad mood. He was hungry and thirsty. Finally Eva showed up, breathless. Volodia seated himself near her in the buggy, looking genuinely worried.

"What happened?" he asked. "Are you always so prompt?"

"They have bookkeepers without my experience. Their balance sheets, reports, and forms were wrong."

"What did you do?"

Eva looked at him with a twinkle in her eyes. "I put their books in order. I couldn't seem to break away."

"Did they thank you for it?"

"Oh, yes. See, here are some grapes. Delicious. Sweet. Try some."

The horse was tired.

"He ate too much," Eva joked.

So the buggy traveled slowly back on the same sandy road to Kyzyl Kishlak.

"We will stop at the hospital center and give some fruit to

48

my mother," Eva said quietly.

With one hand she was holding the reins and with the other she was throwing grapes into her mouth. Volodia kept looking at her face -- big, dark brown eyes, long eyebrows, a small nose and a tiny mouth. In the two hours while he was attending to his task in Chinabaad he had been thinking of her, waiting for her to come back. He looked at the thin blouse she was wearing. He felt an urge to move closer to her, to be able to gently caress her hair, but he was shy and reserved.

Eva felt his eyes, his gaze, and instinctively moved away.

"Stop looking at me like that."

"Are you scared of me?"

"Why, no."

"You moved away."

"I don't trust myself with you," Eva said honestly. "The sight of you, the way you talk, makes me think the craziest things. You know, Oleg looks at me this way."

"All I did was just look at you. I was really worried about you."

Eva moved close to him.

"You know, Volodia, I hoped you would like me. We are so very lonely here."

"Yes, we are. We work hard, have no one. We have no time for a moment like this."

Eva sat up, took a deep breath and turned her face to him.

"You call this happiness? We hardly know each other. And why do you keep looking at me like that?"

"I don't know. I was just thinking why I was so worried about you not being on time. A girl traveling alone ... or was I so anxious to see you again?"

They stopped the buggy near a stream and let the horse drink. Eva washed her face and feet and sat down waiting for the horse to finish drinking.

Volodia was holding onto the reins and kept looking at Eva. Her voice was sweet, calm, low. He thought that her voice was a harmonious accompaniment to the loveliness of the rest of her.

"I'm glad I went with you today. I was very upset this

morning, but traveling with you, Eva, I almost forgot some of
my worries. You know, sometimes you meet someone, and
you hope that time will stand still and that person will never
leave."

"It was a good day for me too, Volodia. But it's getting
chilly. Let's hurry home."

Eva settled herself close to Volodia, holding his arm.

"Funny, we were two strangers in the morning, and now I
am holding your arm."

"Nothing funny about it, Eva. Sometimes things happen
this way. Tell me. Who is Oleg? Is he here in the village?"

"He is a man from my hometown and he works here in the
local militia in charge of the marriage license office -- ZAGS.
His name is Oleg Polishenko. Do you know him?"

"No, I've never been in ZAGS. Is he your friend?"

"Yes, he has been my friend since my school years, but not
my boyfriend."

"Have you got one?"

"I get many offers, notes, poems, but I am still free."

"How did Oleg get here? Did he follow you?"

"Oleg was wounded in the first days of this war. When
they released him from the *lazaret,* he searched for his mother.
She was evacuated together with us and sent here. Oleg
wanted me to come to ZAGS with him and get married. We
like him a lot. He is good natured and honest, but his mother
is an old-fashioned woman. She doesn't like strangers, even
Russians, and particularly Jews. My mother knows her from
Malichov, so I politely declined, but I still like him. He is my
close friend. He always looks at me the way you did."

"Maybe he's in love with you."

Eva did not answer.

"What are your plans for the future?"

"What is there to plan? We must wait until the war is
over. I just pray for my mother to get well and for all of us
to return to our hometown. The Uzbeks hate the Russians and
the refugees. They hate you with your Red Cross badge,
regardless of what you do to help them. To them, you are a
government functionary."

"I am not in their government or in their Party. Are you in their Party?"

"I belonged to the *Komsomol* while I was a student. My boss, Naimov, belongs to the Party, but all he cares about is himself, his village. The only thing he is concerned about is Uzbekistan."

"How do you know all this?"

"They think that I don't understand their language, and I hear them talk among themselves. Let me tell you something, Wolf Tarko. They pray to Allah for the Germans to wipe out the Russians in this war. They hope that the English will come from Iran, or the Chinese from behind the mountains, and free Central Asia from the Soviet yoke."

"How do you feel about it?"

"All I care about is that we win this war, that my brother and our soldiers return home, and we can return to our hometown, my Malichov."

"And in Malichov, will they not hate you?"

"Maybe yes and maybe no. Perhaps the end of the war will change some things, unite all people to build a better world. Anyhow, they've always hated us and we've always survived, haven't we?"

They stopped at the center. Dr. Chaidarov was already gone. Vera took the box and bags of medications and signed a receipt for them. Volodia fastened the horse to the railing bar, called Aziz Ali and asked him to return the horse and buggy to the bank yard. Then he followed Eva to the ward to see her mother.

Celia Markes lay flat in the hospital bed. Her thin hands reached for Eva. She looked at Volodia with a faint smile. Her voice was tired and weak.

"How are you Chavele? How is Anna?"

"I was out of the village all day. I got some fruit, Mother. How do you feel?"

"Thank God, better. I got new medication last night, and I can breathe easier. Anna brought me some soup, so I am not really hungry."

"Mother, this is Wolf Tarko."

"I know him. That's the Pole I told you about who comes here and talks with the patients. How did you meet my Chavele?"

"She gave me a ride to Chinabaad today."

"Alone. No father. A sick mother." Celia was on the verge of tears.

"Mom, stop this pity stuff. You're still here and will be with us for a long time. You'll see, Mom, Boris will come back. You will get well, and we'll return home."

"Oy, dear God, I hope soon."

Volodia was exhausted, but the way Eva talked to her mother, the way she hugged her and comforted her, made him feel good. He felt drawn, somehow, to these two women.

"Mom, I will call on you first thing in the morning. I have to go now."

"Go Chavele, take care of Anna. It was nice seeing you, Wolf Tarko."

"I will see you again in the morning."

Volodia walked Eva home.

"Volodia, please come in and share some food with us. Don't say no, please."

He followed her into the small hut, a dark little room with a sandy floor and bare walls. It contained one bed with a large straw mattress, a big old table, some wooden boxes that served as chairs and clothes closets. Those were the furnishings of their mud cabin called a *kibitka.*

In the yard of the *kibitka* was a stream where Volodia and Eva washed their hands and faces. By the time Eva set two bowls on the table, the soup was steaming and ready.

After they ate, Anna came back from her after-school job in the local restaurant. She was sixteen but looked more like a child of thirteen, skinny, pale, the same pretty big eyes as Eva's. They all sat outside talking about the refugees in the village.

"In the restaurant where I work," Anna said sadly, "the refugees are intimidated by our guests, chased and often beaten by our kitchen servants, but they stay there day and night, waiting for the clean-up man to throw out the garbage so they can find some food in the trash. I can't stop feeling sorry for them. I dream about them every night."

Volodia looked at Anna's eyes, so mature, so full of gloom. He was about to say something unpleasant about the leaders of the village when a tall man appeared in front of them. He was wearing the uniform of the local militia. Eva introduced him to Volodia.

"Volodia, this is Oleg."

"Vladimir Tarko."

"Oleg Polishenko."

The two men sat down facing each other. Eva told Oleg what Anna just said. Oleg sighed.

"We haven't seen the worst yet. They are all poorly educated people unfit to run a village. They don't realize that the government is trying to save the people they evacuated here. I think that the reason they resent us is their belief that we are trying to Russianize Uzbekistan. They believe that under the mask of building Communism, our government and Party is exploiting their land. This is the way they look at all white people here, regardless of who they are. They have gardens full of fruit. They divide food, soap, salt, and clothes among themselves. Never mind us -- they think we were discharged here like waste matter, so they let us starve. The Uzbeks are Moslems -- they believe that everything is predestined by Allah. If Allah decreed for us, the infidels, to be homeless and suffer, then so be it. I can understand them as a Ukrainian ... the cruel laws, the barbaric oppression made them fall into complete apathy and hate the strangers among them. They still pray for deliverance and freedom."

"What hurts and shocks me," said Volodia, "is the indifference some local leaders display to the victims of war, the refugees who lie in misery in all the public places. They pass by and don't even look at the despair of the people trapped here."

Anna made some tea and, for a time, the conversation continued. Suddenly, Volodia started to hum a melody.

"Believe not that the world is for naught,

Made for the wolf and the fox, for murderer and cheat.
That the sky is a blind to keep God from perceiving.
The fog that thy hands not be seen,
And the wind just to drown bitter waits.
The world is not a hovel, market or cast-off!
All will be measured, all will be weighed.
Not a fear not a blood drop will fade,
Nor the spark in one soul be extinguished uncharged.
Tears gather into streams, and streams into oceans,
Oceans will swell to a flood.
And sparks burst into a thunder.
Oh, think not there is no judgment or judge!"

Eva and Oleg listened to Volodia singing this strange song by a poet unknown to them.

"Who is the author?" Eva asked him with a shiver is her voice.

"His name was Yitzhak Leibush Peretz, a Yiddish poet in Poland."

"Is he still alive?"

"His poetry and writings are. He died in 1915 in Warsaw."

Volodia said good night to Eva and Oleg and walked back to his little room. He could not fall asleep; he was thinking of Eva and Celia. He walked into the ward in the center and saw Celia peacefully asleep. He talked for a few moments to Fatima and some patients and went back to his room. When he did, finally, fall asleep, a terrible dream overtook him. There was a *pogrom*. Uzbeks, Kirgiz, Mongols, Tatars were killing Russians. The mobs were shouting, "Kill the Russians! Free our lands!" Leading the mob were Babachan and Naimov.

He woke up perspiring, bewildered from the nightmare. He wiped the sweat from his face and drank water to calm his nerves.

"Hold on, Velvel. Don't get so upset over a bad dream," a voice in him kept saying.

He picked up his notebook and started to read his own

writings:

"I can find no adequate words to describe the joy I feel to be able to write on paper, real white paper, that I got by trading away the only sweater I possessed.

"For eight days now, I have been traveling on this refugee train from Kuibyshev to Andizhan. The people in my coach are mostly ordinary factory workers, too old for army duty, traveling with their wives and children. They all keep to themselves and hardly talk to me. They don't trust me because of my accent or maybe because I am Jewish. It's good that I found this notebook and am able to occupy my time by writing.

"Where shall I start? It is difficult to write in a coach when you can feel and hear the breathing of the passenger next to you. The atmosphere is dense, full of anger, mistrust and hostility. Still, the idea that I have clean white paper and a pencil has welled up in me all the loneliness of the last eight days and the past two years and given me the courage to write my recollections.

"September, 1939. The Messerschmidts' blows resound over us with fury. The German onslaught threw back our unit toward the Bug River. A continuing forceful cannonade strafes the strand and makes it impossible for us to cross the River. We are facing an unseen enemy who keeps dive-bombing our position. "

The downpour was continuous. The noise of the falling rain on the roof mixed with the sound of bomb shells and the slow, steady, rattling, clinking of horseshoes somewhere outside.

Our field First Aid *Punkt* is stationed in a little church in the village of Sokolka, near the Bug River in Wohynia, Eastern Poland. The wounded lay on the wet ground, on stretchers and church pews. The only doctor, Captain Jerzy Kocharski, moved from stretcher to pew, followed by his aides tucking tags with numbers on the moaning wounded and removing them to the waiting horse-drawn covered wagons.

The small church was full and the wounded kept coming. The place was muddy, the air choked with the stench of sweat and blood.

We, the med-aides, were exhausted, sleepy, hungry, half-conscious of what was going on around us. We were not concerned with who advanced, who attacked. The radio loudspeaker blared, but we did not listen. The machine guns, the cries of humans and horses, the explosions and the misery around us made the radio unimportant and far away. What counted was to help the wounded -- this was all that mattered. So we moved around the church giving aid, cleaning wounds, washing foreheads.

Suddenly, the door opened and two armed Russian soldiers in ankle-length coats carrying *Tokarev* -- automatic machine guns -- stormed in.

"Ruki wierch! Hands up!"

We continued treating the wounded and observed with amazement the gestures and bewildered movements of the soldiers coming toward us, pushing their automatics to our chests.

"You, *Polski,* don't move. Hands up!"

A Russian officer came in and ordered the soldiers to step back. The officer's manners were courteous, his voice firm.

"Please continue working. All of you who carry arms, surrender them. *Brosaj orusje!* -- You are all prisoners of war."

Captain Kocharski motioned to the corner of the church where his pistol was hanging on his officer's belt and continued working on a wounded soldier. The Russian officer offered *machorka* -- tobacco -- to Dr. Kocharski, who politely declined. He motioned to the Russian to give the cigarette to the wounded. "Doctors may continue to attend to the wounded, all other personnel must leave this place." The Russians marched us off to a forest.

We walked a great distance in darkness. By morning we had loaded the wounded on *britchkas*, and our column of med-aides and disarmed soldiers marched to the woods on the road outside the town of Wlodzimierz -- Vladimir Wolinski.

The wounded breathed with difficulty, moaned, cried for water. I walked beside my wagon of wounded, helpless.

There was nothing we could give them until we were ordered to stop marching. The rain kept falling. I shivered from cold and hunger. Finally, our column stopped in a thick grove of trees.

Captain Kocharski and the wounded were transferred to ambulances. We were left behind with the soldiers in the woods. The Russians kept bringing more prisoners. We all looked tired and hungry, but the new prisoners looked much worse. Their eyes were bloodshot, frightened. Many carried exhausted soldiers on their backs. They fell quietly onto the black, wet ground.

The Russian guards, also tired, sat next to us on the ground. Some smoked, ate dry fish and dark bread, and offered some to us. By evening, we were still sitting in the woods waiting for food. Many of the Polish prisoners went into the woods to relieve themselves and disappeared.

I awoke in the late evening, hungry and aching from sleeping on the wet ground. I went deeper into the woods and loosened my belt. I was so weak that I fell and could not get up. A civilian helped me to my feet and carried me into a little field shack. The gray-haired Polish peasant helped wash my feet and face, and shared bread and milk with me.

"Bog Zaplatch -- God will reward you," I said.

He cried, *"Oh, Jezuniu,* what will happen to our land now?"

I had forgotten the dreadful experiences of the war I had been part of in the last twenty days. All I could think of at that moment was the soul of this Pole who showed me kindness and friendship and shared his bread with a defeated soldier. I repeated to him and to myself, "God will help us."

He gave me some civilian clothes and showed me a side road into Vladimir Wolinskiy.

In town, as if it were pre-arranged, the streets were full of people, red flags, banners, and demonstrations. Pictures of Stalin, Lenin, Timoshenko, Voroshilov, and other Soviet leaders were on all buildings. Youths chanted "freedom for the masses" and shouts of "thanks to the liberator of our land, Comrade Stalin," filled the town.

Simultaneously, the arrests began. Polish officers and clergy, Jewish businessmen, Ukrainian and Byelorussian landowners were marched off to waiting wagons and army trucks marked for distant destinations. The radio loudspeakers blared the joint communique by the German and Russian governments: "The Red Army and the German troops will restore the peace and order which has been disturbed by the disintegration of Poland ... " The radio loudspeakers kept repeating: "We came to liberate you from the Polish capitalist oppressors. Trucks and trains will take you refugees to a new life in the Soviet Union."

A huge red poster was hanging in front of the local synagogue. It read: "RELIGION IS OPIATE FOR THE PEOPLE." Despite the poster there were many worshippers in the small synagogue.

When I came in and inquired about the sexton, a young man noticed my Red Cross armband. I was followed, arrested, and led into a school building. The corridors were full of arrested "hostile" and "disloyal" Poles, Ukrainians, Jews, local intellectuals, teachers, priests, rabbis, and small shop owners.

I was led into a classroom where the Polish eagle lay smeared with paint. The portrait of Joseph Pilsudski, Poland's national leader, lay in the same corner, as if left there intentionally to insult the prisoners. Poland was my country. The Polish Armed Forces were fighting against the Germans and the Russians, against their immense superiority, almost to the last bullet. To see now the eagle smeared with paint hurt me and brought tears to my eyes.

At a table sat a Red Army officer in a green uniform with an oblong insignia on his collar. Near him stood a heavy set young man with a reddish face and snow white tuft of hair. He was wearing civilian clothing and a red armband. Near the officers' table sat a young woman with short bobbed hair.

"Documenti!" commanded the officer.

"Water," I pleaded.

The girl filled a pitcher with water from a pail and gave it to me. The officer examined my papers and gave them to the girl to translate.

"He is a medic, born in Lodz, Poland. A refugee."

"Why did you come here? Are you a German spy?"

"I am a Jew. I worked at a hospital base here in this area."

"Are you a Polish officer?"

"No, I worked with the Red Cross."

"Definitely a spy," the white haired man injected. "Let's get the bastard outside and blow his shit brains out."

The young woman intervened.

"Tell me, what is your name?"

"Vladislaw Tarko."

"What is your Hebrew name?"

"Zeev, Wolf Tarko."

"Recite a prayer in Hebrew."

"Shema Yisroel, Adonai Eloheynu, Adonai Echod."

The Russian officer released me in the custody of the young woman. They gave me a document and changed my name to Vladimir Arionovitz Tarko. They assigned me a room in the same building where the woman and her family were living and told me to report to the militia headquarters in two days.

Outside my window was a banner: "Red Army, you have saved our lives." Daylight, long lines of people were marched off into captivity. Where to?" No one knew. The news of the Molotov-Ribbentrop agreement upset me. The photograph showing Stalin behind Ribbentrop and Molotov when signing the death sentence on Poland depressed me. I dreaded to think what would happen now to my family, to my people in Poland.

When the two days were over, I went to the militia headquarters to present my papers. The officer and the woman approached me and politely asked, "Are you well enough to go to work?"

"Yes, but ... "

"But what?"

"I would like to travel to Bialystok to seek my relatives. I hear that Jews are running from Central Poland to this area."

The officer turned to the woman translator.

"Tell him that there is a war going on. No one looks for relatives now. It is better he should sit on his *derriere*. We need good medics in Russia. If he doesn't want to go voluntarily, we will send him nevertheless. We do not tolerate free eaters, idlers, and loafers. Explain it to him."

The woman tugged at my arm and we went outside. People were standing in long lines in front of the bakeries and grocery stores while the radio blared news about Red Army marches and speeches proclaiming the dictatorship of the proletariat over the liberated territories of Western Ukraine.

We walked in silence until the woman began to speak to me, to my great surprise, in Yiddish. "Our government sends us up here to help establish order on the liberated soil. We came here to protect the population from the reigning chaos created by the war. I see that you are an intelligent person with a profession very much in need here. If you choose to register voluntarily, you can go to any city in the Soviet Union, except to state capitals of the Soviet republics and strategic areas that are off limits for non-citizens."

"I left my family in Lodz."

"My friend, going back to Lodz now means certain death for you. Thousands of Jews are running from Poland to Brest-Litowsk, Vilno and Bialystok. Consider yourself fortunate that you are already here and that you have a good profession. I know you were a Polish soldier. I know also that you are a Jew and that you suffered plenty from the Poles. Listen to me. Register for a year. When the war ends, you will be able to return, or perhaps you will like so well in our country that you will decide to stay. Everywhere in our country there are medical institutes, libraries, and schools. You can work and study in any school if you can prove your capacity and skill, and willingness to work. Education is free in our country."

The young woman looked sincere. She was perhaps no more than twenty-five, short, plump, with an open and honest face. Her dark, sad eyes looked directly at me when she spoke. I found courage and asked, "What will happen if I say I do not want to go? I don't like what I hear on the radio about Hitler and Stalin making deals ... The Nazis are my enemies ... They attacked my homeland. They preach the extermination of my people, our people. I hate the German-Soviet Friendship Agreement. How can you trust Hitler?"

"Listen carefully to what I shall tell you now. In our country, learn to keep your mouth shut and follow orders. Do what you are told and nothing will happen to you. We have over sixty thousand Polish war prisoners. They are sent to special camps. Consider yourself lucky that we are treating you as a refugee and not as a war prisoner. We are sending you to a *Sovkhoz* in Poltawa. Tomorrow morning I will come for you. You will get some warm underwear, shoes, food stamps, and bread cards. We have your documents ready and we will give you money to last you until you reach Poltawa."

"I did not mean to offend you ..."

"I understand. I am Jewish. To be a Soviet citizen is a magic word I cherish and I am proud of. Listen, Tarko. You were a stranger in your own country, frightened, insulted, your rights trampled on. Therefore, today is a new beginning for you. *Dosvidanya. Wsio choroShoho!*"

We looked at each other. Our eyes were full of tears. We shook hands. Suddenly, she kissed me and walked away.

Next morning, together with refugees from Poland, Russian guards marched us off to the railroad station, loaded us on open platforms on a rainy day, guarded by Ukrainian militia. After two full days of train tribulations, we arrived at Sovchoz Lenina -- a prison-farm between Kremenchug and Poltawa, in the Ukraine.

We tried to comfort each other, singing in unison *"Jeszcze Polska nie Zginela* -- Poland will live as long as we live. Someday we will return to a free Poland. We hope some of us will live to see that day."

I was munching a carrot. The carrot was salted from my tears...

Volodia took up his pencil and began again to write in his notebook:

Tanya warned me not to ask for bread delivery to the hospital and center. Party regulations demand that bread be delivered first to the working men and women in the fields and cooperatives. I feel that our first duty is to the patients. Their fathers and sons serve on the front lines of Europe, defending this country. Why should they wait for their bread ration until 1:00 in the afternoon.

We received a new breathing resuscitator from Andizhan which was made in the United States. No one here knows how to read the instructions written in English. Tanya was furious. "Why did they not include a translation in Russian?" I was up all night, eager to figure out how this machine works. With the help of Verotchka we triumphed. It works! We are all very happy. From total inexperience to blind luck!"

* * * * *

CHAPTER FIVE
Fear

Fear

In only nine years, *Kolkhoz* Octiabre had become a strong farm cooperative in the Kyzyl Kishlak area. It was considered among the leading farms in the Chinabaad region. State and Party leaders liked going there for visits or lectures. They knew that on the way home they would find a nice gift in their cart or truck. A bag of rice, flour, dried fruit, or some other gift could be expected.

The government agencies in Andizhan, in order to encourage and increase labor productivity and intensify cotton and rice production, gave the *kolkhoz* many Party benefits. Many were given the title of "Advanced Workers of Communist Labor," and received extra deliveries of clothes, shoes, household utensils, and prolonged postponements from the draft.

The farmers in *Kolkhoz* Octiabre were Uzbeks, Tatars, Kirgizes, and other nationalities from the Soviet Republics. Refugees from Poland, Bessarabia, and Lithuania also worked there in the fields and in offices.

The refugees had all arrived during the war, evacuated by the Soviet government from their native lands. They spoke Russian, Ukrainian, Romanian, Polish, Yiddish, and the dialects of the region from which they came. But no matter where they came from, what languages they spoke, or the color of their skin, the refugees had one thing in common: they all suffered from hemorrhagic fever, malaria, eye ailments, sores, carbuncles, skin rashes and other ailments caused by malnutrition and ticks.

They lived on cabbage and *djugara,* twenty-five ounces of bread, a drop of sugar, and a few vegetables. Twice a day they got a bowl of some sort of soup with little fat or meat in it. Most of the time the cabbage was rotten, and the horse meat or fish stunk. When the refugees complained to the Party leaders, they were told, "Thank Allah for this. We are in a war."

"Vladimir Arionovitz, are you free tonight?" Dr. Chaidarov, looking thin and frail, came through the back door of the center. "I don't feel too well and I have to speak at a meeting in *Kolkhoz* Octiabre. Could you please take my place?"

"I cannot speak Uzbekian."

"You will speak in Russian, and they will translate. You will speak as my voice."

"How will I get there?"

"Vera Alexeyvna is going there to stay overnight and visit some of the sick in their isolation unit. I will arrange for a council member to give you a ride home."

It was a nice evening. Vera and Volodia traveled on the sandy road to Chinabaad in a carriage with some dignitaries from Kyzyl Kishlak. The road was dusty, so hardly anyone spoke. Vera was tired, and she fell asleep as soon as they were on their way.

While traveling, Volodia prepared a brief outline for his speech. He tried to translate Latin words and phrases like malaise, irritability, anorexia, diarrhea into simple Russian words, in order to adapt his remarks to the local audience of *kolkhoz* leaders and emphasize the key point: ticks and mosquitoes are the arch enemy of the people in this village.

At the meeting house in the *kolkhoz,* the guests drank green tea, chewed tobacco, and listened to speeches Volodia could hardly understand. The chairman apologized for Dr. Chaidarov and called on his representative to speak on his behalf. Volodia dutifully walked to the podium and began, even though people kept talking.

He spoke of hemorrhagic fever and typhoid fever in addition to the common local disease -- malaria. He outlined a plan for control of the population and environment, for preventive measures against ticks and the plasmodium parasite.

They hardly understood his pidgin Russian with the Polish accent. Still, when he finished by saying "With the help of the great Stalin, we will beat our enemies at all fronts, and, with the help of the local Party and council, we will win the war against malaria and other diseases," all the guests and local leaders applauded. Volodia applauded himself in the local tradition and returned to his bench to listen to the poor translation of his remarks.

A short, muscular man, with a round, double chin and big, round eyes, dressed in a white silk shirt hanging out over neat European-style pants, came over to Volodia and introduced himself.

I am Ibrahim Bagdayev, a friend of the Chaidarovs. I was asked to give you a ride back to the village. If you are ready, my coach is waiting."

Volodia politely said farewell to the chairman and a few people he knew. He was glad to leave.

They drove for a while in silence. Volodia looked at the man near him. He had never seem him in Kyzyl Kishlak.

"Comrade Bagdayev, are you the new principal in our school?"

"No. I live and work in Chinabaad."

"And you are going to take me all the way to our village?"

"Muhamoud Chaidarov is a very close friend of mine, and he asked me to give you this ride home."

"Thank you very much. Are you working in the health department?"

Bagdayev did not answer. Instead he said, "I compliment you on your remarks about the need for improving the sanitary conditions in our area. I just felt uncomfortable that the chairman did not introduce you properly. He did not even call your name."

"Not important. The main thing is that we should implement the sanitary regulations in our area."

It was dark on the road and it took a few minutes for the horse to get used to the narrow streets of the village. When they got to the wide road, Bagdayev asked, "You work all day at the center. You have many problems there and still you find time to lecture. Why are you doing all this?"

"In order to be successful in our work, we cannot shut ourselves up in our hospital and say, "I'm responsible only for the patients in the four walls of our center," and forget the rest of the people in our region. Sickness, dear comrade, knows no walls. If we have an epidemic, we must fight it all the way."

"Still, I don't understand why you are doing all this for Kyzyl Kishlak. After all. you are a refugee, not even a Soviet citizen."

"I faced a dilemma, either to look back into my past -- and say there is nothing to live for, or to take the other option, to look to the future -- fight the war, help the people around me and make this the justification for my own existence. My hope is to make this village a better place for all people to live."

"Why this village?"

"This is as good a place to start as any other. There are people here from all over the world. They need help. Just to live from day to day, to get a little food, is useless."

"But sooner or later you will leave this place, won't you?"

"And if I do leave, does that mean that I should neglect what has to be done here? At this moment, this is my village. It is up to the population here, to you and to me, to make this the best place to live, and it starts with both of us. If you see me sprinkling the front of my home, cleaning my yard of garbage, so will you do the same. This attitude has nothing to do with politics, native or stranger, citizen or refugee. It is just the simple relationship among human beings. It does not start with a village council order or directives. You must personally dedicate yourself to your fellow man, wherever you live. Then you will be respected by the people who surround you."

"We say the same thing but the other way around. We start with country and Party first, and then we think of ourselves."

"On this we differ, but it leads to the same. In order for me to give myself to this village, it must make me feel needed, and appreciated. When I see my efforts realized, I get more ideas for innovations and better ways of improving the sanitary conditions of this village."

"Sometimes what's good for the village may not necessarily be good for our state."

"For this you have a Party and council to see to it that everything is done within the limits of the law and to the benefit of both. I have to know only what is permissible and what is not. When it comes to politics or laws, I leave that to Dr. Chaidarov. I just do my job among the people."

"What makes you think the local people want you in their *kishlaks?* To them you are still a stranger. They didn't even introduce you by name tonight."

"I'm a stranger to the man in the alley who doesn't know me. But when people meet me, they realize what my job is and they become my friends. They know that what I asked them to do is for their own good."

"Still, what makes you personally do all those things? After all, you are a young man. Others your age are out with girls. You're out every night working, or inspecting."

"My work must come first. As I mentioned before, I need a reason to go on living while my people are being murdered. There is a war going on against a common enemy and I'm not allowed to fight in it. So this is my contribution to the battle we're in -- a battle against malaria and typhoid fever. This is now a daily occurrence, and we are worried."

"Dr. Chaidarov suffers, as you know, from war wounds, and his health is not improved by working fourteen to fifteen hours every day. He has compassion for the sick and they adore and respect him. However, for some reason he doesn't get this respect from the leaders of his own village. They don't answer his requests. They greet him courteously but adjourn their meetings, ignoring his requests. Later, Dr. Chaidarov sends me to try to talk to the village council secretary."

"The council secretary Kozlov is a very conscientious Party worker."

"He is always drunk."

"That is his personal business."

"He is so cold, so cruel to me."

"He does not like foreigners. He does not trust them."

"Why does he drink so much?"

"He lost two sons in this war."

"Oh, I am sorry to hear that, but many families lost their dear ones in this war."

"He lost a high position in our government. He was demoted to the job of village secretary because of his drinking habits."

"Still, my impression is that he does not care much about this village."

"What makes you think so?"

"On a few occasions I went to him to ask for his help in getting food for our medical complex. He hardly looked at me."

"People like Kozlov do not want to be told what to do. They are used to ordering others around. He is a very serious-minded person."

"He looks down on the refugees and on the local people."

"It is in his nature and upbringing. He is here to help, but not to be advised by a refugee. He considers himself too great a man for this."

"Honestly, I don't care how great a man Comrade Kozlov is, I can only judge him by the way he deals with individuals. I respect Dr. Chaidarov ten times more for his actions, if nothing else. He travels in the middle of the night to help a farmer in a remote *kolkhoz,* while the secretaries make long speeches and applaud themselves. People are dying here. For God's sake we must do everything in out power to keep them."

"You believe in God?"

"Why are you asking?"

"You keep saying, 'For God's sake' and 'God willing.'"

"It's just a manner of speaking. I was raised this way. My reliance on my faith is like a ball of cord. The cord is being unravelled by the daily happenings to my people. The ball is getting smaller as my beliefs crumble. Just seeing what is happening in the world, I cannot believe like I used to, but

I still believe."

Bagdayev stopped near the Darya River and waited for a barge to take the coach across. There was a small *tchaichana* -- teahouse -- at the barge station, and the manager offered Bagdayev some tea, while a helper gave the horse a bucket of water. Volodia suddenly realized that Bagdayev must be a very prominent person. Everybody knew him. They greeted him and shook his hands. The servant brought fresh grapes, warm *lepioshkas* and green tea.

The radio's loudspeaker at the *tchaichana* -- tea-house -- blared the foreign news from Tashkent, "London -- The government of Czechoslovakia today characterized as 'the most dastardly German act since the Dark Ages,' the Nazi slaughter of the entire male population of Lidice, a town near Prague. They vowed revenge today for the mounting wave of Nazi executions.

"London -- The Polish government protested in a broadcast against mass shootings of Poles, torture of tens of thousands in concentration camps, and deportation of more than one and a half million people. Only by the announcement of retribution and the application of reprisals whenever possible can a stop be put to the rising tide of madness of these German assassins."

"This is sad news," Bagdayev remarked. "Let's go back to our discussion. You still did not answer my initial question, Comrade Tarko."

"What was it, Comrade Bagdayev?"

"I can't understand why you are doing what you're doing here. You are not even a citizen. What is your goal here?"

"Comrade Bagdayev, if I were not serious in my work, and if I were just interested in having a clean hut, a full stomach, and a girl to sleep with, I would be like an animal or like this barge here cast adrift upon the Darya with no goal, no direction, no harbor, going nowhere. Life would be meaningless. This work gives purpose to my life."

"From what I heard from Chaidarov, you appear to be successful."

"My friend, it is easier to appear successful in the eyes of Dr. Chaidarov than in my own eyes. We have a long, hard way to go."

"You're so right, Comrade Tarko. The march of progress
is crushed by people who don't want to give up their ways of
life. This does not say that the Soviet system, and the new
Party ideas are not good for us. They're just not yet strong
enough here to resist a deeper, stronger tradition that is many
generations old."

They finished the bowls of tea and drove the coach onto
the barge.

"Comrade Bagdayev," Volodia said politely, "I'm so focused
on my own work that I forgot to ask you what kind of work
you do. It looks as if everybody knows you."

"I was born and raised here, therefore, everybody knows
me. Besides, the good and welfare of every citizen and agency
of this area is my concern. This is a border area, the security
of this region is my definite responsibility."

"You work in the border militia?"

"No. I'm the area *sledowatel* -- the district attorney for this
region."

It took Volodia a while to overcome his shock. He looked
again at Bagdayev's round face and did not believe his own
eyes. Bagdayev smiled.

"Comrade Tarko, everybody gets scared when they meet
me. They think of arrests, interrogation. But I am a person
just like you, trained to do a job. There are many enemies
among the people here and, as district attorney, I must keep an
eye on them, all of them. You included. Why are you so
quiet suddenly? Are you scared?"

"I have no reason to be scared. Maybe I talked too much."

"What you said, Comrade Tarko, was noble. But I'm afraid
the odds are against you. You see, we have a system, Party
regulations, village structure, local priorities, and quota
obligations. You see only the sick, the old, the women and
children, and your refugees. You see individual human beings.
We see society, the soldier on the front, the worker in the
factory, or the farmer in the field. We are concerned about the
kolkhoznik who produces the most cotton and rice. They are

our first concern because they provide the food for our fighting men on the front. This is the opposition you face, and you had better be aware of it."

"Don't you think that your workers are farmers also in danger of typhus and typhoid fever if we don't take preventive action?"

"This is exactly why I said you will be only partially successful in your work. I said 'partially' because I can see you're going to be bogged down in defeat on many of your requests, especially on housing for the refugees."

"How did you know about my request for shelter for the refugees?"

"My business is to know what is going on around here. You have nothing to fear."

"I'm not afraid to tackle any problem when I know it is good for Kyzyl Kishlak."

"Unfortunately, only Chaidarov, myself, and a few more like us, realize that what you're trying to do is good for the area. The majority of our people still need education to understand what the danger of epidemics is. Some say that you just care about your refugees."

"I don't deny that."

"Don't get carried away by their problems. You will be blown way off course. Stick to your work. Let the Party and village council worry about them."

"We delivered a petition to the Party secretary weeks ago and as yet there was no action."

"Comrade Tarko, it's not indifference on their part. The Party knows the significance of the refugee problem. They are all concerned, but the local secretary cannot react personally to your petitions. He must forward them to the Refugee Control Commission in Andizhan. The refugees are not a local problem."

"But what shall I do? Let the lice eat them to death?"

"Let Chaidarov sign all your petitions requesting medicines and food for your center. Your name or your signature on letters can only delay your petitions. They will be put aside for double checking."

"Why?"

"This republic is run by people with Uzbekian names, by Uzbekians, sure, with the help, advice, and supervision of our Party, but certainly not people with names like yours. Now can you understand?"

"Thank you. I'm please to have met you. I have learned a lot tonight. Thank you for the ride."

"You're welcome. Don't avoid me when you see me. You are an efficient worker, but I suggest that you discuss all your steps and needs with Dr. Chaidarov. It's preferable that way. *Salaam. Dosvidanya.*"

It was almost midnight when Volodia got to the center. He went to bed but could not fall asleep. He could not forgive himself.

"How stupid can you get? Why did you talk so much? Why trust a stranger with your enthusiasm just because he said he is Chaidarov's friend?" Volodia kept arguing within himself. "I hope I did not say anything to hurt anyone. My God, was I in the lion's cage?"

He was tired and tense. Then Eva floated into his mind and slowly the fear and fright disappeared. He thought of her cheerful laughter, her voice saying, "The worst thing is to worry alone. When you worry, come and share it with me."

The loudspeaker blared the news, "The English Air Force bombed Munich, the city is in rubble and flames ... The heroic defenders of Stalingrad are surrounding the Germans. Fighting goes on in the streets of Stalingrad ... "

The communique ended with, "We will counterattack on every front. Victory will be ours."

Volodia opened his notebook and started writing:

"I feel like I am possessed by a Dybbuk, *a ghost who constantly pushes paper and pencil into my hands and forces me to write. I feel empty, depressed, lonely, and tired, still I have this urge to write. A voice in my brain calls constantly: Keep writing. Often I dread to read the*

written words, but there is nothing I can do. I am possessed by a ghost.

"Can you love and hate a place at the same time? With every passing day I feel more love and more hatred for this malaria center. With my limited knowledge I suddenly became an expert in difficult diagnoses. Even Chaidarov calls me for consultations about problems for which only he and Tanya know the cures.

"Quite frankly, it scares the life out of me. I spent six months taking a medic course. I worked in an ambulatorium for contagious diseases, war-related communicable epidemics. I worked in field headquarters in a sanitary battalion. Now, every time there is an emergency, every time they are short-handed, they call on me.

"It is no good that my kibitka -- *room -- is adjacent to the center. It's like being on frontline duty; every time I try to take a rest, someone is pounding on the door.*

"I have no formal medical education and the patients confuse me with the medical staff. They expect me to be everywhere, do everything, and know all of the answers to their questions. What a heavy burden! Some patients think that I am a snob, pompous, but the honest truth is I don't know many of the answers to their questions ... "

* * * * *

CHAPTER SIX
Oleg

Oleg

Several weeks later, Eva's mother was allowed to come home. Each night it was the same: Celia would complain about not receiving letters from Boris, and Eva would sit on her bed, hold her mother's bony hands in hers, and whisper:

"Mom. The war will be over soon. Our armies are winning. Boris will come home."

After Celia fell asleep, Eva would come out of the *kibitka* and sit on the sandy ground. On this night, Oleg, Anna, and Volodia were there, and the conversation, as always, turned to memories and dreams.

Eva talked about the years of the great famine, the year 1933, when she used to go to school hungry.

"It was a terrible time then in our hometown. Mom was swollen from hunger, and father justified our sufferings by quoting Lenin: 'We must make sacrifices today in order to build a better tomorrow.' We were afraid to go out in the evening; people killed each other's children and ate them ... "

Oleg sat for a while in silence. Then, turning to Eva, he said in a quiet voice, "Yes, I remember you in school, nibbling on your black bread, picking up lost crumbs from the floor. Millions perished in the Ukraine in those years. The peasants wanted to starve the city population; they were against the collective farms -- the *kolkhoz*. Still, we survived. We built factories, clubs, new buildings, until this damned war came!"

Soon they were making up poems and singing the "Fisherman's Song," about the heart of a girl, dreaming about her lover who sailed to far away waters. They sang about Katiusha, the maid who sits at the river and sings to her boyfriend, "You protect our Homeland. Katiusha will protect your love."

76

Oleg sang in Ukrainian:
"The world is full of nice young men,
Good looking, with nice manners.
Only one disturbs my peace,
Makes my heart tremble, flutter faster.
Serdce -- Heart! I don't want any peace.
It's wonderful to feel your heart beat,
Stronger, alive. Thank you, heart, for love."

Volodia sang a Yiddish song he remembered from Poland,
a poem by Joseph Papernikov:
"Maybe it is castles in mid-air I'm building,
Maybe my God is nowhere to be found;
But, my dreams are bright, my dreams are true.
In my dreams, the skies are clear and blue.
Maybe my goal will always escape me.
Maybe my boat no port will attain.
It is not the achievement that will please me,
It's the struggle and striving, the high to gain."

"I like that song," said Oleg. "It reminds me of my
hometown, Malichov, the Yiddish."
Oleg Polishenko is my friend now, thought Volodia. The
two had mutually disliked each other at the start, Oleg eyeing
him disdainfully, Volodia resenting his tall good looks. Still,
Volodia was cautious.
After meeting Bagdayev, he made up his mind never to
discuss politics with the people here, regardless of who they
were, Uzbek, Jew, Pole, or Russian. Not only did Volodia see
people dying, he saw many arrested and some just disappear.
He had the feeling from his conversation with Bagdayev that
from the moment he had arrived in Kyzyl Kishlak, he had been
watched, spied upon, but by whom? He did not want to know.
Actually, he did not care. Volodia did his share at his
center position, keeping receipts for every pillow, blanket,
sheet, and towel stored in the warehouse. He trusted Dr.
Chaidarov and Dr. Ivanovna with his keys to the drug cabinets.
Aziz Ali liked to change his old towels for new ones or take

some green, soft soap home, but the old man always asked for permission to do so.

Still, ever since the ride with Bagdayev, an uneasy feeling of mistrust and fear crept into Volodia and kept him on alert, even with Dr. Chaidarov and the staff.

Oleg had a wound in his shoulder and Volodia changed the bandages for him. He took his time and gently removed the bandages, washed around the wounded area with vodka, and powdered it with streptocide dust. He followed this procedure every second day. Volodia and Oleg hardly noticed that the wall between them had disappeared and they became friends.

They shared memories of their past, recalling childhood years. Oleg talked of harsh winters, drifting snow, frosted breath on window panes, frost bite, trees and little houses all robed in white moonlight. He loved his Ukrainian countryside.

Volodia talked about his school years, teachers he had honored and admired, how he had dreamed of becoming a medic, his thirst for knowledge, his search for books, and his faith in a better world after this war. He shared with Eva and Oleg his poems about his grandparents.

Oleg's mother, Ekaterina Efimovna, always insisted, after Volodia had changed her son's bandages, that he try some of her *pirogi* -- potato-filled pancakes. When she saw the Red Cross on Volodia's arm, she crossed her heart, saying, "I left my possessions in Malichov; a home, a husband, two other sons. God in heaven knows if they are still alive. One thing I do have with me. It has been in my family for generations. Let me show you, Volodinka, my precious possession."

Ekaterina Efimovna went to the wall and removed the portrait of Joseph Stalin, revealing under it an Icon, a colorful image of Mary holding the child Jesus.

"Why do you keep it covered with Stalin's picture?"

"I'm an old woman. I will die in the faith of my forefathers, but Oleg is a Party candidate. He works in the ZAGS at the militia and we have to be careful."

She held her small, dry hands out to Volodia, saying, "Oleg said that you always say 'The Lord willing.' Please, will you recite a prayer with me?"

Volodia felt a surge of pity for this lonely woman and said in a low voice, "Oh, Heavenly Father, give us the strength to survive this war, to be helpful to all the suffering people here, to be strong and calm in the face of so much misery and disaster. Give us the strength to spread love and hope among the unfortunate refugees in this village."

Tears ran down Ekaterina Efimovna's face.

"May the Lord give you happiness and strength."

Oleg came in dressed, and he and Volodia said goodnight to Ekaterina.

On the way back to the center, Oleg took Volodia's arm.

"Now you see why my mother will never agree to let me marry Eva. What would you do in my place?"

"She is your mother. You lost your father and brothers. Why hurt her?"

"But, I am hurt too. I love Eva."

"I know. Eva likes you too. She's known you since childhood. This makes you more like a brother to her."

"Did she tell you this?"

"Yes, she did."

"Volodia, I'm going away for four weeks to Kokand."

"Why are you going? For what?"

"To take a special course for militiamen in border areas. Volodia, I want you to know that I am your friend. If I can't marry Eva, you should."

"I have nothing to offer her."

"Listen. I know that you keep company with Dr. Ivanovna. I noticed the way you two walk together."

"Tanya lives in a world of her own. She has her own love, Mischa, a refugee who is now at the front. She has her own convictions and her own ideas of morality."

"She seems like a snob, always walking by herself, living by herself, and always giving orders."

"You're wrong, Oleg. Tanya is a very humble person, always criticizing herself. She is very gentle with people. She has a goodness in her and is capable of sacrifice. She can work without limits to save a human being. She stays alone because, in a sense, she is a tragic person. She is full of desire for love and does not have a man to share it with. She is fond of children and does not have a child of her own. As hard as she works, she remembers every morning to leave some seeds and bread crumbs for the birds on her porch. Tanya has an inborn yearning to help people."

"They say she has a temper."

"Yes. Tanya can explode at anyone who hurts her hospital or her patients, but then she gets sad, moody, until someone says a nice word to her. A friendly gesture or a smile brings her around again."

"Sounds like you are in love with her, Volodia."

"I like her very much. She is warm, gentle, and lonesome, like me. We try to stay away from each other, and yet we know we need each other, too. Can you understand this Oleg?"

"I can't. If you feel that what you are doing is wrong, why do you continue this relationship with her?"

"Tanya and I work very closely in the center and hospital and share many problems. We are very good friends, that's all."

"I think Eva is in love with you."

"Did she tell you so?"

"No, but I can see."

"Do you hate me for it?"

"No. Not any more. I have gotten used to the idea."

"Thank God."

"Why do you thank God?"

"Because I want you as my friend. I haven't a soul left in the world."

"Neither have I, except for my Mother. Will you look in on her while I'm away?"

"Yes, I will."

They stood awkwardly at the doorway of the center. Then Volodia reached out and put his arms around Oleg.

"Dopobatchenya -- goodbye," Oleg said, his voice trembling. "Take care of the Markes family."

"Dosvidanya. Take care of your wounds."

"I will."

Volodia was concerned that the Kyzyl Kishlak water supply coming from the *ariks* -- the streams, was polluted and not safe to drink.

He took samples of the *arik* water and sent them to Andizhan for bacteriological analyses. The results of the laboratory findings never came back to the village.

Volodia constructed a small storage reservoir for water. The water was purified through a thin cotton net. One of the large barrels was used as a source for drinking water and was covered with silk and cotton nets for filtration. He used empty glass jugs and alcohol bottles for boiling water for the patients in the clinic.

Every evening he made sure that enough fresh water for the patients was available for the next day's needs.

Volodia went to the center. Aziz Ali helped Fatima serve hot water with small squares of hard sugar. The red cabbage sent by *Kolkhoz* Octiabre to the hospital never reached the center. So instead of soup with barley and red cabbage, they served fish soup for lunch, and for supper, hot water with a lump of sugar. Disgusted, Volodia went to his room and listened to the latest news.

"Yesterday, our heroic fighters of the North Division captured Demiansk, north of Smolensk. The Germans and their allies lost 700 tanks, 400 planes, 1,700 guns; 700,000 enemy soldiers were killed and 300,000 taken prisoner. Mass expulsion of the enemy from the Soviet Union has started, but the real struggle is only beginning."

As Volodia lay on his bed, a thought passed through his mind.

"I'm a refugee. I have my papers as a medic. What if I jump on the next military train going to the front with the Red Cross badge on my arm? Who would miss me?"

* * * * *

CHAPTER SEVEN
Mischa

Mischa

Tanya was resting on the old couch in her little room at the hospital. She tried to read an outdated newspaper, but the dim light hurt her eyes. Fatima knocked twice and then popped her head through the door, asking if she was going home.

"I'd rather stay here tonight." Fatima, knowing better than to ask questions of Tanya, bid her a good night and left.

Tanya read Mischa's letter again. And again:

"I'm sitting with my unit in a grove of trees. Actually, this was once a grove of trees; shelling and fire left only shallow holes and burned trees and bushes here. Within minutes, we will attack the enemy. All I can think of at this moment is you, your face, your hair, your eyes. If I live until tomorrow and win this battle tonight, it is because I will go into the battle fighting for a better world for you and people like you. I have an intense desire to see you again and, like the night we met, to loosen your braids. Dearest Tanya, I am thousands of miles away from you, yet I feel your presence day and night..."

Tanya read the letter over and over again. How long has it been? A year? Fourteen months? She had been on a train to Andizhan, working in the fourth coach which had been blocked off as a first aid station.

A long line of people had stood waiting by that coach. Mischa was among those waiting.

She was standing with her back to him, washing her hands in a bowl of carbolic solution, and she heard a quiet voice.

"Excuse me. Can you help?"

Tanya turned sharply.

"I thought I had taken care of everyone. Sit down a

minute."

She dried her hands and came over to Mischa.

"What happened? A wound? It looks bad. How did it happen?"

"Some young girl was trying to grab a seat on the train and hit me in the eye with her bundle. There must have been something sharp in it."

"You're lucky. You could have easily lost that eye." She dipped a piece of gauze in boric acid and wiped lightly around the wound.

"Does it really look that bad?"

"Bad enough to keep you from work."

"You must be kidding?"

She smiled, revealing pearl-white teeth. Her blue eyes met his gaze, and she blushed like a young girl.

"You'll have to come to see me several times so I can change the bandages," she said after a moment. "The salve I'm applying now doesn't smell too good. However, it will soften up the scab and draw out the pus."

"Ichthamnol ointment?"

"Yes, how did you know?"

"It comes from bituminous rock. It is used as an antiseptic."

"You speak a perfect Russian, but with an accent. You're a foreigner, aren't you?"

"Yes," replied Mischa, "from Germany. I'm a Jew. May I go now?"

"Why are you so touchy? You're not in Germany now. And if you're a Jew, so what? Most of my professors and colleagues were Jews. Did you ever hear the name of Dr. Winogradov?"

"Dr. Vladimir Winogradov, the famous medical scientist?"

Her eyes lit up. "He is one of the greatest heart specialists. He lectured to us at the Moscow Medical Faculty. He too is a Jew. But where do you know him from?"

"I also studied."

"Well, in that case, we've got to get to know each other. My name is Tatyana Ivanovna. Call me Tanya."

"My name is Mischa -- Michail Wengrov.   Call me Mischa," he said.

"You have the hands of a piano virtuoso," Mischa murmured.

"Is that a compliment?"

"It's the truth, the pure truth."

"Thank you." She asked him to sit at the edge of the bed, then brought two saucers of *kipiatok* -- boiled water, spread out a small, white cloth on the bed, and placed on it several hard biscuits and dried apples. "Please, eat. Be my guest."

The train started to move. Mischa stood up.

"Sit down. It's too late. I won't let you jump from a moving train. You'll just have to be my patient and guest for the next few hours."

He sat again, took a dried apple, and slowly started to eat.

"You went to college?" Tanya asked.

"Yes, I studied commerce, international relations, and languages. I dreamed of becoming a doctor of law, but my father died and I had to take over the family business."

"And Hitler confiscated the business?"

"Yes. I left it to the Nazis and ran away. Just as you see me now."

"Excuse me. I would like to change my clothes. This coat itches me."

She disappeared behind the curtain and returned shortly, wearing a thin, beige colored blouse and a blue skirt. Mischa noticed that one of her legs was bandaged and that she wore an elastic stocking.

"You're hurt?"

"It's nothing. A souvenir of the Finnish front."

"Your medals are also from that time?"

"Yes." She sat next to him on the bed. "Better still, tell me, how do you like it here with us?"

"To tell you the truth, it's strange to me. But I respect people who believe in something and who will sacrifice themselves for their country. After Hitler's annexation of Austria, the Munich Conference, and after your Molotov and Ribbentrop were photographed together, I lost all trust in ideals.

Under the disguise of a temporary and false peace, the world leaders have misled the individual, the downtrodden, the oppressed."

"Do you feel this way because you yourself are one of those?"

"No!" Mischa insisted. "I always had my own yardstick of what is right and just. Even during the time when I was one of the privileged few, I always helped the hungry. Not because any system, party, or religion made me do it, but because I have always hated oppressors, bureaucrats, whether they were leaders of a corporation with whom I did business, whether a 'fuhrer' or whatever they called themselves."

"But our system wants to uproot and destroy all such oppression."

"No, my dear, I am not impressed by a system that would bury the freedom of millions of people today in order that tomorrow our great-grandchildren will live in a better world." Mischa hesitated. "But on second thought, you may be right. I may be so untrusting and pessimistic toward all ideals and isms because of my own sufferings. To tell the truth, I envy your love of country, your belief in your future. I no longer believe in anything. I live without a goal, a future, a hope."

"Terrible," Tanya said. "How can one exist like that?" Don't you have any desires?"

"I exist. That is all. I did have one wish: to go to the front and fight against the oppressors of my people."

"Which people? The Germans or the Nazis?"

"No difference," Mischa replied. "The Nazis want to destroy the Jewish people physically; the German people want to destroy us spiritually. They dirtied German soil for generations to come with the onus of the *Herrenvolk*, the master race. Where was that precious cultural heritage of Goethe, Schiller, and Beethoven when we needed it? No, Goebbels, Shirach, and Himmler, and all the others have poisoned Germany for generations."

"Why don't you volunteer for frontline duty?"

"Your 'Genius Father of the peoples' doesn't trust me. He refused my request."

"He's right. With thoughts like yours, you'd be killed at the front the first day."

Mischa remained silent. He thought awhile, then quietly conceded. "You're right, Tanya. I'm not even good for that."

She took the empty plates from the edge of the bed and again sat next to him.

"How can you live like this, Mischa? How can you go to work when you are so depressed?"

"Your people gave me a temporary roof over my head. You have shared the little that you had with me, a stranger. And ... "

He wanted to say something but caught the gaze of Tanya's blue eyes and fell into silence. She tenderly put her arms around his shoulders and he felt the round softness of her breasts, heard the beating of her heart.

"Yes, Mischa ... what else?"

He touched the soft satin skin of her face. She did not stop him, but stared questioningly into his eyes.

"And," he said, "in the depths of my heart, I feel that burning of one small spark of hope. The spark becomes inflamed when I meet people like you. You're talking to me now as one human being to another, equal to equal. That gives me hope. Hope that evil will not long endure, that perhaps there will yet be a better and a more just world without war and oppression, without terror and the threats of concentration camps and prison areas. There will come a time when one human will be able to befriend another without inquiring into his religious beliefs and without looking at the color of his skin or the shape of his nose. One nation won't build its successes and happiness at the expense of another nation. It's possible, Tanya, that we won't be around to see this. And if we are around, we'll be old and broken. Still, we'll have some satisfaction in knowing that we, in our days, lived to see a better world."

"I also believe in that. Somehow it seems our dreams are the same. I've got to tell you that your words give me greater courage to work, to want to live, and to help people. I, too, see wrongs, injustices, suffering among my own people and elsewhere. But mankind is full of such things. You have reminded me that those of us who have ideals must remain true to them. Thank you."

"And I thank you for listening to me, Tanya. You're the first person to whom I have opened my heart. I feel much better already. Even my forehead doesn't hurt as much as before. You will have to tell me more about yourself. You're an interesting woman."

"Not today. I have to lie down and rest my feet because we'll soon stop at a station, and I will get another load of patients."

"Well, in that case, don't move. I'll sit at the door of the coach."

Tanya lay down on the bed. "You know something? I've a funny feeling that I have known you for a long time."

"Odd! I have the same feeling." Mischa reached for a case of bandages, shoved it over to the bed and sat down next to her.

"What are you looking at, Mischa?"

"I'm looking at your hair. You have beautiful hair, Tanya."

"Yes? I always wore my hair in long braids, but beautiful? No. That's the hair style of an old maid."

"You're an exceptionally beautiful woman and a wonderful person."

"You're complimenting me. That seems so bourgeois."

"But it's the truth."

"Thanks." She was quiet for a while, listening to the clatter of the train. "What are you thinking about, Mischa?"

"I can't tell you."

She passed her hand over his badly shaven cheek.

"You can tell me. I'm a grown woman."

"May I loosen your braids?"

"It'll be hard to do them again."

"May I touch them?"

She did not answer, but took his hands and drew him close to her. He caressed her blond silky hair, her face. She closed her eyes and lay quietly.

"Mischa, what will the people in your wagon think? They

will wonder where you've disappeared to."

"I don't care what they think."

"Tell them you were hungry and I invited you to supper."

"They won't believe that."

"You'd be ashamed to tell them that you were with a woman older than you?"

"I don't have to report anything to anyone. I am not even worthy enough to kiss you, although I have had the desire ever since you lay down."

She opened her eyes. Tenderly, she took his head in both her hands and softly pressed a kiss on his lips. She lay back on her pillow and took his hand to wipe away her tears.

"Tanya, you're crying?"

"Dear Mischa. You don't know how hard the life of a woman with a crippled leg and medals on her chest can be. In addition, there is the title 'her majesty comrade doctor.'"

"And I thought that you lacked nothing. You have intelligence, beauty, grace. You have a country, people to love, help and heal."

"Yes, that keeps me going during the day. However, my nights are terribly lonely. Oh, Mischa, how often I yearned for such a moment as this. Someone to want me for myself, not for my doctor's title or my medals, and not to pity my crippled leg. A man to desire me as a woman. Sometimes I forget I'm a woman and that I have my own desires. Hold me, Mischa, in your arms. Oh, yes. Kiss me. Undo my hair."

She fell into his arms and bit his lips, drinking his love, like a nomad at an oasis.

Later that night, the transport train ground to a halt on a siding in order to let another train pass. Mischa got up from the bed.

"Will you come again?" Tanya asked.

"If you want me to."

"Please."

She accompanied him to the door and gave him her hand.

"Thanks for giving me these hours."

"The pleasure was mine. Good night."

"A quiet night. Sweet dreams."
"You too."

For the next ten nights, they were together. In the mornings, he returned to his wagon and Tanya busied herself with her patients.

One day, Tanya lay in her car, watching the passing rice fields and thinking about Mischa.

Is it fleeting, she wondered, like the landscape flying past the train window? What ties me to Mischa? What do I feel for him?

Until now her life had been so simple, so smooth, so uncomplicated. She was the daughter of a coal miner from the Don region. She had finished public school and high school. Later she had studied in medical institutes in Zitomir, Kiev, and Moscow. She loved her profession as she loved her people and her land. She had learned the languages of the peoples of her land because she was preparing to go to Central Asia after completing her studies and do volunteer work in a hospital there.

How did she get wounded? Then the Russian-Finnish War started. On the front, at Koralya, she had been wounded in the leg. In a Leningrad military hospital she had met Serge, a young officer who had just been released from the hospital after having a bullet removed from his shoulder. Serge was of medium build, strong, and broad shouldered. He would come to the hospital every evening and play his accordion for the sick, singing for hours in his pleasant baritone voice.

During the day he began to visit her, bringing sweets, perfume, and silk handkerchiefs. He spoke of his hometown, Minsk and the factory where he had worked. He read her the long letters his mother wrote to him. He told her about his father who had died from hunger in the thirties.

When she left the hospital, she visited him in his small room. Serge submitted a request to go to a higher officers' candidate school, where he hoped to continue his military career when his shoulder wound was completely healed. In the meantime Tanya worked and lived in the same hospital where she had been a patient.

Once Serge came to visit her, bringing along some vodka and cakes. She fried some potatoes and cut up a herring, and both sat down to eat and drink. In the morning, she awakened and found Serge in her arms. Everything occurred so simply, without romance, and she had been disappointed.

And so months passed. Tanya was too busy to think much about herself. She would visit Serge from time to time, and he would sometimes visit her in the evening. They would finish eating, read a bit, talk, listen to the radio, and go to sleep.

Serge went home for a visit to his mother. He wrote Tanya long, warm letters quoting the poets Pushkin and Mayakowskiy, and asking her to come to meet his mother. In his last letter, he had written that he was about to enter the White Russian University in Minsk. The higher military academy refused to admit him, because the deep wound in his shoulder had also damaged a lung. He asked Tanya to come to Minsk and marry him.

Serge had become dear to her. But she needed something more. She wanted the kind of love she had read about but never felt in her relationship with Serge. They were too much alike. There was no contrast, no friction to make their love catch fire.

She held off answering him for months, stalling as long as possible. She finally wrote him a letter in June of 1941. Then the war broke out.

She was evacuated to Kuibyshev. She wanted to go home. The Germans had overrun the entire area between the Don and the Volga. She volunteered to accompany this refugee train to Central Asia.

Did she still yearn for Serge? Yes, until the night Mischa came to her.

She attempted to analyze herself. "Did I yearn for Serge or for a manly touch? Was Serge the fantasy I was seeking, or merely the first man in my life?"

And Mischa? Why did she still want him? Why did she feel more than a physical desire for him? Why would she not hesitate if he asked her to marry him? Why did she feel such a fountain of joy from every touch, his gentle embrace? She had read about women who sacrificed themselves for their beloved, given up roots, home, and country. Would she give up her land, her work, and her future for him? Would Mischa be ready to take her?

"Mischa, your eye is healed. You won't need to care for it anymore. Do you capitalists pay for such a service?"

"I don't have anything to pay with."

"I'll take a kiss."

Mischa bent over and kissed her on the cheek.

"Mischa, don't you love me anymore?"

"Why do you say that, Tanya?"

"I feel it in your kiss."

"Did you study psychology? Freud? Jung? Adler?"

"We don't believe in their theories."

"Then what do you believe in?"

I don't want to enter into this kind of discussion with you. Why are you so touchy, Mischa?"

"I heard that tonight we will reach our destination."

"Tonight we will just arrive at the beginning. You ought to be happy that this trip has finally come to an end. How many people have the strength to torture themselves?"

"My dear Tanya, you'd be surprised at what people can endure."

"I'm not surprised at what people can endure. I was at Saumusalmi in Finland. Besides almost 50,000 dead, we had 160,000 wounded. The Finns used our tactics. They burned everything that might be of use to us. I took care of people with frostbitten hands, noses, and feet. People with burnt ears, faces, entire bodies. I dragged our wounded from the Mannerheim Line through snow and fire in minus 40 degree cold. Therefore, please don't tell me that I don't know about human suffering. But I don't make such a big thing out of it. The world will not go under because of it. Relatively speaking, we have it good here in comparison to what is happening at the front." Tanya sighed, "Mischa, dear," she continued in a softer tone, "I want to help you."

"I don't need pity. I don't need anyone's sympathy. I want someone who needs me."

"Mischa, you crawled into my heart, came close to me. I dreamed, built castles in the air. But in the hours that you weren't here, I had a chance to think about our relationship. To be honest with you, I am married to my profession."

Tanya went over to Mischa and kissed him. "I can't tell you how happy I was to be with you these past few days. Your opening your heart to me, your reproaches, your making me realize the truth about the world and people, everything brought me closer to you. I didn't count the hours that we were together. I had the feeling that it had been years, years of happiness and joy. Perhaps the first night was the natural expression of a physical urge of two grown people, but with each passing hour, it became more noble, more elevated, to such a degree that mere words cannot express it. No, Mischa, I didn't give you this out of pity. I, myself, did not know how you felt toward me. Were you paying me back for my services to you, or were you satisfying your own physical desires? I never thought that you felt more than gratitude toward me. But for this alone I was thankful to you. After all is said and done, I'm still as lonely as you, despite the fact that I am surrounded by my friends, my country, my children. I dreamt many times about going through the pain and suffering of carrying and delivering a child. But my profession became the main goal of my life. If I were to come and live with you, you would always feel that I am supporting you."

"Oh, Tanya, if these were normal times, I would go to your father and ask him for your hand in marriage."

"In normal times, we would never have met, Mischa."

"Do you know that after our first night together I wanted to ask you to marry me?"

"I'd marry you now if you'd ask me."

"Life with me wouldn't be easy. Don't forget, I'm a foreigner."

"Then become a Soviet citizen."

"I don't want to marry the Soviet Union. It's you I want. After the war, I'll be able to travel where I want and not where you'll be sent to serve your Motherland. What will happen if they won't let me live in the big city? Would you come with me wherever I was sent?"

Tanya remained silent a moment and then answered quietly. "Mischa, I would deny myself all the pleasures of the world if only I could be with you. But I would never deny my medical profession. I would never denounce my citizenship, and I would never desert my people. Serving and helping the sick is part of me. I would never be happy with you in any country if I were not able to practice medicine. This is not a trade that I have learned. You may call it patriotism, nationalism, whatever you wish, but my knowledge, my know-how, is tied to my people and my land. My father was a coal miner in the Don region. He was sold to the mines like someone sells a pig or a dog. My grandfather was a peasant, an illiterate serf, owned by some prince from the Tzar's household. Thanks to this government I had the opportunity to study in the best medical institutes. If not for our system I would have been sold to some household as a servant. I owe my country everything. I love my work so much that I am willing to drag you along into my sea of love for all my people in this land. I would never be happy if you took me away from my camphor, carbolic acid, and bandages. You could offer me the most beautiful palaces of Europe, but without my stethoscope, tweezers, and scalpels, I would die spiritually and physically.

"You are right, Mischa, I am married to my country and my profession. Go wherever you're sent. When I have some free time, I will visit you. And whenever possible, you will visit me. I can write to the authorities; perhaps they can help you, but I am going to my hospital. I can hardly wait. After all, who has the right to enjoy so much happiness when one's country is aflame?"

Someone knocked on the sliding door. A train crew member brought a plate of steaming hot rice. He informed them that the train commander had sent some *plow* for the comrade doctor, and that tomorrow the train would arrive at its destination. He set down the food, bowed, and left the car.

Tanya handed Mischa a fork and said, "Come, dear, let us eat our last meal together."

"We should use our fingers."

"If you want to eat with your fingers, be my guest," Tanya said heartily. "I'll eat with my fork. Would you like a drink?"

They chatted and drank past midnight, finally falling asleep in each other's arms.

They were awakened not very early in the morning by a sudden jolt of the train.

The transport train had stopped in the city of Andizhan. It was still cool and dark. The locomotive pulled the cars onto the spur tracks and disappeared. An official went down the line of cars telling everyone to get off. Mischa helped the people in his wagon climb down, took their baggage and placed it alongside the car. The passengers embraced, many stammering, *"Wsio Choroshoho Wam* -- all the best to you."

An officer and two Red Army soldiers came over to Mischa and held a lantern to his face.

"Documenti! All men over here! Documents, passports, travel permits -- *comandirowkas!"*

They took Mischa and the other men and led them to a group of passengers already gathered from other cars.

Tanya was busy loading her first aid station onto two wheeled carts, but she noticed that the two soldiers were marching all the men in the opposite direction.

"Where are they taking the men?"

"To the front," answered the station master.

For a moment she was sad. Then she remembered Mischa's desire to go to war. "He has gotten his wish," she thought.

*   *   *   *   *

"Tanya, do you plan to stay here all night?" Volodia's voice sounded firm: "Why don't you go home and rest?"

Rest? What sort of rest? Tanya thought as Volodia's voice brought her back to the present. "I was just too tired to go home. Volodia, I got a letter from Mischa."

"Good. We will read it when you get home."

"Sorry, I can't go now. I had such a good dream and you interrupted it. I was with Mischa."

"I'm sorry, but Fatima and I are concerned about you. Do you want me to walk you home?"

"No. I'd rather stay here tonight. Maybe Mischa will come back."

"I hope so. Sweet dreams." Volodia left and Tanya picked up Mischa's letter and started to read it again:

"Dearest Tanya ... "

* * * * *

CHAPTER EIGHT
Verotchka

Verotchka

It was past midnight when Anna came running to Volodia's room.

"What on earth happened?"

"Volodia, come quickly. Eva has been bitten by a scorpion."

Anna and Volodia went running in the dark to the Markes' hut. Outside they could hear Eva crying and shrieking. The small room was dark, for there was no kerosene in the lamp. They lit the room with candles. Still, it was difficult to see.

Eva had been sleeping on a blanket on the ground. She had been stung on the shoulder. Volodia knew that the clinic had no anti-scorpion serum, so he quickly kneeled down on Eva's blanket, uncovered her shoulder, and sucked out the poison from the wound.

"Do you have any alcohol in the house?"

"No, we've used it all," Anna said.

"Then do you have iodine?"

"Yes!"

Volodia washed the wound with iodine and told Anna to hold the candle. He picked Eva up from the floor and carefully turned over the blanket. The scorpion was still alive; he quickly grabbed a shoe and killed it. Then he retrieved a bucket of fresh water from the stream and washed Eva's forehead and shoulder. After examining the wound, he noticed that there was still a red spot around the sting. He squeezed out the poison and again put some iodine around the wound. Eva, like a child, kept yelping and crying. Volodia sat near her on the floor and kept soaking the wet towel in water and holding it to her forehead until she fell asleep. At daybreak he returned to his room at the center.

Next morning, Volodia went to see Comrade Naimov, the bank director. Naimov was a chubby little man dressed in a well-tailored Stalin jacket. He greeted Volodia warmly and invited him to his office.

"Citizen Tarko, where are you going to travel today? We have only one horse."

"I did not come here today asking for a ride, Comrade Naimov. I need a favor of you. You are an important leader in this village, and a man of understanding and culture. I need your help."

"If you came to me about housing for the refugees, you came to the wrong man."

"It is about housing for Eva Markes and her family." Volodia told him in detail what had happened last night.

"Eva Markes is one of my best accountants. She never complained about anything."

"Eva is not a complainer. The Markes family is satisfied that they have an opportunity to work for a man like you, a man of understanding and generosity, who upholds the real Uzbekian traditions."

Later the same day, Naimov sent Volodia a horse and cart, two beds, a couple of straw mattresses, blankets, two wooden chairs, a table and a permit for a one-room flat in the building for village employees. A room with real floors and electricity. Eva and Anna cleaned the room, scrubbed the floor, overjoyed that Volodia would move in with them.

"This will keep the men away from my children," Celia cheerfully chattered to her new neighbors. "Now, they will leave us alone."

Volodia got them some carrots and onions, then went back to his room at the center. He did not feel it was right to move in with Eva. He had Oleg to consider.

Volodia made his rounds at the center and soon was listening to complaints about food. Aziz Ali, as a matter of pride, followed him, showing off the cleanliness of the ward. Some of the patients asked that the loudspeaker be turned down, others asked for help in writing letters to their sons in the army.

Volodia stopped in the morgue. Someone had died last night, and Volodia gave orders to Vera to notify Dr. Ivanovna and to remove the corpse.

He went to the warehouse to give Vera new sheets and pillows for the Clinic. There were also new admissions to the hospital and they needed mattress covers, sulphur, and other medications.

The new admissions were suspected typhoid cases. Vera waited for Dr. Ivanovna to confirm the diagnosis. She prepared reports on the blood, feces, and urine tests.

"I hope the tests are all negative. If not, we will have our hands full ... We are short on bichlorides and other disinfectants. We must visit the families of the new patients, disinfect their homes and, protect them with vaccinations," Vera said quietly.

"We received some gauze netting screens to keep out mosquitoes and flies. You can use them in the isolator."

Vera did not respond to what Volodia had just told her. She picked up the sheets and started to walk away. Volodia stopped her.

"Please wait ... I want to ask you something. How are things going, Vera? Do you still hate me?"

"*Hospodi Pomiluj* -- God forbid, Vladimir Arionovitz. I just don't like men."

"You've said that to me before. Why do you hate men?"

She swung around and looked Volodia squarely in the eye. "I've never told this to anyone. I don't like pity. But you, Vladimir Arionovitz -- I trust you."

"Thank you, Verotchka. You're the most qualified nurse we have here. You know how much I respect you. I realize that you have scars from something in your past. So, if you'd rather not discuss it ...

"I want to tell you what happened if you are interested."

"Verotchka, we are like comrades in arms. We work side by side every day. Of course I am interested in what bothers you."

Vera had lived in a dormitory room at nursing school.

"Well, after my graduation, I was invited to a party. Some of the guys got us drunk. I couldn't stand on my feet. Four of them helped me get home and they undressed me. I struggled desperately -- scratched and screamed, but no one heard me cry out. The four overpowered me, and I passed out. After the incident, I had a nervous breakdown. I also had an abortion and remained in the hospital for seven weeks."

"Did they arrest the bastards?"

"They investigated. I didn't remember exactly who they were because I was drunk. The case was dropped. I was reprimanded by the *Komsomol* for immoral behavior and given a chance to rehabilitate myself by working in this remote village."

"Don't you think, Verotchka, that this was just one unfortunate moment and you should not accuse all men for the crime of four? You said yourself they were drunk."

"Yes, I think this way many times, but I feel differently. I can't stand when a man touches me. I have no desire left, no urge for a man. I can't banish from my mind this 'one unfortunate moment.'" Anyhow, I can never have any children, so I devote my life to my work."

"You have the courage to forgive the four?"

"I already forgave them, but I can't forget. It always comes back. That night left a scar on my mind, body, and soul, that no therapy can erase."

"Still, you can't go on living all alone with this horrible nightmare. It can destroy the strongest person."

"Not when you have strong faith in the work you're doing. I gave up my personal happiness to help the unfortunate in this area, just like you, Vladimir Arionovitz. In a way, we were both raped. I was raped bodily and you spiritually. Your beliefs, your people, have been persecuted for generations and are being destroyed now by the fascists, like our people all over European Russia."

"How do you know all this?"

"I listen to my patients when I'm on duty. They talk about their lives in Poland, Rumania, Lithuania. The more they talk, the more I love my country. We are a poor country. Many

of our citizens are still illiterate. We have just begun building
a new life for all inhabitants of this land and it is our own.
When we win this war, we will build a better world for all our
citizens."

"I'm glad that you can talk about the horrors of your
personal life in the same breath in which you talk about the
virtues of your homeland."

"After all, what are the sufferings of one single person in
comparison with the suffering of our people in Leningrad? I
keep my emotions to myself and go on working."

"Verotchka, you're a great lady. I'm glad we had this talk."

"I'm glad too. I did not want you to think I have
something against you personally."

Aziz Ali came running with a scared look on his face. He
was sweating and his voice was trembling. *"Chozain* Tarko."

"What's the trouble, Aziz Ali? What are you trying to tell
me?"

"Chinabaad is calling you, NKVD. Hurry to the
telephone."

Volodia was trying to calm down and to convince himself
that this must be some error. Still, he went to the phone and
asked the operator if someone had been trying to call him.

"Yes," replied a friendly voice. "I'm calling for *Sledowatel*
Bagdayev. He would like you to come to Chinabaad this
morning. He hopes you can make it."

"I will come before noon."

"Can't you make it sooner?"

"I don't think so. I have to arrange for transportation."

"We know. We have arranged with the bank and they
have a horse already saddled for you."

"Then I'll be there as quickly as possible."

Volodia locked the storeroom and went to the office. He
pulled out the drawers of his file cabinet and glanced through
his papers. Everything was in order. Volodia thought fast.
There was nothing to be distressed about.

Still, ever since he had met Bagdayev, he had anticipated

that sooner or later he would be called. Volodia heard of the ruthless interrogations by the NKVD. He had been warned that the same fate was in store for him, unless he took out a Soviet passport or volunteered for service in the army. Lately, he had noticed more and more searches for deserters and black market operators. Arrests of Polish refugees were a daily occurrence.

The military draft board had a quota to draft soldiers and workers for the coal mines and forced labor camps. Volodia feared that even with his privileged status as a medical worker, he too would be drafted. He picked up the saddled horse at the bank and called on Eva.

"I've been called to Chinabaad."

"Is this so new for you?"

"The area district attorney wants me, the *sledowatel* in Chinabaad."

"For what?"

"I don't know."

"You look pale."

"Do I?"

"And you sound scared. Don't worry. This is not the way they work."

"How do you know?"

"If they want to arrest you, they send a militia escort to accompany you."

"A good time for your jokes."

"No, seriously, Volodia, I know their system. We live with it."

"Really! Then I'll see you this evening, if I come back."

"You'd better. We need the horse."

"Thank you."

"Horses are needed here more than refugees."

"Why are you so cynical?"

"We'll talk about it when you get back."

"Good day, Eva."

"Come see me, please, when you get back, Volodia."

Volodia noticed how Eva's small mouth trembled. He bent to kiss her. After he mounted his horse and was on his way, he heard Eva's voice calling, "Wolf Tarko! *Gott is mit dir!*"

God be with you!

Volodia rode at a breakneck pace to the militia building in Chinabaad. A sentry took the horse. Volodia washed his face and hands at a hot water fountain. Soon, a uniformed guard showed him into a small room. On a table was food set for two. There were fresh *lepioshkas,* baked fish, melted butter, and bowls of tea. Bagdayev came in and greeted Volodia with a smile.

"You didn't eat breakfast today, did you?" he asked warmly.

"No, there was no time."

Volodia felt more at ease. This is not the way they arrest people, he thought.

"How is your health, Comrade Tarko, *Yakshi misis?"*

"Tuzuk! Thank you. And how is yours?"

"I'm as hungry as a dog. Please join me. This is also my breakfast. You know we work late too."

They both ate heartily, dipping the *lepioshka* in the butter and downing some tea. Bagdayev started the conversation.

"How is our public health care program in Kyzyl Kishlak?"

"It has not yet passed its initial development stage. Actually, we are trying to develop a method of preventing and controlling communicable diseases."

"Our Party and government published textbooks and laws on public health."

"Administration of health care cannot be regulated by textbooks alone, or some formula or law. It is too broad a field and too enormous a job. Each Soviet Republic with its own climate, religious, and racial customs has its own way of acting and thinking. What is suitable for the Kirghizs is not acceptable to the Uzbeks."

"Our Party and leaders think for the good of the people. This is why we have laws and books."

"The books are good educational guides, but health care ideas are changing constantly. Often, we must discard old practices and accept new points of view from more competent workers in the field of preventing epidemics and infectious diseases."

"This is exactly why I called on you this morning, and I'm glad you came."

"I felt if you wanted to see me, it must be important."

"Yes, Comrade Tarko," Bagdayev's face got serious, "very important. Remember our talk on the barge? I was thinking of it constantly. It bothered me, and with the help of our *rayonkommat* (regional commandatura), we decided to help local refugees. However, we need your help. There are many elderly Jews from Poland, even the Russian Jews can't understand them well."

"What can I do?"

"We want to transfer the unfortunate people from all public places to the old school dormitory."

"I will be glad to help."

"After you disinfect the dormitory and give the refugees a good cleaning in the bathhouse, we will supply you with clean shirts, pants, skirts, even some shoes for the school-age children. All these things are gifts from Comrade Stalin."

"When do we start?"

"Right after we finish eating?"

Volodia supervised the transfer of the refugees from the *chaichanas* to the dormitory. The building was old and dilapidated, but it was a roof over their heads, an address where the people could be registered as living there. They would now be able to get mail, breadcards, even work. The regional council provided old, rusty, iron bunk beds and clean, straw mattresses. The local health center sent a nurse and some volunteers to help.

The nurse was an expert in the diagnosis of contagious diseases. She carefully examined the children and the elderly. She discovered a child with tuberculosis and elderly refugees with dysentery caused by food poisoning. They were sent to the local hospital.

Bagdayev personally directed the placing of a huge barrel for water storage and the placing of large kettles for cooking in the dormitory yard. Volodia subdivided the old building into three separate residences, for men, women, and women with children.

The bathhouse was opened. Getzel, the barber, with the help of a local woman barber, gave everybody a short haircut. The refugees' belongings were disinfected. Clothes that were beyond repair were burned and the people were given a gift of clothes from the "Great Benevolent Stalin." When the Polish refugees came back from the bathhouse, they were admitted to the new home, the dormitory, and given breadcards. Volodia set up a special committee from among the refugees to direct their own affairs. The committee set to work, registering the people, isolating the sick and old who needed special care. Spirits were good. The poor refugees from Poland who had felt abandoned before, now felt suddenly something had changed, somebody cared. Was it Stalin? Or was it the 'Organization of Polish Patriots?' What's the difference, they thought, as long as they have given us a roof over our heads.

By late evening, Volodia had finished his assignment. Before returning to Kyzyl Kishlak, he called on Bagdayev.

"Thank you for coming down to help. Actually, it was you who made me go out and see them. How is my friend, Muhamoud?"

"He works too hard. He is a sick man."

"We know. That's why I asked. Babachan told me that he hardly eats." Bagdayev talked in a warm, familiar voice. "Please, can your Dr. Ivanovna do something for him?"

"Dr. Ivanovna tried to convince him to go to Andizhan and see a specialist there. He needs another operation, but refuses. He wants to wait six months."

"Why?"

"Dr. Chaidarov plans to reorganize the whole health service in our area. We are in danger of a typhus epidemic. I really wish he would go. He is such a good man, may God help him. Oh, sorry. I always say this."

"Don't apologize, Tarko. May Allah help him. We all need him. Say *salaam* to him and Babachan when you get back."

"I will. I wish I could do the same thing for the refugees in our village."

"Why don't you build some temporary, provisional shacks?"

"We need permits and materials for that."

"Let Chaidarov write a request to the area council. We will see what we can do."

"Spasibo! Thanks again."

Volodia sang as he galloped back to Kyzyl Kishlak. He rode straight to Eva's to tell her of the day's unexpected events.

"There'll be no more homeless souls sleeping in the streets of Chinabaad."

"They arrested them all?"

"No. They gave them a school for shelter."

"So that they can keep a better eye on them? What other good news have you got from there?"

"Stalin himself bestowed the title of 'Hero of the Soviet Union' on Air Force General Jacob Mushkewitz for his victory over the German Luftwaffe. Mushkewitz is a brilliant officer and he is Jewish."

Eva was unimpressed.

"My Boris is a common soldier. He also fights for this country and makes his contribution to this war."

"But this is the second high-ranking Jewish officer honored in a month."

"Who was the first?"

"General Jacob Kreiser. He counterattacked the Germans near Moscow and smashed their army."

"Why are you so excited by Jewish generals? We Jews have a great share in this war. Just because someone is a general does not make him more special than the common soldier."

"Why are you so touchy?"

"I was damned worried about you, that's why."

"I just wanted to share the news with you. We always hear remarks that the Russians are fighting this war for the Jews and the Jews are hiding in Tashkent. So, I want the whole world to know that there are Jewish generals giving the Germans a smashing defeat as well."

"You don't know our country, Volodia. The people here

don't read newspapers. The radio commentators don't say that Kreiser is Jewish. *Pravda* is used only to wrap trash in, or for cigarette paper. Secondly, even if a million Jews got the 'Order of Lenin' or the 'Order of the Red Banner,' they would still hate us. Can't you understand? Before it was the czars, now it's the Politbureau. They have always used us as the scapegoats for everything. *'Yak bida to do Zida'* -- when there's trouble, blame the Jews ... They always settled all revolutions, demonstrations, uprisings of the peasants here by *pogroms*. Stalin is not better than Plehve and the Politbureau is not better than the 'Black Hundred' of prerevolutionary fame. The people of this country hate the Jews as they hate the system. All of them, including your new benefactor in Chinabaad. They all want Russia to lose this war. Their loyalty to Stalin and to the Party is a fake, a cover-up just to survive. We Jews are caught between the Communists and the anti-Russian feelings. This has been going on here since the revolution and it is continuing even now. Give those people here a free hand and they will attack and plunder us now."

Volodia looked at Eva with astonishment.

"My God! So whom can we trust? Is everyone our enemy?"

"Yes, Volodia. Everyone here cares only about himself, his own skin, and you must be careful whom you talk to, what you do, and whom you befriend. We are uprooted from our homes; they evacuated us in cattle wagons like animals to this area and they look at us like animals. Look at your work, Volodia. You worry, beg for food, soap, or a grain of salt for your patients, while the Party members have cellars full of rice, and feast on chicks and lamb. And they have feasts every time our country loses a city or a division. Look at the refugees. Their husbands and sons are fighting for this country, and they are treated cruelly every time they need something."

"What will happen when you get home?"

Eva sighed. "We are not back yet. The war is not over. Volodia, the reason I told you all this is that I see you killing yourself in your work. Start taking it easier. They will use you as long as they need you and then toss you away."

"Let's listen to the late broadcast."

The communique was joy to Volodia and Eva:

"Seven thousand Germans killed on the Central Front ...
The Red Army offensive reached the Don River ... The second
Red Army surrounded twenty-two German divisions."

* * * * *

CHAPTER NINE
The Refugee

The Refugee

Life for the Markses began to look up. Celia's health improved so much that she began working in the restaurant while Anna went to school. Eva got a better job at the bank, where she gained the respect of the clients and the confidence of Naimov, the bank director. When Naimov had to leave Kyzyl Kishlak for meetings or conferences in Chinabaad, Chakulabaad or Andizhan, he entrusted Eva with the bank's rubber stamp and the personal stamp with his signature.

In addition to her salary, Eva received small gifts from the *kolkhoz* accountants for helping audit their ledgers and balance sheets. They often left her little bags with dried *uruqs*, raisins, onions, salt, vegetable oil, or a cup of melted butter. Sometimes, thank-you notes were attached to the gifts.

In comparison with the other refugees, the Markeses lived well. All they worried about was Boris.

When Volodia was busy at the center or away in a village, Eva would bring food to his little room and wait for him so that they might have dinner together.

One night, while Eva was waiting for Volodia at the center, a strong wind knocked down the electric line and the power went off. It was raining outside and the downpour came in through the window and door. Eva could not bear to wait alone in the darkness. She was about to leave when Volodia opened the door. The wind slammed the door behind him. Volodia lit the small kerosene lamp and warmed his hands at the flame. Eva mopped up the water coming in from the door and turned to find Volodia trembling from the cold.

"Volodia, I've got some food for you. Do you want to eat?"

"You're an angel."

"What have you been doing?"

"We had to move some patients to the isolator."

"Do you want to wash up?"

"I took a shower before I left; new emergency regulations."

"Would you like me to make some tea while you change?"

"No, thanks. Let's just get a bit of food. I'm hungry and tired."

"I'd better run home before the rain gets worse."

"It is bad already. Let's eat. You can stay here tonight."

Eva kicked off her shoes and sat down on his bed.

"I don't want to eat. The smoke of the kerosene is hurting my eyes."

Volodia ate and then turned off the lamp and sat down on the bed listening to the rain. There was no need to talk. He gave some grapes to Eva, which she ate slowly. His hand fell on her knee.

"Oh, God, how tired I am."

Eva got up quietly and took the grapes back to the basket. She locked the door and came back to the bed. Volodia was asleep. Softly she slid onto the bed cover beside him. For a moment he opened his eyes and then took her into his arms.

"Volodia, are you asleep?"

"I'm dreaming."

"Me, too." She stroked his hair and face.

Volodia delicately touched her neck. She sighed with delight.

"Volodia, do you like me?"

"Yes, very much."

Volodia was happy to hold her like this. For weeks he had dreamed about her, imagined holding her in his arms. However, now that the moment had come, he was reluctant to do more than just hold her. He stroked her smooth skin.

"Volodia, do you want me?"

"I need you, Eva. I need you more than you realize."

Eva sat up and took her clothes off. By the dim light they looked at each other. Then, trembling, she pulled herself to Volodia and he took her in his arms.

"You're shivering, Eva. Do you feel cold?"

"Yes, cover me with your body. I've wanted this for a long time. I love you, Volodia."

When they awoke in the morning, the room was full of rain water. Volodia didn't have the energy to get out of bed. He looked at Eva and kissed her tenderly. He just wanted to touch her, caress her hair, embrace her.

"Eva, we've got to get up."

Eva groaned, "It was so good, so warm. I dreamed of my hometown and you were with us."

"Come, Eva, we must get up."

Volodia bent over and kissed her forehead.

"Get up, little girl. Look at the mess here. Get dressed. We will eat breakfast together."

"Stay here today, Volodia, Let's call in sick."

"No, Eva. Come by after work and we will go out for dinner."

"How about Mother?"

"We will take Mother and Anna too."

Eva jumped out of bed right into his arms.

"I'm so happy."

Volodia ran his fingers gently through her hair.

"Me, too. You know, Eva, somewhere now there is a war going on and we are here practically singing, enjoying each other so much. We delight in making love while the radio brings news of war, death, and wounded. What a paradox is my life."

Eva shrugged and said, "Maybe this is what life is all about. It's stronger than war, destruction, and misery. Maybe love is stronger than all human suffering?"

She rested her head on his chest.

"Oh, Volodia, I want you so much."

They made love again in the damp, cold room.

It rained for days, stopping and starting again with a new force. The storms created a shortage of drinking water and flooded alleys. The streams reeked, huts caved in. There was a lack of food and medicine and a lack of wood for the center's furnaces. Every evening, Volodia returned soaking wet to his little room to be greeted by Eva's outstretched arms.

Aziz Ali changed the linen on their bed, got an extra pillow, a new pitcher for water, extra tea bowls, cups, and a small kerosene stove. Volodia became aware that something new was happening to him. Not only did he care about Eva, he wanted to be with her constantly. He missed her during working hours. Eva seemed to feel the same.

"Volodia, I can't wait to get home from the bank, I just want to be near you, hear you talk, and just be in your arms. What would I ever have done without you?"

"You would have married Oleg Polishenko."

"Mother would never have allowed it."

"Would you have done it anyway?"

"If I wouldn't have met you, it would have made no difference. I've known Oleg since kindergarten. We've always been friends, but I would not hurt Mother."

"Does she like him?"

"Yes, very much, like our own Boris. But, she keeps saying she wants her children to remain Jews. Besides, Mother likes you very much."

"Is this the reason you cook for me, because I am good to your mother and Anna?"

"And me."

Eva leaned her head on his shoulder.

"Volodia, I struggled for weeks not to fall in love with you. You Polish refugees are so different. You're all waiting for the war to end, to go back to Poland, to your girlfriends, your families. I will never leave my mother alone. She is a sick woman and she needs me. Still, it happened. I'm twenty-one years old already. Many time I've longed for a man, but meeting you, I experienced something new, something that never happened to me before. Even though I saw you walking and holding hands with the Russian doctor."

"I've told you already, we are just good friends. She has a friend in the army."

"Many women have husbands in the army and live with any man they can get."

"Tanya is different."

"How do you feel about her?"

"What kind of a question is that?"

"Well," she paused. "You seldom kiss me."

"Stop talking foolishness. You know that I love you."
Eva closed her eyes, a smile on her lips. Then she reached
out and embraced him. Happy, but tired, she fell asleep in his
arms.

During the following weeks, Eva and Volodia stayed
together every night that Volodia was free. When he received
a note from the draft board to register at the *Woyenkomat* --
the military registrar's office -- Eva went with him. In the
column in the questionnaire reading 'whom to notify in case of
emergency,' Volodia wrote 'Eva Markes, c/o Kyzyl Kishlak
Village Bank.' One morning, before leaving for work, Volodia
attached a note, written in Hebrew, to Eva's dress. It was an
old poem he remembered from school written by Judah Halevi:
> *"Awake my fair, my love.*
> *Awake, that I may gaze at thee!*
> *And if one fain to kiss thy lips,*
> *Thou in thy dreams dost see,*
> *Lo, I myself then of thy dream*
> *The interpreter will be!"*

Before leaving for the bank, Eva stopped at the malaria
center.

"Volodia, you know I don't read Hebrew. What is this
note about?"

"Just that I love you and I want to marry you." Volodia
said earnestly, "Let's go to ZAGS and register."

"We will get married after the war. If I marry you now,
I may lose my job. You are a foreigner, a refugee, and not a
citizen. I will lose my security clearance in the bank. Please
understand. I can't do it now."

"Maybe it is dangerous for us to see each other at all!"
Eva's eyes filled with tears.

"How can you say this to me? You know I love you."

"I'm tired of being called stranger, refugee, *brodiaga*,
untrustworthy, stateless. I'm fighting your epidemics, cleaning

your lice, and killing your mosquitoes, and no one is going to tell me I can't marry the girl I love. I work as well as any of your native-born citizens, and all I ask is to be treated like a decent human being."

"I am sorry, Volodia. You're too naive and too honest to understand our system. But, thank you for the poem."

A Party directive was sent to all agencies in the area stating:

"(A) Make more public health help accessible to wider sections of the local and evacuated citizenry; (B) Set up a network of lectures to explain ways of developing a campaign against disease."

As a result, a flood of people began coming to the malaria center. Some of them required immediate help and were referred to the "quinine window." Drugs were given to them without prescription; they just signed their name or made an 'X' and received their dosage.

The directive was sheer nonsense to Volodia. The Party was trying to monopolize control over the lice and mosquitoes. He knew an epidemic could not be stopped by issuing decrees. The Party directive made the practical implication of this order the responsibility of the local Party committees and village councils. However, the leaders ignored the directive that all people be given equal help and service. The refugees waited in line for help, but were ignored. They were looked upon as something unwanted, unclean, strange. Many of them stood in line for days waiting, starving, fainting. They complained bitterly that they had had to walk in the extreme heat for miles, hungry and thirsty, to get medical help, and when they finally got there, they were told to wait ... no room ... no food ... no drugs.

Many of them had diarrhea from drinking contaminated water. The lack of salt in their diet gave them swollen bellies. Others complained of high fever, malaise, vomiting, rashes, bleeding, shock.

There was no vaccine to immunize them. Andizhan promised some new drugs, new insecticides. Nothing arrived but 'special orders,' announcements that sounded like war bulletins: "Beware of ticks, mosquitoes ... they are your enemies."

Volodia sprayed the clinic and center with carbolic acid. But the disinfections did not help, and the mosquitoes and ticks returned.

Dr. Chaidarov ordered the isolation of infected individuals. There were no extra rooms and no screens available for effective isolation. Scores of sick people from nearby villages lined up outside the clinic.

Those with dysentery waited in long lines at the open shack with the big hole in the ground, the center's additional toilet. Some of them, after a visit to the toilet, were in no condition to walk back to the line. They required immediate help, hospitalization, but only a few were admitted into the hospital, clinic, or the center. The majority were sent back or had to walk back to their *kolkhozes*.

From day to day, things got worse, and the lines grew longer. They sent Volodia people with sore arms instead of sending them directly to the clinic. These people came to him speaking Russian, Polish, Yiddish, German, Uzbekian. If a man was reluctant to let Dr. Ivanovna look at his swollen, inflamed appendix or hernia, if some refugee was scared when Dr. Chaidarov had to open his carbuncle, they sent for Vladimir Arionovitz. He always had some kind words to say to them, to pacify their fears. Volodia knew that kindness would not fill their stomachs and would not cure their wounds. Still, his expressions of sympathy helped. There was no clergyman in the Kyzyk Kishlak area, so in their last moments, they asked *Pan* Vladislaw" to say confession with them. *Pan* Vladislaw -- Volodia -- Wolf Ben Aharon, recited prayers he remembered from his childhood, prayers he learned when he was a student at a religious school in Lodz.

"Hashem Melech -- The Lord is King. The Lord was King. The Lord shall be King forever and ever."

For the Uzbeks, Tadziks, and other Moslems, he recited from the Koran a line he learned from Aziz Ali. "The noblest of you in Allah's sight is he who fears Him most."

"You sound like a *Muezzin,* calling the faithful to prayers," Tanya giggled.

"I'm not a *Muezzin,* not a rabbi, and not a priest. I am just helping those unfortunate people to die peacefully."

In the beginning, Volodia feared someone might report him for practicing religion, a punishable offense. Finally, he decided he had nothing to lose. The refugees came here to be helped and all that was given to them were promises. They suffered and died. Volodia was not religious himself. His beliefs and confidence in the Almighty were shaken, intimidated by insults and suffering. How could He let the sun shine over His people while they died from lice and hunger? Where were His justice and mercy?

Still, Volodia kept coming to visit the sick -- Jews, Christians, Moslems. They all believed in God and murmured their prayers with their teeth chattering, trembling. He whispered to them long-forgotten prayers that suddenly came back to him.

"May the Almighty in Heaven have pity on your soul, pardon you all your sins, assuage all your pains, remove all your diseases, and lengthen the years of your life, Amen."

"May the Merciful Father grant you complete restoration of your health, even as it is written. When He calleth upon me, I will answer Him: I will be with Him in trouble, I will deliver and honor Him. With length of days will I satisfy Him and let Him see my salvation."

The most beloved prayer for the Catholic and Jewish refugees is Psalm 23, "The Lord is my Shepherd."

" ... Yea though I walk through the valley of the shadow of death, I will fear no evil, for Thou art with me ... "

Even Tanya expressed a liking for the words of that Psalm. "Your prayers don't help, but they can't hurt. Still, I fear that someday they will cost you your job, if not worse."

"Tanya, all I am interested in is helping those people. If I can cheer up a patient either by talking to him about his family or praying with him, I do so gladly. Can you understand this?"

"I know, Volodia, I understand. But will they?"

"I will fear no evil, for Thou art with me."

"Who? Me?"

"Not you, Tanya, God!"

"So, you do believe?"

"I'm bitter, disappointed, doubtful, hurt, humiliated, nameless, stateless, but deep in my heart, I believe."

Food shortages caused an outbreak of illness among the children. Every day groups of them came, alone or with adults, looking pale and pasty. Their bellies were swollen and many were suffering from hookworm, which they caught from walking barefooted around infested, polluted streams. Prayer could not help them. What they needed was food, milk, fresh fruit, and green vegetables. Again Volodia called on Secretary Kozlov. The secretary had a short answer: "There is a war going on. We must send all the food to the soldiers. We have written instructions from the Party and the government."

"Written instructions are one thing, but watching children die from hunger is something else. I wish, Comrade Secretary, you would visit the clinic and see for yourself."

"Sorry, I'm busy with very important matters."

After conversations like this, Volodia would return to the center upset. Yet he would not allow himself to be discouraged. On his own he gathered some food for the children. Tanya, Eva, Vera, Getzel Gold, and other refugees all contributed. Still it was not enough.

Tanya happened to see him returning to his office on one occasion with tears in his eyes.

"Volodia! You're talking to yourself!"

"No, Tanya, just praying."

"For what?"

"For this war to stop. For our soldiers to defeat the enemy. For some food for the children and the other patients."

"Pray for me too. I'm suffering with them. I'm desperate. Whoever heard of a hospital without a pharmacy, without a bloodbank? We need more nurses, orderlies, and another doctor. Dr. Chaidarov needs surgery. I closed the nursery. I told them it is safer to keep their babies at home. We have cases of tuberculosis; we must isolate them. We have a woman, a lunatic, whom we must remove to an asylum. Typhus is at our doorstep. The situation is terrible. The tubercular patients are in a contagious stage. I have a refugee who is mentally ill. Where shall I send him, to the street or to jail? Last night we had a case of appendicitis and we did not have any sterilized instruments. Fatima was away, Verochka was too busy. Volodia, I can't function like this. I feel I'm breaking down."

"What can I do? Talk to Dr. Chaidarov?"

"Volodia, we must get a supply of medicines, of anti-typhus serum. We need new syringes. I'm getting so tired and disgusted that I can't work any more. Damn all this. My legs hurt so much, up to my spine."

"Why don't you go home and rest? I, myself, am so angry that I'm ready to leave this whole damned village and join the Polish army."

"You can't leave us, Volodia. We need you here."

"They don't appreciate you and they don't value my work. Look, there are 11,000 inhabitants in this area and they send close to 600 refugees here. They keep sending them like junk to the garbage dump. The *kolkhozes* don't want them, the council can't stand them, and the Party doesn't trust them. They are mostly women, war widows and children, and they can't work in the rice and cotton fields. What do you want me to do? I can't work eight hours in the center, then stay in my room and close my eyes to the suffering. Tanya, they are my people! If I can't help them, what am I here for?"

"Volodia, they are my people also. Everybody here is my people. But so many refugees! We have twice as many refugees as local people in the hospital. That's why there is constant friction and tension between the village council and the refugees. The council resents the refugees -- they think of them as inferior. That's why they are so indifferent to the suffering of the sick and the needy."

"Still, the Uzbeks have their homes, their own little gardens, vineyards. They have as many as four wives and plenty of food. Chinabaad did something for the refugees. Even the local militia helped. Why can't Kyzyl Kishlak do the same?"

"Chinabaad did it because they had help from Andizhan."

"They gave the refugees clothes, shoes, food, a gift from Comrade Stalin himself."

For the first time in many weeks, Tanya burst out laughing.

"What is so amusing?" Volodia asked.

"Who told you that the food and clothes were from Comrade Stalin?"

"The *sledowatel* himself."

"The transport of food and clothes were sent to Chinabaad by the Andizhan Committee of the 'Union of Polish Patriots,' gifts sent from America for former Polish citizens."

"How do you know all this?"

"We had a letter asking us for a list of patients in our clinic and hospital who are former Polish citizens."

"Did you send them this list?"

"We prepared the letter, but the local NKVD asked us to remit the letter to them. I forgot to mention it to you. I'm only a doctor fighting diseases. I can't fight with the Party or our Soviet security directives."

"Damn! You gave me an idea. I'm leaving for Andizhan to join the Polish Patriots."

Tanya came over close to Volodia and said emphatically, "We need you here. Don't you realize how much you care for the people here? You will not and must not leave them." She put her hands on his face. "You need a shave. Soon you will really look like a rabbi or the Pope."

"I wish they had a rabbi or a priest here."

"I wish we had two more doctors and more nurses. What

are you planning? You are going to abolish the revolution and reestablish religion?"

"No, but so many people are dying, why not help them die peacefully?"

"Let's concentrate on helping the living. Come! Let's go home. I'm very tired."

"I'm going to visit the Markes family."

"The widow or her daughter?"

"Are you jealous?"

"Me? What right do I have to be jealous?"

"You're a woman."

"I'm a doctor first. I have patients, my work. I have Mischa. All I want from you is your friendship."

Volodia walked Tanya home.

"Go get a shave. I will take a shower."

Tanya undressed, covering her body with a sheet.

"Volodia, if I ask you to scrub my back, will I be betraying my Mischa?"

"I don't know, but I feel I will be betraying Eva. I'm in love with her."

"Are you going to marry her?"

"I asked her and she refused. Will you marry Mischa when he returns?"

"He will probably marry Esther, the girl who lives in Andizhan. Mischa helps her. She gets his army paycheck."

"How do you know?"

"I was the one who got her address for Mischa."

"Why?"

"He left his things with them when he was mobilized. It was at the railroad station in Andizhan. He asked me for their address. He needed some of his documents."

"How do you know he sends them his money?"

"In a way, he adopted them."

"Them?"

"Yes, Esther, her mother, and her sister."

Tanya and Volodia stepped into the small shower room.

"He adopted them? And you?"

"We had a momentary love affair."

"Momentary?"

"Yes, but it will last a lifetime."

The telephone rang. Tanya answered it and came back to the shower room.

"We must go. It was Fatima. Something has happened to your widow Celia."

They dressed hurriedly and walked back to the clinic. Tanya picked up her medicine bag and, leaning on Volodia's arm, rushed to the Markes' home.

* * * * *

CHAPTER TEN
Grief

Grief

People were clustered outside the house chattering in low voices. Their faces were so somber and gloomy, Volodia thought for a moment that it was too late.

Celia was lying on her straw mattress bed, covered with a cotton blanket. Her breathing was labored. Anna was off to one side, weeping, while Eva sat on the floor near her mother, holding her hand. In a shaky voice, she told Volodia the news.

"Volodia, Boris was killed in action."

"Oh, no," Volodia cried.

He pulled Eva into his arms. She wept bitterly, openly.

Tanya injected a pain reliever into Celia's arm and in minutes the injection took effect. Celia opened her eyes and began mumbling.

"My Boris. My only son. He was only nineteen last September. In the battle for Moscow ... my child." Tanya, too, was overcome by their tragedy. Eva asked Volodia to take Tanya home. "Thank you, Dr. Ivanovna, for your help," said Eva after a time. "You can do no more for us now. Please, Volodia, walk the doctor home."

Tanya walked slowly.

"Remember what you said this morning, Volodia, it is one thing to read about so many killed, so many thousands wounded, but when it happens to you, when you see it and you actually feel it, it's just terrible."

Gently, he helped Tanya up the steps to her home.

"Would you like me to make you some tea? You look so pale and tired."

"Thank you, Volodia, no. You go back to Eva. She needs you now more than ever."

It was unbearable for Volodia to see Celia is so much pain. He prayed that Celia would fall asleep. Maybe a few hours of rest would weaken the shock and ease the grief. Volodia sat down on the edge of the bed near Anna and Eva. He put his arms around them both.

In the middle of the night, Volodia awakened. He found Celia sitting up, her hair disheveled, gazing at the sleeping Eva and Anna, with tears running down her face. Gently, he covered her hands with his, whispering, "Please, Celia, calm yourself. I can understand your grief, but remember you still have two children. Boris will go on living in your thoughts as long as you live. He will live in your memory, and in Eva's and Anna's. Can I give you anything?"

"No, thank you. I am grateful that you are here with us."

Volodia helped her stagger out of bed. She was weak and could hardly walk. He helped her to the door and she went outside to the outhouse. When she returned to bed, she was calmer and soon fell asleep.

In the morning, Volodia went to the center. He gave Aziz Ali and Vera all they needed for the day, then went to see Tanya and got some drugs for Celia. He picked up milk and his bread ration and went back to Eva and her mother.

Volodia was glad they did not know about the traditional week for mourning and prayer for the dead. They were so lonely in their calamity that this one night of grief was already too much.

This was war time. Everyday someone received the pink and yellow notifications delivered by a special messenger from the *Voyenkomat* -- Military Commissariat. People were used to living from day to day with hunger, sickness, dirt, lice, but when grief struck, it was suffering shared by all.

Still, after a few days of sympathy visits, the families where a son or husband died were left to suffer a permanent loss, that only they had to live with, like the amputation of an arm.

After they finished eating, Volodia helped Eva remove all the food that friends and neighbors had brought for them.

"Why do people think that a bereaved family deserves more food than others?" Celia said sadly. Her face looked gray and pale. "My son fought for his country against Hitler. At least if I could have told him how much I love him, how much I need him ... Oh, I wish I were a man and younger. I would go to the front to take my son's place and fight the Nazis until victory." She hesitated and began to cry again. "There are so many widows and hungry children in the village, please take all this food to them."

"I will take the food to them, Mother," Eva said, holding back her tears.

Volodia was back in his office going over some of his notes, bills, and a letter he had written to the Party secretary. Tanya came in excited, nervous.

"Volodia, they lied to me outright. They promised to send us some volunteers and not one person has come."

"I've written a letter to the Party secretary. Please sit down and read it carefully. I have to leave for Chinabaad. You can make any corrections you want. Here are the pens and ink bottle."

Volodia left and Tanya sat down to read.

To the First Party Secretary
Village Kyzyl Kishlak
Chinabaad Region
Comrade A. Rachatayev
We are facing a disastrous situation in Kyzyl Kishlak. We are dealing with an impoverished group of refugees who face unparalleled hardships.

The Kyzyl Kishlak Malaria Center, with the help of the Regional Clinic and Hospital, has utilized all possible resources to help these people. Still, the unsanitary conditions in which the refugees live have produced lice and bacteria, the cause of diseases.

We appeal to the Party Secretariat to take into consideration Paragraphs 135, 136, and 137 of the Party Program in the interest of protecting public health and safety

of the people of Kyzyl Kishlak. We ask you to assist us by
providing the following:

1. *An extra supply of food for our Hospital and Center.*
2. *Soap, alcohol, and DDT in large quantities to meet the*
   new circumstances.
3. *Dwellings, homes for the refugees who live in the*
   chaichanas *and public places.*
4. *Prompt opening of the bathhouse on a 24-hour basis.*
5. *Mobilization of volunteers to serve in the Hospital and*
   Center.
6. *Boiled water used in public places. All collective kitchens*
   must ensure that food is hygienically prepared.
7. *Obligatory disinfection of wearing apparel of any man or*
   woman who comes in touch with a sick person.

We hope the Party Secretariat will give this urgent message
the utmost attention.

Dr. Mahomoud Chaidarov
Director, Health and Welfare
Sel-Soviet Kyzyl Kishlak
Copy to: State Health Commissariat, Andizhan

Tanya made some corrections, stuffed the letter in an
envelope, and called Aziz Ali.
"I want this letter taken to Dr. Chaidarov. After he signs
it, deliver it to Comrade Rachatayev."
"Shall I wait for an answer?"
"No, just leave it with him."

Eva came to the center and sat on the step outside
Volodia's room. She looked pale, still grief-stricken. After
awhile, Volodia came. His hair was wet from the shower and
he was wearing his white, long coat.
"I didn't know whether to come in or wait outside. I didn't
know if, after our argument, I have the right to see you, but
I had to get away a little. My eyes hurt and the sun was
blinding today."

"It's good to see you, Eva, really. I'm not angry with you at all. It was hot today. I just got back from Chinabaad. How is Mother?"

"I wish you could see her just for a few minutes. She is asking about you constantly."

"Is she still so depressed?"

"She makes an effort to be calm, in front of us. It's so hard to accept the loss. Many people come to see us. It's good to feel that we have friends, but like Mother said, you are the closest and dearest among them." She moved closer to him and took his hand in hers. "You smell from Carbol. You're still wet."

"I was full of dust and sand, so I took a shower with green soap and carbolated water."

He was tired. He knew Eva needed to talk, to open up. He tried to think of a word, a line to say to her which would console the pain.

"Volodia, you're so quiet. I want you to know that I'm very thankful to you for what you did for us when this catastrophe came."

"I did what I was supposed to do."

"Mother said you cried."

"So I did. It is hard not to cry when you see a mother suffer the loss of her only son. You know how much I care about your mother. She is my friend."

"And are you still my friend?"

"Yours, Anna's, everybody's."

"And Dr. Ivanovna's?"

"Yes, and hers."

"Mom said that Boris is still alive and that he will never die as long as she lives. She knows she will never see him again, but she will never cease to yearn for him, love him. You know, Volodia, I myself see him as if he were still alive. I can't imagine him as no more."

Again the tears streamed down Eva's face. Volodia put his arm around her. Eva leaned her head on his shoulder and let the tears flow.

"Eva, you've got to be strong."

Volodia tried to say something more. Deep in his mind he was searching for words to express something warm, genuinely human.

"Eva, you refused to accept me as your husband. Will you accept me as your friend?"

"You're saying it out of pity, to soothe my grief."

Volodia took her pale face in his hands, looked in the big, sad eyes and touched her mouth with his lips.

"No, Eva, not just pity. I really feel close and care about your family. You refused my offer to marry you, but I still love you."

"What about Dr. Ivanovna? You went back to her after our argument."

"Eva, believe me, we are just good friends. Tanya has someone. He is on the Leningrad front now."

"Did you ever live with her?"

"Yes, I did. I used to."

"Just like that?"

"We are grown people. Sometimes she needed me just because she was lonesome. We are fond of each other; we needed someone to talk to. Loneliness is a terrible thing and we feel good with each other. Many times when I was discouraged, she gave me confidence in myself."

"Are you in love with her?"

"In all honesty, in a way, yes. She is a remarkable human being, a devoted doctor and a very beautiful woman."

"Don't you feel that you are stealing someone's love?"

"She is not married to him and he will never marry her. He sends his check to a girl and her mother in Andizhan."

"And Dr. Ivanovna knows about this?"

"Yes, she knows."

"And she still loves him?"

"Now more than ever."

"To be truthful, I couldn't live like that. I would not want only part of a man I love. I dream of the whole man."

"Do you have one you dream about? Is this why you refused to marry me?"

"Yes."

"Where is he?"

"Oh Volodia, you're so smart and so stupid. I know you're preoccupied with your work, with your daily problems, but don't you realize that you're the man I dream about? You, Volodia, are the one I'm waiting for. Do I sound silly, after refusing to marry you, to say all this? Did I carry my dreams too far? Didn't you feel I love you when we were together in this room? The only reason I did not want to go to SAGS was the fear that you will go back to Poland after the war and I will have to leave my mother alone. Also, I had heard about your relationship with Dr. Ivanovna and wasn't sure whether you were all mine."

Volodia just sat there and listened.

"Look how selfish we are. I just lost my brother, the whole world fell apart for us, and here, during this saddest week, I think and talk about love."

"We are lonely, Eva, and young. We have our longings and desires, our dreams of a little happiness. That doesn't diminish your love for your mother or the pain of your brother's death."

"Volodia, will you be offended if I tell you that I'm terribly jealous of Dr. Ivanovna?"

"You don't like her?"

"Yes, I do. My God, all the house calls she made to mother, all the help she gave us, of course I'm appreciative. But I feel that her sleeping with you is an offense to her lover fighting on the front."

"Eva, you have misinterpreted her relationship with me. You would be surprised to know that sex was the least important part of our relationship. We just got accustomed to each other."

"You said you love her."

"I love you too. I have never spent the night with her since I met you. Don't eat your heart out about it, really. I'm not worth all this trouble."

Volodia kept stroking her hair. Eva was leaning against him. He could feel the warmth of her ample breasts. All the time she was talking he wished he could just hold her close in his arms. It felt so good.

"Volodia, will you visit Mother tonight? It's getting late."

"No, not tonight. I haven't eaten anything since noon. Come to my room and join me for some fruit."

"They got up holding hands. Eva closed the door.

"What do you want, Eva? Grapes, apples, raisins?"

Eva pushed herself back into his arms.

"I want you, Volodia. I need you so much."

That night, Eva and Volodia were drawn to each other with a new power of love and desire. She kept holding onto him, plunged herself into his arms.

After midnight, resting on his chest, happy and satisfied, Eva babbled, "Volodia, I never realized I could be so wild about anyone. Please, tell me more about yourself, about your life. I know so little about you."

Volodia closed his eyes, pulled her closer into his arms.

"There isn't much to know."

"How did you become a medic? I want to know everything about you. Everything."

"I don't remember exactly how I got into this profession. It seems such a long time ago."

"Oh please, Volodia, try to remember."

"My parents died when I was a child. I was raised by my grandparents in the city of Lodz. My grandfather was an orthodox Jew. He sent me to Hebrew school. Because I was an orphan, I became *bar mitzvah* at the age of twelve and was sent away to study in a yeshiva in Piotrkow, a small city not far from Lodz."

"What is *bar mitzvah?*"

"The word means 'son of the commandment' and every Jewish boy, when he becomes thirteen years old, takes on responsibilities of a religious nature. He begins to pray every day in *tefillin* -- phylacteries. He must give charity on his own and perform all traditional duties of a Jew."

"I don't understand, but please continue."

"My teachers and tutors predicted that some day I would become a rabbi, but the more I studied the more doubt I had about social justice, about the 'heavenly blessing of being poor,' and I started to read Polish and Yiddish books: Mendele, Peretz, Slowacki, Mickiewitz, Gorki, Tolstoy. One of my classmates took me to a meeting of a youth group and there I heard about Nordau, Herzl, and Gordon."

"Were they all writers?"

"They were writers, political leaders, dreamers, and planners of a Jewish homeland in Palestine."

"Zionists?"

"Yes. My grandfather was a poor man, my grandmother a sick woman. I did not want to be a burden to them. I left the *mesifta* in Piotrkow and went to a textile factory to learn a trade, how to make sweaters. I didn't like it. I dreamed about going to Palestine. I have an aunt there, my mother's younger sister. But I needed a trade, a vocation to make myself useful as a pioneer. I heard about malaria and swamps in Palestine, that pioneers die there in the infested swamps, and my dream was to become a medic. I shared my dream with a friend, who was like a father to me. He was a great Yiddish poet who lived on the same street where my grandparents lived. He was a great friend of young students and poets. His wife was a famous actress in the Yiddish theater in Poland and their home was always a center of culture and art."

"What was his name?"

"Moshe Broderson. He is now somewhere in the Soviet Union with his wife, Sheine Miriam, and daughter, Hanka. Anyway, Broderson worked as editor in the local *Folksblatt*, the Yiddish newspaper, and knew many doctors and administrators. He gave me the address of a clinic in a nearby town where orderlies and sanitary workers were needed. They offered free training, free uniforms, room and board. I registered. The registrar and the doctors had strictly Polish names, but they looked Jewish. When I got home for the weekend, I had mixed feelings, to tell or not to tell my pious, religious grandparents that I had quit the textile factory and had become a *sanitariusz*. Luckily they didn't ask me. I was able to continue on-the-job training, and dreamed about the day I would get to Palestine and work in a hospital with doctors who don't have to hide their Jewish names.

"After six months of training at the ambulatorium, my relationship with the staff and patients became bearable. Most of them were Poles, so I avoided conversations about race, religion, politics, and Jews. I didn't want any confrontations. I did my job well, studied hard and learned many things related to my new profession. Every two weeks, I received an envelope with my pay, which I handed to my grandmother, keeping enough for the streetcar and small expenses. I was a loner. All I cherished were my books, reading and writing poetry. I belonged to our youth group and on weekends, attended some meetings, but my mind and heart belonged to my grandparents."

Volodia paused for a moment and then continued.

"I had a girlfriend. Her name was Machcia. She was pretty, smart, full of life, always singing, always dancing. She was as poor as I was. They lived seven people in one room; her parents, two brothers and two sisters. Machcia was a seamstress and worked in a shirt factory. In the evenings, she sewed at home. Her father, once a big businessman, had lost everything in the depression. We loved each other and dreamed that someday we would save up 200 *zloty* (a fortune of about $70), and get a visa for Palestine."

"Every free moment I had I studied. Dr. Miecislaw Krassner and his wife, the head of the ambulatorium, often invited me to stay at their house for the weekend, while they went away on short vacations. They had a large medical library, and my knowledge increased with every passing weekend. Dr. Krassner was influential in all the local hospitals. My close relationship with him helped shield me from the anti-Semitic remarks made by some of the staff people. Most of the Polish staff were good, honest, and helpful, especially the nuns. They gave me good advice. Sometimes, they shared some fruit, or a glass of homemade lemonade, or lent a helping hand when I was carrying a heavy load of linen, aprons, or medical supplies. When my grandmother became sick, I gave up my activities in the youth group. I gave up extra reading and studying, even my

weekend visits to Machcia. I needed money and worked any
hour, any overtime available. My grandmother was bedridden
and my grandfather stayed home to take care of her. He was
too proud to ask for help, so we lived in two little attic rooms
on the money I made and shared the little food we could
afford.

"In the beginning, my work was just to learn a trade, a
way of making money to support my grandparents, but working
in the ambulatorium and part-time in the hospital, I started to
like what I was doing. The patients started to have special
meaning to me, not just merely charts, bed and dispensary
numbers, or a list of prescriptions or treatments to be given to
number so and so. I developed an ability to work day and
night and not get tired. I just needed to sleep a few hours,
shave, shower, and be back on the job. Many cold weekends
I did not feel like traveling home. There were seminars and
lectures on hospital management for volunteers and I attended
them. I gained popularity with the staff in the hospital for
volunteering to work on Christmas Eve. Once a patient, in his
hour of dying, asked me to recite with him the last rites, "to
cleanse his soul from sin at the hour of death."

"What did you do?"

"I called for the priest and while the patient was holding
onto the Red Cross on my arm, I started to recite Psalm
Twenty-three...The priest came and he continued the psalm to
the end, said some prayers in Latin, and the man died
peacefully. The next day, everyone in the hospital knew about
the incident. The young priest, Father Gursky, complimented
me saying, 'You serve God in a special way.'"

"Father Gursky asked me why I took on additional burdens
in the hospital. I told him I had a strong desire to help. He
said he would like to have me by his side when we go to
war."

"Are we going to war, Father Gursky?" I asked him, and
he said "Yes, the situation with Danzig doesn't look good. Let
us pray that this new year, 1939, will be a peaceful year."

"God willing."

"Nu, Eva, this is enough for tonight. Tomorrow morning

I must go to Andizhan. Look, here is a notebook with some of my life stories and my poems. You can read them while I am gone."
"What is it about?"
"My first love story."
"How many did you have?"
"Many, but this was my first one. Are you jealous?"
"Yes, I am..."
Volodia kept stroking and kissing her hair.
"There is no reason, Eva. I love you."

* * * * *

CHAPTER ELEVEN
Sharing Memories

Sharing Memories

Eva picked up a copybook with yellowish pages and read the small lines written in Yiddish:

I. Two Velvels

I was showered with love by my grandparents, pity and sympathy by my teachers; what I really needed was the affection and attention missing since my parents died.

I enjoyed being a student at the Yeshiva Beth Meir in the town of Piotrkow Tribunalski, run by the Orthodox Agudas Israel. We were free to choose the books and tractates we liked to study and we learned *Talmud, Midrash* Commentaries in Yiddish translation, but not in Hebrew; the "Sacred Tongue" was too Holy to be used in daily conversations.

I had been a pupil in Machzikai Hadas Yeshiva in Lodz and was transferred to Piotrkow Tribunalski to study until I would be ready to enter the Seminary of the Lublin Scholars founded by Rabbi R. Meir Shapira, of Blessed Memory, after whom our Yeshiva was named.

My teachers were mostly *Gerer Chasidim* -- pious and learned rabbis. They were followers of the Rabbi of Ger, Rabbi Avraham Mordechai, of Blessed Memory. I was fascinated by their sharp minds, humility and passionate love for learning Torah. Many of them looked like my father, of Blessed Memory, whose picture I kept in the table drawer in my room.

I was lonesome and fell into the habit of talking to myself, arguing or singing in two voices. Sometimes we talked to each other, asking questions about *Gemara* and commentaries. We studied together *daf yomi* -- a page a day of *Talmud*, recited to each other pages of the *Mishna* or chapters from The

142

Ethics of the Fathers, quizzing each other on who said what. But one Velvel inside me was always creating friction. Like a disciple of Satan, he argued with the pious disciple of the *Gerer* Rabbi. The other Velvel was overwhelmed by feelings of tension, irritated by the people in whose homes he ate free meals.

They were fine, compassionate people, good, gentle and curious Jewish mothers, or overgrown daughters who served the food with a sigh, grieving over the "poor orphan." I was smothered with so much pity that every spoonful of borscht they served was hard to swallow and every morsel of bread stuck in my throat.

The first Velvel was a God-fearing, pious student, sitting in the Yeshiva from morning until late evening, showing competency, a degree of enthusiasm in his studies, to the satisfaction of his teachers and the delight of his grandparents, who dreamed their only grandson would get a scholarship to the great Yeshiva of Lublin.

The other Velvel in me had sinful dreams, feelings of inferiority for being so poor, so shabbily dressed. His shoes and clothes were falling apart at the seams.

I was now going on seventeen, growing tall, and outgrowing my overcoat which was old and too tight and from which the buttons kept falling off.

"It is true," I argued with the other Velvel, "our rabbis don't care about *chitzunius* -- exterior dress, the most important is *pnimius* -- inner strength, willpower to study and do good deeds."

Both Velvels were lonely and homesick for my grandparents, whom we had not seen for more than a year.

Last *Pesach*, I was ready to walk home the 47 kilometers to Lodz, but the weather was nasty and my shoes had holes.

II. The Twins

I had two days of two meals at the home of Reb Simcha the butcher. Leah, his wife, a fine woman, was possessed by a craving to do *mitzvot* -- good deeds, give charity, help others. She always carried small change for the poor.

They had twin daughters, Feigele and Chanele, both good-natured, always giggling, fresh and aggressive. They stared at me with unconcealed desire and always found a way, while serving my meals, to lean on my shoulders so that I could feel their warm breath on my neck. They served my food as if they were stuffing geese before taking them to the ritual slaughterer, always making remarks:

"Velvel, won't you come tonight and help me with my Yiddish lessons? I'll be nice to you ... "

"Velvel, why don't you come and work for my father? You will have plenty to eat here ... We like you."

Little remarks like those gave me sleepless nights. I dreamed about the two identical girls, laughing, their dark brown hair draping all over me. I woke up bewildered, trembling all over, murmuring prayers, asking for God's forgiveness, and quoting Reb Jacob: "One hour spent in repentance and good deeds in this world is better than the whole life of the world to come. Yet one hour of satisfaction in the world to come is better than a whole life in this world."

But the other Velvel in me was happy with the dreams. They satisfied my desires and were good substitutes for loneliness.

III. The Kosher Inn

I spent two days in the kosher guest house. I helped serve meals from noon to two o'clock and in return got a free meal and one *zloty*.

The waiters and waitresses would save leftover bread for me, pickles, sometimes a chicken leg, a piece of brisket. They wrapped the packages with little notes attached which I considered temptation of Satan himself:

"Dear Velvel, you are as poor as we are. Quit wasting your life with the fanatics. We're all living in an uncertain future here. Join the Labor Movement. Together, we will fight and build a better future for the Jewish masses of Poland. Take this note with the food to the other poor students of your Yeshiva. Come join us. We need you!"

It was disturbing to receive this type of message. The girls and the men who worked at the Kosher Inn were all very nice to me. They never made fun of my earlocks. Just once, a young girl caressed my light chin whiskers saying, "Get rid of the earlocks and I'll marry you tonight, even if you are only seventeen." Her remarks made me blush to my ears.

On my way back to the Yeshiva, I kept repeating: "Rabbi Yoshua ben Levi said: 'Eat bread with salt, drink water by measure, sleep on the bare ground, and live a life of hardship while you toil in the study of *Torah*. If you do this, happy shall you be in this world and in the world to come.'"

At the Yeshiva, I shared with my rabbi the conversation with the waiters at the inn. He said: "Worldly intellectualism, political movements, estrange our people from their heritage. Our *Torah* movement holds onto the principles of love of God and humanity. Your waiters are good-hearted people, but they came too late. Our *Torah* teaches justice for the poor."

IV. My Attic Room

I lived in an attic room at the home of Reb Shmuel Isaac, a devout, observant Jew who had inherited the carpenter shop from his father, going back in the mastery of the trade to the seventeenth century, when the first Shmuel Isaac the Carpenter helped build the famous Moses Kazin Synagogue in Nowa Wies, a suburb of Piotrkow.

The home was an old, one story house with an attic converted into a room. Reb Shmuel Isaac's father renovated the house, adding a tall wooden fence to keep the noise and thieves out. He built a side door from the kitchen leading to the outhouse in the backyard.

Reb Shmuel Isaac added a white tiled oven with a chimney reaching high above the ceiling of my attic room. The back porch had a sliding roof which could be moved back to show the sky, and during the *Sukkoth* holiday, was covered with pine branches and green leaves and used for a *Sukkah* -- booth.

Reb Shmuel Isaac was very proud of the fact that he managed to work from dawn to dusk, never forgetting to pray three times daily, attending evening study at his prayer-*shtible* and frequently visiting his rabbi, the *Tzadik* of Ger.

While working he sang Chasidic melodies and recited psalms. He always thanked heaven that he was able to work with his hands, creating foot stools, milking stools, rocking chairs, and doing furniture repairs in peoples' homes. Mostly he worked in his shop in the backyard of his house, while he repeated chapters of the Bible or his beloved Ethics of the Fathers.

From the moment I stepped in their house, I felt a closeness to Reb Shmuel Isaac and his wife, Rebecca. He was a gentle and tactful man, tall with blond hair and gray eyes. His small beard was trimmed and his face was tanned and rugged from working outside. His eyes were always underlined with dark bags from the heavy glasses he wore while sawing material in his shop, and they were always red from the sawdust. His perpetual smile endeared him to his customers, Polish peasants and peddlers from nearby villages.

Rebecca, a shapely woman who wore a blonde wig over her blond hair, spoke with a melodious Warsaw accent. Her blue eyes laughed at me with goodness. Rebecca helped run her husband's business, selling 'his creations,' as she jokingly called them, at a stand in the market place.

I was to help Rebecca and Reb Shmuel Isaac every morning to carry their wares to the market and pick up orders for their peasant customers from shops or the apothecary. For this I got my attic room and breakfast every morning, and I would be a "welcome guest" at their *Shabbat* table if I so desired.

I was glad of their hospitality from the moment I stepped into their house. On Friday nights the aroma of the sizzling *cholent* and *kugel* in the oven would tickle my nostrils, the kettle of *Shabbat* tea was singing *zmiroth* -- Sabbath songs -- all night ... It was good to be with them and they liked having someone in their home.

They were lonely people, devoted to each other, with no close relatives or friends in town. Their only daughter, Brachale, was away. She had graduated from the Sarah

Schnirer Teachers Seminary in Cracow and was now teaching at a Beth Jacob School for Girls in Lodz.

Rebecca would get up in the morning at the first sign of daylight and would cook for the whole day. I helped her bring in the fire wood from the shop and carried water from the well when the water barrel was low, especially during the winter season.

Sometimes a peasant would get drunk and Reb Shmuel Isaac would let him rest on the wagons in his yard. I helped feed and water their horses.

At mealtimes they would ask me about my parents, grandparents, what I wanted to be in life, how I was doing in my studies ... There was no pity, no crying over me -- the orphan. They would ask me to read to them again the letters from their Brachale and would show me her pictures with her class of students. It was inscribed "To my Tateshi and Mameshi from their loving daughter, Bracha."

Piotrkow Tribunalski

The provincial town of Piotrkow was the site of the General Assembly in prepartitioned Poland with a long history going back to the year 1578.

Jews had played a role here in the struggle for independence and in the economical development of the area. They had lived in harmony with the Poles for hundreds of years.

Piotrkow is located on the crossroads between Lodz and Warsaw, linked by good roads to many of the small villages and farm communities.

Every day was a market day here and this kept Reb Shmuel Isaac and Rebecca very busy.

The shrill of horses, geese, and pigs, the hustle of merchants with the peasant women and the constant cry of beggars excitedly arguing with each other, screaming for help, could be heard from dawn until long past dusk.

Peasants with their horse-drawn wagons and coaches came directly to the shop or to the market stall, trading farm products for milking stools and merchandise that Rebecca sold "on consignment" for small shop owners, items such as barrels, pottery, brushes, kettles, saddle goods and other farm utensils. The farmers liked to deal with Rebecca. She looked Polish and spoke with a Warsaw accent. They often asked her for advice in personal matters or left her orders for materials and merchandise to be picked up by them on the next market day. The Polish peasants, themselves poor but very religious people, shared their meager belongings with the less fortunate among them. The farmers always kept bundles of fruit, vegetables or homemade bread with them on the coaches and generously gave it to the beggars and poor at the market place and to the invalids sitting on the steps of the parish church on Farna Street and the Bernardine Monastery on Kosczuszko Square.

Whenever I helped Rebecca pick up merchandise for the farmers from the shops or apothecary, the farmers always rewarded me with an apple or pear, a tomato or a bundle of carrots, which I shared with my rabbis and the other students.

Rebecca had her favorite customers and was ever ready for them with a little tobacco, a piece of egg *challah*, honey cake or a bottle of *bimber* -- vodka, as little tokens of appreciation. After a while, the farmers knew that I was studying to be a *Rabin* and they would leave an extra egg, flower seeds, or fruits for that 'poor orphan.'

And the two Velvels in me kept rebuffing each other: "Are those the habits you will get used to? Is this your future? Proclaiming to the world that you are an orphan? What will become of you?"

"I get paid for pick up and delivery of the farmers' orders. What's wrong with that? Thank God I don't have to carry back any merchandise in the evening."

Rebecca knew exactly what would sell on what day, as her husband Reb Shmuel Isaac knew the exact prayers for sickness, rain, the evil eye, and thanksgiving. I didn't see anything wrong with earning some food as long as I did not neglect my studies.

At the Yeshiva I was in another world. Here both Velvels had inner peace. I paid attention to my rabbis who frequently explained or defined a comment in the *Mishna* or *Gemara* with a parable or fictitious story. The same Rabbi Yakov Yochiel who told us moving stories about the *Tzadikim* -- saintly rabbis of Kotsk and Ger -- and brought us to ecstasy by the passion of his stories ... The same Rabbi Yakov Yochiel who sang melodies of the Rabbi of Modzice, pouring out his heart to God *Meshiach Zol Shoin Kumen* -- that the Messiah should finally come ... The same Rabbi Yakov Yochiel pursued the studies with a methodology of a genius; every law of the *Torah* was explained with logical concepts. Not only did he know the *Turim* and *Shulhan Aruk* -- books of Jewish law -- by heart, he knew exactly where to find specific passages, and what were Rashi and the Tosafists' comments on those passages.

I was delighted just to sit there and listen to them unravel passages from Maimonides in such logical terms that a child in elementary school could understand.

When I was allowed to study on my own and put my heart and soul into the books, the other Velvel in me, with all his desires, dreams, and complaints, had no entry here. This was a sacred place of Divine Spirit. Here my soul thirsted for God.

Dreams of Flesh and a World to Come

But the nights were terrible. Dreams ... May God forgive me. Why is he teasing me? Girls ... The Kosher Inn. Waitresses ten years older than I. The butcher's daughters, Feigele and Chanele. All of them in such perverse dreams. And lately, this Brachale. All I saw of her were pictures. All I knew of her was that she was a teacher at a girl's school in Lodz. She had been away from home for years now. She spent her vacations teaching in a summer camp in Bielsko-Biala.

Rebecca would let me read Brachale's letters to her. I knew Brachale was engaged to be married to a student soon to receive *Smicha* -- ordination as a rabbi at the Sfat Emet Yeshiva in Ger. I knew that they registered at the Palestine

Amt in Warsaw for a marriage license and a certificate to go to Palestine, and hoped to teach there at the General Orphan Home in Jerusalem. In my mind, she belonged to someone else; still I dreamed about her, asked her silly questions like, "Why do you have to be three years older than I? Why don't you come home to visit your parents, you, their only child?"

Rebecca would say how terribly lonely it was when Brachale left. But they got used to it. "She was a bright student, always reading, studying, and dreaming of being a teacher. Now, thank God, she is a teacher and her groom, they say, is a giant in *Torah*. Hopefully, when they settle in *Eretz Yisroel,* we will follow. My Shmuel Isaac has a good trade, two golden hands, *kein eyin horo* (no evil eye), and they need carpenters everywhere ..." Rebecca kept herself busy with her customers and her spotless housekeeping. She was always baking bread, braided *challah,* honey cakes for her clientele or her Brachale, who received them by special messengers or merchants who also had daughters studying in Lodz.

Every Friday evening when greeting the Sabbath with the blessing over the candles, Rebecca would set aside small change for charity for the Yeshiva of Reb Meir the Miracle Man in the Holy land, and some silver coins for *Hachnasat Callah* -- poor brides' fund of Piotrkow. She chanted her own special prayer in Yiddish for the poor people of the world, for her daughter, Brachale, and her groom Lazar -- the scholar -- for her husband, Shmuel Isaac, her customers, her boarder, the orphan Velvel and *kol Yisroel.*

"May the Lord bless and protect you;
May the Lord countenance you and be gracious to you;
May the Lord favor you and grant you peace."

Many times the other Velvel in me stood under the window before going to the *Shtible* for Sabbath services, just to listen to Rebecca's prayer, waiting to hear her mention, "My boarder, the orphan Velvel ..." Rebecca prayed with so much sincerity that many times I cried ... Why, I never knew.

As time went by and I progressed in my studies, I was able to spend more time helping Reb Shmuel Isaac and

Rebecca. They dictated all their letters to Brachale to me, and I dutifully wrote them and sent them off.

My life was divided now between the Yeshiva, my attic room, and the Kosher Inn where I still worked twice a week for two hours. I was so immersed in study that the outside world did not exist for me. All I cared about were my meditations, and memorizing the commentaries of Rashi and the Tosafot. We sat at long tables on hard wooden benches, singing out our special melodies for chapter after chapter of *Mishna* and *Gemara* from morning until night, our bodies rhythmically swaying back and forth to a melancholic, sweet sing-song of *"Omar Abayah* -- Abayah said..." Here, every day was Sabbath and on every Sabbath we were blessed with a Divine Spirit, an extra Sabbath soul.

Even on my way to the Kosher Inn or while carrying loads to the market for Rebecca and Reb Shmuel Isaac, the two Velvels in me argued back and forth about tractates in *Midrash* -- the interpretation, commentary of the Bible, trying to solve problems, explaining meanings of words in the Babylonian or Jerusalem *Talmud.*

People on the street pointed and stared at me, though I was too busy arguing with myself or humming a tune of a *Gemara* melody to pay much attention to them. Sometimes they would stop in astonishment and look curiously at my long black coat, earlocks, and fringes, but, again, I did not pay any attention. I went back to my *Tannaim* -- the sages and teachers of the past. I did not care about the outside world.

The only one who really disturbed me was the other Velvel: "You don't care about the world you say ... How about me? I am almost barefoot. Grandfather writes that grandmother is ill. How can you isolate yourself from everything? Is the Yeshiva the boundary of the universe? How about the demonstrations in the marketplace against *pogroms?* Why aren't we part of it? The waiters at the inn care about you. Do you care about them? What is our future going to be? Even if you get a scholarship to the Lublin Yeshiva, will you marry a girl and be supported by your father-in-law? We are living two thousand years in the past, in Babylonia, in the Temple of Jerusalem. We are studying laws of no meaning to present-day life."

I did not let the other Velvel in me dominate my thoughts: "What we are studying is for the perpetuation of the Jewish people. We hold on to our traditions, to our laws from generation to generation. We see life constantly changing, but we continue to hold on to our sacred books, to our moral values, we hold on to our joys and sorrows, to our festivals and Sabbath, until the Messiah will come ... "

"The Messiah will come in a generation, and all mankind will be judged guilty or righteous. With hunger, persecution, and injustice in the world, the Messiah could show up any day now -- God willing. Stop your disputations, let's continue. Remember the Baal Shem Tov said: 'Do not mortify the flesh, pity it.'"

Longing
    The Messiah did not come, but notes and letters from my grandfather in Lodz kept arriving. Written in a beautiful Yiddish with Hebrew quotations, letters full of love. They penetrated the heart and soul of both Velvels in me.

"Your *Bubeshi* -- grandmother -- is ill. She feels guilty before our Heavenly Father and your mother's soul in heaven for letting you live so far away from us. She feels an unbearable longing to see you once more. We hope you will come home for *Pesach*."

The "once more" was not good news to me. Heaven knows how much I wanted to help them, comfort them, be near them, and I was so helpless. What could a Yeshiva student do for them besides reciting psalms and prayers? Both Velvels in me felt inadequate, inferior. Here I was, almost seventeen, at the level of self-study, and I could not figure out how to help the only people left in the world who were my family, my own. I was so helpless and ignorant of what was happening around me in the outside world. All I knew was *Olam Haba* -- the world to come -- but there was a reality, the *Olam Hazeh* -- this world. My grandparents.

Wait for the Messiah? According to my Rabbi Yakov Yochiel, "There is a Messiah in every human being." He quoted the *Zohar* saying, "Redemption is not a thing that will take place all at once at the end of the days; it is a continuous process taking place every minute. Man's good deeds are single acts in the long drama of redemption."

"All the world -- could it be that the 'Bundists' and the 'Zionists' have a part in the coming of the Messiah? Could it be that the outside world has a part to play in the redemption? Could it be that I am holding back the Redeemer by doing nothing but just studying?

Piotrkow had a Jewish community with thirty *Talmud Torah*s--Hebrew elementary schools, two Hebrew-Yiddish schools, a Yiddish newsweekly, and an ORT (Rehabilitation through Training) School. Maybe I could apply for a part-time *Melamed* -- teacher's job? There were organizations from Agudas Israel and *Mizrachi* -- Religious Zionists -- and Youth Groups like *Hashomer Hatzair, Gordonia, Zukunft*. There were *Kibbutzim* where young people, my age, learned trades, preparing themselves to go to Palestine. They worked in local lumber yards and textile factories. The *Bund* and Agudas Israel had summer camps and trade schools and they helped young men and women acquire skills and find jobs. Perhaps they would be able to help me.

What good is it that I know the *Tannaim* -- the sages of the *Mishna* -- the sayings of Rabbi Yehuda Hanassi, the birthplaces of Abayah and Rava, the names of cities in Babylonia, Pumpedita and Mahoza, but don't know what is taking place in the world around me. There is an enemy of the Jewish people rising in the world named Hitler, and I try to fight him by fasting Mondays and Thursdays and reciting psalms. What good is all my study if I don't know how to earn enough money for a pair of shoes, a decent coat, a clean shirt? And I can't even afford my own food?

The two Velvels did not wrestle on this subject any more. We decided to find a new direction. We started to read, to look outside ... to the world around us.

Brachale

One day, after the High Holidays, Brachale came home. While working at the summer camp in Bielsko-Biala, she became ill and was bedridden all during the *Yamim Tovim* -- the holidays. The doctor advised her school principal to send her home to recuperate for a few months.

I found her in the kitchen preparing lunch for her father.

"You are Velvel?"

"Yes, *Sholom Aleichem,* Brachale. Welcome home!"

She greeted me with the familiarity of an older sister who had returned home. I knew she was three years older than I, but she looked much younger than the picture in her room.

"Are you very *frum* -- religious? Do you talk to girls? If you object, I will try not to talk to you."

"Brachale, we were all waiting for you to come home."

"You too?"

"Me too."

We all finished eating and said the final blessing. Reb Shmuel Isaac took some food to the market to Rebecca. I was reluctant to say anything. I just observed her washing dishes. Her light brown hair was woven into two braids which she wore like a crown around her head. Her eyes were blue-gray with a dark frame under them. She was soft spoken, but firm.

"Velvel, what are your plans for the future?"

"I hope to study at the Yeshiva in Lublin."

"And then what?"

"Maybe I will go to Palestine. I have an aunt there."

"What is she doing in *Eretz Yisroel?*"

"She is draining swamps in the Valley of Jezreel."

Brachale looked at me and said, "Velvel, I don't know how many pages of the *Talmud* you can recite by heart, but they will not help you dry swamps and rebuild the Jewish Homeland. It is very important to have a trade. There are many Jewish organizations here that could help you. Our own Agudas Israel or ORT can advise you what to do. Please go see them ... will you?"

"I will. I was there already, but they told me to come back next week."

"My *mamashi* told me all about you and I feel as if I've known you all my life from your letters. I don't want to get you out of here, but honestly, I want to help you."

I thanked her for her meal and the advice and went back to my studies at the Yeshiva.

The following morning, the two Velvels started another argument. One wanted to get up, wash his hands in the basin on the wash stand in the attic room, and say his prayers. The other Velvel was just lying in bed looking at the wall, observing a spider spinning a web. He was full of envy:

"This spider is working, creating his nest. What is it that I will do today? I am a parasite, just eating other people's food. Brachale is right ... What is my future going to be? Selling *mezuzahs?*"

"God will perform a miracle as he did with Elijah. He ascended to heaven in a flaming coach-carrier."

"Stupidity! How can you believe in all those stories you are reading? These are fantasies, folklore, written by many people in different times."

"Time to get up and pray."

"I am following Kotzk's tradition ... spontaneity in prayer, pray whenever the spirits move you."

"Have you seen Brachale's delicate hands? Her voice is ..."

"She is someone else's bride."

"She is not married yet. What if her groom will not get *Smicha,* will not graduate. Will she change her mind?"

Suddenly I heard Brachale's voice.

"Velvel? Good morning. Are you feeling well? It's late."

"I will be down in a few minutes."

"I said my prayers, ran out of the house to the yard and followed Reb Shmuel Isaac with his merchandise-loaded wagon to the market. I unloaded the hand wagon and helped Rebecca display the goods.

"Velvel, are you feeling well?"

"Yes, thank God. I just overslept."

ORT

The man in charge of the ORT School was tall and skinny

with a clean shaven face and a head of thick black hair. He spoke Yiddish with a Lithuanian accent. He was polite, but serious. He offered me a chair and listened attentively to my answers to his questions.

"We have many *Chedorim* -- elementary schools -- here. Would you like to be a *melamed?*" he asked piercing me with his small brown eyes.

"I'd rather learn a trade."

"He gave me a brochure in Polish and Yiddish, a listing of trades I could learn locally, or I could be sent to an ORT School in Cracow, Lodz, or Warsaw.

"You can learn to be a tailor, a meat cutter, a textile worker, or a watch maker right here in Piotrkow. We have people in the lumber business who will teach you how to do carpentry or be a lathe operator. Nevertheless, I advise you to go back to Lodz. You have more opportunities there, but if for any reason you want to stay here, I will help you."

For some reason I was in no hurry to leave. Brachale was an avid reader of Hebrew, Polish, and Yiddish books. She kept saying that every tongue people use in reading is a vehicle to better human relations. Languages spread ideas and books bring inspiration and knowledge. The main object is to make good use of what we read in our daily lives. She did not object to my taking books to my attic room to read.

I swallowed the contents of her books with the thirst of a lost wanderer in the desert. I began to read and recite poems by Tuwin, Slonimski, Bialik, Peretz, for the benefit of the other Velvel. I saved up a few *zlotys* and was able to send some *Hanukkah Gelt* -- Hanukkah gift money -- to my grandparents. I was so proud of myself that for the first time in many years, I carried Reb Shmuel Isaac's milk stools to the market loudly chanting a Chasidic song the entire way.

"Hey you, crazy earlocks, what is it today? *Purim?*"

"Yes! I sent *Shlach Mones (Purim* gifts) to my family."

I was really as happy as a Jew on *Purim*.

The Winter Season

Winter came early that year. The old houses were buried

under the snow, and the streets were icy and treacherous.
The more I advanced in my studies, the more time I was
allowed to study alone or at home. Because of the weather,
many students did not come to the Yeshiva, but just showed up
twice a week to be examined by our rabbis.

But, Heaven forgive me, instead of studying *Talmud*, I was
reading books of Jewish history by Dubnow and Balaban;
pamphlets by Max Nordau, Rabbi Zvi Kalisher; and books by
Theodore Herzl, Borochow, and Zeev Zhabotinski.

Every morning, after helping Reb Shmuel Isaac carry his
creations to the marketplace, I helped Brachale carry wood
from the yard to keep the fire going in the potbellied stove.

Rebecca came home exhausted in the evenings. After
counting the daily earnings, she warmed her feet in a bucket
of hot water and went to sleep.

Reb Shmuel Isaac returned home from evening services at
his Gerer *Shtible* -- prayer house. He ate his supper and went
back to the shop to work until very late.

"This is the season when you must make up for the slow
days in January and February," he kept saying. "God will
forgive me for not studying *Torah*. I will do it after Christmas
when things get slower."

I would sit in my attic room reading books, writing to my
grandparents, or relax in the kitchen and chat with Brachale.

Aches and Pains

One day during the week of *Hanukkah*, Brachale returned
home from the marketplace coughing and complaining that
everything hurt. Her hands were ice cold; she was so unsteady
that I removed her coat and galoshes and helped her to the
sofa.

"Would you like me to make some tea?"

She was shivering all over and her face was as pale as
porcelain.

"I have painful cramps in my shoulders ... Please call my
father."

I called Reb Shmuel Isaac and he helped Brachale to her
room and put her to bed.

"Velvel, please stay downstairs. Brachale may call for something. A good rest and some tea will relieve the pain. I must finish an order for tomorrow morning. God help us." Reb Shmuel Isaac started to recite prayers and psalms for her recovery and returned to his shop.

Brachale called me. "I can't move my arms and ankles. I can hardly breathe ... Everything hurts."

"Shall I call Dr. Malewski?"

"Not now, it's snowing too hard, it's too icy. We will wait until morning."

I made her some aspirin powder with tea and lemon, and then washed her forehead with a towel. She was trembling.

"Where is my *mamashi?* My head is burning."

When Rebecca returned, Brachale was asleep. "My Brachale, the light of my eyes," said Rebecca, tears filling her eyes. "I'd rather be sick than you." She sat all night on the old sofa, lamenting, praying, finally falling asleep from exhaustion.

Growing Up

I sat all night at Brachale's bedside, adding wood to the stove, giving her tea, changing the wet towel on her burning forehead.

I must have grown up that night. For the first time in my life I was taking care of somebody else. For the first time in my life I was sitting close to a young woman in her bed. She kept pushing away the heavy feather quilt, uncovering her nightgown.

It was past midnight when Brachale awoke complaining of severe cramps. She was burning with fever. She asked for her mother and wanted to go to the bathroom. But Rebecca was fast asleep. I covered her with her father's coat. She held onto me with her arm around my waist. There was no bathroom in the house, so I took her to the kitchen and sat her on the chamberpot covered with a special chair made by her father for use on cold winter nights. I waited outside the kitchen until I heard her voice calling me. I took her back to her bed, covered her, and stayed near her, listening to her rapid breathing. I added some wood to the stove and returned to her bedside.

For some reason I was not tired. I watched Brachale shiver as if she were having convulsions. I was plain frightened, but also felt stronger than Rebecca and Reb Shmuel Isaac. I felt like their guardian, capable of protecting Brachale until morning naturally -- with God's help.

"Father in heaven, please help her."

I looked at her feverish face and suddenly realized how dear this young woman was to me, how precious and close, and how dangerously ill. Again I turned into a boy ... I cried.

Dr. Stanislaw Malewski

Dr. Malewski came in the morning and locked himself in Brachale's room. He came out drying his hands with a white towel, his gray eyes looking sad.

"I can't give your Bella a complete physical examination in her condition." His old, wrinkled face looked anguished. "Shmuel Isaac, I want to be as truthful and accurate as possible. I am afraid Bella shows all symptoms of pneumonia. I want you to bring me some of her stool and urine as soon as possible."

He left some powders to give her every two hours and wrote a prescription to be picked up immediately from the apothecary.

Dr. Malewski spoke Yiddish like a Jew. He stroked his gray hair and mustache.

"Shmuel Isaac, you did the right thing by giving her aspirin and sponging her. Continue with the tea."

Reb Shmuel Isaac pointed at me saying, "He did all this, our Velvel."

"A relative?"

"No, a boarder, a student at the Yeshiva."

"He will make a good *Feldcher*. Give her plenty of liquid and keep sponging her. This helps keep the temperature down. I will come again to see her this evening. You, Velvel, when you're ready to take a job in a hospital, come see me."

"Me in a hospital?"

"Why not? Isn't it God's command to help people in need? When you are in the apothecary, pick up a thermometer and a bed pan. Don't let Bella out of bed until I say so."

I helped Dr. Malewski with his fur coat and opened the door for him. Reb Shmuel Isaac and Rebecca followed him to the door with thanks and blessings.

Convalescence

For weeks, Brachale was ill and Dr. Malewski came almost daily to visit her, including Sundays. There was no bed available in the city hospital, so Dr. Malewski arranged for a nurse to care for Brachale at home. Even though it was cold, the nurse insisted that the window be kept open for a few minutes for ventiliation.

Reb Shmuel Isaac raised the bed with wood blocks to make it easier to feed Brachale. The sheets and pillow cases were changed daily. The floor was cleaned with carbol acid.

I assisted the nurse with everything and, after a time, no longer blushed when I saw Brachale's body uncovered. The nurse thought I was a relative and called on me any time she needed help.

At night, I frequently smoothed her lips with petroleum jelly because they were chapped from the fever. When I did, Brachale would hold onto my fingers.

Dr. Malewski ordered that I wear a face mask and a white gown when I fed her or rubbed her with alcohol, or when I turned her from side to side to prevent bedsores. He would often tease me, saying, "How is Velvel the 'doctor' today?" He brought medicines, homemade preserves, and sometimes a real orange and juices in corked bottles with French writing on them.

Love Thy Neighbor

Dr. Stanislaw Malewski lived only two small streets from Reb Shmuel Isaac, in a home centuries old. He was a Pole born in Piotrkow to a family who had lived here for many generations. His forefathers were the founders of the Farna Church and Polish Patriots.

Everybody knew Dr. Malewski -- the missionaries, the textile workers, the Jews, and the peasants from nearby villages. He was a friendly man, short, with gray hair, a gray mustache, and gray eyes. People greeted him with respect. Even orthodox Jews lifted their hats in reverence and respect for him. Many times, he helped the poor by providing them with money for medicines.

Dr. Malewski had known Reb Shmuel Isaac when he was still in short pants. He remembered his late father who left the Rabbinical School to become a carpenter as had his father before him. Reb Shmuel Isaac did a lot of work in Dr. Malewski's old home. He built shelves for equipment, book cabinets, a diagnosis table, desks and benches for the doctor's waiting room, and a fence for his little yard.

When Dr. Malewski insisted that he pay for Reb Shmuel Isaac's services, Reb Shmuel Isaac resisted, saying, "We are childhood friends, neighbors for a hundred years. You delivered my Brachale ... Take money from you? Never!"

So Dr. Malewski, the most distinguished practitioner in Piotrkow, felt at home in the house of the humble carpenter.

With Brachale so ill, Rebecca stopped taking her wares to the marketplace and asked her steady customers to come to the shop. The farmers brought chickens, butter, flour, winter fruits for "Brachale, the Bride," but Brachale, on the advice of Dr. Malewski, only drank milk with butter and honey.

I neglected my studies. I told my rabbis that there was sickness at the home of Reb Shmuel Isaac and they needed my help. My rabbis praised my charitable deed. They agreed that I was performing a great *mitzvah.*

Rabbi Yakov Yochiel blessed me: "The Almighty will reward you for helping a family in need, but I want you to take the Holy Books and study at home. God willing, when all is well, you will come in and we will examine what you have learned."

A New Vision
But one Velvel in me did not follow the Rabbi's advice. Instead of learning my discourses on the *Mishna,* the allegories

of the *Midrash*, I read books published by the Polish Red
Cross, pamphlets about home care, chronic diseases, and first
aid. Dr. Malewski urged that I read a book about
communicable diseases and share my findings with Reb Shmuel
Isaac and Rebecca, not Brachale.
New words became part of my vocabulary -- bacteria,
germs, streptococcus infections. As Dr. Malewski ate a piece
of honey cake dipped in Passover Wishniak liquor, he
explained to me the difference between bacilli and spirilla
bacteria.
A new world opened for me in the medical texts and
magazines. I gorged myself on books. The trouble was that
Brachale knew she did not have the necessary resistance to
ward off pneumonia. Her groom kept sending good wishes for
a speedy recovery from the Rabbi of Ger.
Reb Shmuel Isaac was delighted with the beautiful letters
from his future son-in-law. But Brachale was having pains in
her lungs and chest. She smiled for the benefit of her mother
and father, but she walked around the house like a shadow, sad
and quiet. She had a difficult time adjusting to being served.
She was used to serving and helping others. She was anxious
to get well and leave for Palestine. As the day of her wedding
drew nearer, she was still not allowed to go out, even to visit
her school and her future in-laws for a *Shabbat*. Dr. Malewski
forbade her even to talk about such things.
"You think you're well, Bella, but a coach ride to Lodz is
very tiring. I am talking to you not as your doctor, but as
your friend. You are not ready yet."
One day I heard her ask Dr. Malewski, *"Panie Doctorze,*
do I have tuberculosis?"
"Unfortunately, Bella, I must say yes."
"Will I be able to get married this year and leave for
Palestine?"
"No, my child. I would rather advise you to go to a
sanitarium in Otwock."
"Will I ever be able to get married and have a family?"
"Fortunately, we detected your disease early enough and
expect that you will recover fully. There are new drugs

available. I'll start you on them as soon as they arrive. Plenty of fresh air and a lot of milk will also help you."

"Dr. Malewski, you are avoiding my question. Will I be able to get married this summer?"

"No, Bella. A change in climate, plenty of rest, and you will ..."

"Forgive me, Dr. Malewski." Brachale ran out of the room sobbing.

Dr. Malewski looked after her sadly. I helped him with his coat.

"Velvel, do not leave her alone today, and let me know tonight how she is. Sometimes it hurts, but I believe in telling my patients the truth."

The next morning, Brachale wrote a long letter to her groom and enclosed the *Tnaim* -- the engagement contract.

"You are free from the 'word or honor' we gave
each other at our *Tnaim*. You are free to go to *Eretz
Yisroel*. My blessings and good wishes go with you.
The Almighty destined otherwise for me. Please, pray
for my body and soul. Bracha."

Low Spirits

The task of getting Brachale out of her room to eat or drink fell on me. Reb Shmuel Isaac swallowed tears and recited psalms. Rebecca talked to the customers, scrubbed, cleaned, and cooked. She did not realize the grave state of mind Brachale was in, and kept saying, "Dr. Malewski said that millions of people in Poland have lung trouble and are cured. It just takes time. Brachale, have confidence in God. He will help. The Rabbi of Ger himself prays for you."

Brachale just sat in her room withdrawn, expressionless. Not even a nod.

"Mamashi, please leave me alone," she said quietly.

I had no desire to read or study or even to say my evening prayers that day. All I could think of was Brachale sitting in her room, motionless, like someone dying. I asked myself what I could do for her now.

I couldn't just do nothing, knowing she hadn't eaten or

drunk anything since Dr. Malewski left.

The other Velvel crept into my thoughts: "For weeks now, I've been praying for her recovery. Her father, the Rabbi of Ger, the rabbis and students of his Yeshiva ... why did God not answer our prayers? She is a pious girl. She wanted to give her life for *Am Yisroel* -- to the teaching of *Torah* to orphans in the Holy Land. Why does He punish her? Her parents are God loving, honest people. Why were they chosen for such sufferings?"

"You blasphemer! How dare you ask yourself questions like these? God, blessed be His name, will punish you for this ... Remember what the *Gemara* in *sanhedrin* says, 'And he that blasphemes the name of the Lord shall surely be put to death.' You recall it?"

"All I did is ask a question ... "

"You must have more faith, just simply faith, 'Love God and have faith in Him.'"

Quietly I opened the door to Brachale's room. She was stretched out on her bed. Her face was pale, her eyes half-closed.

"Brachale, can I come in?"

"Please, Velvel, sit here," she whispered. "Velvel, did I ever tell you how I met my 'chosen' -- my Lazar?"

"No, Brachale, you did not."

"Would you like to hear?"

"Yes, very much."

"I have a girlfriend in our seminary, Goldie. Her father is a rabbi in Pabianice. One day she invited me for *Shabbos* to her house and there he was, Lazar, her oldest brother. He was tall and handsome, with dark eyes, long earlocks and a small black beard. Goldie arranged the seating at the table so that we faced each other. I knew her parents were in on this -- and the dean of our seminary, too. He made *Kiddush* -- the prayer over the wine -- and we all sang *Zmiroth* -- Sabbath songs -- between courses. There were many people at the Sabbath table, a house full of children, a poor wanderer -- an *orach* they brought home for the Sabbath feast. I did not see anyone. I was hypnotized by his looks, fascinated by his voice. That night, for the first time in my life, I dreamed about a man and the man was Lazar. I was ashamed and felt sinful for having this dream, but I was happy. The next morning I spent more time looking at myself in the mirror, trying to fix my braids more perfectly than ever before. After the *Shabbat Tzimmis* -- meat with plums and carrots -- dessert, and grace, Lazar asked Goldie and me to stay at the table while his parents and the children left the room. Lazar talked to us looking at his sister: "Goldie, our rabbi brought his brother here, the rabbi of Pabianice. He asked us, a group of students, if we are willing to go and teach in *Eretz Yisroel* at the General Orphan Home in Jerusalem." He pretended not to notice my reaction and continued. "Maybe you and some of your seminary graduates would like to consider going?"

Lazar moved back his black velvet skullcap, touched his earlocks, and turned his eyes on me.

"I am an only daughter. I don't know if I will be doing the right thing, leaving them. But, if our rabbi, be he blessed, asks us to go ... Still, I must first ask my parents."

"Naturally."

"I don't believe my father will let me go, even with our rabbi's blessing ... Not as a single girl."

"Naturally. There are good students in our Yeshiva who would feel honored to have you or Goldie for a wife."

I felt my pale face start to blush. Goldie kept silent. She did not utter a word. Lazar continued: "The Rabbi of Pabianice feels that I should also get married before leaving for Jerusalem, but not before I have *Smicha.*"

He sat for a few minutes, looking at Goldie and me, then stood up. "Please, think about it. It is a great *mitzvah* to help orphans and go to *Eretz Yisroel.*"

Two months later I was engaged. Lazar went back to Ger to study. We saw each other only four times at his parents' home and once at the seminary where he came with another student to visit Goldie. Lazar took care of all the details, applications to the Palestine Agency for a certificate, a permit to enter Palestine. We wrote to each other twice a week. I have all his letters. But now this ... " Brachale started to cry.

"I am not strong enough to face it." Her trembling hand
reached for mine. "God, what am I doing to my poor
parents?"

"Dr. Malewski said they now have new drugs, and with
proper treatment, you can be cured."

"Not enough to go to Palestine with my Lazar."

"Maybe it is God's will that you should stay here with your
parents. They love you so much. Your mother cries all day.
You do not take your medicine and you do not eat. She is so
depressed."

"I am so selfish. All I was thinking about was my
magnificent future with my Lazar in Jerusalem. How
everything has collapsed. Oh, Velvel, the pain is so great. It
is impossible to describe how I feel. The training in the
seminary was hard, and I prepared myself for service to our
people. Now, I can't even go near children. What is the point
of living?"

Brachale, still holding my hand, turned her face to me as
though she were seeing someone for the first time.

"Yes, Brachale," I continued. "My life was wrapped in a
fog. All I knew was God, the rabbi, and my studies. You,
Brachale, made me see reality and distance, a vision of
tomorrow, things my eyes could not see ... "

Brachale listened hungrily to what I said, took my hand
and leaned it against her cold cheek. "Velvel, I wish you ...
" and she stopped. "Would you please give me some water.
I want to take my medicine."

Shattered Dreams

Reb Shmuel Isaac and Rebecca insisted that I not sleep in
the attic any more. I slept instead on a folding bed in the
living room.

Rebecca, sick from aggravation and "God's punishment"
was no longer able to tend to the business. She stayed in the
house, took care of Brachale, and cried. I gave up studying at
the Yeshiva and worked full time with Reb Shmuel Isaac in
his shop.

He himself spent less time now in the *Shtible* and devoted

more time to his shop and his family.

Since the yard bordered on the heavy wall of the Bernardine Seminary, he asked the priest for permission to build shelves and a stand leaning against the wall. The priest, in turn, hired Reb Shmuel Isaac to fix all the broken pews and doors in the old church.

The farmers and small shop owners now came to order and buy the merchandise displayed on the wall shelves. Brachale and her parents insisted that they pay me a regular salary. I was reluctant to take any money from them, but Brachale insisted that I take it.

I bought new shoes, shirts and socks, a real woolen sweater, and an overcoat. I showed off my new clothes for Brachale and for the first time in many weeks, I saw a gleam in her eyes and a smile on her face.

After *Purim,* I received a letter from my grandfather, "Please, you must come home, grandmother is ill. She wants you home for *Pesach.*"

The week before *Pesach,* Dr. Malewski came with the news that he arranged for Brachale to go to a sanitarium in Otwock. She had to leave the day after Passover.

I started packing my belongings in a wooden suitcase made especially for me by Reb Shmuel Isaac. I said goodbye to Reb Simcha, the butcher, and his family; to the innkeeper and waiters at the Inn. I also said goodbye to my beloved rabbis, the students at the Yeshiva, and to Dr. Malewski. They all gave me gifts for my grandparents and books for me.

After night services, I spent my last evening with my rabbi, Reb Yakov Yochiel. He spoke of ethical conduct, fear of God, the importance of honesty, indulgence in good deeds, prayer and learning *Torah:* "Constant study is the most important thing in life."

I sat near him answering questions. The other Velvel in me was far away, praying fervently for Brachale, "O, please, God, restore her health. Make her dreams come true."

Reb Yakov Yochiel blessed me. He sent greetings and a blessing for my grandparents and gave me a sealed letter of praise.

Two days before *Pesach* I said goodbye and kissed Reb Shmuel Isaac and Rebecca. I kissed the *mezuzah* on their door and went to the Piotrkow market place. I got a seat on a coach ready to leave for Lodz.

Brachale insisted on seeing me off. She was still very weak and leaned on my arm for support. I was afraid to look at her face. I did not want her to see my tears. We walked without saying a single word.

When the driver was ready to leave, Brachale looked at me with her great, tearful eyes and said, "Velvele, please write to me. Have a good kosher *Pesach*. I ... I will pray for you ... always."

I could not speak. The tears were running down my face. Brachale wiped them off with her fingers. She leaned forward and kissed me on the cheek. Both Velvels in me cried, aware now of how much Brachale really meant to both of us.

The driver cracked the horses with his whip. I sat on the coach looking at Brachale's figure disappear behind the old houses of Tribunalski Square.

Both Velvels prayed, "Heavenly Father, please watch over her and restore her health."

* * * * *

CHAPTER TWELVE
Mutual Hatred

Mutual Hatred

Volodia and Vera traveled to Andizhan to pick up provisions for the hospital -- paper goods, antiseptics, drugs, ointments, and other medications. When they returned early on a Sunday morning, Volodia discovered the kerosene light was on in his room. Eva was sleeping in his bed.

"I read your life story and dreamed about you all night," Eva said sleepily.

"I don't find this amusing. Why did you leave the door open all night?"

"I was waiting for you. I'll get up and make you something to eat."

"I'm not hungry, just tired from the all-night ride."

Eva's hands reached out to him.

"Please come over here."

Volodia sat on the edge of his bed. Her arms reached him and he buried his head on her chest. Eva stroked his hair.

"You know, Volodia, I don't like this room without you. Do you want me to undress you?"

"At eight o'clock in the morning?"

"Today is Sunday. I just want to be near you. I've been thinking about your life story and I want to hear more if you're not too tired."

"Okay. Where did I stop? Do you remember?"

"Every moment. You talked with Father Gursky about why you like to serve people and he told you if war comes he would like to have you near him."

"God, what a memory you have. Father Gursky always quoted a man named Albert Schweitzer, who said, 'No man is ever completely and permanently a stranger to his fellow man. Man belongs to man. Man has claim on man.' With the help of Dr. Krassner and Father Gursky, who claimed me as his personal friend, I was transferred from the ambulatorium to the hospital.

"It was tough for the first few days among the nurses, nuns, maids, and interns. There was much more pressure there. The rotational hours of floor service made it impossible for me to come home regularly for every second Friday evening meal. I shouldered more administrative responsibilities, more complicated tasks. I was no more a *sanitariusz* or orderly; I was *Pan* Vladislav of the administration office. I had full understanding of all hospital needs and functions, the patients and staff. I was proud and happy in my work.

"The interns liked me. Some of them were frightened when they first came. They needed advice and help on purely technical things. I was fortunate to know where to direct them. Many patients had their private doctors. There were some elderly Jewish patients who did not know the Polish language. My help was constantly needed. They joked about me. They would say I was "the special administrator for extraordinary assignments."

"I had to take an examination to enable me to handle the administrative unit on special hours, and I had good marks.

"Father Gursky, Dr. Krassner, the nuns and nurses complimented me on my achievements. However, I still felt that some people looked down on my job.

"Dr. Krassner once remarked, 'Don't feel embarassed. This job will someday save many lives, including your own. Would you rather have my position?'

"Not with my poor background."

"It has nothing to do with background and it is not too late. I will speak to Rabbi Joseph Feiner, the district army chaplain. I will recommend you to the Army Medical Corps. Will you serve?"

"I'll do anything you say, Dr. Krassner."

"Before the week was over, I received a letter from the draft board to come to the 32nd Division for induction. The doctors' examinations, the tests, the recommendations, the physical ... I survived it all. I was grateful to Dr. Krassner,

Father Gursky, and Rabbi Feiner for their favorable opinions and commendations. I said goodbye to my grandparents, Machcia, and the hospital staff. The Army barracks were only a few blocks away from my grandparents' home, but a world apart.

"I could not get used to the handful of sergeants who were always cursing. The basic training period was child's play compared with the brutal name calling directed against the recruits. The food was the best I had ever tasted, but I couldn't swallow it with the insults directed at every meal toward the Jewish recruits. I was infuriated and bitter and said so to my benefactor, Chaplain Yosele Feiner.

"Tarko, we must remember that we are a minority here. We have taken abuse and insults for generations. You're not the first one to complain. But remember, only a few sergeants are at fault."

"Rabbi Feiner, on every roll call, they make fun of us. I can't stand being insulted every day. They use inhuman methods to degrade us."

"We will survive them."

"What about human dignity, Rabbi?"

"When we return to *Eretz Yisroel,* we will have human dignity. For the time being, no matter what happens, you must remain calm, strong. God will guard you."

"After basic training, I worked in a small hospital on a military base in Konstantin. Most of the personnel did not know that I was Jewish. The conversations were now about war with Germany any day. Maxim Litvinov resigned, Molotov was appointed as the commissar of foreign affairs. People talked about Ribbentrop, Memel, Beck, Marshal Rydz Smigly. ("I will not give up one button of my uniform to Herr Hitler. We are strong, ready and able to meet any challenge.")

"Even with bad news about war, the Jews were made the scapegoats. Everywhere were slogans such as "The Germans and Russians were the external enemies. The Jews are the internal enemy." "We fight for our honor against the Germans, for our freedom against the Russians, and for our soul against the Jews."

Those slogans made me tremble with anger. I was biting my lips, and my ears were burning. I wanted to shout: "God! Is this my country? Why? Why so much hate?"

"Eva, I think I told you too much already."

"Volodia, I'm listening to every word you say. I'm learning who you are inside. It seems Jews had it bad in other countries also."

"We were hungry and poor in Poland. Still, we lived our own lives."

"To be cursed and insulted? I hope after this war, when we return to Malichov, we will be able to build a better life for our people, for all people. Will you come with me, Volodia?"

"We will talk about it tomorrow. It is past mid-day and I'm hungry."

"What happened during the war?"

"I served in the Polish army, in the Carpathian Infantry Division. Our unit was captured by the Russians at Wohlynia, Eastern Poland. I was sent to a *sovkhoz* -- a prisoner of war camp -- near Poltava. When the Germans attacked in June 1941, our camp was evacuated to Kuybyshev. For a while, they let me work in a hospital, but as a Polish subject, I had to leave. From Kuybyshev I was sent to Tyumen, from Tyumen to Irtish and from Irtish I came here. Maybe it was fate for me to come here and meet you."

Eva looked at him skeptically.

"I really think so," he said earnestly. "You are a good reason for me to want to live, to survive."

"I think I'm dreaming," she whispered.

Volodia took Eva in his arms and kissed her tenderly.

"Let's get dressed and go visit your mother."

"Why now?"

"I have to see her. I'm thinking of my grandparents."

Dr. Chaidarov showed all the symptoms of a very sick man. His stomach looked swollen; his face had an unnatural redness. He had heat spells, pain, nervousness. He was upset because all his requests and letters were unanswered. He developed a feeling of unworthiness, a man ignored and insulted. Dr. Ivanovna said that he suffered from a blood infection brought on by the wounds he received in Finland. The infection produced an inflammation of his stomach tissues. "He is in trouble. He must have surgery," Tanya said. But Dr. Chaidarov did not complain about his injuries. He lived only for his patients, for his community. He lost confidence in his village council, as well as in himself. His ego was further aggravated by Babachan, his wife. She loved him as her husband, but disagreed with him in all his plans on how to solve the critical health situation in Kyzyl Kishlak. Babachan's view was that the needs of the local school should come first. Dr. Chaidarov felt his wife's ideas were narrow-minded and jingoistic in the face of the severe epidemics they faced.

Volodia came to visit him. Ninotchka served tea.

"What brings you here so early in the morning?"

Volodia waited until Ninotchka left the room and began, "Dr. Chaidarov, it's been weeks now since we sent the memorandum to the Party Secretary and no answer, no one was called to a meeting, to a hearing. Again, we have new cases of typhus."

"What do you want me to do?"

"Maybe your wife can say something at the meeting. We have so many new casualities that there is no more room in the cemetery. Aziz Ali has started to use the pit in the backyard of the Center to bury the dead."

"Babachan will not say anything. Medical care must be made available to all people in our area. If not, the epidemic will spread rapidly. How is Dr. Ivanovna? What is she saying?"

"Tanya agrees wholeheartedly with you, but she has decided to leave all troubles and complaints to me. She is determined to go on just being a doctor."

"Why is she not going to the council meetings?"

"She understands that all Party and government rules are being broken. Taking this to her heart means headaches, pain in her legs. So instead of attending Party meetings, she works overtime at the hospital and center, and makes routine visits to nearby *kolkhozes."*

"I don't blame her. I myself will not attend any more village council meetings. I still have confidence in our Party, but I'm terribly disappointed in our local leaders. They are narrow, egotistical people. Just fancy talk, big phrases, nothing concrete."

"Dr. Ivanovna still believes the local council serves and protects the people."

"Nonsense. They protect only themselves, their own round, fat bellies."

Volodia drank his tea. He looked at the way Dr. Chaidarov's hands trembled as he held his cup of tea. He agreed with him: all the talk here about the working class, the masses, frontier armies, it was all just talk. He, Volodia, was interested in the individual. A village consisted of human beings. All other things -- schools, clubs, clinics -- were created to serve the people. Volodia felt that there was no conflict between his work at the center and his great concern for the homeless refugees crowded together in public places under unsanitary conditions with no food, no soap, no clothing. The refugees, like the local people, were sick, injured, confused, and suffering.

The problem here was just plain antagonism to the refugees. Still, self-pity or anger would not accomplish anything. Calmly he said to Dr. Chaidarov, "If you, your wife, and Dr. Ivanovna can't do anything, I will. I'm not afraid of losing my job. What I am scared of is that by doing nothing for the refugees, I'm losing my self respect. I will call on and write to every available agency and ask for help."

"You can lose your freedom, Vladimir Arionovitz."

"What freedom do I have? To stay and watch my people starve to death? See them perish from lice and worms? The refugees use incredible substitutes for food. They hunt for dogs, cats, catch crows. They make soup out of fruit scraps found in the garbage dumps. Refugees are falling down and can't get up again."

"Your task is to get enough drugs and food for the center.

You can't fight all the village problems."
"I can't, but I must. I will reach their minds. I will feed
them hope."
"My dear friend, Vladimir. May Allah help you."
Dr. Chaidarov was incapable of getting up from his chair
to escort Volodia to the door.
"Why didn't Dr. Ivanovna come?"
"She was busy with the delivery of a premature baby."
"Poor child. She rushed to get here. To what? To such
a life? Tell her *salaam.*"
"I will, Dr. Chaidarov, and you take care of yourself."
"The devil will not take me."
When Volodia was able to get a little food or a few rubles,
he gave it to the refugees. He listened to their narratives,
which were so much like his own life. Some of the Polish
refugees were gifted people, writers, former teachers. Some
were Jews in name only, having become fully assimilated.
They were sent here from strict regime camps in Irkutsk or
from hard labor camps in Vorkutka, in Kalima -- freed after
the Sikorski-Stalin Pact as Polish subjects, rejected by General
Anders for being Jews. They were mistrusted by the Russians
and accused of being German spies. They were exhausted,
hungry, mentally deteriorated, praying for death. And when
they died, their corpses were abandoned on the open *chaichana*
yards, merely covered by a burlap sheet. Volodia talked,
reasoning with them, trying to awaken in them a desire to go
on living.
"Have hope. Someone, somewhere is waiting for us when
we return. We must be strong."
"Hey, Tarko. Why talk about yesteryear and some day?
What can you do for us now? Now? Give us a bath, some
soap, a meal. Give us a roof over our heads."

Celia was depressed and sick for weeks, but after a while
she began to move around the house. Slowly her strength
came back; her spirit improved. The grieving for her lost son
was still deep in her, but she recovered from the shock. Time
and the determination to survive were strong factors, as was

Volodia's presence.

He often stopped by during the day while Eva and Anna were at work. Sometimes he brought food. He would sit beside her bed, smoothing her hair, holding the palm of his hand against her face.

"Why did my Boris have to die?" she cried bitterly.

"Why do so many thousands die every day? That is the way of life. Actually, your son did not die. His soul will live in you as long as you will live."

"Oh, how cruel God is to us."

"Perhaps. But I think of him as a God of mercy. He gave you two fine daughters to live for. You must have faith to raise them, protect them."

Volodia could see that his words had somehow reached her.

"Here," he said. "Good. Here, I've got some rice and oil. You want to do a good deed? Get up and cook it for me. We have some hungry refugee children at the teahouse. I'll stop by later and take it to them."

"I will cook it and take it to them myself. Oh God. How selfish we are. Just thinking of our own grief."

Volodia rubbed his cheek against Celia's face.

"I'll see you later."

The *chaichana* -- teahouse -- "Kyzyl Octiabre," had a long veranda along the backyard. The veranda looked like a roofed balcony furnished with square boxes, covered with old pieces of carpet, mats, and rugs. Before the war, on days when the temperature reached 100 degrees, or more, young people used to come here, drink green Uzbekian tea, and listen to songs and music. This teahouse was the pride of the village.

Now the young were gone away to war. Many had died or were wounded, disabled for life, or lived far away in army *lazarets* and sanitariums. The teahouse had gone unused until the refugees were dumped there.

It could hold maybe fifteen to twenty people, but the village council had decided it could harbor thirty families, mostly women, children, old people, and invalids. The *kolkhozes* in the area wanted only able bodied men or single

women who could work in the cotton and rice fields, or who
had skills to help in the offices or kitchens. The women and
children suffered from a variety of illnesses. Their isolation
was tragic. Though their husbands and sons were soldiers of
the Motherland, here no one cared about them. They begged,
not for medication or food, but for poison. Starved and
distressed, they dragged themselves to the center crying, "Give
us something that will put an end to our suffering."

Many of the refugees were unable to leave the veranda and
stand in line to pick up their meager bread rations. They were
too weak, too sick, and too scared to leave their poor
belongings. Some of the elderly men were too ashamed and
embarrassed to come to the center, their only pair of pants
threadbare from too much heat in the disinfection chamber at
the bathhouse. The village youngsters would torment them,
throwing stones at them, playing hit and miss.

In the front of the veranda was a red banner with a slogan,
"We thank you, Comrade Stalin, for our happy life." Under
the banner and the red flag, the refugees lay lethargically, while
lice, gnats and blood-sucking mosquitoes crawled all over the
children, the old people, and all over the red banner.

Every evening, when the *chaichana* was ready to close, the
refugees waited in a line around the garbage hole, looking for
leftover food. They picked up bones, rotten vegetables,
watermelon rind. Sometimes, after eating the waste, they
collapsed in pain and died the same night. Their bodies were
taken to the "Garden of Eden Boulevard." Their belongings
disappeared, and their place was taken before sunrise. No one
missed them. No one even registered their names.

In the backyard of the hospital compound was a stream.
Along its banks was a deep pit, dug by youth pioneers and
school volunteers in 1941, weeks before the war. This was
supposed to be the foundation base for a new "Pioneer Palace
of Culture," built in honor or the 20th anniversary of
Uzbekistan's independence. It was to be dedicated in 1944.
The planned palace, a large building with spacious dormitories,
classrooms, and a sports field for pioneers of the whole
Andizhan area, was given to Kyzyl Kishlak for "implementing

Comrade Stalin's Socialist offensive in collectivizing the area, increasing production of cotton and rice, and transforming the border area of Kyzyl Kishlak into a fortress of Marxist-Leninist idealism."

Kyzyl Kishlak was advancing rapidly and the local leaders hoped their youth would stay in their remote area, or come back here after wandering off to schools and military service. The war in June, 1941, stopped the digging. All plans were postponed until after the victory, but the long deep pit remained. The pit became a graveyard for the refugees and homeless from the *chaichanas*, an internment place for known and unknown patients of the hospital and center. Early mornings or late evenings, Aziz Ali and a helper covered the bodies in burlap sacks made of jute, sprinkled carbolic on the sacks, and let them down into the pit, covering them over with sand or mud. The local Uzbeks and Tatars took their deceased back to their own cemeteries, so the pit was the burial place for the refugees. They called it by different names: "Stalin's Alley of Happiness" and "Garden of Eden Boulevard."

The odor of the disinfectants contaminated the air. Dogs and rats made the area their home; nearby dwellers and residents made the pit a disposal place for ashes, garbage, and excrements. The rain made the pit muddy and swampy. Sometimes dogs would get trapped there, they would go down into the pit but would not get out. After a day or two without water, they died squealing, drowning in the mud, suffocating from the smell of decomposed rotting corpses.

Little by little, the deep excavation filled up with dogs, rats, ashes, and burlap sacks, including unknown patients who had died from typhus, typhoid fever, and malaria, even before they were admitted to the hospital. In the spring, wild grass and flowers covered the whole boulevard, and the stench disappeared. Someone put a cross and a Star of David near the plate commemorating Kyzyl Kishlak as a "Fortress of Marxist-Leninist Idealism." Some atheist village officials or devout Moslem Uzbeks found the cross and Star of David repulsive signs. To have such a foreign symbol on their sacred land was unbearable. They felt it their duty to remove it. But the next day, a new cross and Star of David would appear. Finally someone had the right idea and got hold of a red banner reading, "Comrade Stalin United Us All. We Thank You, Great Leader, For This Happy and Peaceful Life." The banner was attached to the cross and Star of David. No one dared now to remove the red banner, the cross, or the Star of David.

Special Broadcast:
"Rokossovsky gave the German 6th Army an ultimatum: "Surrender, there is no way out for you at Stalingrad." Field Marshal Paulus surrendered together with 24 other generals and 91,000 prisoners. The 6th Army has ceased to exist. This is the beginning of the end for Hitlerite Germany."

Volodia wrote in his notebook:

> *Life in this village is full of drafts, dust, dirt, sickness. Days are gray, hard. Life here is a road full of deep holes very difficult to pass, to overcome.*
>
> *My days pass here without seeing sunlight and the nights have no moon. Often I get lost in the darkness, feel lonely, disturbed, and very sad.*
>
> *My only companions are memories, deep-seated recollections of my childhood. They are deeply infused into my soul: the love and compassion of my grandparents. In moments of despair they help me overcome all hardships, isolation. They are my constant companions in these days full of challenge."*

*   *   *   *   *

CHAPTER THIRTEEN
The Party Secretary

The Party Secretary

The policy of the Party and village council was that whatever food came to the magazine-store must be given to the working people first, women and children next, and what was left to the old or sick, and then to the refugees. The locals considered the refugees *darmoyedy* -- unnecessary, free-loaders. "The one who does not work, does not eat," was the slogan. Volodia made a list of all the people who were homeless and without bread cards, stating when and where husbands were mobilized into the army or work battalions. He gave the list to two women who, with their children in their arms, went to the militia.

"We want bread, food for our children. Give us food stamps or arrest us."

"Noan Kilde -- bread will come later," the Uzbek officer promised. "You all go back to the *chaichana.*"

"Send us back to Andizhan!" the women demanded. "Our husbands are soldiers. Our children are starving."

"If you organize demonstrations here, we will arrest you all."

"Good! Then you will feed us and we will have a roof over our heads."

In a matter of hours the women received bread.

Volodia went to the teahouse in the evening with Eva, Anna, and Oleg. Oleg ordered all the refugees off the benches, and Volodia sprayed the place with carbolan and lime. The *chaichana* manager was fuming.

"Murderer! Mule ass! You're ruining my business with this smell."

Oleg took the manager aside and explained, "Don't scream. He is killing the lice and mosquitoes. He is protecting you."

182

Next evening, Volodia came with a four-wheeled wagon and took all the sick to the bathhouse. Fatima washed the women, and Aziz Ali washed the men. Getzl Gold, the refugee barber, shaved the men's heads, underarms, all body hair. Fatima did the same to all the women. Those who were able to walk back on their own did so. Oleg and Eva were stationed at the veranda to watch the bundles of belongings. Those who had lost their clothes in disinfection got fresh shirts and pants from Aziz Ali. They were "inheritance gifts" from victims resting on Garden of Eden Boulevard.

When the refugees got back, Celia and Anna served barley soup with real horse meat. Volodia spoke to them. "Friends, the war is going in our favor. Your husbands and sons will return soon. They want to find you alive. Those of you who feel strong and are able to move around must help the others. We need those with skills to take care of the sick. We need people who will go and pick up your daily rations. We need someone willing to prepare warm meals for the children and the sick. We need volunteers who will take the elderly to the bathhouse and clinic. It is up to you to stay alive, to save your families. You must live to see victory for all of us."

Volodia could see a spark of hope in their eyes. They elected a delegation of three men and two women to represent them. For the first time, there were some smiles. Someone was singing, *"Kogda Tovarish, moy domoy vierniotsa* -- When my friends soon return home."

The change, the tumult in the veranda yard, attracted some Uzbeks from the *chaichana* and nearby restaurant. They gave the refugees bread, grapes, raisins, and brought some milk for the children. The Uzbeks were good people by nature, compassionate, friendly, religious. Their help was welcome; it helped the refugees believe that they were human beings.

Volodia had to leave again for Andizhan and Oleg took over the daily visits to the refugees. When he got back, the committee proudly presented him with a surprise. Six refugees had found jobs in the local bakery and restaurant. The refugees by now knew each other's first, middle and last names. Not only did they feed the sick and elderly, but they helped each other write letters to relatives or to the military agencies, searching for their sons and husbands on the front. At night they organized a guard to protect their belongings from dogs and thieves. From somewhere the refugees got old boxes, benches, pieces of carpets. They organized an evening club, which gave them a place to talk, listen to the latest news, and sing. The letter writing to relatives brought new hope and rekindled spirits in some of them. Checks and parcels began to arrive from sons and fathers. The money helped them buy a little extra food, a piece of soap, or an Uzbekian silk scarf to protect them from the sun.

The refugees built a toilet in the yard. They dug the big hole themselves with tools borrowed by Oleg from the local militia. They surrounded the walls with mud brick, old pieces of wood, broken boxes and cans, and they disinfected the area with lime, tar and carbol. They invited Dr. Chaidarov to have the honor of being the first guest to use it.

More letters came from relatives on the fronts. For the refugees it was a transfusion of new hope and willpower to live, to endure. Some of their sons were listed as heroes, officers receiving medals. The parents were proud and shared their joy with Volodia.

However, new refugees were now arriving from Tashkent, Kokand, Fergana, and Andizhan. The rains had started and there was no place in any public premise to house them.

They were willing to work without money, just for a little borscht, *kasha,* and a bite of bread.

Some of the young women, weakened from malaria, sun, and asthma, sold their bodies for a cup of tea and a piece of *lepioshka* -- bread. They seemed oblivious when people called them *djalabs* -- prostitutes. When the Uzbek or Russian "benefactors" (after using them) called the militia to have them arrested, and they seemed glad -- at least they would have a roof over their heads, a meal, and security for the night. Some of the girls committed suicide; some just lost their senses, walking around half naked, cursing, stealing fruit from the bazaar.

After a while they discovered that stealing an apple or

watermelon was not worth it. One got a beating from the vendor, a kick in the stomach from the militiaman, and only one meal in jail for it. They discovered something much better. They came to the bazaar and started screaming, "Stalin is a fake! The communist party leaders are parasites, blood-sucking ticks!" They got arrested and were sent to jail to serve hard labor. They received beatings, but also two meals a day. Some of them were lucky. The male guards adopted them as their maids, to clean and wash for them. The women got enough food to sustain themselves, and from time to time they even helped their countrymen, the Polish refugees who were starving on the outside. But only a few were so "lucky."

In those surroundings Volodia lived a reasonably comfortable life. Aziz Ali kept his room ventilated, swept, spotless. Eva had a warm meal ready for him any time he came back from traveling to the villages. He had real friends in Tanya, Eva, Celia, Oleg, Dr. Chaidarov, and Vera. Still, Volodia was unhappy, restless, disturbed by what he saw and heard in the bazaar and *chaichana*. The plight of the refugees made him want to scream with rage.

He started to accept gifts from the farmers he visited and gave all his food to the children, women, and sick at the *chaichanas*. When Oleg invited him home for freshly baked *pierogi* -- horsemeat-filled potato cakes -- Oleg asked his mother to make some extra for his close friend. The *pierogi* were delicious, but Volodia could not swallow them, thinking of the people who died every night of hunger, and of the burlap sacks with refugee cadavers filling up a new row at the Garden of Eden Boulevard.

Volodia felt he was beginning to break down. The suicides of two young women in one week were too much to bear. He felt resentment and bitterness against the local leaders. He disapproved of Babachan, who could have helped but refused. He was irritated by the inaction of Tanya and Dr. Chaidarov. He felt he was fighting a losing battle against ignorance and petty nationalism. He lived like a beggar-king in a little room the size of a jail cell, with two clean shirts as a bribe to look the other way. He had food. He had a girl he made love to.

Were these the important things in his life? Actually, all he
got from Dr. Chaidarov and Tanya was moral support, just
words. Was this also a bribe to keep him there at the center?
But leaving would not solve anything either. The only real
reason for him to stay on was to help the refugees get housing,
clean up the streams, the yards and shacks they lived in, give
them vaccines, help them find jobs so they could receive ration
cards, give them courage to live and make this place bearable
for them to subsist.

As for Babachan and her "quasi local patriots" who put
stumbling blocks in his way, to hell with them! Certainly, it
hurt to see all the patriots living in comfort, all types of food
delivered to their homes by the truckload, but this was their
country; this was the way it was. In a way he was proud that
he had changed the conditions of the area, had helped the
refugees in some small way. The patriots hated him. So
what? The Poles hated the Russians, the Russians looked
down on the Uzbeks, who mistrusted the Tatars. Still, when
they were sick, they were all human beings and helped each
other. He, the sanitar, responded to their needs, their misery,
and pain.

Volodia thought to himself, "I'm like a soldier on the front
line. The threat of imminent death hangs over all of us. It is
a test of my own abilities to see if I can win this battle. My
weapons are broom, disinfectant, vaccine, education. I'm ready
to fight and win, until peace comes. Then I will go to the
land of my dreams and, together with the refugees, survive."

Volodia prayed, "Bring us in peace from the four corners
of the earth and lead us upright to our land. Recall our
dispersed from among the nations, and gather our scattered
people from the ends of the earth."

He felt better now. An old, reliable friend was back with
him now; he was back in alliance with God.

The rugged mountains surrounding Chinabaad produced an
equally rugged and varied population in the valley. The
Chinabaadians were husky, strong, and hardworking. They kept
their camels, horses, and *ishaks* -- donkeys -- clean. They

watered their sand roads early every morning to keep the flies, mosquitoes, and dust away. They built sturdy and strong *kibitkas* -- huts -- using more stones than dung and straw. They worked in the cooperatives in town and still had time to attend to their private vineyards and vegetable gardens. Their forefathers were Uzbeki nomads, a good-natured and proud people, free as the Tien-Shan Mountains that surrounded them.

With people like these, Chinabaad was able to solve its refugee problems of housing and isolation of the sick, and to find work for all able-bodied persons.

By contrast, the people of the Kyzyl Kishlak valley were lethargic and lazy. Their goats and jackasses were always dirty and full of flies. Their women worked hard and the men sipped green tea, working just a few hours in the morning before the sun hit the valley. Still, this valley produced its share of rice, cotton, and other crops. No one had to be machine-gunned here in the time of Stalin's class struggle in the countryside. No one was sent away to forced labor camps in Siberia to the Gulags.

Instead of burning their crops like the poor farmers in the Ukraine, they collectivized, delivered to the government the fixed amount of produce, and got back all the benefits of socialism. Kyzyl Kishlak always managed to get high praise and recognition from the Party and government. The residents neglected their local needs as well as those of the refugees. The local slogan was "Everything for the heroic defenders of our Motherland." There was talk that the *kolkhoz* manager regularly delivered bags full of rice and flour directly to the homes of the Party functionaries, where the local leaders divided the incoming goods among themselves before they reached the cooperative store.

However, it was hard to substantiate these rumors by other jealous functionaries. After all, what do refugees need shoes for when they can hardly walk? What do they need oil for when they have no flour, no barley, no rice? Why sell them silk or dishes when their stomachs are empty, when a loaf of bread costs twenty-five rubles, a cup of rice ten rubles, and all you get from the army for your son's or husband's military

service is ninety rubles a month, if you get the check at all?
Ekaterina Efimovna Polishenko, Oleg's mother, took a
liking to Volodia. She called him *sinotchek* -- son. Oleg often
traveled to Kokand and Andizhan and Volodia picked up her
bread and food rations at the militia store. Ekaterina spoke
only Ukrainian and it was difficult for her to understand the
Uzbeki-Russian.

She complained of headaches and a sore throat, and
Volodia got her some streptocid tablets and aspirin. When her
temperature rose, she was so weak she could hardly stand up.
Volodia called for Celia and Eva to come over and help her.
Thanks to the two women, Ekaterina got back on her feet.
The nostalgia of their common past, their talk about Malichov,
their home town, created a new closeness between the women.
They dreamed together of the moment when they would return
home. Eva, with her straightforward way of speaking, told
Ekaterina about her deep friendship for Oleg, but assured her
that she would not 'steal' her son away from her and admitted
that she loved another man.

"Does he love you?"

"He loves the whole world. I hope he has something left
for me."

Ekaterina hugged Eva and started to cry.

"I lost my husband and two sons in this damned war. I
don't want to lose my Oleg. That's all I have left -- my son
and my God. Who is this man your God sent to you?"

"The Polish Army sent him. Volodia."

"Volodia? *Hospodi!* God have mercy! As for a Pole and
a Jew, he doesn't look different than any other man. My, he
almost looks like my Olesha."

When Oleg returned to Kyzyl Kishlak, he was delighted to
see the new relationship between his mother and the Markes
family. Nevertheless he looked sad, serious, more somber. He
thanked Volodia for taking care of his mother.

"How was school, Oleg? You look so discouraged."

"I didn't learn too much."

"What were you doing there for so many weeks?"

"Can I trust you?"

"I don't know. How do you feel about it?"
"I'm writing reports on anyone I know in this forsaken village."
"Just like that?"
"Yes."
They walked for a while quietly. Oleg broke the silence. "I wish I could get the hell out of here. I can't stand this anymore. All my life I hoped that my country would change. My father was an honest, poor peasant who worked his piece of land outside Malichov. So they expropriated it. Seeing what happened to our neighbors, how millions of people were deported to Siberia or killed, made my family leave on their own. For a while we lived in Kiev, a beautiful city. I started school there. My father worked on the railroad and Mother kept going to the many churches there. My brothers studied in trade schools.

"Then came the building of the Dnieper Dam. We moved to Zaporozhye. When the dam was finished, we received permission to move back to Malichov. There was hunger all over. The famine killed millions of people, but millions more were killed by the "reformers" -- the secret police. They said that the Jew, Leon Trotsky, wanted to sell Russia to the foreign capitalists and we believed it. Many of my father's friends were slaughtered or sent to desolate places in the name of a new world, a new socialism. But the better life never came. Then came the war. I was mobilized and my father and brothers were sent to blow up the dams and plants at Zaporozhye and they never returned. You can imagine how my father felt. He was so proud to have been one of the builders of this dam. He considered it a great achievement for the Ukraine. We suffered much during all those years, but we never complained.

"Sometimes it was as though we were living a nightmare. Always accusations, condemnations, deportations. Near the end of the war I hoped that all this would change, that we had learned our lessons in madness and inhumanity. I dreamed of going back and building a new Ukraine, without the miseries of people spying on each other, without arrests and purges.

And here they've asked me to serve my country by informing on my friends, the few that I have left."

"Did they ask you about us?"

"You, Eva, Dr. Chaidarov, Babachan, even my own superiors at the militia. Also, Dr. Ivanovna and just about everybody I know or have met. You should watch yourself around Aziz Ali; he informs them of every step you take."

"I have nothing to worry about. I do my job. I haven't a kopeck of my own."

"I know that Eva stays in your room overnight. I know you are visiting Dr. Ivanovna."

"What does this prove? We are friends."

"Immoral behavior."

"What else did Aziz Ali report?"

"You are giving away center food to former criminals."

"First of all, they are not criminals, and, secondly, I give them my own rations."

"Can you prove it is your own food?"

"What about Dr. Chaidarov?"

"He's got a little bitch in his house, some homeless kid. They picked her up among the homeless children, treat her like their own child. Babachan was even talking about adopting her."

"Ninotchka?"

"That rotten kid reports on every step they make, every personal argument they have, even on their bedroom habits. She hides behind doors and listens to their talk."

"What can one say that is bad about such fine people as the Chaidarovs?"

"They have lavish parties in their home for Party and village leaders. You and Dr. Ivanovna are also mentioned in her reports. You criticized the local government and Dr. Chaidarov agreed with you."

"What do you suggest, Oleg?"

"Stick to your work. Stop complaining, and don't discuss politics with anyone. Keep your eyes open when you are around Aziz Ali."

"What will you do? Keep informing?"

"Yes, until I resign. I have a good excuse to quit: my mother's health. You'll help me get the proper papers from Dr. Ivanovna and we will ask for a transfer to Russia."

Oleg and Volodia walked in silence. Both were in a gloomy mood.

"Volodia, now you understand why my heart is sinking so low. All this is lying heavily on my mind and conscience. I often feel like screaming. You know now that I am your friend. Please, don't stay away from me. I need your friendship. What are you going to do?"

"I wish I could join the Polish Army, go to the front, and fight the Germans. But I can't flee like a deserter and leave the refugees at the mercy of the heartless Village Council. I have an obligation to my people here. I started something for the refugees and I plan to finish it, even if it kills me."

They arrived at the center.

"Stay well, Volodia. Thanks again for all that you did for my mother. I love her so dearly. She is kind of old fashioned, too religious, but she is a good hearted woman."

"I know. I love her too. Oleg, will you have to report our conversation tonight?"

"Yes. I am going to report exactly everything you told me."

"What's that?"

"That you are sick and tired of seeing people dying on the streets here and that you'd rather join the army and fight against the Fascists."

'Wsio Choroshoho, Oleg, all the best."

"All the best to you Volodia."

Tanya came out of the center and was astonished by the look on Volodia's face.

"Volodia, what happened?"

"Nothing. Who said anything happened?"

"You look as if you've seen a ghost."

"Do you believe in ghosts?"

"Come on, are you sick?"

"Yes."

Tanya put her hand on his forehead.
"No, not here." Volodia pointed his finger to his heart.
"Here."
"Stop playing games. What happened?"
"Don't talk so loudly; we're being watched."
"So what. Everyone in our country is being watched. A
large part of the population in this remote area is made up of
people forced to come here or run from Europe because of the
collectivization of their lands. Some had their houses
confiscated and were deported to this region. We don't know
what their feelings are towards our government and Party. We
have many enemies, and we have to be on the alert. As long
as you and I obey the laws and work, we have nothing to be
afraid of. Did you say anything wrong?"
"Of course not."
"So why are you so worried suddenly?"
Aziz Ali came to the door leading a saddled horse.
"Doctor, this is the best horse in the bank's stable."
Aziz Ali helped her up on the horse.
"Where are you traveling to so late?" Volodia asked.
"I have some patients at *Kolkhoz* Lenin. Do you want to
join me?"
"No, not tonight."
"Go rest. You seem very depressed."
"I'm tired, that's all. Be careful."
"I will."
Aziz Ali asked Volodia if he could make some tea for him.
His very presence was so annoying that Volodia had to turn
away so as not to show his feelings, but he replied, "If you
would be so kind, just bring me some boiled water and an
aspirin."
Volodia went back to his room. He did not turn on the
light. He sat there in the dark, motionless. Aziz Ali returned
with an aspirin and a cup of water. Volodia's hand started
trembling.
"*Chozain* got malaria? Sick? No good mood? *Yamon* --
bad?"
"No, Aziz Ali, just very tired. Too much work. I will rest

tonight and be as good as new tomorrow.   Good night.
Thanks for the aspirin and water."
"Hope you feel better.   *Salaam.*"
Volodia could not understand.   Such a good, warm, honest
man like Aziz Ali, an informer.   God, what duplicity from a
man who acted so sincere.   What makes them do this?   Who
manipulates their lives like this?   What system is it that turns
good people into poisoned souls?
He looked around his little room and was afraid of his own
shadow.   He felt as if someone were hiding behind his little
window watching, listening to him.   He fell asleep dreaming
he was in a cell, on a bed surrounded by doctors, nurses, and
militiamen -- people and faces he knew.   They were all holding
hearing devices, telephones, microscopes, stethoscopes, listening
to every part of his body.   All were dressed in white,
mumbling, talking.   What were they saying?

* * * * *

CHAPTER FOURTEEN
The Epidemic

The Epidemic

The words "Red Cross" had a certain respectful ring for the refugees. The locals, too, respected the Red Cross workers, even though they were Moslems. However, the Party Secretariat avoided the Red Cross workers like the malaria epidemic itself. Every request and memorandum was ignored and refused for "lack of funds" or "unnecessary improvements in time of war."

Volodia told Dr. Chaidarov frankly, "I always believed in the goodness of the Russian nature. They gave us aid and food even when they themselves did not have enough. I saw their kindness and mercy before I was sent there. Now I see harsh treatment from a Russian like Kozlov, ill-concealed hatred and quarrelsomeness toward you and the hospital. He refuses to see you without even an explanation. It infuriates me to see how he ignores and humiliates you. I can't work under such unbearable conditions any longer. I want a transfer."

Dr. Chaidarov argued with him. "Kozlov knows nothing of village work. He was sent here against his will, because of his drinking problem. He is bored here and we are disgusted with him. We detest one another and we can't do anything about it. He is part of the Party hierarchy. Frankly, we hope the alcohol finishes him off someday. Notwithstanding all your just complaints, I can't let you go. I would be the worst enemy of this village if I signed a transfer now."

"Did you tell them about the refugees? Did you tell them that if they don't stop the epidemic among the refugees, it will reach their own homes?"

"They say the refugees are strangers, that they brought this typhus epidemic here, and instead of spending money for beds, more food rations, take them all and send them back to Andizhan."

"Then why don't they do it?"

"They're scared. They're afraid that it's against Party instructions."

"I've heard this before. There is a strong anti-refugee feeling here from some of the Russians who lived here before the war. The refugees are insulted and are pushed out of the lines at the food store."

"So you see yourself what I'm up against."

"Every demand we've made has been rejected. Your health reports were not forwarded."

"I know and it upsets me, but what more can we do? I want you to know that you're doing a good job at the center."

"Dr. Chaidarov, compliments and back-slapping will not help the refugees, and all my skills did not help the hundreds of refugees at rest now on the Garden of Eden Boulevard. Your village leaders' refusal to deal with the refugee problem is an insult to me."

"It is a blow to me also. I can't accept your resignation. Take it up with the village council or Party secretary."

"I will. *Salaam.*"

Dr. Chaidarov did not answer. His face was pale. He just sat breathing heavily, listening to the radio.

"Radio Moscow Operational Bulletin. Our troops on the Voronezh Front captured the important regional center of the Ukraine, the town of Sumy. The whole region has been completely liberated from the Fascist invaders. Our troops destroyed or disabled 108 tanks and shot down 51 planes."

Around midnight, while Volodia was walking through the center talking to patients, Vera came with the message that Comrade Rachatayev, First Party Secretary, wanted to see him right away.

"Now?"

"Yes."

For weeks Volodia had tried to see him. He was always

busy, out of town, or in conference and would call back. He
never did. Now he wanted to see him immediately.

"Comrade Tarko, sit down. I have heard you are a
competent worker at the center, but a bit too energetic. Who
appointed you to write requests for the center? Isn't that
Comrade Chaidarov's responsibility?"

"Dr. Chaidarov was very sick. He knew that I signed his
memos."

"Did he tell you to send copies of your letters to
Andizhan?"

"No. Your office never answered any of our previous
letters. We called many times asking for permission to see
you."

"We are fighting a war and we must concentrate all of
efforts in this direction. Those are Party orders directly from
Comrade Stalin."

"Comrade Secretary, we are fighting a war here also, and
the casualties are the wives and children whose husbands are
dying for this country."

"We gave you this position and we will decide when you
can leave."

"I am thankful to Dr. Chaidarov for giving me the
opportunity to work here. I know I am an outsider in your
midst. I am reminded of it constantly. Still, I have taken
responsibility for everything that needed to be done. But some
of your local leaders have obstructed my work. Comrade
Kozlov mistrusts and hates us refugees."

"Comrade Kozlov is a very important Party leader."

"To me he is a small, irritated man, always drunk,
insensitive to the needs of the people in this village. I don't
care that he insults me personally. What I demand is that he
let me do my job. I will not hesitate to say to the people in
Andizhan what I said here to you ... I am a refugee. This is
not important ... It is important to me not to betray the people
here. Let me work or let me go."

Rachatayev looked like any upper-class Uzbek -- well-fed,
full-faced, shaven head. His Russian had a heavy Uzbek
accent, his manners were slow, his questions clear and to the

point.

"Comrade Tarko, we have received your resignation. We consider this desertion, and your memorandum to Andizhan a disrespect to our local Party authority. As an outsider in our midst whom we entrusted with a position of responsibility you have acted like an enemy."

Volodia kept his temper as much as he could.

"Comrade Secretary, before you blame me, read my last memorandum. Your own staff, your own life was what I wanted to save."

Rachatayev lowered his voice. "Let's stop this argument. I want you to know something. I approved all your requests for the hospital. All the items you asked for arrived here a week ago, but all the new blankets were stolen. We are conducting an investigation, but in the meantime you must have patience."

"In the meantime people are lying on bare floors, being bitten by scorpions, dying in dirt. There is not a block of soap in the whole center. We are forced to use soap liquid and animal disinfectants to wash the patients."

"There was soap in the village cooperative last week."

"You were out of town and the secretary of the village council was drunk. By the time he sobered up, all the soap was gone."

"Kozlov was drunk in the daytime?"

"Yes."

"You see, Tarko, we can't even trust a Russian, a Party member. I want you to withdraw your resignation. I personally promise you a supply of soap, some beds, and salt."

"How about housing, some shelter for the refugees?"

"I can't promise you what we don't have."

"Can I get a truck to pick up some drugs and merchandise for the hospital?"

"We have no right to take away any trucks from the fields. They are delivering cotton to Kokand."

"If your drivers get sick, your trucks will not travel by themselves."

"I will try to supply the trucks also."

"Comrade Secretary, mere promises will not help us. You, me, all of us here are confronting an epidemic of such proportions that many people will die."

"Is this why you want to resign? You want to save your skin?"

"Comrade Secretary, you really know how to hurt someone, don't you? If I wanted to save my skin, I could have picked myself up and left when I was in Andizhan. I have no family, no baggage, nothing."

"They could arrest you and send you to a hard labor battalion."

"Believe me, I might be better off. I'm a qualified medic. You see, even in prison they will respect my Red Cross badge."

"You don't feel we treat you with respect?"

"I could not get a meeting with you since I arrived here."

"From now on, any time you have something important, you just walk in. I will tell my secretaries the same."

"Comrade Secretary, I wish you could find time to visit our center and hospital. I also hope that the village council will take a walk around the yards and *chaichanas* and see the conditions the refugees live in."

"Good idea."

Rachatayev handed back Volodia's resignation papers and they shook hands.

"*Salaam.*"

"Goodnight."

It was very late when Volodia returned to his room. Tanya, in a starchy white uniform, came to his door.

"It's open, come in."

"Dr. Chaidarov said you're leaving."

"Not for a while."

"Where have you been until now? It's so late."

"Been out shopping for the center."

"In a speculator's home? Be careful, don't get anything from the black market."

"This one is legal."

"Come on, where have you been?"

"To see Rachatayev."

"*Hospodi Pomilui* -- Merciful God."

"Yes. He will deliver the things we need."

"See, I told you our Party looks out for the people."

"I hope you're right."

"Do you want some tea?"

"No. I want to rest. Thank you anyway. Why are you up so late?"

"Verochka is sick, so I came to help. Anyhow, I'd rather stay here than be alone at home."

"Get anything from Mischa lately?"

"Yes, a very sad letter. I'll let you read it. I also got a letter from the Gittermans. They received a letter from him. Are you sure you don't want any tea?"

"No, Tanya, thank you."

She left. Volodia undressed, dumped his clothes on a chair, stretched his bony body on the clean sheet of his bed and read Mischa's letter.

Dearest Tanya,

This letter comes to you from Belgorod. I will not write about myself this time but share with you a traumatic moment I lived through in this war.

The whole civilian population of Belgorod was taken prisoner and marched off to a pit, without consideration as to who was loyal, who was a quisling, who was still able to work, who was a patriot; the village priest, the cooperating militia and police, school-age children and women -- all were given iron picks, shovels and ordered to dig. They were ordered to take off their coats, their hair-coverings, their hats and carry the dirt in it, hand it to the next person.

Half naked they worked day and night digging the deep pit.

Then, without warning, the armed guards pushed the mass of ragged, barefoot men, women, and children into the pit. To make the ground melt, they poured gasoline over the frozen ground and set it afire. The people, the rags, were set aflame, beards, hair were firebrand torches.

The Wehrmacht kept pushing the people into the pit with their rifle butts and whips. Some people fell under the blows from the rifles. The other men in line dragged the corpses with them to the pit. From the flames the snow melted, and the water which was mixed with blood kept rising. Children were drowning.

We attacked the German trenches. Only a few hundred yards from the trenches, we discovered the dugout. We stood for a moment at the brink of the pit in deep shock. Despite the screaming orders of our field commander to move forward, despite the artillery and *katyusdza* fire we were so terrified, we could not move. The harrowing stench of burning flesh choked our throats. Our units were ordered to attack. The Germans retreated, leaving the people in the pit drowning, wailing, smoldering.

Snow was falling when our unit reached the pit. We found long wires and tried to pull up those who were still alive. They were so weak that they were unable to lift themselves, grasping the wires ...

The next evening, to Volodia's amazement, medical supplies and soap arrived from the local cooperative warehouse. Dr. Chaidarov's face glowed when Volodia handed him a cake of soap, a new towel, and, miracle of miracles, a roll of real toilet paper.

"I'm glad you got to see him. I hope things will change now for the better."

Just then, Dr. Ivanovna came in looking worried.

"I heard what you just said, Dr. Chaidarov. Sorry to say that help came too little, too late. I just had a call from two *kolkhozes*. People are complaining of unusual headaches, pains in the back and legs. They stopped eating and are walking off the rice fields. Chakulabaad reports high fevers, nausea, hemorrhages and people walking around delirious. People collapsed while working in the fields."

Volodia listened carefully.

"What do you think it is?"

"From the symptoms they describe, it sounds like typhoid fever."

"From the little I know, it sounds like typhus."

There was a long moment of silence. Dr. Chaidarov turned to Volodia and said, "I know what you're thinking. You told us so. What do you suggest now?"

Tanya spoke first. "Dr. Chaidarov, what is the use of making suggestions when they go unheeded? Suggestions were fine when we were planning how to prevent an epidemic, but now it's here and we need action. Are you ready to fight it?"

"Yes. I want every child, man and woman in the valley to get an anti-typhus vaccine shot. I want all public places disinfected with any available insecticides."

"We have only a few cases of vaccine," said Volodia.

"Give it to our staff, militia, military, public workers, and restaurant personnel. Close all outdoor toilets, order all water used for drinking to be boiled first. We must proceed without panic."

"I suggest that by official order the cinema, Pioneer Club, and school be closed and all public meetings be cancelled," Volodia said. "The public bath should be opened 24 hours a day, with separate hours for men, women, and women with children."

"Only one man is employed at the bathhouse."

"I know," said Volodia. "I can find volunteers among the refugees who will work without pay. Just give them their food rations and a place with a roof over their heads."

"I would like to see that soap be given directly to the refugees," Volodia continued. "Lice and ticks are the carriers of the epidemic. I ask you to order isolation of the sick in every village and *kolkhoz* in the area. You, Tanya, had better inform the school board and the militia of the situation and let Dr. Chaidarov handle the Party and village council."

Dr. Chaidarov sprang up. "Why me?"

"You are the head of the local health department. I'm fed up with doing the dirty work all the time," Volodia said in a sudden burst of anger.

"Don't explode, Vladimir Arionovitz. I admit, we all have little love or respect for the bureaucrats."

"I'm sorry, Dr. Chaidarov. I lost my temper. But the situation is so serious! I wasn't exaggerating when I sent that

memorandum to the Party. I saw it coming. Now it is here
and we must act."
    "What more do you suggest?"
    "I don't suggest anything. I want action now! Today!
You are responsible for this area and you must start acting this
very moment. If you feel sick, and we know you are sick,
call Andizhan and ask for more doctors, more nurses, more
typhus serum and more disinfectants. This area has too many
diseases for only two doctors to handle."
    "Calm down, Volodia," said Tanya. "You always say 'with
the help of God' we will work it out some way."
    "Damn it! This epidemic is not the will of God. The
Party and council leaders are the ones who neglected this
village by not answering our requests. I heard clearly what
you ordered, Dr. Chaidarov. Sorry to say I want certain things
done differently. I hope you will agree with me."
    "Let's hear them."
    "All people working around the sick must get antibiotics
and vaccination shots first. The Party and village council
bigwigs can wait. They are isolated from the people anyhow.
Every person on our staff must take a shower and dust himself
or herself with DDT before leaving the clinic, hospital or
center. I don't want our staff to become carriers of germs to
other people, even if we have had vaccinations. In the next
twenty-four hours, all refugees should be removed from all
public places, bazaars and *chaichanas*. The sick are to be
taken to an isolator where they can be helped. This will help
stop the epidemic from spreading."
    "I agree with Volodia," Tanya remarked. "We must isolate
the carriers."
    "The whole staff, even if they have had vaccinations,
should be vaccinated again. Let's prevent recurrences."
    Dr. Chaidarov made some notes and then spoke. "I'm
calling Andizhan now. The first thing I want from them is to
stop sending more refugees here."
    "Wait, Dr. Chaidarov, please ask them for some plasma."
Tanya stopped him as he was about to pick up the wall
telephone. "We have many patients with schistosomiasis. We

found the parasite that spreads it in the irrigation ditches around the rice fields. They suffer from swollen livers and intestinal hemorrhage and they can only   be saved by transfusions."

"With a war going on, you're asking them to send us blood plasma?" Dr. Chaidarov said wearily, "We must do our best right here with what we have."

"How can we help them without the needed medications?"

"I will give some of my own blood. Who is the patient?"

"Karabov, a local young man working in the *Kosomol* -- youth organization. But I will not take blood from you. You look too worn out yourself."

"Who is the other patient?"

"A militiaman's mother, Ekaterina Efimovna."

"Oh my God," cried Volodia.

"What happened, Volodia? Do you know her?"

"Her son, Oleg, is my friend."

"I will not take your blood either. You're too anemic."

"But Oleg can't give her any blood. He has open wounds from the war."

"I know. That's why I wanted some plasma from Andizhan."

"I will get some refugees here to give blood. How long has she been here?"

"Since yesterday morning."

"I have to go and see her."

Volodia made a short visit to Ekaterina and then went to see the refugees in the teahouses and marketplace.

"*Panie* Tarko," a Polish refugee addressed him, "why did they bring us here from the prison camps? Are we to die here from starvation and lice?"

"Why do you ask me?"

"You work for them."

"No, friend, I work for you. Instead of complaining, get all able-bodied people together and come with me. We are going to build a *succah*."

"You're out of your mind?"

"No friends.   In fact, I want you to build three or four *succot*.   We will use mud, straw, dung, everything we can find. I've got some heavy canvas we can use for walls and roofs. We will build on the ruins of the old school."
    "It is hard to dig this ground."
    "It is better than digging graves.   The Garden of Eden Boulevard is already full.   There is typhus here in the area. You must isolate the sick, build a roof over their heads before the rains start, and cleanse yourselves of germs."
    "Give us soap.   It is easy for you to talk about hygiene and sanitary conditions.   Give us some food, some clothes. Look at our women and children.   Street beggars in Poland were better dressed.   We're better off dead from typhus."
    "I'm not the one to judge how you will be better off.   All I want is to try and save as many of you as I can.   So, who is coming with me?"
    "Will you give us something to eat?   We have no strength to dig.   We don't need your vaccinations.   Give us some food..."
    "I will.   Let's start moving before the rains hit."

* * * * *

CHAPTER FIFTEEN
Anger and Depression

Anger and Depression

The rains and the flood lasted for a full four days. They swept over the area like a typhoon, washing away many of the gardens and seed fields; the mud walls were dissolved by the violent downpour and the mountain winds did great damage to the village water canals.

The water *ariks* receptacles were contaminated by human and animal waste that was spread in the fields. It smelled awfully and infected the whole region with the typhoid bacillus.

Day after day new lines of *kholkozniks*, refugees and villagers came to the clinic complaining of headaches, pains in their arms, legs and backs. People began to die daily.

Day and night Tanya and Dr. Chaidarov walked the wards, marking the same symptoms over and over on little blackboards in front of the patients' beds: nausea, high fever, red spots on the abdomen, neck, shoulders, chest, severe ulceration, intestinal pain, hemorrhages.

A big sign outside the clinic read: "Beware! Communicable Disease!" It hung at the entrance warning people to stay away. Still, the *otshereds* -- long lines -- kept getting longer until they extended all around the building. Often, completely exhausted from waiting in line, people collapsed and died. Their corpses lay abandoned until Aziz Ali disposed of them.

Volodia kept begging for volunteers from the local youth organizations, from the *kholkozes*, but no one showed up. They were scared. Many died during the epidemic and those who survived developed a wild appetite for food, but no fats or meats were available. Once in a while horse or sheep guts were delivered from a *kolkhoz*.

When not working on the ward, Volodia traveled from the

208

kolkhoz to the village, asking and looking for handouts of any edibles to feed the hungry patients.

For many days Volodia did not see Eva. Miraculously, all her family was well. Eva left some homemade soup or curdled milk at his doorstep, and he gave it to the clinic. He warned Eva and her family not to visit him or their neighbors.

Every night a note was attached to his meal: "Oh, Volodia, I miss you. Can I see you tonight?"

The answer was, "No darling. Even though God has spared me and I do not have the disease myself, I can be a carrier of the typhoid bacillus."

I woke up this morning with an anti-typhus serum reaction from a shot given me by Tanya three days ago. All my body is one mass of red blotches. I feel shortness of breath and my throat is dry, swollen, my head is burning. I tried to get up but my legs were too weak.

I trailed along the walls to the outhouse. I asked one of the patients passing by to call Aziz Ali. I had almost fainted from the smell in the latrine. The odor of urine, carbolic acid, and chloride disinfectant took my breath away. I hardly made it back to my *kibitka*.

I lay down on my back and waited to die.

Suddenly the door seemed to open and my grandfather came in, dressed in his black, silk Sabbath caftan and his round, velvet Sabbath hat.

"Velvele, I came to chant with you a prayer for your recovery. Please repeat after me: Grant me, Oh God, faith and hope; help me to bear the ills of life with patience and resignation."

"Chozain Tarko, wake up! You are talking in your sleep."

Aziz Ali came with hot *kipiatok* -- boiled water -- and freshly washed shirts. For a moment I was confused. My whole body was hurting, but I was pleased with the vision of my grandfather.

"Thank you, Aziz Ali, for the tea and for washing my laundry. Please tell Dr. Chaidarov that I will return to work tomorrow."

I closed my eyes hoping that the image of my grandfather would return.

After the epidemic subsided slightly and the rains stopped, the malaria sickness spread with new force. Mosquitoes around the canals were breeding and growing by the billions, biting the farmers as they tried to repair the canals and replant the fields.

Dr. Chaidarov and his staff worked for days on end, sleeping in Dr. Chaidarov's or Vera's room for a few hours, when possible, only to be called back to the emergency room or ward as soon as they had closed their eyes.

Most exhausted was Tanya. She did not go home for days. She worked at the clinic for long hours without any rest. Often, she came to Volodia's little room shivering in pain, her face and eyes flushed with fever. Sometimes Volodia came in to rest for a while and found Tanya on his bed sleeping, her face as pale and yellow as the hospital gown she was wearing.

Volodia sat beside her and prayed, "God, save this brave, courageous woman."

He looked at her disheveled hair and tired face. All these weeks she never complained...just that her legs hurt...

He fell asleep sitting at the edge of his bed beside her. When he awakened, Tanya was gone. He found her moving among her helpless patients in the clinic.

Typhus followed the malaria epidemic · like a violent hurricane. Every morning the two-wheeled wagons picked up corpses in and around the village and buried them on top of the pit at the "Garden of Eden Boulevard." All the talks, the appeals to the local Party and village leaders fell on deaf ears. The official attitude was "All efforts to win the war."

Every morning long lines of feverish children, women and men were waiting in front of the clinic and center. The people in the growing lines were wet to the bone from the rain. They lacked strength and burned with fever. Many of them collapsed at the entrance to the center.

Volodia tried desperately to see some officials, but they were hiding in their homes and vineyards.

The new shacks he helped to build for the refugees protected some of them. However, trucks from nearby villages started to bring the sick refugees from the *kholkozes*, dump them off and leave them at the center's entry room to die.

It made Volodia furious.

"Dr. Chaidarov, what are we going to do for these people?" Dr. Chaidarov was upset, angry. He started to feel uncomfortable in Volodia's presence and told him so.

"You make me feel guilty."

"You belong to the Party. You belong to the village council. You are the regional doctor," Volodia cried.

"I am one man alone, doing the best I can. You think I like to see many people dying?" Dr. Chaidarov started to tremble. "We have failed the people here. We have neglected the individual needs of the people. It's frightful. I do not have the courage to confront my own wife."

After this encounter with Dr. Chaidarov, Volodia went back to his little room. Eva was sitting on the step waiting for him. He hardly said a word. Eva leaned her head on his shoulder and asked him if anything was wrong. He did not utter a sound.

"Volodia, you don't love me any more, do you? You hardly speak to me."

"What is there to say? People are dying here by the cartloads, two, three members of the same family. It is impossible to get help."

"Our people are dying everywhere. It is a war, Volodia. It is a great misfortune which has befallen the world."

"No, Eva. We. The refugees. We suffer more than anyone. No one has compassion anymore. Even some of our own refugees who have jobs and work will not help. It is unbelievable, Eva, how little they care for the other refugees from Poland, Lithuania, Rumania. They treat us like a herd of homeless dogs."

"But why are you blaming yourself for their misery? You did not ask them to come here."

"I'm surprised at you. You are talking just like the Uzbeks and the Russians. They also ask who sent for them."

"There is a shortage of food and of medicine. Whom do you blame for that?"

"There is no shortage of food. There is a shortage of human compassion here and no pity for human suffering."

"It makes no sense to blame yourself for all the failures of the village leaders. We are in a war...After this ordeal is over, maybe life will be better in our country, as you always say -- God willing."

"Eva, please go home. I have to be alone."

"Where are you going?"

"I'm just going for a walk."

"Let me walk with you."

"No, Eva. Go home and rest."

"Tomorrow is Sunday. I can sleep late."

"No, dear. Just leave me alone."

Volodia got up and started walking quietly in the direction of the Garden of Eden Boulevard. Eva watched him disappear, waiting and hoping that he would return soon.

When he did not return past midnight, she went to look for him at the center and the clinic. No one had seen him. Next morning Eva and Oleg as well as Dr. Chaidarov searched for him all over the area, but Volodia seemed to have vanished.

Finally, Dr. Chaidarov found him wandering aimlessly on the sandy road near the Darya River.

"How dare you disappear like this?"

"I needed a day of rest. It's Sunday today, isn't it?"

Dr. Chaidarov remained silent. Volodia continued, "I don't want to go on living like this. I can't stand by and see my people die."

"So you escaped?"

"Yes, I escaped to the Darya. When I saw my face in the river, I began talking to myself."

"I called myself egotist, privileged fool, scoundrel, *sukin-sin* -- son-of-a-bitch."

"But why? Why?"

"Because I'm eating every day and they are starving. I'm sleeping in a bed and they lie in alleys. I am incapable of functioning any more in the center. It's just impossible for me not to care for them. You must understand this. You are a doctor."

"You cannot be responsible for everyone, everywhere. Thousands of people died building the Fergana Canal. In a *sovchoz* -- government farm -- more than 200 people died last week from food poisoning. Andizhan and Tashkent have hundreds of lorries of dead every week. All of this is certainly not your doing."

"I told myself the same things, but to stay and work in the center and see people dying and not be able to help them is what I consider a crime."

"I can't pass judgment on you, Vladimir Arionovitz. I can't belittle your feelings, beliefs, but reality..."

"Dr. Chaidarov, I had nothing to live for in this world until I became a medic, concerned with helping the sick and the helpless. Besides all this, I am a Jew. I can't close my eyes to the suffering of other Jews here in my own alley."

"Why do you Jews have to make us feel so guilty, so uncomfortable? Do you think that we are indifferent to human suffering and only you have compassion for other people? We Uzbeks here have suffered and still suffer. Thousands of us were killed, sent to Siberia to die in the cold for holding onto our way of life, our religion and culture. Thousands died digging canals and are dying now from malaria because of the same canals. The Party and government care only about the cotton and the rice fields, about quotas, norms and production and not about our people. We are at war with a system that rules and regulates our lives from above. We have learned that in order to survive, we must follow the Party line and obey Party orders. You think we like to see people die in our villages? We are Moslems and to help a stranger is part of our culture and religion. I think I've already said too much, Vladimir Arionovitz. If Tanya, Eva and I mean anything to you, forget what I have said. Come back and continue your work. We need you. I need you, but for Allah's sake, you mustn't try to solve all the problems."

"I know I can't save all of them, but I can save some of the refugee children at least. I will go to Andizhan, directly to the Health Commissariat."

"I am warning you again, this desperation of yours will lead you to jail."

"If my going to jail can save some lives here, I'm ready to take a chance."

"They say Jews are supposed to be smart. You're a fool, Volodia. I can see you're headed for trouble. Many people will suffer if you are arrested."

"Why should anyone suffer because of me?"

"You're plain naive and stupid. May Allah protect you. God protects the fools."

They traveled in silence the rest of the road. When they reached the center, Dr. Chaidarov looked at him with pity.

"What we talked about on the road, leave it in the sand and in our hearts."

"Thank you for the ride. You made me feel needed here."

"You made me feel guilty."

"Sorry."

"I'm still your friend. See you in the morning. Better go wash up. You look awfully dirty for a medic."

***

After the epidemic subsided, there were still a thousand and one problems in the center, isolator inspections in the area, visits to the new refugee shanty-dwellings. Volodia and Eva renewed their discreet affair.

As busy as Volodia was, he still found time to see her. When he felt depressed, a word, a gesture of hers rekindled hope in his heart. Gradually, she even stopped objecting to his friendship with Tanya. Still, she refused to marry him.

"Not yet. We must wait. The piece of paper from the ZAGS-Marriage Office is of no importance. The most significant thing is that we belong to each other. I only wish you would give us more of your time. Mother hardly sees you, and I want you."

"You have me now."

"I want you every night. I need more than just moments

together."

"In this dirty little room?"

"This is the most beautiful corner in the whole world, Volodia."

"You talk like a poet."

"Don't forget, I'm a school teacher. Literature and poetry were my favorite subjects at the teachers' technicum."

"I'm not in the mood for poetry."

Tenderly he took her in his arms. Just holding her gave him delight and pleasure. Though many weeks passed and they hardly spoke, still they knew they meant everything to each other. Volodia stopped talking about getting married and Eva stopped asking about his visits to Tanya.

In the weeks ahead, Volodia spent his daytime hours working at the center and evenings on Eva's front steps, talking of the past with Celia, Eva and sometimes, Oleg. He declined invitations to attend meetings or to speak at *kolkhozes*. He remembered, when he had first arrived how full he had been of plans, ideas, and enthusiasm, impressed by the passionate speeches given by the Party and government. There had been directives on how to win the war, unite the people, help our brethren, the refugees. Volodia realized now that he had confused speeches and promises with reality. There had been a lot of steam, mere bubbles and empty lines in all those speeches and Party promises. He knew now that only action could be effective. He was no longer the idealistic medic who worked day and night, traveling to all the *artels* -- small shops -- and cooperatives, speaking about sanitary conditions. He had become a man of deeds. His task was saving patients not through prayers or speeches, but with food, fruit, a little sugar or an extra bite of bread.

Ever since his conversation with Oleg and then with Dr. Chaidarov, suspicion riddled his mind like a poison. He did not trust anyone around him. The matter-of-fact way in which Tanya took his discovery that they were being watched cooled his unlimited trust even in her. He could not talk to her as freely anymore. Wherever he went, he checked to see if he was being followed. He kept all his opinions to himself. At the center he did only what he was supposed to do. He kept his books in order. Everything was accounted for, locked up. Every capsule, sheet or apron given to a nurse or helper was listed by day, name and hour. He politely declined dinner invitations from Babachan. He stopped escorting Tanya or going to her home. Tanya had guests from Andizhan, the Gitterman family, whom she invited to live with her.

The only places he felt good were his little room, at Celia's and at the home of Ekaterina Efimovna, Oleg's mother. His mind became as dry as the desert sand. He did not read, write, or listen to the radio. Every opportunity he had he spent with Eva, or visiting the refugees from Lithuania, Rumania and Poland. He had a sincere interest in learning the Russian language. Oleg and Eva kept asking him caustic questions and Volodia tried to give them grammatical, amusing answers.

"Why are the lice so big on the billboards which read KEEP CLEAN?"

"Those are not lice. Those are undercover agents."

"Why is there no milk for pregnant mothers?"

"We have milk only for children."

"So why don't the children get the milk?"

"The Party leaders get the milk. They have first grade educations."

"Then what makes them Party leaders?"

"They know how to stand up and applaud."

Volodia was surprised to find out from Oleg that Aziz Ali was reporting regularly on his much improved, proper behavior.

Tanya worked herself to exhaustion. She had kidney failure, high blood pressure, headaches. She lost weight and was extremely weak. However, she kept working twelve hours a day.

The Gitterman family was a big help to her. Mrs. Gitterman kept the house clean, cooked home-made meals. Her daughters, Esther and Chava, worked in the hospital. They learned to do the work of practical nurses. Their coming was good for Tanya. Their common immediate past, their longing for Mischa, improved her spirit.

Tanya kept saying how happy she was now, having her

own family. Esther, out of gratitude to Tanya, was truly devoted to her, and did everything she could to make Tanya feel better. Moreover, the more Esther did for Tanya, the more Tanya did for the sick.

One night, Volodia came back from Ekaterina's home and found Tanya resting on his bed.

"You're avoiding me, Volodia. Are you no longer my friend?"

"I will be your friend as long as I live."

"Why don't you come over and share tea with us?"

He mumbled an answer.

"Are you happy with her?"

"What are you talking about?"

"Eva. She is so pretty."

"Thank you."

"I'm glad for you, Volodia. Please close the door. I have something to tell you."

"No, wait, I just told Aziz Ali to make some tea."

Tanya got up and sat on the chair.

"What are you doing evenings? I don't see you anymore in the wards."

Aziz Ali came in and served tea.

"Are you planning to leave Russia when the war is over?"

"Oh no!" Volodia practically shouted. "This is my country now. I like the people here. I want to serve this village."

"Volodia, I'm grateful to you for saying this."

Volodia felt like a jerk. He knew that what he had said was something for Aziz Ali to report.

"Tanya, you wanted to tell me something."

"Volodia, I have a kidney inflammation. It could be that it's the result of my war wounds or an infection I got working with the typhoid patients. There is no way for me to have an operation here and my blood pressure is sky high."

"What are you going to do?" Volodia asked, badly shaken by the news.

"Nothing. I can live with one kidney and will work as long as I can. I want a promise from you. If anything happens to me, keep the Gittermans in my home and let them continue working at the clinic. Don't say a word to Dr. Chaidarov; he himself is very sick."

Tanya got up to leave. "My dear Volodia, I have frightened you. After Mischa, you're still my closest friend, my only friend. Anyway, no use feeling sorry for myself. I am a soldier on a frontier."

"Isn't there any doctor who can help you?"

"I thought of that and decided it was too late. I would have to travel to Tashkent, but I'm so exhausted that I just can't take the risk. Anyway, how can I leave a hospital without a doctor?"

"Dr. Chaidarov is here."

"He needs surgery himself. He is a competent doctor but not a surgeon. I've got to go back. We have a full house tonight."

"You're still joking?"

"You don't want me to cry, do you? Have a good night, Volodia."

"Wait, I'll walk you back."

"No thank you. No pity please. I can find my way."

Tanya left, but Volodia ran after her.

"We must tell him."

"God forbid! He is fighting a war. Why upset him?"

They walked in silence with Tanya holding onto Volodia's arm.

"Remember, Volodia, the first time we walked together here? We were so full of plans and hope."

"Tanya, perhaps you made a mistake in your diagnosis."

She shook her head. "I was too good a student in diagnostic studies. The only thing I regret is that I will not see and hear the sound of victory of our armies over our enemy. There is so much to do, so many wounded to heal. You know, Volodia, you would have been a good doctor. You love people and you care."

"Just to care is not enough. To defeat human misery, we must act, learn, do things."

"You did things for me. You were here when I needed you. I needed you tonight and you were with me."

Tanya turned her face toward Volodia and she saw tears in his eyes. She held out her arms to him. Volodia bent over to kiss her cheek, but Tanya put her arms around him and kissed him.

"Volodia, you're a kind, sweet man. You will make a perfect husband for Eva. I must go."

* * * * *

CHAPTER SIXTEEN
The NKVD Pigpen

The NKVD Pigpen

Things started to happen in Kyzyl Kishlak. The tragic months of the epidemic had convinced the local leaders that they could not hide from the refugees. Typhus, typhoid fever, and dysentery had reached every place, even the village council and Party secretariat. The local leaders had storage rooms full of rice, alfalfa, barley and flour and were not able to eat. They needed drugs and medical care. The hospital and center had drugs, a staff of personnel and volunteers, but they needed food.

One result of the epidemic was that the local people started to respect the medical staff. The village council admitted that Dr. Chaidarov, Dr. Ivanovna and Vladimir Tarko were right in their demands, warnings and requests. But their support came too late.

Dr. Chaidarov remarked sarcastically that public hygiene is in the last paragraph, last chapter on the program of the Communist Party of Russia, the reason being that after the struggle with the Party to impose the laws for prevention of epidemics, no one is left. The physicians died from exhaustion, begging for legislation on sanitation, and the population died from contagious disease.

The staff worked on rotation around the clock. They had many new problems. Confusion of languages and dialects, arguments among patients, fights for food rations or for better floor space were just a few. There was a shortage of surgical instruments and food was not delivered on time. Some patients wanted the loudspeaker on all the time and some complained that the sound drove them crazy.

The isolator for typhus patients was a gloomy place. A shadowy aura of sadness pervaded the ward. This was now

Esther Gitterman's domain. When she had problems, and she had them all the time, she called Volodia. The patients confused her and complained a lot. Volodia tried to comfort her. Esther helped Vera and Fatima keep records of every pill given to a patient. She learned responsibility and compassion.

There was a patient in the isolator named Karabov, a leader of the *Komosol*, a very quiet young man who had been there many weeks but was still very weak.

Late one evening while Esther Gitterman was on duty, Karabov had a visitor. She greeted him politely in her limited Uzbeki-Russian:

"*Salaam Chozain, Yakshi missis*? Whom do you want to see?"

"Comrade Karabov."

"Have you been vaccinated against typhus?"

"Yes, *Barishnia*."

"Please, we want you to wear this white coat. This is for your protection." She handed him a clinic robe.

"*Chozain*, what do you carry in this towel?"

"Some fruit for my friend."

"Sorry, patient Karabov is still very sick. Doctor's orders, no food, just fluids. He sleeps constantly."

"So you take the fruit."

"No, many thanks anyway. We are not allowed to take fruit from patients or guests. You can leave it at the kitchen door on your way out of the ward. Fruit must be washed, boiled and given to the patients only. They come first."

"Why is your loudspeaker on?"

"It helps the patients get better. It keeps them informed about the war. Our armies are winning and this is good for their morale."

"Do you like this kind of work, *Barishnia*?"

"*Chozain*, at first it was just a way to get my bread rations and a little money, but now we get paid hundred-fold by the patients. They smile at us, they call me *dotchka* -- daughter, and are very thankful."

"Everything looks so clean."

"We clean everything ourselves. We need more workers,

but our village has no funds. You know, *Chozain*, there is a
war going on and everything must go to the front."

"How many hours do you work?"

"As many as we can stand. Ten, sometimes more."

"A pretty *barishnia* like you? When do you have time for
fun?"

"There is a war now. There is no time for fun. My man
is at the front. We must help him win this war so he can
come home."

"What is your name, *Barishnia*?"

"Esther, Esther Gitterman. Why do you ask, *Choazin*?"

"I'm very much impressed with your work."

"It's not I alone. All of us work together. Sometimes, we
get very tired, so many people die because of lack of help and
food. Many times patients are not able to eat because there is
no one here to feed them. You will excuse me, I have work
to do. It was nice talking to you, *Choazin*. You speak
Russian very well. Come again. Who shall I tell Kabarov was
here to see him?"

"Rachatayev, Party Secretary."

"Kabarov will be very happy. He is a good patient, but so
weak, he can't eat. I hope God will help him."

"Esther, you are a very sincere worker."

"Thank you, *Choazin* Rachatayev."

Rachatayev came again the following evening. He
unloaded two sacks of rice and vegetables from a small wagon.

"This is some food for the sick."

With him was a tall, skinny girl in Uzbekian clothes,
wearing a multicolored silk dress and a *tupiteika* covering her
hair.

Fatima, who was on duty that night, recognized the Party
Secretary and requested that he wait where he was while she
fetched him a white coat.

"Is it necessary?"

"Absolutely, Comrade Secretary, for your own protection.
It's a great honor for us to have such a distinguished visitor."

"How is your father, my friend, Aziz Ali?"

"Thank Allah, he is well."

"Where is Sister Esther?"

"Esther is a volunteer here. She is working day shift. Do you need her?"

"This is my daughter, Sulichan. I want Esther to teach her how to take care of the sick here. Give her an anti-typhus vaccine first, of course. She just needs some training and practice to be a good volunteer. She was a good student in school and has a good head. I've brought you some food from my garden, and I will try to get more. If a refugee like Esther can do it, we local people must do it too. Can I see Comrade Kabarov?"

"It would be better if you didn't. He has a high fever. He won't even recognize you. I'm sorry."

The local newspaper printed an appeal by Party Secretary Rachatayev for volunteers to help in the hospital, clinic, center, and isolator. None of the local men or women came, for they were scared they would catch an infectious disease. But the refugees, Ukrainians, Tatars, Jews, by-Volga-Germans came. They registered, were vaccinated, received white uniforms, bread cards, and a warm smile. The volunteers were well-educated, and, like Esther and Chavele, they learned quickly to care for the sick, to wash, sponge and clean them. Even the dirtiest work gave them dignity, self-respect and a new acceptance in Kyzyl Kishlak.

Some of them, working nights at the phone, learned how to advise in first-aid cases and how to fill out forms in the waiting room for the many patients standing outside and inside the cramped center and clinic.

With Dr. Chaidarov and Dr. Ivanovna overworked and sick, Volodia organized all the administrative services of the hospital center. Volodia had help from Fatima and Vera, as well as from a former patient, Karabov.

After his recuperation, Karabov decided to stay on and work as a volunteer. He started by helping the male patients bathe, get haircuts and disinfect their clothes when they were admitted. More and more, he developed an understanding and compassion for the sick, their families and the staff. He worked mostly with Chavele Gitterman and Sulichan Rachatayeva.

Volodia rarely had time to leave the center now. He was always on the move to the adjacent buildings, from the wards to the admission room, from the kitchen to Dr. Chaidarov's office. All beds, bunks, and corridors were filled, but the floors were clean. When inspectors came from Andizhan and Chinabaad, they regarded Kyzyl Kishlak as an outstanding medical complex. Dr. Chaidarov and his staff were praised for their service and loyalty. Never in his life had Volodia worked so hard and carried more responsibility. He saw people recuperating and walking out of the center and isolation unit, weak, but better.

Dr. Chaidarov and Dr. Ivanovna worked long hours, often sleeping in their offices, living on a quick bite of *lepioshka* -- bread -- and tea, a piece of fruit, a few grapes. But they looked inspired, happy that they had licked the epidemic. All they needed now was food -- nutrition for those who had survived.

Volodia decided to see Secretary Rachatayev.

"What are you going to tell him?" Dr. Chaidarov wanted to know.

"That there is a vast accumulation of rice, barley, sugar and salt in the village warehouses. They sell it freely on the black market. Let them give some of it to the sick."

"Who told you that?"

"Karabov."

"Karabov is a nice young man, an idealist, a *komsomoletz*, -- member of the communist youth movement -- but very naive. He can go to jail for statements like these. What a fool. It's a bad idea -- you'd better use another approach."

"I will think of something. Do you want me to walk you home?"

"Thank you, Volodia. I'd rather stay here. You'd better take Dr. Ivanovna home. I don't like the way she looks lately."

"Better, look at yourself, Mouhamud Chaidarov."

"No time yet for looking at ourselves. We still have plenty of patients to look after."

The situation in Kyzyl Kishlak stabilized. There were whole days now without patients dying at the isolator and Center. There was talk about reopening the school in order to normalize life in the area.

Babachan called Volodia. "Mouhamud did not come home last night."

"I know. He was tired and slept here. He feels better this morning. We just had tea."

"Vladimir Arionovitz, I must talk to you. Can you come over to see me?"

"If it's about the school, you can open the first of the month."

"No, it is not about the school. It's something personal."

"Babachan, if this is something personal, I'd rather talk to you here, or I will come to your office at the school."

"Why? Is something wrong with my home?"

"I don't like to talk in front of Ninotchka."

"Why? She is like my own child."

"Babachan, dear, I'd rather see you here. I'm really busy with my work."

"Too busy to help a friend? You said you were our friend, didn't you?"

"Babachan, please come over here. I will give you as much time as you need."

Babachan came to Volodia's little office and sat down on the only bench. Her eyes looked red; she must have cried all night. Her face was a mirror of sadness and despair.

"Vladimir Arionovitz, my husband is a very sick man. I know he will listen to you. I want him to go immediately to Tashkent, before it's too late."

"I'm aware that he is sick, even though he never talks about it. All he is concerned about is his responsibility to his village. I doubt if he will go until we are sure the epidemic is over."

"But hc will listen to what you say."

"I'll try, but who will take his place?"

Her eyes filled with tears.

"I don't give a *kopeck* anymore. I want my husband alive. We gave everything for the *kishlak*, for Uzbekistan. We haven't had time to have our own children."

Her sobs overwhelmed Volodia. He did something that no man in Uzbekistan would dare to do to a married Uzbekistani woman -- he touched her hair.

"Babachan, please control yourself. Stop crying. You know that Mouhamud is like an older brother to me. I know him. You can't change his faith. He loves and believes in his people. This hospital is his blood and soul. If it's taken away from him, he will not last a day."

"There must be something we can do. I can't let him destroy himself. Sometimes I think he wants to die."

"He is disappointed in the local leaders who made promises to him and never kept them."

"He is disappointed in me; I let him down. I kept saying that the future of our village depends on our local people and the Party. He kept saying that our village will develop only if we pay attention to individuals, regardless of who they are. I voted against him again and again. I was busy with my school children and didn't have children of my own."

"Mouhamud has a full life, and I know he loves you. Your husband is an exceptional man."

"He is no more a man. He is dying little by little each day. I know, I see it."

"Babachan, I will talk to him again today."

Her hand was trembling as she said with tears in her eyes, "Vladimir Arionovitz, I hope it's not too late."

"You don't know your husband. He is strong in his will to live and help his people."

"I hope and pray to Allah that you are right."

She walked to the open door and then returned. "I want you to know, I voted at the council meeting to give you the old school for a refugee shelter."

"Thank you, Babachan."

"Why don't you like my Ninotchka?"

"I don't know why, but I don't trust her."

"Why?"

"I can't talk about it. But I'd advise you to send her off to school in Chinabaad or Andizhan. You have a good excuse, your husband is sick and you need the room for a nurse."

"How can I send away a homeless girl?"

"Secretary Rachatayev wants someone to serve tea and clean his office. Why don't you let Ninotchka go there?"

"How do you know this?"

"He wanted me to send him Esther Gitterman, the girl who lives with Tanya."

"I hope you didn't."

"Never on his life. I told him that she takes care of Tanya."

"How is Dr. Ivanovna?"

"Tanya and your husband are a pair. He loves Uzbekistan and she worships Mother Russia."

"She is a great woman."

"She, too, works herself to death."

"*Salaam*, Vladimir Arionovitz. Please talk to him."

"I will."

"You can take the school building today."

"Thank you, Babachan."

Volodia wanted to say, "You're too late, Babachan. We don't need the school building. Most of the refugees are now dead. Many of the refugees are resting forever on the Garden of Eden Boulevard. The few that we saved are patients in the isolator or work there as volunteers, helping, saving the lives of your local people, Uzbeks, Tatars, Tadziks." Volodia was not bitter or angry, just hurt. Poor Babachan, she thought she had done what was best for her village.

Fatima and Kabarov registered in ZAGS, the local marriage office. There was a small reception at Tanya's home arranged by Aziz Ali's wives. Volodia and Dr. Chaidarov arrived after the festivities had already begun. There was a noisy crowd of

Party and village council bureaucrats, school teachers, relatives and musicians. The wives of Aziz Ali, in native garb, their faces partly veiled, served fruit juice, tea and homemade sweets. The crowd chanted, congratulated Kabarov, and teased, "What a sneaky way to get the best-looking girl in the village, get yourself sick with typhus and make the nurse fall in love with you."

"Years ago he would have had to pay a dowry-fortune to her father. A bride like Fatima would have cost him many goats and sheep."

"He arranged this very cleverly. He joined the Party and got her for free."

"Many say that Dr. Chaidarov arranged it. Instead of losing a nurse, he gained an extra helper."

Finally the guests started to leave. Volodia said *salaam* to everyone and prepared to go.

"Would you like to stay for a while?" Tanya asked him quietly.

"Thank you, Tanya, I can't. I have to go back to the center."

"Eva?"

"Yes."

"Why don't you marry her?"

"She doesn't trust foreigners."

"You conquered malaria, but you can't convince a girl to marry you?"

"She has her reasons."

"Good night, Volodia. If you feel like it, come back tonight. I'll stay up. I can't sleep anyway."

* * * * *

CHAPTER SEVENTEEN
The Interrogation

The Interrogation

One evening when they were alone, Volodia asked Eva, "What do you call our relationship, Eva?"

"Friendship, a loving, understanding friendship."

"Do we really have such a friendship, Eva?"

"Yes, Volodia."

"Why don't you want to marry me?"

"The piece of paper from ZAGS will not strengthen our relationship."

"I'm not sure about that."

"Describe how you feel about me," Eva teased.

"I'm not as good with words as you are. You're the waterfall in this desert; the food for my brain and heart."

Eva closed her eyes, "Keep talking, Volodia."

"Really, Eva, the only thing that gave me the power to withstand the pressures here was you."

"How come you never say to me 'I love you?'"

"Don't you feel it?"

"I want to hear it again and again."

Volodia embraced her. "I love you, Eva."

"Why did you keep it to yourself for so long?"

"Saying it sounds so empty compared to my feelings."

"Do you believe in destiny?"

"No, life is not predicted or dependent upon destiny."

"Mother said you were 'destined' for me."

"That's rationalizing. Some people have a tendency to blame everything on destiny. It's a superstition born in the human mind."

"Don't you feel it's strange that we met here, at the end of the world?"

"It is strange, but love is not based on miracles or destiny.

If we love each other, it is for what we are, not because we were destined to."

"You said you believe in God."

"My belief is not based on magic, miracles or destiny. God does not lead individual people to each other. He gives us the strength to choose our conduct, our freedom to act. How can your mother know that the reason for my coming to this village is because of you and not because of the refugees or Dr. Chaidarov? How does she know that you were evacuated here to meet me and not Oleg? What has God to do with our temptation, our forbidden desires? No, Eva, man is his own master and has the power over his own destiny. I came here because here was a place where I was needed, where I could be useful. And here I found, you, your mother, Oleg, Tanya and Dr. Chaidarov. I would like to stay and work but there is too much hate here."

"There's much less here than in your Poland."

"Still, Eva, you claim this is a new world."

"Brotherhoods of nations are not yet brotherhoods of men, of people. Don't forget, Volodia, hatred against us was part of the Russian religion and was official government policy for many generations. Our system is only twenty some years old."

"Why do they hate us so much?"

"It's tradition with them. In the fifteenth century, many of their priests converted to Judaism. Among the converts were many influential and rich families. This created a storm among the church leaders and they started pogroms against Jews. The converts were burned at the stake or sent to Siberia. From that time, the Jews were refused the right to live in 'Holy Russia' until the Revolution."

Volodia listened with admiration to his angered Eva. He did not say a word and she continued.

"After the Revolution, we saw a change for the better. There were Yiddish schools, newspapers, writers and good theaters, but in the last few years before the war they started to close our clubs and schools. They said that the parents themselves did not want Yiddish schools any more."

Eva's face turned sad. "How can we continue as Jews

without our own culture and history? Still, I hope that after
the war, things will get better. Our constitution provides
freedom of worship."

"On paper, everything here looks beautiful, but in
practice..."

"Maybe you're right. Since the Stalin-Hitler Pact, things
have changed. Still..."

"Still what?"

"There is no place in the world for us to go to but back
home. No country wants us. I heard that in the summer of
1938, there was a conference in Switzerland or France of more
than thirty nations and no one wanted the Jews in their
country, even the so-called democracies."

"Eva, they didn't accept any new Jewish immigrants into
their countries, but there were Jews living there already."

"So, why didn't the Jews of those countries fight, protest,
demand that their countries allow immigration of their brethren
from overcrowded Europe?"

"Who knows why? Maybe they did not realize how bad
the situation in Europe was. I, myself, wanted to go to
Palestine. We needed only two hundred *zlotys* to get a permit,
but we were too poor. There were thousands like me who
went to the HIAS, the Hebrew Immigrant Aid Society, to the
Joint Distribution Committee, and to the Agency for Palestine,
but the answer was, 'You must wait. No funds, no money.'
Hundreds of thousands were ready to leave Poland for
Palestine, for Cuba, even for Madagascar and Uganda in Africa,
but our good friends, the French, the Americans and the
English, did not want to help us until it was too late. People
are bad, selfish, full of prejudice and hatred. This is why we
have this war."

"I believe that after this war, people will change for the
better."

"Maybe."

"No maybes, Volodia. We will have to be the ones to
fight for true understanding. All those millions of people
killed, all this suffering, for what? To go back and be hated,
persecuted? I won't surrender to the old ways. Look at

yourself here. You have made friends with Moslems, Christians and Jews. How did you accomplish it?"

"By helping them as individuals and by serving them in crucial times on a purely humanitarian basis."

"Maybe this is what we will have to do when we get back home. We will stop looking at each other as Jews, Ukrainians, Poles or Russians and start looking at each other as citizens of one great country of two hundred million individuals."

"You are too naive, Eva. Not in our generation will every man look at his neighbor as his brother."

"Why not? At least we can hope and try for such an accomplishment."

It was hard to believe, but the patients at the center consumed more food during the epidemic than at any time before. Not only did they eat everything they were served, they stole from each other, often getting into arguments and fights among themselves and the staff. Every few weeks there was a shortage of something. They had flour, but no cooking oil; cabbage, but no fat or bread; rice, but no salt. Deliveries were always in question, and the promises by the village council were often only empty air.

Volodia increased his dependence on the local farm cooperatives, the *kolkhozes* and *artels,* finding the farmers to be more human and more charitable than the officials who always justified shortages with the Party slogan, "There is a war going on."

Still, all was going along fairly well until someone started stealing entire wagons of food designated for the hospital. Two loads of rice left Chakulabaad but never reached the center. Food reserves were running out, and shelves were empty. Volodia called Comrade Kozlov, the secretary of the village council. "Not my business," he said abruptly.

Irked by this callous indifference, Volodia called Dr. Chaidarov. Babachan answered the telephone.

"Mouhamud is in bed, sick. Please give him a day to rest."

Volodia then called *Kolkhoz* Octiabre.

"We would like to borrow a few bags of *djugara* -- barley -- for the hospital until our food allocation arrives."

The *kolkhoz* chairman was polite. "Sorry, we are running short on deliveries to Andizhan. You will have to get special permission from the Sel-Soviet or Party."

Secretary Rachatayev was in Tashkent and not due back for four days. Volodia went back to Comrade Kozlov. The receptionist, a polite Uzbekian woman, went to Kozlov's office and came out with a question. "Why is it so urgent for you to see Comrade Kozlov?"

"Something happened to the food load for the hospital."

Comrade Kozlov, in his unbuttoned Stalin-jacket, came to the door and asked, "Why did you not go to Dr. Chaidarov, your superior?"

"Dr. Chaidarov is sick in bed. We have a hospital with patients to feed."

"Come in."

"Thank you."

"We have a Party Secretary, a militia, why do you have to come to me with your problems?"

"The hospital is part of the village council's responsibility. Hungry patients can bring disaster. This is the second time that food sent to us has disappeared. I can't let patients starve."

"Why don't you try to get food from the local cooperatives?"

"They are ordained to serve only the people who work, and, sorry to say, they just promise and never give us anything."

"They follow directives of our government and Party. Are you criticizing the directives of our Party?"

"Comrade Secretary, I'm not criticizing anyone. I'm responsible for a malaria center and a hospital which the local leadership has turned into an asylum for the mentally ill, incurably sick and now a dumping place for the typhus epidemic. We have an isolation unit full of patients. We need food for them immediately. I don't care who stole the transport. All I need is food."

"But why me? Use some money from your budget until your food arrives."

"The cost of bread is staggering. We can't buy food at the bazaar. We stopped the epidemic, but if the patients that are in the isolation units, who are still carriers, go back to the *kolkhozes*, you will have a new typhus outbreak. We still have loads of refugees coming here now from area *kolkhozes*."

"We did not send for them."

"You did not send for me either. We were sent here by the order of the Soviet government. I resent your remarks. The refugees have husbands and fathers fighting for this country."

"Where? At the bazaars of Tashkent?"

"Comrade Kozlov, I don't have to stay here and listen to your insults. They were forced to flee, to leave their homes. If I don't get food by sundown, I will call the Commissariat of Health in Andizhan."

"You would not dare. I'll send you to the front."

"Don't try to scare me. I'd rather go to the front than hear you, a village council secretary, insulting his own citizens. By your ignorance you jeopardize their lives."

"I have orders to follow."

"You have paper orders. I have living people to fight for. Can't you see what will happen if we do not feed the sick and the staff?"

"I can see that you are an enemy of our system. We have ways to deal with your kind."

"Are you threatening me?"

"You were threatening me with calling Andizhan."

"If I cannot have food here, I will."

Kozlov's face turned red. "We shall see." He picked up the phone and said something in Uzbekian.

Volodia started to leave and the militiaman stopped him.

"Citizen Tarko, you'd better come with me."

"Citizen Kozlov, do you realize what you are doing?"

"Yes. I am making a citizen's arrest. You are an enemy who has insulted our government and Party."

"I want to call Dr. Chaidarov or Dr. Ivanovna."

"Dr. Chaidarov will be reprimanded for having an enemy
of our system on his staff, I assure you. We will deal with
you effectively."

"There are important things to do and you..."

"Someone else will do them. You are under arrest."

The Militia Detention House looked more like a pig pen
than a prison. It had the pervading odor of a stable, smelling
of human sweat, unwashed mouths and bodies, mixed with the
strong stench of ammonia. Volodia felt he would choke from
the unbearable smell. His eyes were burning. It took him
awhile to get his breath. It was dark in the cell. He saw
shadows of bodies sitting and lying on the bare ground. He
heard voices talking in familiar languages, Russian, Polish,
Yiddish and Uzbekian. He sat down in a corner where there
was a little space available and closed his eyes. Volodia
suddenly realized that the place he had found was the location
of the barrel used by the prisoners for urination. He moved as
far as he could from the stinking barrel and leaned his head
against the wall. Soon bugs started moving on his body, gnats,
flies, lice. Volodia tried to move away, scratching his neck,
his hair, but it did not help. He felt the bugs under his shirt,
in his pants.

In the evening, the prisoners were marched in groups to the
backyard latrine by a guard. Volodia and another prisoner, an
Uzbek, were ordered to carry the enormous barrel to the yard.
Volodia forgot for a moment that he was a prisoner; his
vocation was too much a part of him. He took a fistful of
weeds from the stream and sprinkled the barrel, drowning the
bugs and flies nesting in the cracks.

The guard and the Uzbek looked at Volodia with pity, and
with hand gestures motioned to each other that he had lost his
mind.

The prisoners were served some bread and a watery soup.
Volodia refused to eat and demanded to see the militia
commandant or militiaman, Oleg Polishenko.

The guard gave the food to Ahmedjan, the Uzbek who
helped Volodia with the barrel, and promised to find Oleg.

After the meal, most of the men were led away to work -- to clean yards, the bazaar and local offices. The Polish refugees were left to clean the yard and lavatory around the militia grounds. Volodia and all those who came in during the day remained in the cell.

Volodia made up his mind not to talk to anyone. A man he knew from the bazaar, a speculator, tried to get him into a conversation.

"Why are you in here, Tarko?"

"Some mistake."

"You say they make mistakes?"

"I don't say anything. There's just been some misunderstanding."

"Scared to talk?"

"Why? I didn't do anything wrong."

"You sold something at the bazaar?"

"No, did you?"

"Yes, I did. I did not know the rice was stolen. Did you steal something?"

"I'm not a speculator. I work."

"Doesn't everybody work? But a kilo of bread costs more than two days' pay. I had to do something to supplement my poor diet. I have to eat, don't I? So you were honest and worked your ass off and you're in the same trouble as I am."

"I'm not in trouble and have nothing to fear. Just some misunderstanding."

"You look worried."

"Yes, I am, but not for myself. I'm worried about the people in the center and the hospital, about my friends."

Oleg came and brought some food with him. The guards took Volodia outside.

"Don't come near me, Oleg. Stay where you are. I am full of lice and bugs."

"God have pity. Who did it?"

"Secretary Kozlov. Please call Dr. Chaidarov and if Babachan answers, tell her what happened."

"I will. I will."

"How are Eva and Celia?"

"Very upset. So is my mother. Why you?"
"I made a mistake and lost my temper."
"Did you insult the Party?"
"I did not. Maybe I insulted Kozlov."
"He is a bastard. I'm with you, Volodia. We will get you out of here."
"Thank you, Oleg. Go now. I can't eat anyhow."
Among the prisoners that came back in the late evening was the barber, Getzel Gold. He was a tall, skinny, handsome young man from Lublin, Poland. He worked in the local barbershop and was a favorite among the refugees and Europeans in the village. He was always singing, telling jokes. He had a wife and three children, all girls, all beautiful like his wife, Elka. Getzel spoke Polish, Russian, Ukrainian, and Yiddish, even though he had never gone to school. Getzel had given free haircuts to the refugees at the local bath.
"Getzel, what are you doing here?"
"I came to pray with the morning quorum. Why are you here? To study the lice?"
"I came here to be the cantor at the prayers."
"Will we have a quorum?"
"We can count the Uzbeks in, they are circumcised. No kidding, why are you here?"
"I told one too many."
"What?"
"A joke. Oy, am I an idiot. But I told the joke in Polish."
"Who was there."
"The same people. Our crowd, Poles, Jews, Ukranians."
"Why don't you keep your tongue, Getzel? You have a wife and children."
"I'm stupid. All my life I tell jokes. What is a barber without a fat joke? I kept my steady customers that way."
"Did they interrogate you?"
"Yes, once. They wanted to know the name of the person who told me the joke. I really don't remember where I heard it. They told me they would keep me here until my brain rots and my memory falls apart and opens up. What will I do?"

"What will your wife and children do?"

"Who is the Uzbek near you, the one with the bandaged arms? Did they do it to him?"

"No, he did it himself. He tried suicide. He killed his wife and stabbed his brother."

"God, why?"

"He got back from the army hospital unexpectedly and found his wife in his brother's bed. Someone must have written to him, because he knew exactly where to find them."

"How do you know all this?"

"He talked to me. He was at Stalingrad, received medals. Some welcome home for a hero."

"Why do they keep him here and not in a hospital?"

"I asked the same question. He must have said something against the militia or government when they came to arrest him. Those dirty bandages will give him gangrene. He can't eat either. I fed him. His arms are swollen."

"Why don't they take him to the hospital?"

"Ask them."

Ahmedjan, the Uzbek, came back from cleaning the school building. He sat near Volodia and asked in correct Russian, "How is the Markes family?"

"How do you know them?"

"Anna was my student. I met you at their home when their brother was killed."

"Oh yes, I remember you. Why are you here?"

"I was arrested for parading in a *parandga* -- women's clothing."

"Why would you disguise yourself as a woman? Is something wrong with you?"

"No, Allah forbid. I'm a school teacher who objects to being taken to the Red Army. I don't eat pork; I'm a Moslem who lives according to the Koran."

"But your country is at war."

"My country is occupied by the Russians."

"Didn't the Revolution free you and make you your own masters?"

"Nothing has changed here in the last twenty years. We

are still an occupied country. Let me tell you something. I trust you, because I know you did good things for our village. No one can hear us here except Allah. I want you to know that there is no difference between the cruelties in the time of the Czars and those of the Marxist-Leninist masters who are holding power now. My people are choking in an atmosphere of Party rivalries, always accused of plots, always being charged with counter-revolution. There is constant friction between Party and government leaders."

"I don't think all the people here are so bad off. Some of you have a good life. You have nice homes and vineyards."

"Only the Party privileged. You say something against them, or against their actions and you've insulted the sacred representative of Stalin. Any insignificant remark we make is considered by the secret police to be an act of treason, Paragraph 58 -- a plot against the state, against the army, against the leader Stalin himself. The result? We mistrust all Party bureaucrats. We hate the Russians among us, the good and the bad ones. We don't like their culture, their manners or their way of life."

"Still, the Soviets did many things for Uzbekistan, didn't they?"

"After my return here from the teachers' institute, I was impressed by what the system had done for my country, the development, electricity in every remote place, schools, hospitals, cultural centers. Our population was ninety-five percent illiterate, and our youngsters started to learn to read and write. But millions of people had died building canals, developing mines, collectivizing our farms, and everything we produced went to "Mother Russia." Most of our people in the cities live in misery, exactly as under the Czarist empire. Our people were once a free and happy people. We traveled wherever we liked; now you can't get a permit to visit your own dying mother in the next city. They say there is war now and we must mobilize to win this battle, but after the war they will continue to Russify Central Asia. Under the pretext of building Communism they spread Russian chauvinism. They killed our writers and our national poet, Tschulpan. They murdered our *Mullahs* -- clerics -- because they were too religious. Many of our leaders are corrupt and misguided; even in our village there is mistrust and hatred."

Volodia listened closely. A teacher in the Communist system talking to him like this? And where of all places? In a prison cell.

"Our vocabulary has great phrases and lines for banners, but our language is false, false as the smile of the Russian prosecutor's face who will investigate you, so watch out."

"It seems to me that the struggle between Communism and nationalism is taking place here, in Uzbekistan; both ideas expect recognition. What is the way out?"

"This is our tragedy. There is no way out. We must stay on this path. All I want is to survive. This is why I dressed in women's clothing. Let them think something is wrong with me. All I want is not to get killed in their war."

"Why did you tell me this?"

"You saved many lives in this village and I heard that you believe in God. I hope that someday you will be free, so you will tell the world on the outside about our tragedy -- the great tragedy of the people of Central Asia."

* * * * *

CHAPTER EIGHTEEN
Off to the Polish Army

Off to the Polish Army

At midnight, a guard awakened Volodia and led him to the yard.

"You wash. You are going to see the *sledowatel.*"

"Who?"

"The interrogator, the investigation inspector wants to see you."

"Good."

"Good? You fool. They're strict. You'd better tell them the truth."

At the NKVD building all offices were lit. The long entrance lobby was carpeted with a heavy floor covering and on the white walls were portraits of Beria, Lenin, and Stalin. A uniformed guard asked Volodia's name and asked him to follow him. He was taken to a small room, clean and furnished only with a wooden bench. Water was still dripping from Volodia's hair. He straightened his hair with his fingers and, using his shirt for a towel, dried his neck and face. A warden opened the door.

"Vladimir Arionovitz Tarko?"

"Yes."

"Come with me."

In a small office behind a desk covered with a red cloth, three uniformed men faced Volodia. Among them was the familiar face of Bagdayev. The table lamp was set on Volodia's face and he kept his eyes closed to the strong light. Behind a curtain Volodia heard voices and movements like someone turning over pages in a book. When the warden left, Bagdayev adjusted the lamp away from Volodia's face.

"Thank you."

"Want to smoke?"

"No, thank you."

"Did they treat you all right here"

"Yes, considering ... "

"What do you mean by 'considering?'"

"Considering this is not a hospital or hotel, but ... "

"But what?"

"I am very unhappy about the sanitary conditions here. We are fighting an epidemic and the bugs here can spread to the guards and wardens and they will carry it to the village."

One of the officers, a tall, thick-necked Russian with broad shoulders, athletic arms, and deep voice interrupted him. "We will talk about this later. We did not come here to consult you."

"I wish you would, for your own protection."

"Are you being disrespectful?"

"I'm being concerned, Citizen Natchalnik."

"Do you know why you are here?"

"No. I never did anything to deserve detention with speculants, burglars, drunkards, and sex perverts."

"You insulted our Party and criticized our system. You insulted the village council secretary, who has been a Party member since the Revolution."

"I don't judge him by his years in the Party, or as a Party member. I see him as a small man with a mentality to insult other people, to trample on human values. He insulted me personally and insulted my people."

"You were trying to influence locally established politics."

"Never. I am not a political person. I am a medical corpsman who serves this community. Ask your Party leaders and members who are familiar with what I did here. Ask your health department in Andizhan. They came here and recognized my work."

"Your work is not under investigation here, but your background and anti-Soviet statements are."

"My background was checked by the state office of the health commissariat in Andizhan; so were my qualifications in every detail. I'm proud of my background and proud of my job as a health worker."

"Why haven't you become a citizen of our country?"

"I was a medic in the Polish Army fighting against the German fascists. I was taken prisoner by the Red Army and sent to a *Sovchoz* and later to a village for war prisoners. I hope that after our victory over the German fascists, I will be able to return to my homeland, to a free Poland."

"Don't you know that in Poland they don't want you, that they hate your kind?"

"I hope that when this war will be over, there will be a new, free Poland, without hate and discrimination against any minority groups."

"How do you feel about the people here?"

"My work, my activities here speak for themselves."

"You insulted an official of this village and a veteran Party member."

"I asked him to feed a hospital full of patients. You call that insulting?"

"Why didn't you go to your superior, Dr. Chaidarov?"

"I did, but his wife told me he was sick in bed."

"Did Comrade Chaidarov advise you to go to the village council and force your entry to the secretary's office?"

"No, she did not, and I did not force myself into his office. In fact, he came out to the waiting room and asked me to come in."

"Did you say that you would call Andizhan if he didn't give you the food?"

"Yes, I did. After he insulted me, my people, and all the refugees."

"What did he say?"

"When I told him that our patients are men and women whose sons and husbands are fighting for this country, he said, 'They are fighting in the bazaars in Tashkent.'"

"He has been a Party member for twenty years and you are a stranger here. It is his word against yours."

"Not a word he said is true."

The other investigator, holding open a file, interrupted, "We have information that you asked the local bakery to deliver bread to your center before delivering it to the village council, and they delivered bread to you under the threat of closing the bakery."

"I never threatened them. I forced them to clean up the yard of the bakery; the ditches were full of flies and mosquitoes. I gave them three days to clean up or be reported to the village council."

"Did you report them?"

"The manager of the bakery -- *artel* -- begged me not to. They did clean up. He asked me what he could do for me. He wanted to give me some bread."

"Did you take it?"

"Yes, I did. I gave it immediately to Aziz Ali, our center's helper, and he gave the bread to the patients."

"Did you instruct Aziz Ali to give the bread to your friends, refugees from the Ukraine, a patient by the name of Celia Markes?"

"He divided the bread among all the patients. When he offered some to me, I told him to give my share to Celia Markes."

"When you came back to the bakery on the third day, what happened?"

"The yard and premises had been cleaned up completely. The manager thanked me for not reporting him and again asked me what he could do for me."

"Did he give you bread again?"

"No. I told him that if he really wanted to help us he should try to deliver the bread a little earlier in the morning."

"Did you realize that you broke Party regulations on priorities of services to the working population?"

"Sorry, all I wanted was to help the sick and the elderly. I really did not know that I was breaking any laws." Volodia was tired, nervous. His voice was trembling. "May I have some water?"

The investigator kept looking at the file and continued the questioning, ignoring Volodia's request. "Did you conduct religious propaganda among the patients? Did you say prayers regularly with the patients?"

"Propaganda, no. Prayers with patients, yes. They were

near death. They asked me to say the prayers with them."

"Do you believe in God?"

"Yes. Sometimes I have my doubts when I see what is happening in Europe, but deep in my heart, I believe in God."

"And you still say prayers with your patients?"

"I'll do anything to make it easier for them to survive their diseases or die peacefully."

"Even if it breaks Soviet laws?"

"No, but according to the Soviet Constitution, freedom of worship is allowed as long as it does not interfere with the state."

"I see from your papers that you have done some good for this village. So why did you act so stupidly?"

"Like what?"

"You went to the village secretary, a Party member, a Russian who was sent here to lead this village in the path of Communism and advise his Uzbekian comrades, and you, a stranger, a refugee, you insulted him."

"I did not intend to insult him."

"You called him a murderer of women and children."

"Honestly, I never said such a thing. I said that it is like cold-blooded murder to let women and children starve and not do anything about it."

"So what do you suggest we do with you?"

"I couldn't care less what you do with me, but for God's sake, I hope you have delivered some food to the isolation unit and center."

For the length of the investigation, Bagdayev did not utter a word. The Russian officer rang and the warden came in. He told Volodia to follow him to a small room next to the interrogation office. Bagdayev followed them.

"Tarko, you have done something so absurd, so surprisingly stupid in our system, that you will have to pay for it. No one criticizes a Soviet official, a Russian, and gets away with it. I know what you have done for this area and my Russian friends know also. Dr. Chaidarov called me, as well as Dr. Ivanovna. They would give their right arms for you, but you can't stay here any longer. We will not send you to a hard labor camp as Comrade Kozlov wishes. We cannot send you to the army since you're not a Soviet citizen. So, to satisfy Kozlov, and the rest of the Russians on the council, we are sending you to a work battalion at the Angren coal mines in upstate Tashkent. With your qualifications, you'll survive anywhere. We will prepare documents that you volunteered to work in the coal mines."

"I have friends here. I have a girl here whom I love."

"I know. I'm sorry. Sooner or later all you refugees will go back to your homes. We have to stay on and live with the Kozlovs. I know he is a drunkard, a son-of-a-bitch, but he represents the regime. Do you understand, Tarko?"

The warden came back with tea.

"Drink now. We will call you back to sign the protocol."

Volodia tried to sip the green tea. But he had a lump in his throat. He waited a long time and almost fell asleep from exhaustion when the warden touched his shoulder.

"Poshli -- Let's go"

The same three officers were in the room. The curtain was removed and the Russian officer handed Volodia a two-page hand-written document. Volodia asked for a pen.

"Don't you want to read it?"

"What difference will it make?"

The officer read the last two lines on the page from his copy, "Everything said, discussed, mentioned here, under the penalty of the criminal code, will never be told to anyone."

Volodia signed the paper.

"We are giving you three days to transfer all your responsibilities and papers in the center to Dr. Chaidarov or his delegated representative. Tomorrow, you will appear at the military draft board for your destination papers."

"Thank you."

Bagdayev followed Volodia to the street.

"Tarko, I'm sorry it happened this way."

"Thank you for what you did for me tonight."

"No. Thank Babachan Chaidarov and some militiaman named Oleg Polishenko. If not for them I would not have had your case for weeks. They are all good people, but your Dr.

Ivanovna is a very sick woman."

"How do you know?"

"They came to see me today. I'm glad I was not away somewhere at a meeting."

"Thank you for coming here and helping me personally."

"This is my job, Tarko. Because someone is a Party member, it does not necessarily make him a good man, and because you are a refugee, it does not make you an enemy."

"Thanks again, and as a last favor, would you do something for a woman and three children?"

"Who are they?"

"The wife and children of the local barber, an illiterate refugee from Poland, Getzel Gold. He is in the Militia Detention House."

"Whom did he insult? The village council chairman?"

"No, you know how barbers are, telling dirty jokes, trying to be funny. He told a client a joke about a *kolkhoz* and was arrested."

"First time?"

"I don't know."

"Is he a friend of yours?"

"Yes, besides being the local barber, a refugee who helped out at the center and the *Banya* -- bath house -- anytime we needed him, he also was on my team of workers who came to help you in Chinabaad when you cleaned up your town."

"I remember him. I will see what I can do."

"Thank you."

"Good night."

Eva was sitting on the step of her home when Volodia returned. She jumped up, shouting, "Volodia!" Celia and Anna woke up, weeping, hugging him. Celia kept repeating, "God heard my prayers." Eva chattered, "I knew they would let you go."

There was some *kasha* soup left. Eva had not eaten supper. They sat down and ate.

"Was it bad, Volodia?"

"It was very depressing."

Eva noticed that Volodia hardly ate and was not anxious to talk.

"Volodia, would you like to sleep here?"

"No, I have to go to my room and get rid of my clothes."

"I'm coming with you. They messed up your room when they searched it. I will help you clean up. Volodia, is everything cleared up?"

"I'm out of here for good. I have to leave this place in three days."

"No. I will talk to our bank director. Naimov can help."

"It's no use, Eva, the papers are already signed. I'm going to the coal mines."

When Volodia opened the door of his room, he was surprised.

"Looks like Aziz Ali cleaned the place."

Volodia undressed and asked Eva to take all his clothes outside.

"They are full of lice and bugs."

"In one day?"

"It doesn't take long to get lice, in that hole."

He washed, changed into clean underwear and went to bed. Eva undressed and lay beside him. He was tired. They both fell into a deep sleep. Volodia slept for some time and then something woke him up, like someone crying inside him. There had been sickness around him when he had arrived here, human misery. He had done everything to help the people here; now he must leave. A voice inside him told him, "You've done your chores, now you can be disposed of." He remembered the saying of his grandfather who always quoted Rabbi Akiva: "Whatever the All-Merciful does is for the good. In pleasure or pain, give thanks."

Volodia looked at Eva. Gently he stirred her hair and softly touched her face. He felt her warm body beside him and realized that this young woman had given him complete happiness in the past days and nights. All the disappointments of the last days, all the aggravation he had suffered were not as strong as the quiet breathing of this gentle woman. "Tomorrow I will be gone," he thought to himself. "Will I

live to see her again? Her face, her dark brown hair? I have
given so much time to the sick and the poor, I have argued
with the mighty and important ones. I earned hate and respect,
and now everything is gone. Everything was in vain, except
she, beside me."

"Oh, how happy he was in the hours they shared." He
remembered reading somewhere that "Happiness is something
you don't realize you have until it is taken from you." It is
like walking in a garden blindfolded ... the flowers are there,
but we don't see them."

"Eva dear, my flower ... You were here all this time and
I passed you by."

He remembered their argument the night before he was
arrested. She had said, "Our *shtetl*, our town was poor, the
people plain, honest Jewish and Ukrainian men and women.
It was good to live among them, sing songs, read poems, play
in Yiddish shows. We did not know much Jewish history or
religion, but we knew that our fathers were good husbands,
worked hard, sent their children to schools. When this war
started, our men were the first to volunteer for the army.
Many were killed or wounded. Here in Uzbekistan, many
Uzbeks and Russians I work with made fun of us."

Through the small window, a ray of morning light shone
on Eva's sleeping face. Volodia felt a need for air. He
jumped out of bed, dressed, and went outside. Cold air and
drizzle greeted him. He began to shiver and went to the
center. Fatima, who was on night duty, greeted him sadly.
She was afraid to talk. Aziz Ali came running, but could not
look Volodia straight in the eye. Volodia knew from the first
moment of the interrogation that Aziz Ali must have been the
informer. He was the one who divided the bread he had
gotten from the bakery.

"Impossible," Volodia thought to himself. "Such a good,
old man, so humble, religious -- an informer?"

Volodia asked Fatima to write down all the merchandise
assigned to her. "I need all my stock and supply lists by
tomorrow. I am leaving. They don't want me here anymore."

"We do need you, Vladimir Arionovitz." Fatima turned

around and walked away crying.

Aziz Ali came in and asked, "What did *Chozain* say to Fatima to make her cry?"

"Nothing. I said *salaam* to her."

"Chozain Tarko, by Allah, Fatima is innocent. They called me yesterday morning and asked questions about you. The bakery manager was there too. They wanted Dr. Ivanovna to come, but she refused. She is very upset and very sick. Her eyes are red and swollen from much crying. I swear by Allah, I told them you are a good man."

"Thank you, Aziz Ali. You and Fatima are very fine people."

Volodia walked to the bazaar, got a fresh *lepioshka* -- bread -- a bowl of yogurt, and went back to his room. Eva was awake.

"Where have you been?"

"At the center and the bazaar. Get up and we will share breakfast."

"What are you going to do today?"

"Say goodbye to your mother, Oleg and his mother. I also want to see Tanya and attend to my last duties at the clinic and center."

They ate in silence ... just a few bites ... they could barely swallow. Suddenly Eva burst into tears. "I've got to go to work. See you." She ran out of the door.

Volodia dressed and walked over to Tanya's home. He knocked on the door and heard her voice, "Come in. It's open."

"Where is Bella Gitterman?"

"I sent her to the hospital for some pain relievers. They let you go, I see."

"Until tomorrow."

"Why did you have to threaten him?"

"I did not threaten him. How did you know?"

"Mouhamud Chaidarov called me."

"He believes them?"

"Yes, he does. He has to. You're strangers here, stateless people. This is his town, his Party. Where are you going?"

"They gave me no choice, hard labor or the coal mines. Why are you sitting in the dark? Why don't you go to bed?"

"I made an effort to get up but I couldn't."

Volodia kept questioning her gently. "How is the food situation?"

"We called Rachatayev in Tashkent. He was furious. He himself called *Kolkhoz* Octiabre and made them deliver rice and oil."

"Why didn't you go to bed?"

"I came home so tired last night that I fell asleep in the chair."

"Do you want me to help you?"

"No. Don't come near me. I think I've caught something bad."

"Let me call Dr. Chaidarov."

"No, not now."

"I will call him right now."

Tanya was shivering. Volodia wrapped her in her army coat. He went to the telephone. Babachan answered. "Vladimir Arionovitz? It's good to hear your voice."

"Forgive me for calling so early in the morning. Dr. Ivanovna is very sick."

"Mouhamud is not well himself. Let me wake him up."

Volodia also called Aziz Ali. "Get me a cart immediately. I have to get Dr. Ivanovna to the hospital."

"The bank will not open until eight."

"I want a cart now. Call Kabarov, but hurry!"

Despite Tanya's objection, Volodia picked her up and carried her to her bed. She seemed terribly light. Her breathing was quick, and she was still shivering.

"My God, how much weight you've lost."

"Good. I look younger and can move around faster. Do you still like me?"

"I don't know. I'll think about it."

"You bastard! Why did you have to insult him? Go over to his office and apologize. Maybe he will let you stay. We need you here. I need you here."

"Tanya, if I do this I'll hate myself for the rest of my life.

Anyhow, all the papers are already signed and I have to leave in forty-eight hours."

"I hope you will be well, Volodia. I loved you in my own way."

Volodia sponged her forehead with a wet towel and gave her some water.

"Volodia, I hope you don't leave as our enemy. We all suffer from this war. We struggle to survive even when it kills us. See Volodia, I'm a simple woman, a straight person. I believe in my country. I'm weak and strong, part of the wheel. I will work until I fall, then rise again to do my job. I will shriek and weep and save the last man, woman, and child to the last aspirin tablet and then, slowly, I will die. In fact, I feel I'm dying now. However, I'm not sad because I have served my people."

"You're an unselfish woman, Tanya."

"Don't be foolish. I'm a doctor. Sometimes we come across false people, misguided ones. They bow to themselves. This is why others must suffer. We Party leaders have a war in Europe and a war here, against ignorance, illiteracy, mistrust. I truly hate to see you go. I know you loved the people here as we do. Will you write to us?"

"I will. Just try to get well."

Aziz Ali came to the door. *"Chozain* ready?"

Volodia wrapped Tanya in her military coat and carried her out to the cart.

Dr. Chaidarov came. He was sad. "Sorry, Volodia. I meant to come when you called, but I couldn't get up. I've been sick myself."

"No need to apologize. I understand."

"Thank you, Volodia. I can take no chances here. We must get her to Andizhan."

"So take her! Please, save her!"

"I'm not well enough to escort her alone. Can you leave today instead of tomorrow?"

"I planned to spend this last night with Eva and her mother."

"I understand."

"But I will leave today. You get a stretcher and a truck."
"I will be ready by noon."
"I will be here."
Volodia picked up his papers from the military board, gathered his bundle of belongings from his room, and walked to the bank.
"Eva, can you come outside? I'm leaving today."
"Why today?"
"Tanya is very sick and we must take her to Andizhan."
They walked in silence.
"I was foolish to fall in love with you," said Eva. "I'm a selfish person. I wanted you all to myself. You never fully belonged to me anyhow. You were married to the refugees and to the center."
"Maybe I was foolish to be so concerned with this village and its people, but you have a mother and sister to live for; I had nothing. Now, when I have you, I must leave. However, I don't regret what I did for this village, and I don't regret meeting you. I really love you, Eva. Eva, I've memorized the name Malichov in my heart and mind. As soon as the war is over, if I survive, I will come to your hometown."
"Volodia, let's be honest with each other. You know I love you, but I will never leave my mother."
"We'll talk about it then."
"I will wait for you, Volodia. Please write."
Volodia took her in his arms.
"Volodia, try not to give all your strength to your job. Leave some for after the war," Eva said quietly, the tears coming down her pale face.
"I will, Eva."
"I was happy with you, Volodia."
Eva walked away, smiling through her tears. Volodia remained there until she disappeared. He was thinking, "Will I ever see her again? Oh God, I hope so."

They cleared the approach to the hospital entrance for the truck. Volodia helped arrange the stretcher on the truck. He fastened the chair for Fatima who was to accompany Tanya

and hold the bottle of plasma. Volodia paused just long enough to say goodbye to the Gittermans. With the competence of an experienced nurse, Verotchka made Tanya as comfortable as possible. Volodia signed some forms and gave them to Karabov. Old Aziz Ali kept nervously pulling his mustache. Oleg came running when the covered truck was ready to leave. He could hardly talk. "Volodia, take care."
"Take care of Eva and her family."
"I will." Oleg had a lump in his throat. "I will miss you, my friend."
Say *Do-Pobatsienia* to your mother. God be with her and God be with you, Oleg."
Dr. Chaidarov and Volodia took their places in front, near the driver.
Babachan came running. She handed Volodia a silk handkerchief with freshly baked *lepioshka* and some fruit. *"Salaam!* Allah bless you." She walked away sobbing.
Volodia looked at Kyzyl Kishlak for the last time. The center, the people, the *kibitkas,* bazaar, the Garden of Eden Boulevard with the red banner side by side with the cross and the Star of David. No, he wasn't sorry for the time he had spent here, the sleepless nights and long days he had worked. He really loved the people, the refugees, the local villagers, and above all, Dr. Chaidarov, Tanya, Oleg, and Eva. Thinking of her made him burst into tears.
Sitting next to Volodia and seeing him so grieved was too much for Dr. Chaidarov. He needed all his strength and self control not to shed tears himself. He realized that he was losing two close friends. Tanya was a tireless doctor, and Volodia an efficient technician, and they could not be replaced. His own body was sagging with weariness and pain. He felt like taking Volodia's hand away from his face and closing it with his fingers to show him that he shared his grief and to assure him of his friendship.
Someone was standing in the middle of the road motioning with his arms for the truck to stop. The driver slowed down and stopped. The tall, thin man came over to the side where Volodia was sitting.

"Tarko, forgive me for stopping you. I heard you're leaving. I'm leaving also. They let me go under the condition that I would go voluntarily to a state-owned farm. I can take my wife and children. I was in the militia office to get my papers and saw Oleg Polishenko. He told me the sad news. God be with you, Wolf Tarko."

"God save you and your family, Getzl Gold."

"Fur gesund! Travel in health!"

* * * * *

CHAPTER NINETEEN
Frontline Notes

Frontline News

It was a long way from Kyzyl Kishlak to Andizhan. The truck had to travel slowly. They stopped every hour to put water in the radiator and to check on Tanya. Dr. Chaidarov and Volodia were worried about Tanya's condition because it was getting worse by the hour. Her temperature would not drop. Fatima kept sponging her with water from the stream along the road. Tanya slept as if in a coma.

Dr. Chaidarov was silent and gloomy. He was holding his chest and kept biting his lips.

"I hate to see you go this way, Volodia."

"I hate to leave, Mouhamud. I loved this village."

"You overstepped your authority."

"It was a dangerous situation. There wasn't enough food left for two days."

"I know, but it wasn't your fault."

"Who cares whose fault it was? I had to do something urgently. You were sick."

"Babachan is always overprotecting me."

"It was not Babachan's fault either. You worked like a slave, and you're not in any condition to do so."

"I don't mind working like a slave. The trouble is we live like slaves, always told what to do and always following orders."

"You told me yourself that in order to progress, your people had to learn from the Russians."

"You're naive, Volodia. Some Russians like Kozlov act like masters in an occupied country."

"I don't understand you. You're a leader here, a Party member. You see a drunkard ruining your village and you don't say a word?"

262

"Sorry, Volodia, I've talked too much already. Let's change the subject. Here is an envelope with a *characteristica* -- an evaluation of your work in our village, a travel permit to Tashkent and some money. I don't want you to go to the coal mines. I have some letters addressed to you from the Union of Polish Patriots. I hoped all the time that you would not get their letters and would not discover them. I know I did wrong in not giving them to you, but I needed you here. Now you can go and serve your own Polish Army.

"Volodia, our village would have been a better place with more people like you."

"The world would have been a better place with more doctors like you."

Dr. Chaidarov's eyes were tearful. "Volodia, it's written in our Koran, 'O man! We have created you from a male and a female and divided you into nations and tribes that you might get to know each other.' Indeed, my friend, divided as we are, we have gotten to know each other. I will never forget you, Vladimir Arionovitz Tarko."

They arrived in Andizhan late in the evening. Tanya was in a coma and was immediately admitted to the hospital. Fatima gave Volodia her hand.

"*Salaam*, Allah be with you. Please write to us."

"I will."

"Mouhamud, if something happens to Tanya, take care of the Gittermans. As for me, I can only thank you for being my friend. Thank Babachan for all the *pilaws*, fruits, and this silk handkerchief. I will keep it as long as I live."

"I will keep you in my heart, Volodia, and Kyzyl Kishlak will remember you."

The two men embraced. There were so many things Volodia wanted to say, but he could not utter a word. He walked away quickly, holding back the tears. He rushed to the railroad station to make the night train to Tashkent.

At the station a militiaman stopped him: "Citizen with Red Cross, *documenti* please."

Volodia showed him the envelope Dr. Chaidarov gave him.

"Your name please!"

"Vladislav Tarko."
"Where do you travel?"
"To Riazan, Polish Army, Kosciuszko Division."
"Come with me. I will help you get on the train."
"Thank you officer."
"Slavic armies united will win this war."
"Sure we will win, *doswidanya.*"
"*Doswidanya,* in captured Berlin."
The Russian militiaman gave Volodia a warm handshake,
saluted and jumped off the train.

The friendly handshake reminded Volodia of something he
had read or heard many years ago while working at a hospital
in Poland. It was a quotation by Albert Schweitzer that said,
"No man is ever completely and permanently a stranger to his
fellow man."

Dear Eva,

*With incredible difficulty I managed to get to the Polish
barracks at R. I've been busy from the moment I set foot
in this pine forest. I have the ambition to fight and win
and return home to help build a new free Poland. With all
my experience I have to train again. They have many new
American and Russian ambulances, emergency equipment,
new instruments for treating the wounded in the field and
in the dispensary. They are sending me for special
training to Kuybyshev.*

*All my love to Mom, Anna, Oleg and his mother.
Please write.*

Miss you so much.
V.

———

*I'm finishing this letter that I started a month ago. Our
division fought against the Germans in the Kursk offensive.
I hope you heard about it on the radio. We had many
heroes in our division. They are the same Polish refugees*

who, just months ago, were prisoners in hard labor camps
all over Russia. We had them in our malaria center. I
remember their dried-up faces, eyes sunken in their sockets,
burning with fever, hungry and diseased. Now they are
people again, men fighting for honor, country and freedom.
I am so proud I was part of this fight. We were close to
fifteen thousand former Polish citizens from Western
Belorussia, and the Ukraine, and a little over a thousand
of us are Jews. Many were killed and wounded in this
battle. The Russian officers were really brave and
aggressive.

Our team of doctors still works day and night in the
field ambulatoriums, and field stations, but we are never
tired. We saw evidence of what the Germans did to the
people here, to prisoners of war.

Everywhere we march we find vast pits of bodies, mass
graves of people buried alive. Here and there we find a
survivor. They look completely debilitated. All villages
are obliterated, doomed. We share our rations with any
survivor and we share our hatred for the enemy. We all
have one desire -- Revenge! Victory! I will keep writing
to you as long as I have strength and a piece of paper to
write on. When my letters stop coming, let Mother Celia
say a prayer for my soul. I probably will have died
saying, I love you, Eva.

Volodia

Dearest Eva,

So many weeks have passed and not a word from you.
I often dream and think of you, still holding you in my
arms. The soldiers here receive letters from their parents,
wives and children. It is necessary to have someone
somewhere. For days now we have been traveling on the
road to Belgorod. The villages are burnt out and only
fragments of houses with their chimney stacks remain.
Before departing, the Germans blew up all the buildings
and drove off the inhabitants. The only things they left

were delayed action mines which are difficult to detect, and they cause many casualties. Tonight we cleared a partially blown up church building and set up a medical station and feeding point. The soldiers coming here for help look exhausted and need baths. Their uniforms are riddled with bullet holes and are soaked with mud, dust and blood, but they are all in high spirits. The smell of victory is in the air. After we saw what the enemy did to the people here, we have only one answer for them -- revenge!

You know, the rumble of artillery fire shatters the ground. I have grown used to the roar of planes, to the sound of bursting bombs, but I can't get used to the misery and suffering of the civilian population.

I wanted to finish this letter yesterday, but the wounded kept coming, often two wounded carrying their comrade. We have many casualties waiting outside the church. The benches are red with blood. We are tired, yet, every moment we can spare we build barricades and trenches around the church. We have six orderlies here in our unit; all six are of different nationalities. We work as a team, helping and protecting each other and sharing our meager rations. Our doctors, some of whom are women, often shout and curse. Some surgeons are frustrated by the lack of elementary medical instruments and supplies because much was lost in the heavy bombardments. However, all of them do a great job serving day and night to save young lives. We work by candlelight or with kerosene lamps. Sometimes our patients get delirious from pain and shock. Oh God, so many amputations, and they suffer horribly. All we have for the wounded soldiers is a little morphine. It makes them feel better for a moment, but later they wake up to reality. This medical station will be our home for a while. Heavy fighting is going on in this area. Our soldiers will never retreat again. We are pushing the enemy to their defeat.

Please write. Regards and love to all.

Volodia

Dear Mouhamud,
No letters from you for a long time. Eva's silence hurts me very much. I have sent her telegrams and letters, but never received replies. Did they leave Kyzyl Kishlak? How is Babachan? Tanya Ivanovna? Vera? How is your health? Our N. base is on the banks of the Oka River. Our barracks are clean. The food is good. My new uniform and square Polish cap remind me of home. Many of the soldiers are still sick; their wounds and experiences in faraway places like Vorkuta, Kalima and other labor villages of this great land are still in their memories. They lack enthusiasm to serve or to fight. Their dear ones perished in Katyn or froze to death in Siberia, so they have no taste for the speeches, parades and sermons. The officers are mostly Russians, or Communist-dominated elite who exercise authority and control training, supplies and political indoctrination. I work hard from morning bugle call until I sign off at midnight. Our units are well-trained and our hospital is equipped with modern trucks and ambulances.
We are getting ready for the battle of destiny. My love and indebtedness to you and Babachan.

Volodia

At the end of July 1944, the Third White Russian Army, under Marshall Konstantin Rokossowsky, continued to advance at great speed and encircled the German garrison at Brest-Litovsk, the last Wehrmacht stronghold on the Belorussian front. The vigorous attack on Poland and Lithuania was accelerating with great speed. The Red Army destroyed and annihilated whole German divisions. The offensive of Rokossowsky's Army was followed by convoys of medical aid stations, Evako units, to help treat the wounded soldiers and remove them from the battle areas to hospitals.

Volodia's Evako unit moved slowly on the side roads of small destroyed towns, hamlets, and villages that were littered with thousands of human corpses, local peasants and Germans.

They set up watch stations in burned-out farms which were covered with destroyed military hardware and the trampled bodies of soldiers trapped by explosions of mines and often run over by their own advancing tanks.

Volodia's Evako unit gave aid to passing soldiers with minor wounds. His unit had trucks, horse-driven wagons and an ambulance full of casualties.

On the morning of July 28, his unit advanced into Brest-Litovsk. While giving first-aid to a soldier, one of the horse-drawn wagons struck a mine. The explosion overturned the ambulance and Volodia and his patient were hurled off the road. Volodia was thinking of his patient, still breathing, his patient's arms blown off. He tried to move, to crawl, and then he felt the blood coming from his mouth and nose. He started shaking in shock, felt feeble and lost consciousness.

When he awoke, he started to move his hands in the direction of his face. All he could feel were bandages. He tried to move his legs, but to no avail. He could not recall what had happened. A strange, dreadful feeling overwhelmed him. "Am I dead? Paralyzed? Legless?" Stubbornly he moved his hands against his face again and touched his right ear. Suddenly he felt a sharp stinging pain all over his head. He wanted to scream, to call someone, but no sound came from his mouth. His lips were dry, burning; he wanted to touch them, but they were covered with cotton and bandages. Two tubes were attached to his nose and throat.

"Where am I? What happened to me? Am I dreaming?"

It soon became obvious that he was in a hospital room and that he was wounded. Again he moved his hands in the direction of his legs. There was no pain, no cramps. He panicked. "Are they amputated? No, they're here. But why can't I move them?"

A woman in white came in. He was still in a delirious state. Verotchka? Tanya?

She was tall, blonde. Her eyes looked at him with solemnity mixed with delight. "Good, Comrade Tarko, you are alive. You made it. We tried everything on you. Can you hear me?"

Volodia motioned with his eyes that he could.

"You almost died. Do you want something?"

Volodia tried to say, "I'm thirsty, fire, dry, burning." He could not find the word "water."

The nurse left the room and came back with a wet towel. Volodia felt miserable.

"My name? She called me Tarko. Tarko? Why can't I talk or hear? What do you call that stuff she is holding in her hand? Glass, yes a glass." Volodia tried to say it with his lips, "G l a s s." His tongue suddenly felt a spasm of pain. He pointed his hand again to his lips and finally it came back to him, "W a t e r!"

For many months, Volodia received treatment. Eventually the tube was removed from his windpipe. His ear healed, but his hearing was impaired. He received a new kind of drug to relax the muscles in his legs. Though he exercised with a physical therapist, he had a difficult time standing up without support. The doctors and medics were all good to him. They all worked on his legs, his wounds, and his lacerated spirit. Many times he stumbled and fell or had muscle spasms. Slowly his speech was restored, the splints removed, his front teeth fitted. He walked around the ward with a cane, doing his best to help other wounded soldiers. His memory came back and he started to remember things, people, and places. He started to write again.

One morning, Dr. Kirpanowa, the woman doctor, came to his room followed by four officers wearing long white coats over their uniforms. Dr. Kirpanowa unceremoniously pulled off the bed sheet and said something to a short, distinguished-looking man with piercing, brown eyes and thick, graying eyebrows.

"Incredible! A real miracle. I treated him, but I never believed he would make it." He took the information chart and handed it to the other officers. Volodia was frightened. "Another operation?"

"No, Comrade Tarko. You've had your share. Soon you'll be back fighting the enemy. How did they treat you here?"

"Just wonderfully, *Spasibo*. The doctors, nurses,

everybody."

Next morning he was taken by ambulance to a military *lazaret*. Here Volodia learned to control his facial muscles, to swallow without grimaces and pain. He learned how to eat, a difficult problem for his swollen jaws. His throat still bled daily, but with the help of an ever-changing staff of doctors, orderlies, and therapists, all of them friendly, he was able to break the tension when the bleeding occurred. He gained confidence in himself and the world around him. He roamed the ward holding onto his cane and helped the other patients.

After many months, Volodia was finally told: "You will be ready to go soon. We've done everything we can to help you."

"Yes, I know and I'm thankful."

For the next few days Volodia practiced walking without a cane. All his muscle reactions were normal, except his impaired hearing and the throat bleeding. He took a bath all by himself, was able to dress and did not feel the stiffness and pain in his legs as before.

The next morning they handed him his discharge papers, food cards, letters and citations. He also received a new uniform, his Red Cross badge and a *naprawlenie* -- an assignment-travel permit to Lublin, Poland. Volodia said goodbye to the staff and patients. He was happy to leave the *lazaret* and to realize that he was capable of going back to the army. Inside this *lazaret* he had seen so much human misery and suffering. Young men, some of them still boys, were without legs, arms, paralyzed from the waist down, blind, or deformed. Often he heard men scream, cry, groan, or shout at the top of their lungs from pain, calling their mothers in all languages of the Soviet Union and its allies. Many times he cried with them or lifted himself out of his bed supported by his crutches to try to calm them.

Volodia went to say goodbye to the chief surgeon, who gently checked his ears, the mark of the tracheotomy, and his pulse.

"Comrade Tarko, you are still very weak. I suggest you stay here for more rest. Your knowledge of languages can be of great help here. Please stay on."

"Comrade Doctor, I'm thankful to you for saving my life, but I must go to Poland now. I heard that Marshall Zhukov is already on his way to Berlin. I want to be part of that battle."

"I'm immensely happy for you, Comrade Tarko. Take care of yourself, *dosvidanya*!"

Volodia walked out of the *lazaret* to the sound of army trucks, and people shouting. He was happy that he was able to hear them, and able to walk. He prayed, "Oh God! Help those young wounded soldiers I left inside those walls as you helped me."

* * * * *

CHAPTER TWENTY
Majdanek

Majdanek

On a cold January morning, Volodia arrived in Lublin, Poland. He walked down the train steps onto the platform bedecked with Polish and red flags. The loudspeakers announced that Cracow, an ancient capital of Poland, forty-six miles from the German border, had been captured, and that the Red Army, in another day of great triumphs, had swept twenty-five miles along the highway of Warsaw and advanced to within two hundred miles of Berlin.

"The conquest of Germany is here."

It was snowing. Volodia loved the snow under his feet. More news came from the loudspeakers. "Armored North Divisions from Marshall Ivan Konev's Army overran Silesia. General Eisenhower's Armies on the Duesseldorfer Front reached the Rhine River and are attacking from the Moselle River to the north."

Volodia looked around the railroad. The platform was full of Russian and Polish soldiers, also German war prisoners in their green and light brown army coats. They looked starved, their cheeks deeply hollowed, eyes sunken, rags bound on their feet.

In spite of all the suffering they had caused his people, despite his hatred of all the Nazis, he looked at those starved prisoners with pity. "What did they accomplish with their horrible crimes against the people of Europe? Did the Fatherland improve the lifestyle of this prisoner in rags? What will he receive for his patriotic deeds when he returns home to the Reich, if he ever returns?"

He turned up his coat collar against the cold wind and together with two more passengers, he stepped onto a *droshka* -- a horse-drawn carriage -- to Lublin.

The city of Lublin, the streets and old buildings were all intact, full of people -- women, children, soldiers arguing with the vendors, old black-shawled *babushkas.* Young girls leaning on soldiers' arms were strolling in the snow, smiling. Volodia wondered at the differences here compared to one of the devastated cities in Russia. Everything looked the same as before the war. Those who had survived, lived, loved, and smiled. Only the dead soldiers, the killed civilians, the Jews lay in the mass graves of Kursk, Oriel, Babi Yar, Rovno, Lutzk.

After he had walked a few blocks, his legs started to hurt. The fresh air made him feel hungry. The smell of hot cabbage and *kelbasa* hit his nostrils. He stepped into a small restaurant and sat at the far corner near the back door.

A waitress came and took his order: a glass of warm milk and a piece of honey cake. He looked around the tables. People were drinking beer or lemonade, eating omelettes, knockwursts, *kelbasa,* and chatting raucously.

Volodia looked for a familiar face, familiar eyes. There were none. He was a stranger here, an alien in his own country. He was glad to hear Polish, to walk on this snowy soil, but the faces, the loud laughter of this throng of people, the old familiar slang, did not bring him any closer to the people here.

Volodia paid for his meal and left the restaurant. He walked along the street in the snow still searching, looking for a face he would recognize as Jewish. A young, tall woman with laughing blue eyes walked by his side, "Would you like to love me, *Kochany* -- darling?"

"No, dearie. I have to go to Majdanek."

"Jesus Maria! Why do you want to go there?" She shrugged her shoulders and walked away in the snow.

Volodia hired a *droshka* and asked the driver to take him to Majdanek.

All he was told was that he should go to an army unit stationed near Lublin by that name. When his Evako hospital had advanced in the spring of 1944 into the Ukraine and Belorussia, he had heard of atrocities and mass murders committed by the Nazis. He had seen the mass graves and had heard of deportations of whole communities to concentration and forced labor camps. However, he had never heard of this murder factory six miles outside Lublin. He had seen villages burned down, inhabitants murdered and hanged. He had heard about Babi Yar, about terror and humiliation, of whole towns starved to death. Mass graves of women and children and the smell of decaying corpses had followed him until the day he was wounded. When Majdanek was captured by the Red Army in July 1944, Volodia was in a Vitebsk hospital half dead.

The gates looked like all army settlements or bases, fenced with barbed wire. A long line of civilians with travel bags on their backs were standing there waiting for the sentry to let them in. There were many Russian, American and French officers walking in and out of the gates. Volodia noticed some Jewish eyes among the crowd and he asked *"Amcho?"*

"Yo!" they answered in Yiddish, "we just returned from Russia."

Volodia looked at their faces. They looked worse to him than the war prisoners he had seen in Lublin; faces yellow and gray from tuberculosis, starvation and frostbite, wounds that had left holes in their skin, their toothless jaws. However, their eyes held a gleam of hope. Volodia must have looked very ill to them. One grabbed his arm. "Hey, brother, you look terrible. You're bleeding from your mouth."

"It's nothing."

Volodia looked at the man. He was young, in his early twenties, gray-haired, yellow-skinned, a bluish-black shadow around his eyes.

Volodia presented his documents to the officer at the inner gate. With his papers in his hand he was sent to the ambulatorium, the medical complex, a block of green barracks. There he joined a group of newly arrived recruits and was marched to a barrack named *Bad und Disinfektion* for a shower.

"In this concrete barrack," explained the accompanying sergeant, "the Germans daily gassed thousands of Jews with

Zyclon gas. From here the *Zydys* -- Jews -- were shipped by lorries to the crematoria and mass graves."

So here he was, Volodia -- Wolf Ben-Aharon Tarko, ready to take a shower and cleanse his body for service to the New Democratic Republic of Poland in a barrack where his people had died. And here were his fellow soldiers around him joking, making wisecracks. Their laughter made him tremble almost convulsively.

Volodia picked up his new uniform and a Red Cross first aid kit of his own. He got a bed with a blanket and small pillow in a clean barrack near the ambulatorium building. Then he went to the mess hall. It was crowded, thick with warm steam and the smell of cigarettes, smoked meats, and sauerkraut. He entered the ambulatorium and asked the nurse for a glass of cold milk. Volodia pointed to his throat, "I have difficulties swallowing." The nurse came back with a deep dish of oatmeal and milk. Volodia was grateful.

"Thank you, sister. I'm Vladislaw Tarko. I'm assigned to work with Major Gurewski in this ward."

"Oh good. We are short of help here. A lot of emergencies and we're short of everything, even bedpans. Some of the patients are so weak they can't walk to the toilets. Oh, forgive me. I'm Sister Helena Janicka from Czestochowa."

"How did you get here?"

"In 1939, I went to look for my father who was a war prisoner in Belorussia."

"Did you find him?"

"No, but I was arrested and sent to Siberia. I returned with the Polish Army. I have to go now. It was nice meeting you, *Panie* Tarko."

"Thank you for the *kasha* and milk."

Volodia worked the midnight shift. A truckload of Polish repatriates was delivered in great secrecy after midnight. Only a few of the patients were able to walk in by themselves. The rest had to be helped or carried on stretchers. The orderlies put them up temporarily on cots and served them tea with crackers. Volodia organized an emergency bath in a nearby barrack where they kept the ambulatorium laundry. He was

exhausted, his throat was twitching with a gnawing pain, but
the faces of these wounded repatriates were so shocking to him
that whatever he had seen in his years as a medic looked
insignificant by comparison. He tried to talk to them, but to
no avail. It seemed that their long experience in Russia had
made them fearful to say anything to the strangers in white,
even if they spoke to them in Polish.

After duty, Volodia went back to his room. As tired as he
was he slept only a few hours. Something in him was pulling
him again to the *Bad und Disinfektion Kammer*. He walked
around the barracks following a crowd of people and listening
to a guide describing Majdanek.

"The concrete barracks were served by civilians. When the
transports arrived, they invited the people to sit on benches to
rest and leave their belongings. They undressed here and were
asked to step into the windowless bathhouse; first the men,
then women and children. The dark, concrete boxes were
locked and the gassing took place. First some hot air was
pumped in, then the Zyclon gas was showered down on them.
It took only a few minutes and two hundred people were
killed. One and a half million Jews died here.

"Six gas chambers worked here constantly. From here the
corpses were carted to the crematorium. The victims'
belongings were sorted here and shipped to Germany."

Volodia found himself trembling again. He was hungry,
but he did not feel like eating. He went back to his barrack,
took his shoes off and lay down on his bed. He closed his
eyes, but was awakened by a call to a paramedics orientation
meeting. Captain Szymanski provided information on personal
needs for active duty in the new frontier areas. The briefing
was short, no discussion, no questions. On the way out of the
session, a priest offered his thin hand to him.

"Tarko!"

"Father Gursky! Oh, thank God!" The two men embraced.
"Chwala Bogu! You're alive! What happened to you?"

"Our ambulance was blown up by a mine. I was
wounded."

"Are you all right now?"

"Thank God, still weak, but thank God."

They walked slowly to the barracks. Father Gursky appeared very thin in the oversized army coat he wore.

"Father, why don't you go on ahead without me. It is nasty, and I have to walk slowly."

"Tarko," he said softly. "I have plenty of time. I'd rather walk with you. Do you mind?"

Volodia's hand trembled when he opened the door. "Please, come in."

It was dark in the barrack and cold. The wind blew through the window frames. Volodia took off his coat and shoes and lay down on his bed. Father Gursky did not utter a word. He just sat there, murmuring quietly to himself, "Holy Mary, Mother of God."

Volodia must have fallen asleep. His thoughts, and now his dreams, were of gas chambers, the repatriates, the Garden of Eden Boulevard, Kyzyl Kishlak jail, Kursk mass graves. He opened his eyes. Father Gursky stood beside his bed staring sadly at him.

"Tarko, how do you feel now?"

"What did I do?"

"Your cry pierced the heavens. You searched for God."

"What did I say?"

"'God, where are you?'"

"Where is He, Father Gursky? Where was He when all this around here happened?"

"Tarko, He is here with us. He returned us from the most remote corners of the Soviet Union, a crowd, ragged and hungry, sick, and humiliated. We're joining together to rebuild our country, our army, our shattered beliefs. God is with us Tarko. Our country will rise again. We must hope. We're going to be free again." Father Gursky sat on the bed, tired and sad. "Talk to me."

Volodia could not find a word to say. His heart was empty. He had no energy to get up when he was called to duty.

Volodia worked all night in the ambulatorium, a hospital in miniature. Orderlies and nurses rolled stretchers in and out.

Doctors were working around a metal operating table. The corridor was full of waiting wounded soldiers.

Volodia fed the patients who were unable to move their hands, and helped them to the lavatories. He felt dazed and moved as if asleep, dreaming. Soon things fell out of his hands. His white coat was red with blood. He did not remember eating anything that day. His legs hurt, but he managed to work through the night. He went back to his barracks. The only thing he felt he had in common here was the *Bad und Disinfektion* chamber.

After a week of briefings and lectures about the Kosciuszko Division, after parades and sermons, Volodia got an assignment to the Polish Army hospital in Neugard, a small town on the frontier near Stettin. He was also given thirty days leave to go anywhere he wished. He questioned going back to Lodz. Father Gursky had told him that all the Jews of Lodz had died in Chelmo, Auschwitz, Ravensbrook, and Sackshausen. The last Jews of the Lodz Ghetto were murdered and buried in mass graves on January 17, two days before the Russian Armies entered the City.

"Maybe there were some Jews left, hidden somewhere."

"I walked in the ghetto streets ... nothing except rats, flies, and corpses." Father Gursky was depressed. "All my family were killed, deported to Germany. They robbed our hospital clean."

"I still would like to go. I must."

"God be with you, Tarko."

Before leaving, Volodia went to the "museum" again. He had to go, as much as it grieved him. Again he followed a group of Russian officers and listened to a guide, a middle-aged civilian, gray-haired and gray-faced, explaining the "system" of the death factory. "Only a few minutes and they were gone."

"They! They! They!" Volodia's imagination saw his family, his grandparents, uncles, aunts, neighbors, his girlfriend and her parents. They all were 'they' and they had perished here, or in Chelmo, Auschwitz. What other camps had Father

Gursky mentioned? Volodia still suffered from a loss of hearing and temporary blackouts. Still, he followed the Russians and the guide to the end. They all walked on a field where white ashes had melted the snow. They stepped on bits of bones, skulls. The guide expertly explained, "A layer of manure and then the cabbage seeds -- good *capusta* -- sauerkraut. It is used to feed our soldiers now."

Volodia felt as if someone were strangling him. "For a week now you've eaten borscht and cabbage soup fertilized by the ashes of your own people," he cried to himself.

He followed the group to the crematorium and the furnaces. The smell of carbol and the odor of decomposed human bodies was still there.

"Normally," the guide explained, "two thousand bodies were burned here daily, but the Germans were not satisfied. They were eager to kill more, so they shot and burned whole transports of men, women, and children outside in the woods. They sprinkled gasoline over them and set them afire while many of them were still alive."

A Russian officer walked away bewildered and started shouting, "Filthy Fascist Murderers! I will kill! I will kill the sons-of-bitches! *Yey Bogu* -- By God!"

"I knew I would find you here. Come on, I'll take you back to your barracks." Father Gursky took his arm and led him away.

"Tarko, are you awake?"

"Yes, Father."

"Why are you sitting in the dark?"

"My eyes hurt."

"We've had enough darkness in our lives, haven't we?"

"We still have."

"With the Lord's help, we will see the light soon."

"Where is the Lord? In *Disinfektion Kammer II*?"

"He is in you."

"I am death and so is He."

"So why did you come here?"

"I hoped God was still alive."

"He is Tarko, He is."

"Where? In the barrels of human fat? In the mountains of children's shoes, in the mountain of ashes? Perhaps in Chopin Warehouse among the balls of human hair?"

"Tarko, I understand. You're tired and sick, but this is not the way to think and feel. You're a Jew, the eternal Jew who survived the Romans, the crusaders, the Russian Czars, the Bolsheviks and now the Nazis. I heard in Lodz that your people fought back in Warsaw, Vilno, Bialystok. They had nothing to fight with and fight for, but they did fight back. Now, on the threshold of a new beginning, you don't want to live? Tarko, what's happened to your spirit? We are winning this war, victory is near. I remember you used to quote from the Sayings of the Sages, By force you must live."

"I cheated and fooled my patients, my wounded soldiers. I don't believe in it."

"It helped your patients, it helped me. Many times I was thinking of you."

"One and a half million people died here. Why? Why?"

"I don't know the answer. Ten thousand Polish officers died in Katyn. Hundreds of thousands died in Warsaw, in Siberia, in German Labor camps. Why?"

"Why do people kill each other?"

"They are blind with hatred. God forgive them."

"God needs forgiveness himself. Where was He when all this happened?"

"Tarko, can I turn on the lights?"

"I don't care."

Father Gursky switched on the light bulb.

"Jesus Maria! Look at yourself!"

The pillow was soaked with blood coming out of Volodia's mouth.

"What did you do?"

"Nothing. My wound is bleeding."

"Why did you come here? Why didn't you stay in the hospital?"

"I wanted to go to the front ... to kill Nazis."

"You never killed before, did you?"

"I will now, until I die."

"Stop talking. Don't move."

Father Gursky ran out of the barrack and returned with Sister Helena Janicka. "Please, come with us."

Sister Helena and Father Gursky helped him get up and walked him to the ambulatorium. Major Gurewski, a stocky man, gray-haired and pale, talked with Father Gursky, "This exhibit of Nazi bestiality should not be shown to wounded soldiers. I have been here for two months and still can't look at that inferno." Dr. Gurewski gave Volodia an injection to stop the bleeding. Sister Helena came back with a clean khaki shirt.

"Did you eat anything today?" Dr. Gurewski asked in a friendly voice.

"No, Major Gurewski. I didn't feel hungry today. I saw the Jew-cabbage fields."

Dr. Gurewski swallowed hard.

"What do you feel like?"

"Drowsy."

Father Gursky helped him back to his barrack. The injection started working and in minutes Volodia was asleep.

When Volodia woke up, Father Gursky was at his bedside.

"Feel better, Tarko?"

"Yes."

"Here is some cold tea."

"Is that all a base chaplain has to do? Watch over me?"

"I'm partly responsible for making a medic out of you, remember?"

"Oh yes, I remember and I'm thankful."

"I spoke to Major Gurewski and he said the sooner you leave this place, the better off you'll be."

"When can I leave?"

"As soon as you feel a little stronger."

"If I survived *Disinfektion Kammer II,* I'm the strongest man on this planet."

"Stop talking about it. Look to tomorrow. Forget the horror."

"Never! I will live with it forever. I'm sorry for them.

How dare we forget?"

"You must if you want to live."

"Who said this world is worth living in?"

"You must live. There are so many wounded. They need you."

"Forgive me for being so bitter. I was so glad you were here when I woke up."

Father Gursky had a smile on his face. "Are you going directly to Pomerania?"

"No. I have four weeks leave. I'm planning to visit some friends."

Father Gursky whispered, "Holy Mary. I hope you find them, someone."

"I hope so, too."

"I hope we meet someday, Tarko, in a better world."

"God willing, Father Gursky. You gave me courage."

"You gave me my confidence back as a servant of my faith."

"You know that I am of another faith."

"No, you're wrong. We are all of one creed, one belief. We are all children of one Heavenly Father."

Volodia stretched out his hands. "Help me get up."

"With pleasure."

* * * * *

CHAPTER TWENTY-ONE
Malichov

Malichov

Even with Father Gursky's care, Volodia was dangerously dispirited. Father Gursky's dream of a new, free world to come was overshadowed by the memory of the crematorium and the faces of the Polish officers, the returnees from Siberia. What a fraud and deception to talk to those people about a new Slav Brotherhood and eternal friendship. He tried to think of Zhitomir, Malichov, his new assignment in Pomerania, but Majdanek obsessed him.

Volodia had now one spark of hope, Eva. What a long time since he had left Kyzyl Kishlak, months in training, on the front lines, in battle, in hospitals. He felt impatient with the train for Malichov moving so slowly. He was afraid he would not make it to Malichov and that Majdanek would overtake him before he would get there. Would Eva be there? Would she recognize him? She had heard nothing of him and he nothing from her for so long. Would she be surprised? Shocked by the way he had changed?

The train was speeding through a countryside of bare fields. People were working on the road repairing telegraph cables, rebuilding destroyed bridges. The train stopped at many out-of-the-way stations to wait for military transports to go by. People jumped off the train to get hot water, or to buy a potato pancake. Passengers sat on their bundles drinking *kipiatok* -- hot water -- or vodka or just rubbing hands to keep warm. Many were sitting on the wagon floor huddled together sleeping. Volodia was hungry. In his Red Cross kit, he had some bread and lumps of sugar, but he was afraid to eat, afraid he would start bleeding again. His lips were dry from thirst. He needed to go to the washroom, but he realized he would never be able to reach it in this overcrowded wagon. An old, friendly *babushka* offered him some *kasha*. "You look pale, my son. You should have stayed some more at the hospital. But I know you are anxious to go home, huh?"

After Majdanek, it was good to travel in this overcrowded compartment. The warm expressions of the travelers' hungry faces, their friendly gestures, their naturalness was a good sight after the horrible things he had seen. Volodia looked at the face of the old woman who had offered him some *kasha*. She was wrinkled, gray, her eyes expressed suffering, and sadness, but she showed patience, kindness, and warm generosity.

Volodia's mind carried him away in dreams. She could be the mother of Tanya, of Oleg, of Father Gursky, Vera, or Sister Helena. She looks like my own grandmother, the same sad, kind, and loving eyes. What divides people so that they hate each other and make war? What makes mothers raise sons who murder children, who wipe out whole cities, who make soap from human flesh? He remembered Kursk, the outflanked Germans retreating, leaving completely destroyed cities, villages full of women's and children's corpses in mass graves, hanging men, raping children, starving Red Army prisoners to death.

Again the shadow of Majdanek haunted him. The *Bad und Disinfektion II*, the *Effekten Kammer* with the mountains of women's clothes, the barracks full of baby shoes, boots and galoshes, the acres of cabbage fields fertilized by human ashes, human dust, the furnaces and the concrete operating table where educated men had extracted gold teeth from the victims before they were burned in the ovens. What would happen after the war? What would happen to people like himself? He had heard that nothing was left in Lodz. Where would he go? Would Eva be there, in Malichov? Maybe she was still in Kyzyl Kishlak? Or somewhere in Russia? Perhaps Oleg was back and he knew where Eva was.

Someone was singing a sad song in the back of the compartment.

"Znayt vse moyu kvartiru -- Everybody knows my dwelling, *Tam shivu sredi mogil* -- There I live among the graves."

Would they continue living among the graves, with walls separating them, with mistrust, hate, and fear of the NKVD, the

secret police? Or would the past disappear like a nightmare
and a new dawn come?

"Know the night itself will vanish
Cloud lands drift and melt away;
Once again will skies shine azure
Stars by night and sun by day?"

Who wrote this song? Where did he hear it last? In
Riazan at the Polish Army barracks? In Ekaterina's home?
Why can't the people of the world be as close as the people on
this train? Like the people in the army *lazarets* and hospitals?

Time, dates, had never had any significance for Volodia.
During the years in Russia, he had not looked forward to the
next day, but just hoped for the next hour to go by. He had
no calendar, no watch. He had celebrated no holidays and no
birthdays.   He had little time for newspapers, and if a
newspaper had gotten to him, he had never looked for the date.
The important thing for him was to have things done, behind
him, past. A day gone was a day nearer to victory, closer to
Poland. Now, for the first time in years, he traveled eastwards.
Time and distance became important to him.   How much
longer would he have to wait to see Eva? How many more
miles to Malichov?

Zhitomir had suffered severely from bombings and fire.
The city had changed hands in fierce attacks and counter-
attacks until the Germans were wiped out. Now people, mostly
women, were working, rebuilding the devastated railroad
station. Volodia looked around the platform. It was cold and
windy. The women were drawing, hauling little wagons with
bricks, cement blocks. Some were dressed in rags, but they
sang while working in the cold.

The restaurant was closed, but some women were selling
hot borscht and baked turnips.   There was no train to
Malichov; the bridge had been blown up and was being
repaired. Volodia was advised to wait on the road and get a
ride by truck, horse wagon, or tractor.

So this is Malichov, the beautiful village that Eva and her
mother were longing to go back to, the *shtetl* she was singing

and dreaming about. The driver of the wagon, an old, Ukrainian, kept preparing Volodia.

"All Jews who did not escape were shot. Malichov is almost completely destroyed. The remaining population perished from hunger and cold. The young ones were taken to Germany to work in ammunition factories or mobilized forcefully into Ukrainian units in the German Army under Bandera. Whatever the partisans did not have time to destroy, the Germans sent to Rovno, to the German headquarters, and from there to Germany. The Bandera soldiers helped the Germans hunt out Russians, Jews, and Ukrainian Party members, and hang them. Now we are free again. We still suffer from hunger, but we have hope now that the war will be over soon, that many of our sons will return home and rebuild our villages."

"Have some of your people returned yet?"

"Only a few came back from Russia and Asia, but they did not stay. No homes, no work here, and no food."

The wagon stopped in the center of Malichov. The whole street of houses was burned out. Old men and women collected pieces of wood in the rubble of the wrecked houses.

"Citizen, where is your village council or militia station?"

"Who are you looking for?"

"A family named Markes. A widow and two daughters."

"Oh yes, a half kilometer from here. You can't miss it. The only two houses on the road. Got some *machorka* -- tobacco?

"Sorry, I don't smoke. Would you like a lump of sugar?"

"Anything will do."

The old man took Volodia all the way down the road as far as he could. The mud was deep and covered with snow.

Volodia paid the man and thanked him.

"Hope your folks are alive and well."

"Thank you."

An uneasiness gripped Volodia. He walked in the snow directly to the door, his heart beating quickly. He felt dizzy and was shivering with excitement. He knocked. A tall, skinny man opened the door.

"Does the Markes family live here?"

Someone inside the house heard his voice and came running, pulling him into the dark room. A woman with a familiar voice embraced him and cried, "Oh Volodia! Volodia, you're alive! Oh God! Come in."

The tall man lighted a homemade candle and Volodia recognized Celia. A large room with windows, covered with tin to keep the wind out, a small old table, a box that served as a dresser, and two beds were the only furnishings. Celia, gray-haired and thin, was shaking her head crying, "Volodia, Volodia!"

Between the exclamations of Celia, her greetings and crying, the tall man carried in some wood and made a small fire on a wood stove. Volodia hoped he would not start bleeding for he felt his wound starting to hurt.

"Where are Eva and Anna?"

"Anna stays in a *kolkhoz* here. Eva is working in the bank. She will be home soon. God, you're alive. We had a letter from Kyzyl Kishlak that you were killed in action. We did not believe it, but God, it's more than a year now. Why didn't you write?"

"I did. I did. But I never received any answers."

"Our mail was held up. We had it bad after you left. Naimov was transferred out of the bank and Eva lost her job. If it hadn't been for Oleg, we would have starved."

"How is he?"

"A sick man, but good to us. He got us back home. It took us weeks and weeks. Our home is in ashes. Oleg got us this roof over our heads."

"Did many return?"

"Only a few families came back. They don't stay. They move to Kiev, Korostin. Our village is destroyed, no petrol, no food, no coal, no firewood. Can I give you something? How about some tea? Wait, someone is at the door."

Eva!

She was wearing a shabby old coat, a headcover and heavy boots. When she came in, Volodia got up. Neither of them could utter a word. He took her in his arms. She was shivering; her hands were frozen. She looked thin, undernourished, but beautiful.

"Eva. How are you."

"You look pale, Volodia. How was it?"

"Horrible."

"We got a letter, a yellow slip, that you were killed."

"I know. Celia told me."

"I still have it. Do you want to see it?"

"No. Please sit down. I want to look at you."

"Why didn't you write?"

"I did, Eva, until I got hit."

"They must have kept our letters."

"You still don't know?"

Celia brought some tea. Volodia unpacked his little bag with bread and sugar.

"What kind of work are you doing, Eva?"

"Same old stuff. The money isn't much, but once a day we get a hot meal. If it hadn't been for Oleg ... "

"How is he?"

"The same. His mother is very sick. When he is away working in the villages around the area, I stay over at her house. Ekaterina now calls me 'daughter.'"

"She is a fine woman."

"She is, and so is Oleg. We are very close now. He is all to me, a father, brother, friend.

"I was very sick when you left. For weeks I suffered from depression. I lost my job. Oleg supported me. He got papers for our return home. Oleg was near me when I needed him. We both mourned you. We both loved you."

"I still love you."

"You're still dear to us, to me. But Oleg can't live without me. He really loves me. He is good to Mother. He is decent. I'm sorry, Volodia. I hope you understand and forgive me. I loved you and was happy with you, but now everything has changed. I changed. I know I sound cruel. Reality here is very cruel. There are thousands of women here without husbands, men. The girls here are jealous that I have Oleg who is young and decent. I'm sorry, Volodia, that I have to say it. I was always honest with you."

"How is life here now?"

"Miserable. We are all sick -- there is so little food, clothing. There are thieves, plunderers, and murderers wandering around. Oleg has a hard job. Some Ukrainians hate him because he married a Jewess."

"Are you married to him?"

"No, but they think we are. He doesn't want to hurt his mother. Besides, we don't want to bring children into such a world of suffering and hatred. So much jealousy, suspicion. There are secret Ukrainian nationalists who hate the Russians, murder them. They even threatened Oleg's life. No, this is no place to have children."

"Must you stay here?"

"Maybe we will move to Kiev or back to Russia. The man who lives here with us has a home in Saratov. He works here on the railroad, repairing the bridge. He offered us his home there. He is Russian. What are you going to do?"

"I'm on my way to Germany now. God willing, if I survive, I will leave Europe."

"Where will you go? No country in the world wants the Jews."

"I will go to Palestine."

"The English will not let you in."

"I will fight the English."

"What happened to the new, free Poland you were always talking about?"

"Nothing is left there for us. My city remains, but the Jews were killed. I've had enough of Europe."

"Do you think it's worth living at all?"

"I don't know. On the front line, in the hospital, I was hoping to live for you, but now I want to live to see our victory over the Germans."

"Volodia, don't feel that anything has changed between us. We are as close as we were in Kyzyl Kishlak, but then we were selfish and just wanted to have our own happiness. Now I share it with Oleg and with our mothers. I care more. Believe me, Oleg comes home so tired, sick, and weak that our living together is not important. What counts is mutual devotion. This is what keeps us alive. Oleg hates to work at the militia. He wanted something better, but he does it for his mother and me. He actually supports both families."

"Where did your mother go?"

"To lie down. She is a very sick woman and the excitement was a little too much for her. Besides, she thinks you will not understand the situation here. Volodia, do you feel strong enough to walk with me to Ekaterina's house?"

"I can try."

"Oleg will be very happy to see you. Besides, I saved the manuscripts and documents you left in Kyzyl Kishlak. I am sure you want them."

Volodia and Eva got dressed and quietly left the house. It was cold and dark. Eva held onto his arm as in the old days in Kyzyl Kishlak. They walked slowly and in silence. Eva knew all the mudholes in the road.

"You know, Volodia, I'm so happy you're alive and so glad to see you. You look awful though."

"Eva, will we ever meet again?"

"I doubt it. We can't even get permits to visit Kiev. Look, Volodia, this was once a beautiful town. Here was our club, our Yiddish school, our Pioneer Palace. The Germans hanged the remaining Jews from this building. Later they killed the others outside of town in the brewery where my father used to work."

Eva kept talking and holding onto his arm. She carried his Red Cross kit. They came to a small house. Eva quietly opened the door. It was a side door, a stairway to the attic.

"You go up there and rest for a while. Ekaterina is very sensitive and religious. She thinks you're dead, and seeing you will be a great shock to her. Here are some wood matches."

The attic was clean. The neatness reminded him of his little room in Kyzyl Kishlak. The large metal bed was covered with a colorful bedspread. Volodia turned on the kerosene lamp, sat down on the old chair, exhausted. "Why did I come here? What have I got to offer her? I'm wounded, sick, still in the army. Where can I take her? To what country? What right did I have to come here without writing to her first?"

The door opened and Oleg came in. They embraced and cried.

"Volodinka!"

"Oleg! So good to see you."

"So good to see you alive. Come on down. We've told Mother already."

Eva served potatoes baked in fatback, homemade bread, fried dry-fish, and vodka. Volodia could hardly eat anything. Everybody was chattering, asking, sharing. There was talk about the war, about Dr. Chaidarov, and about Tanya Ivanovna, who had come back to Kyzyl Kishlak after surgery in Andizhan, and died at work in her hospital. Oleg talked of poisoned minds, enemies, lack of safety, and lack of food, of Jews returning home and running away scared. The excitement and the vodka made them talk until the kerosene lamp burned out. It got cold. Ekaterina went back to her room. Eva prepared a pillow on the sofa.

"Volodia, stay here overnight. It's much warmer here. The toilet is outside to the right. Watch the mud."

Oleg and Eva disappeared. He heard them go up the steps to the attic. He turned off the lamp, sat down for a moment to think, and fell asleep in his clothes.

It was still dark outside when Eva awakened him. There was hot milk and bread on the table.

"Where is Oleg?"

"He went to get a horse and wagon to take you to Zhitomir."

"Why all the trouble?"

"He wants it this way. You look sad."

"I am just tired. I am deeply content. You are in good hands, Eva. I have nothing to offer you. My future is so uncertain."

"I'm so very happy you're alive."

Eva turned her face to him and he saw she was crying. Volodia was overwhelmed by a feeling of guilt and uneasiness. He felt that he had disrupted a certain calm here, an arrangement by which people live under strained circumstances and daily tensions.

"Eva, are you happy here?"

"It's not exactly the dream of my life. Who is happy now? So much misery. So little food. I thank God for Oleg. He keeps us all alive."

"What is the future for you?"

"Who thinks so far ahead? We are working, cleaning up the mess the war left us. It is still my town, my home, the only one I ever had. Unfortunately, it is easier to clean up the debris and destruction than clean out the hatred among people here. Even if Oleg were not around, I would have no right to ask you to build your future here. These people would never accept you in their midst, and I would never want to raise a family in this place. Volodia, I must say goodbye to you here. I have to go to work. I hope you will survive this war. Thank you for coming to see us. Take my love with you. There is no place here for our love. Time and life are tyrants; they worked against us. Take care of yourself."

"Say goodbye to Mother and Anna for me."

"I know Mother will never forgive me for not bringing you back to see her, but I know her health. It was too much seeing you last night. It will be hard for her to see you leave."

Eva kissed him on the cheek. Volodia controlled his facial muscles so as not to show the grimace of pain, keeping back the taste of blood in his mouth. Eva left. Volodia just stood there silently, swallowing the warm taste of his own blood. Oleg came. They left in silence, quietly so as not to wake Ekaterina. They traveled in silence. Volodia held a piece of folded bandage on his lips. They arrived in Zhitomir. It was still early morning, but the railroad station was already full of people. Oleg put his arms around Volodia.

"I want you to know, I would not be able to live without her. I hope you understand."

Oleg greeted the railroad militiaman and asked him to help Volodia, a wounded officer returning to the front, get a seat on the train. Oleg and Volodia embraced.

"Take care of Eva."

"Take care of yourself. Eva told me to give you this. It will keep you warm."

Oleg took off his scarf and placed it around Volodia's neck. "Thank you. Remember me to your mother. God be with you, Oleg."

"God protect you, Volodia."

Oleg bent over and kissed Volodia on both cheeks. *"Dopobatshienia!"*

The militiaman took Volodia to a side door and from there to a wagon to be attached to the train. Volodia pulled himself together, took a pill from his Red Cross kit and discovered his notes and documents from Kyzyl Kishlak, some sandwiches, bread with thin slices of fatback, neatly wrapped in a piece of newspaper.

He touched the scarf around his neck and felt warm. The scarf felt like the hands of a child encircling his neck in a tender embrace. Wasn't this the scarf Eva had been wearing yesterday when he first saw her walking into her mother's home? Was this all she could offer him at this moment to remember her by? He would take care of it. He would win this war and take this token of her love with him wherever life might lead him.

Volodia sat back in his corner and listened to the radio voice coming from the station, "Danzig is under attack by the heroic armies under Zhukov and Rokossovsky, the enemy is closing in from all directions. Polish Army units are attacking Gdynia. After fierce street fights, the Polish flag was hoisted over the city. Over ten thousand Germans were taken prisoner. The streets and roads are littered with enemy dead."

Volodia closed his eyes. He listened to the railroad whistle and actually heard a cannonade of bombardments, planes, tanks, and artillery. He saw himself in battle, in Berlin, calm, assured of victory. A man with a Red Cross badge on his arm giving aid to wounded soldiers, gathering them into ambulances, carrying them on field stretchers. He heard trumpets shouting, shells bursting. He saw Dr. Chaidarov and Father Gursky, Oleg, and Tanya, but nowhere could he find Eva ... just a scarf wrapped around his neck, protecting him from wind, noise, bullets. He was running forward with his unit, attacking bunker after bunker, street after street. His throat ached; his legs hurt. The wind had torn off his clothes, his uniform with the Red Cross badge, and his cap with the Polish eagle on it. In the battle, Tanya, Chaidarov, Vera, Oleg, Boris, Father Gursky, all fell one by one. They disappeared; Volodia was alone. He moved forward screaming, shivering among tangled flesh, corpses of friends and enemies. Here they were beside him, and here they disappeared, never to be seen again. He was alone on a field, a desert of destruction, alone and naked, he and a scarf that felt like the hands of a child.

Volodia woke up. The train was moving forward to the Polish border. Despite the grim disappointments he had lived through in the last twenty-four hours, he took with him to Poland, to the front, the memory of people he had really loved and over five years of frustration and friendship in Russia -- a gigantic country whose millions of people, he hoped and prayed, would win this war over the enemy.

"God willing!"

* * * * *

Poetic Notes of
Volodia Tarko

Attack

Tanks roar on the roadway,
our ambulance window panels
tremble, the ground rattles,
the icy passage cracks.

The dark horizon is lit by
bursting artillery shells,
our troups furiously attack
the enemy barricades.

We follow the fighting units,
attend to the wounded and fallen.
The roar of the tanks in action
silences the cries for help.

When the morning star rose
we noticed our commanding officer
was missing, the head nurse's face,
her nose and lips bleeding.

She continued moving in shock,
stopping, lifting the wounded,
giving them water, first aid,
suddenly her eyes closed.

She fell asleep, exhausted?
No, comrade. She is dead, expired.
I can't cry, but my hands tremble,
we march on, over enemy barriers.

Lodz

I was lonely, cold, hungry, unhappy.
Why do I remember you so longingly?
My girlfriend is no longer there,
why do I miss the home where I grew up?

On my cobblestoned streets there were
no trees on the sidewalks, why do I dream
of flowers? I grew up with no place to play,
the only game I knew was gazing at the stars.

After school I studied with my grandfather.
He was killed during the war in Chelmno.
In my dreams he's still here, so is Lodz,
my girlfriend, they are all alive and well.

They all walk the streets of my city, Lodz,
a thousand alleys and hundreds of prayer houses.
An amalgam of Jews in long and short caftans,
round, black hats, bearded faces hurrying to work.

Pictures flash in my mind: Holiday parades,
singing crowds carrying flags, icons, placards,
Jews hiding in the gates, afraid of violence,
the beer halls spitting out drunken derelicts.

Fanatics explode with roaring hostility
against Jews on their way to work, to study.
I weep when I remember you, my valley of sorrow.
Despite all sad memories, I loved you.

"I shall deafen the world with outcry
Like a wounded beast in the forest."

Last Hour in Majdanek

A sound reverberates in my ears,
an echo of a discordant trumpet
and a groan of alarming drums.
I heard them on a January morning
Nineteen Hundred Forty-Five.

I recall red-white banners, an eagle
and soldiers taking their vows
to defend their country, fight for
the homeland "until victory."

I uttered the oath, knowing
that the homeland was saved, but
my home, my family was destroyed.

I heard about Treblinka, Chelmno,
Sobikor, Belziec, and Oswiecim.
Only there I was part of it, in it;
my Army base was in Majdanek.

Everywhere I went I smelled gas, the
odor of the "Disenfections Kammer,"
the smell of the barrels of human fat
destined for soap factories in Danzig,
wheelbarrows loaded with human bones,
mountains of shoes, eyeglasses, luggage
destined for the "Fatherland."

I felt a mouthful of bitterness at
the open doors of the crematoria ovens.
I searched for air and ran to the yard.

There stood a gallows. I thought:
what relative of mine swayed
on this gallows? For what sin?

I stumbled upon charred limbs, on
a heap of burnt bodies, soleless shoes,
ripped caps, bloody, torn shirts.
Everything was sprinkled with gray ashes.

I didn't feel fear, hate, pity, or pain,
just a frozen numbness of mind and body,
raindrops ran down my face.
My Army boots stepped on dead shells,
parts of skulls, scattered ties, scarfs.

Every piece of discarded shred had
an owner; I could see their faces, I could
hear their voices; they were my people.

The cold rain clung to my army coat --
cooled my face and made my body shiver.
But my eyes burned like hot tar, my
throat wound bled. I still kept walking.

The trumpet sounded again: Last Call!
Destination: Poznian, Berlin.
My feet marched in formation. It signified
I was still alive. Yet, my soul was dead.

We boarded heavy Army trucks.
Soldiers sang. My throat continued bleeding.

We left Majdanek on the Lublin road.
I swallowed my own blood with the
salted taste of tears and raindrops.

Every time I hear drums or trumpets
Majdanek comes to haunt me.
Faces of men, women, children
march to the beat of the drums.
With fist lifted to heaven: Why?
Asking mankind: Do not forget us!

June 19, 1983, Fathers' Day

Monuments

The Polish White Eagle engraved in black marble
on gravestones of soldiers killed in World War Two,
greet us in Jastrowie, Blotnica, Walcz, and Ploty.

With a Red Cross on my arm we marched this region
in Nineteen Hundred Forty-Five, fought like heroes
from Pila to Szczecin, Lawiczka, Koszalin, Kolobrzeg.

We helped the wounded, buried the fallen under banners:
"For Your and Our Freedom." We buried the flesh
and carried with us their spirit: Hope of Liberation.

The tears in moments of death, hope turned to dust,
Last words: *Mamo, Jezuniu,* Long Live Free Poland! --
still reverberate in my memory, three decades later.

Their tears turned into crystal rock, made monuments
out of grief, cold like ice, still as death, they live
entombed in my heart like a catacomb, a personal shrine.

To the young soldiers killed in the battle of Podgaje,
bound with wire and burned alive by the enemy ...
My chest feels desolate like the monuments we passed.

Partisan Guide Book

As a young man he spoke Yiddish,
in school he learned Polish, Hebrew,
when he escaped to the Soviet Union
he intensely studied Russian.
When he joined the partisans and
was sent as a diversionist behind
enemy lines, he learned German.

From a pocket-sized booklet, he learned
phrases: *Waffen hinlegen, Ergieb dich!*
Halt! *Bei Fluchversuch wird geschossen!*
The booklet was a treasury of instructions
how to use firearms, best ways of wrecking
enemy trains, trucks, motorcycles, and how
to survive on a diet of moss, bark, and snow.

In the forest at night, they listened to
the news, sang songs, and read The Guide.
The songs were about *Zoya Kosmodemianskaya,*
who was executed by the enemy in the village of
Petrishchevo, followed by a chapter:
How to attack enemy lines from the rear;
how to destroy enemy garrisons at night.

One day The Partisan Guide Booklet vanished.
Someone ran out of *machorka* paper and felt
that he already knew enough about sabotage.
Mischa, who knew the booklet by heart, became
the *"politruk"* of the partisan unit.
Every night, after returning from an attack
on enemy positions, he was rereading from memory.

His fame reached Moskow and orders came that
he be transferred to other partisan regions
to teach them the art of blowing up railways,
bridges, and trains. One night, when attacking a
caravan of German trucks carrying food supplies,
Mischa was wounded. His fellow partisans were sad,
but Mischa cheered them up: It was not in vain.

The next morning Mischa was taken to a village
and left there under the care of a "contact,"
the comrade who carried him to the village,
cried when he said goodbye to his *"politruk,"*:
Mischinka *dorogoi,* I have to make a confession,
I was the one who took our Partisan Guide and
used it for cigarette paper for the rest of us.

Platte (Ploty), Pomerania
May, 1945

Warsaw

People like the lifeless monuments,
sit silently on stony benches,
a ghost part in an ethereal sleep
after the rendezvous with war
that left most of the city in ruins.

Only the crows fling around the
stony benches looking for the trees
which disappeared in the April fires,
a light wind comes from the river.

The air still smells from burnt trees
and human flesh, they leave a dryness
in your throat and a burning in your
eyelids. Rats curl near the benches,
little desperados unafraid of people.

From somewhere comes a melodious sound,
a tune from a burning branch
of a chortled tree. An oriole sings
a song of spring, of life, peace, hope.

1945

Ploty Railroad Station

> *"War is waste and murder,*
> *unconditionally wrong."*
> *Throw earth over graves,*
> *cover them with tombstones*
> *of granite -- iron strong,*
> *play the trumpet of acclaim,*
> *praise them with song.*
> *Listen to their echoes:*
> *War is waste. War is wrong!*
>   M. Krause

When you visit Poland, go to Pomerania,
sojourn to the picturesque town of Ploty,
Powiat Lawiczka. There, at the railroad
station, you will see a mass grave with
a monument inscribed in Polish:
"FOR YOUR AND OUR FREEDOM"

In March, 1945, I was digging a common
grave for Russians, Poles, Jews, Lithuanians
and Kirgizians who had been killed on
the road to Sczeczin and Koszalin.

There, at the railroad station, we placed
the corpses in a row. We dug a grave and
laid them out, no prayers, just total silence.

Major Martinow, Military Commandant of Ploty,
himself severely wounded in the war,
walked beside me after the burial.
    "I hope, when peace will come some day,
    we will not forget these young men."

Who Will Mourn

A Russian an Uzbek
a Pole and a Jew
drown in battle
on the Oder River shore
outside the trenches
of the Stettin battlefield.
All four brave warriors
were less than twenty.

"Their destiny was to die
for the Motherland,"
said their commanding
officer at the burial.
They all left mothers
who will mourn, weep and
remember their heroic sons,
except the mother of the
Jewish rifleman from Riga.
The sad news will never
reach his kinfolk.
His mother and family
were all murdered by
the Nazis in December, 1941.

Night Thrust

They moved fast and silently
like ghosts in the night,
across corn and thicket fields
toward the edge of the forest.
Suddenly they found themselves
facing an enemy vigilante patrol,
so close that they all almost
scraped against their three-wheeler
motorcycles and motor-sleds.
The smell of baked potatoes,
fried fish and the resting men
around an expiring bonfire
was both scaring and thrilling.
They opened fire and killed
the roaring mad, suprised patrol.
The partisans grabbed the carbines,
machine guns, leftover food,
bottled drinks and disappeared.
A roar of army trucks briskly
advanced toward the encampment.
The partisans retreated into
forest, they faded away like
shades in the night, walking in
silence, reloading their carbines,
carressing their new machine guns
like men fondle their girlfriends
they were longing for a long time....

December, 1944

The Night of "Liberation"

It is midnight. The moon is hiding
beyond swiftly floating clouds,
total darkness hovers over the rooftops,
of our field hospital buildings.

My voice, crying in the night:
God, my God, where are you?
Did your angels slumber too?
The howling wind rebuffs my cry.

The fury of the rain and wind
deafens the moaning of the forsaken
soldiers, wounded in action, waiting
impatiently, in a daze, to be taken away.

The Russian soldier guarding us,
stays at the door, gazing blindly
into the darkness of the night,
confused and hungry as we are.

He heard his officer addressing us:
Fellow slaves, we liberated you.
You are free to return to your homes.
Yet, he was told to keep an eye on us...

We have flashlights, but no batteries,
no candles. Some of the wounded need
immediate attention, the officer promised
a swift return. All we have is darkness.

No trace of military trucks, no sounds
of artillery, only the sigh of the wounded,
the whistling of the wind thrashing the roof,
the wounded crying: God. Where Are You?

Terespol, on the Bug River.
September 17, 1939.

Leaving A Military Hospital

For long months since I arrived there,
I forgot what a smile looked like.
All I saw were faces resisting pain.
When my memory and strength returned,
when I was able to walk without crutches,
my mood changed, I helped other patients
to their armchairs, to the washroom,
chattering amiably with the hospital staff,
showing an interest im my recovery.
From the radio loudspeaker in our ward
we heard what was going on in the world.
What we learned was sad and depressing:
A globe encompassed in madness and fear,
people suffering, dying without knowing why.
I disguised my despair in silence, inwardly,
and persisted to go on smiling, resisting
nightmares, depression, holding a rein on
my nerves, finding relief by showing compassion,
concern for newly arrived wounded.
There was genuine love in these wards,
many nationalities, all colors of skin, but
their hearts and blood were the same.
I memorized there the word MOTHER in many
languages and learned to detest war.
I was happy when the day arrived and I was told
to get ready to leave, to face the outside
world on my own feet ...
Still, when I said goodbye to the patients,
the nurses, doctors, and staff -- I cried.

December, 1944

Chrabrost -- **Courage!**

Roses are planted where thorns grow,
And on the barren heath
Sing the honey bees.

William Blake

After nine months of misery, despair, near dead,
all the dread wounds over my body were healed.
They clothed me in a new Polish uniform, gave
me a pair of shoes, crutches, a travel permit
and directions to my military unit in Majdanek.
There was only one more important task to perform.

I dragged my feet to an office on an upper floor,
to say "thank you" to a woman who restored my life.
On the gray door was her name engraved on wood:
Valentina Invanowna Korchukowa, Doctor of Medicine,
a simple note was attached to the metal door:
"We will win this war, all we need is courage!"

My feelings were stirred, bewildered, emotions
mixed. I was happy and sad, calm and worried;
For months I prayed, hoped to leave this place,
away from the smell of streptocide, carbolic acid.
I saw people losing arms, legs, dying in pain,
myself having a rough time, calling it H E L L.

I doubted if my limbs would ever function,
whether I would ever walk, ever talk again.
W ould my memory return? the constant bleeding
subside? I was twenty-five when brought in here.
Now, I staggered up to this iron door, to thank
this woman, twice my age, whom I respected and admired.

This hard working doctor controlled my life,
often, when examining me, she cursed, shouted,
but always left my ward stirring my spirit with
a smile on her face and the word: *Chrabrost!*
Many times I cursed her, cried from pain from her
injections, for removing bandages too quickly.

For her demands to move my toes, insulting me.
She called me S.O.B. I called her beast,
But, for some reason, if I hadn't seen her a day
I was miserable, moaning, complaining, missing her.
When finally I was able to move my toes, she
summoned her staff to show them "a miracle."

Some nights she came to our ward, exhausted,
sat on the edge of our beds, quietly saying,
"I know the pain you all are bearing, the grief
and despair you're carrying, worrying who will
leave here without limbs, what future awaits you?
Will you be less the men you all dreamed of?

"A rose can blossom near a stink hole, a pit,
flowers can scatter their fragrance at dirt piles,
what all of you call dew, we call *chrabrost* --
you need courage, will power to endure, don't give in,
humans are like flowers, feed them with perserverance,
this is my prescription for your survival."

Casually she continued her words of comfort,
"People can live useful lives with one arm or leg
and make their contribution to the community.
Even a caterpillar, ugly, deaf, and totally blind,
has its role on this earth, has its own purpose,
not every creature can fly, some of us just crawl.

But with patience, strength, and determination, some of
us caterpillars will wake up as butterflies.
Not everyone can grow to be a tall pine tree;
some of us must be satisfied to be a scrub, a lean
bush, or just low, green grass in a field. If you
can't be a doctor, then serve as a medic. Do your duty!

There is work for all of us, regardless of who we are.
Some of us are leaders, some of us are followers.
Don't complain if you can't be a captain,
a general who controls the wide highways;
be satisfied that you survived and can control
your own trail, your life. Cheer up, courage!"

Now, leaving this hospital and this brave woman,
I realized how much Dr. Korchukowa did for me.
How much I admired and respected her all this time.
I opened the heavy door, swallowing the tears,
I said quietly, *"Spasibo,* Valentina Ivanowna."
She turned toward me, her face, clear and dear, smiled.

She squeezed my hand, grabbed me in her arms and
hugged me. I began to weep, sob loudly.
"Cheer up, Volodia, be a man, show some self control."
The tears streamed down on her white uniform,
"Get out of here you S.O.B. You made me cry ...
Take good care of yourself, *Wsio Choroshoho!"*

This was January, Nineteen Forty-Five, in Europe,
now, four decades later, thousands of miles away,
I still remember this chubby, warm human being,
the doctor with always smiling, brown eyes, open
face. I still hear her commanding voice in my dreams:
"All that counts in life for survival is courage."

Kursk Offensive

Our tired bodies move slowly,
rain is falling without let-up.
The blowing wind sounds like taps,
rhymed with wails of men, women,
cries of children and howling dogs.

The closer we approach the city
the louder the air-piercing shrill.
Even the artillery fire coming over
our heads, the whistling whirlwind,
is not able to suppress the cries.

Suddenly we came close to a ravine,
a deep pit full of people, animals,
children sighing, women loudly moaning,
men shouting, crying, and dogs howling.
This horror scene astonished us all.

The voice of our commanding officer
kept shouting: Don't pause! Keep going!
Remember what you have seen here,
what they have done to our people,
keep marching until victory is ours.

August, 1943

The Partisans

> *"There is no hope, no fear for you.*
> *There is no work, no whisper, no cry.*
> *There is no home, no bed of rest."*
>   Rabindranath Tagore

They fought in the Ostrow Forest,
Survived fierce battle with the enemy
to be slain from bullets in their backs.

The proverb: a Jew is only good when dead,
was prevalent in the Ostrow Forest as in
the surrounding underground fighting units.

So they buried the fallen Jew-partisans
with military honors, a wreath made of
evergreen twigs, inscribed with big letters:

"They served faithfully for our country,
for their and our freedom, their bravery,
their sacrifice will never be forgotten."

Naked they buried them, their shoes,
clothes, their precious rifles were taken
by the partisans' commanding officer.

The nakedness of the young bodies,
the bloody marks were a sad sign
that spoke of betrayal, foul play.

The remaining Jewish partisans
clutched their fists, bit their lips,
silently pressed their teeth in an oath.

Never to forget their brothers-partisans,
who fought for their own freedom and
died from their countrymen's bullets.

Platte, Pomerania, March, 1945

War Prisoners

I have seen Cain, conqueror of Europe,
now a prisoner of war, walking toward
trains destined for Siberia.

He, the son of Das Herren Volk, bent
frenzied body shivering with fear,
the snowy pavement eating his bare feet.

He walked trembling with cold, hungry,
and bleeding, defeated face, stumbling, sighing,
and after all he did, I felt pity for him.

His miserable looks slowed down the wrath,
anger and hate I carried in my breath,
I, Abel resurrected, who saw Europe crumble.

Who buried the Abels he slaughtered in vain,
whose victims' blood was still calling for revenge,
seeing him groan made me feel sorry for Cain.

What was, then, the purpose of war, of burning
cities, of dying children and mothers,
the awful suffering of millions wounded?

Cain, assassin. I hold the spear now,
but my heart is the shield that protects you:
Go on Cain, live! Be witness to the vanity of war.

Let the cry of the widows and war orphans
follow you for generations to come as a sign:
Hakol Hevel! Vanitas vanitatum et omnia Vanitas!

May 8, 1945
Platthe, Pomerania
translated: January 1, 1982

The Crows

Beneath a gray sky
Katiushas pierce the air
firm and loud voices
echo the battle cry:
For the Fatherland!
Fierce warfare: man to man
bayonet duels leave
bloody snowfields.
The enemy flies,
young soldiers in pursuit
follow them.
We, medics, take after them.
We pick up the wounded,
breathing out their last,
gather them from their pools
of blood, load them on
ambulances, half tracks,
and leave. The slain are
uncared for: no one has time
for the soldiers who died,
except the crows.
They are not afraid of
the noise, explosions, fire.
Not even the cold wind
makes them tremble.
With patience and coolness
they watch the dead soldiers,
anticipating a lavish meal.

Poland, 1945

A Farewell at Kiev Railroad Station

A wandering mass carrying bags, knapsacks, boxes,
pushes toward the entrance of the station.
Inside, the passengers wait in lines for tickets,
check billboards announcing train departures,
search for a bench to stretch their tired bodies.

Slogans everywhere proclaim: Kiev is free!
Someone painted under it: "We are marching to
victory." Among the crowd you see young children
press closely around a soldier, an invalid,
who plays on a harmonica a sentimental war song.

The wounds of war are still bleeding, hurting,
but under the pressure of life the tears dry.
Outside the station there are still wild weeds,
reminders of destruction by a vicious enemy,
yet, cheery music comes from public speakers.

It is cold, cloudy, and windy around the station.
People in fur hats, military coats and *kufeikas,*
wait calmly in line for newspapers and *pierogis*
sold by women vendors. Overhead fly wild birds
coming from the Dniepr shore searching for food.

Among the throng of pedestrians hurrying to the
station, in defiance of a militia woman desperately
trying to control traffic at the busy rail platform,
a soldier on crutches and a shivering young woman
stand in silence saying goodbye to each other.

The soldier has returned from the battlefront,
faithful to his promise to come back to his girl;
he was happy that she survived and returned to Kiev,
but saddened that she is leaving him forever:
Thinking he was killed, she married another man.

Trains come and go, people enter and leave the terminal,
the soldier and the shivering woman stay and wait:
Nothing left to say, all hopes are blank, finished,
a pink slip of paper: "Killed in action" wiped out
all dreams. The train arrives, a last embrace ...

The train starts moving, the young woman still shivers,
his last words: "I love you, I'll never forget you."
Through the window he watches her walk away, with her
goes part of his life, his love and dreams. He swallows
his tears and mumbles: "Please, Heaven watch over her."

My *Kibitka* is a two-by-two,
the walls and floor made of mud.
I sleep on a bed infested by insects,
often awakened by painful stings.

Every morning, when the sun appears
over the snow-bedecked mountains,
I am awakened by a melodious tune
coming from horns on top of a mosque.

I wash my face in an *"arik"* -- little
stream behind my *kibitka,* eat yogurt,
dry fruits, *urugs,* and drink some tea.
In minutes I am at work in our Clinic.

The days are long, the work exhausting,
but it is not the heat that is wearing.
It's the lack of food, medical supplies, and
beds that is upsetting and depressing.

Yet, we work with vigor and devotion.
We know that a war is going on in Europe
against a vicious enemy and the sick here
are relatives of the fighting soldiers.

Every evening, on the way back home,
I listen to the radio loudspeaker
blaring the latest front-line news
and I am envious of the fighting men.

I am waiting for the day to be called
to the Voyenkomat for military service.
I will say *Salaam* to my *kibitka,* to my
friends at the clinic. We all will cry.

Loneliness makes us sad
and sad people are lonely.
They hide behind four walls,
withdraw to nowhere.
The only voice they hear is outside breathing;
inside is dullness, impotence.

A shadow hovers around them,
makes their mind freeze,
depresses their senses to a slow, self-destruction;
they don't move, afraid to disturb the ghost of desolation.

Aimlessly they sit like frozen corpses,
pretend they read, think, but their minds are blank;
all they feel is unconscious weakness,
repudiation of will to live, to love, to smile.

They have notions, illusions that, perhaps, they will die,
their dreams are pure vanity.
They go on living in desolation
and make their friends sad.

Memorial Day Prayer

Yisgadal Ve'yiskadash --
Magnified and Sanctified
be the names of the soldiers
who perished in all wars.

May their memory continue
living in our hearts,
may their loss be a warning
to all nations of our globe
to discontinue enmity.

We shall strive for peace
on the ground and in the skies,
never raise the sword of
destruction against each other.

On this Memorial Day, let us
open the gates of justice,
mercy, and remembrance of all
who were cut down in all wars.

May their memory go on living
in our hearts forever with a
message that wars are evil.
Humanity needs peace.